# THE
# WAITING
# GAME

YOU NEVER KNOW WHO'S WATCHING ...

SHEILA BUGLER

BRANDON
AN IMPRINT OF O'BRIEN

First published 2014 by Brandon, an imprint of The O'Brien Press Ltd,
12 Terenure Road East, Rathgar, Dublin 6, Ireland.
Tel: +353 1 4923333; Fax: +353 1 4922777
E-mail: books@obrien.ie
Website: www.obrien.ie

ISBN: 978-1-84717-367-6

1 3 5 7 8 6 4 2
14 17 19 20 18 15

Layout and design: The O'Brien Press Ltd.
Cover photograph: iStockphoto
Printed and bound by CPI Group (UK) Ltd, Croydon, CR0 4YY
The paper in this book is produced using pulp from managed forests

The O'Brien Press receives financial

## DEDICATION

For Seán – there's no one I'd rather grow
old disgracefully with.

## ACKNOWLEDGEMENTS

This book would be nothing without the help of my
wonderful editor, Rachel Pierce. Her honesty, patience and
good humour have got me through a very painful few months.
Thank you, Rachel.

Others who helped kick this book into shape are Chris
Curran, JJ Marsh, Gillian Hamer, Svetlana Pironko, Lorraine
Mace. I owe a huge debt to all of you. A very special thanks to
Gary Friel. Thanks also to Aidan Cunningham for the 'crack
cocaine pizza' reference.

My family: Seán, Luke and Ruby, my parents
(aka the local sales team) and Tom.

My friends: too many to mention, but you know who you
are. I hope we're all still having fun and misbehaving for a long
time to come. There's always a glass of wine waiting
for you in Eastbourne.

Massive thanks, as always, to the great team at The O'Brien
Press. To be published under the Brandon imprint is an honour.

# AUGUST – BRIGHTON

She liked watching people. Liked it best when they didn't know she was there. Watching them go about their pathetic lives, not realising how insignificant, how unimportant they really were.

Today was different. Today she was watching because she was scared. Trying to work up the courage to cross the road. Scared of rejection. It was an irrational fear, she knew that. After all this time, her mother would be just as excited as she was.

Maybe the house was the problem. It wasn't what she'd expected. So often she'd pictured the life her mother had left for. A better life, with a better man than the one she'd had the misfortune to marry. A woman like that forced to endure a life with that useless loser ... well, who could blame her for what she'd done?

Dirty net curtains made it difficult to see inside, especially standing here on the other side of the road. She caught a glimpse of something, a shadow flitting across the grimy glass, but it was impossible to make out any detail.

A trickle of sweat tickled its way down her spine. Hot, even for August. The hottest summer on record, supposedly. She stepped sideways, seeking shade under the bony branches of a half-dead tree, the only visible sign of nature on the street.

In the house beside her mother's, music thumped loudly through an open upstairs window. A young black man stood at the same window, staring down at her. When she returned his stare, he stuck his tongue against the side of his mouth and made a wanking gesture with his hand.

She imagined herself crossing the road, knocking on Wank Man's door and teaching him a lesson. The thought of it made her smile. The stupid wanker smiled back. Getting it wrong, the way men always did.

She looked back at her mother's house. A dirty-white terraced house in a row of identical dirty-white houses. Cheap and nasty. Not at all the sort of place she'd imagined for her mother. But maybe her mother had a perfectly good explanation for what she was doing in this dreadful, depressing place. The thought perked her up, shook her out of the dark mood that was threatening to ruin everything.

She smoothed down her dress – black, sleeveless, classy – and adjusted the red silk scarf at her neck. Her mother's scarf. The only thing she'd left behind. The silk was embroidered with thousands of tiny black butterflies. She could feel them now when she rubbed her thumb across the delicate threads. She anticipated her mother's joy when she realised she'd kept the scarf for all this time.

She'd imagined this moment so often, different variations of it playing out in her head over the years. Now here she was, about to turn all that desperate longing into a reality.

She stepped off the pavement onto the road, never once taking her eyes off the house. Suddenly, she was there, standing at the front door, pressing the doorbell, hearing it ring inside the house. A moment later, the sound of footsteps ...

# OCTOBER – LONDON

# ONE

*Hush little baby, don't say a word*
*Mama's gonna buy you ...*

Someone was in the house. Chloe's eyes shot open, her mother's voice fading, replaced by other sounds. The rustle of tissue paper. The clang of water hitting the inside of the metal kettle. The *slip-slap* of leather-soled shoes on the lino floor. The soft, wheezy whistle of the kettle as the water started to warm up.

He was here again.

She opened her mouth to scream, but nothing happened. Her mind was awake, but her body was still asleep. She clenched and unclenched her hands, wriggled her toes, sensation coming back slowly.

Downstairs, the water had started to boil. The noise of it loud, even up here in the bedroom. Taking her chance, she threw back the quilt, jumped from the bed, grabbed her bag and ran out of the bedroom, along the corridor and into the bathroom. There was no lock, but she closed the door and pressed her body against it, as if her weight could hold off the attack.

She was shivering, fear and cold making her teeth chatter. She clenched her jaw shut, top teeth grinding down on bottom teeth. A wooden floorboard creaked, too loud and too close. She recognised the sound. The second step on the staircase creaked like that. He was on the stairs. Moving towards her bedroom.

Quietly, quietly, she climbed into the bath, took the edge of the shower curtain and pulled it across. She lay down in the bath, arms clasped tightly around her shivering body, breath held, waiting.

She could hear him through the thin wall that separated the bedroom and the bathroom. Heard the *shuffle-shuffle* of his feet and the heavy in-out, in-out breathing that didn't sound much like Ricky. But then she remembered what he was like when he got angry. Red-faced and the breath snorting through his nose. Angry because she wasn't there, in her bed, where he'd been expecting her.

She fumbled in her bag. Fingers found the phone but couldn't hold onto it. The phone slipped deeper into the bag. She turned the bag upside-down. The contents spilled onto the bath in a discordant clatter.

A flash of light along the corridor. Footsteps moving faster.

Into the small spare bedroom and out again.

She brushed a tube of lipstick out of the way and grabbed the phone. Finger punched 999. Seconds later, a woman's voice: 'Emergency services operator. Which service do you require?'

'Police,' she whispered. 'Get me the police. There's someone in my house.'

The bathroom door slammed open. She put her hand over her mouth to cut off the scream. On the phone, the woman was still speaking, asking for Chloe's address. She hit the End button, terminating the call.

He came closer, his shadow on the shower curtain huge and distorted. He would kill her. He'd told her that's what would happen if she ever tried to leave him.

Fingers curled around the edge of the shower curtain.

The scream came now, roared out of her, blocking out everything else. She dived out the other side of the curtain. She'd dropped her phone. It didn't matter. She raced forward, bare feet slipping on the cold bathroom floor. A hand grabbed her arm. She shook it off, still screaming, and ran faster.

She stumbled down the stairs and along the narrow corridor to the front door. The bastard had locked it. She swung around, saw the shadow of him moving down the stairs. Something not right about it, but no time to think about that. At the back door she tugged the bolt, used both hands to open it. Nearly there now.

Something struck the back of her head. She stumbled against

the door but didn't fall. Still standing, fingers still gripping the handle. She could do it. She pulled the handle, felt the door start to open.

Another crack across the head. She fell, face first. The black-and-white pattern of the lino floor rushed up to meet her.

# TWO

Ellen stood at her bedroom window, watching the line of trees
fade to black as night moved across the Greenwich skyline. It
made her sad, this gradual descent into darkness. Perverse, she
knew, to want to prolong each shortening stretch of day. It was
the trees, she decided. In the burning glow of autumn glory, they
were at their very best at this time of the year. It seemed unfair
not to be allowed to gaze at them a while longer.

'M-uuu-m.'

The voice drew her attention from the beauty of nature to
another endless fascination. Eilish stood in the doorway, waiting
until she knew she had her mother's complete attention.

'Yes, sweetheart,' Ellen said. 'What is it?'

Eilish walked across the room and settled herself on the end of

Ellen's bed. The expression on her little face was perplexed. It was a look Ellen recognised. A frown forming, brown eyes half-closed in concentration as she tried to work out the exact way to phrase whatever question she was about to ask. Decision made, a flash of clarity behind those eyes and she was off.

'Pat says babies come out of your bottom. But that can't be right, can it? A baby's way too big to fit through your bumhole.'

She cocked her head to one side and waited. The look on her face challenged Ellen to come up with a satisfactory answer. When she did that, she looked so like Vinny it hurt. The pain was physical; an ache across the chest that spread down into her stomach and still had the power to consume her even now, almost five years after his death.

'It's not your bumhole,' she said. 'There's a special baby hole that women have. You know that already, Eilish.'

'But that doesn't make any sense,' Eilish said. 'I mean, how would I get a baby out *down there*? And anyway, you still won't tell me how the baby gets into the tummy in the first place.'

Surely, at eight, Eilish was too young to be told the facts of life?

'It's the special baby kiss,' Ellen said. 'Just like I told you. The mummy and daddy decide to have a baby and they have a special kiss and then the baby starts growing in the mummy's tummy.'

'Are you going out tonight?'

The sudden switch in subject would have been a relief if Ellen didn't know what was coming next.

'Yes,' she said. 'But just for a little bit. I won't be late.'

'With Jim?'

Ellen nodded. 'I sort of need to get ready, actually. Will you help me choose a top?'

She turned from her daughter's inquisitive stare and went over to the built-in wardrobe.

'This one?' she asked. 'Or this shirt? Which do you prefer?'

'Is he, like, your boyfriend then?'

Ellen carried the blue linen shirt across to the bed and sat down beside Eilish.

'He's a friend, Eilish. That's all.'

'Pat says he's your boyfriend and you're probably going to marry him and he'll move in here or we'll have to move to his house. Which we'd hate because Jim's house is way smaller than ours and this is our home and we don't want to move. We really don't, Mum. It's not fair.'

Dear God, Ellen thought, give me strength.

'Eilish, listen to me.' She took her daughter's little hand in hers and squeezed it. 'Jim's a friend. Nothing more than that.' Liar, liar. 'And even if he did become my boyfriend – which may never happen.' Pants on fire. 'Then there's no way in the world I'd ask you and Pat to move out of this house. This is your home. And it will stay your home. Do you understand?'

Eilish smiled and some of the tension across Ellen's shoulders disappeared.

'Will you have a baby with him?'

'No.'

'But it'd be so cute,' Eilish said. 'And you could do it tonight. You know, one of those special baby kisses?'

Ellen wasn't sure if her daughter was taking the mick or not.

'Anyway,' Eilish continued, 'it's not a kiss, Mummy. Maria told me what really happens.'

'Oh yeah?'

Eilish nodded, face full of confidence. 'Yeah. The daddy and the mummy have to take their clothes off and lie beside each other and make noises. That's how babies are really made, isn't it?'

Sometimes, what she missed most was having someone to share these conversations with. She pictured telling Jim later that evening, but it didn't feel right. She wasn't sure why. He was great with the kids and seemed genuinely interested in them. But he wasn't their father.

After Eilish wandered off, Ellen got ready for her night out. Blue shirt over a new pair of jeans, make-up, including a new lipstick she'd bought earlier that day. It was a rich red colour and she hesitated, wondering if it was a little OTT for a casual drink.

Except it was more than a casual drink. She was starting to really like this guy. And all the signs were that he felt the same way about her. In as much as she was capable of reading the signs. She'd been with Vinny since she was twenty-two. Which made her as out of practice with the whole dating business as it was possible to be.

Make-up applied, she gave her face a final once-over in the mirror. The make-up did little to hide the tiny pattern of lines at the corner of each eye, but apart from that she didn't look too bad.

Blue eyes, clear and bright. Dark, bobbed hair framed a face that was, possibly, a shade too pale. More blusher, perhaps? No, best not. She'd end up looking like a clown.

Enough. Time to go. She pushed her chair away from the dressing table and stood up. As she left the bedroom, her eyes drifted, like they always did, to the family photo on the small bedside table. Her, Vinny and the children. Vinny's arm draped over her shoulders, smiling out from the photo, like the happiest man in the world.

She smiled back, briefly, and her eyes slid to the sheet of white paper lying beside the photo. It was folded over but she knew, by heart, what was written on it. She'd only folded it to stop herself from looking at the words over and over.

She looked back at Vinny's smiling face. 'What do you think I should do?' she asked.

Unsurprisingly, there was no answer from her dead husband. Letting her eyes linger on his face a moment longer, she eventually turned away and left the room, closing the door behind her. As she approached the stairs, the doorbell rang. Pat ran to answer it. Goosebumps skittered across Ellen's skin when she heard Jim O'Dwyer's voice.

She stood for a moment, looking down at him. He looked

up, smiling when his eyes locked with hers. She walked down to meet him, giddy at the prospect of an evening with him.

Her whole body tingled as he walked forward to greet her. She was grinning like a fool, but she didn't care. He was grinning, too. Like a pair of besotted teenagers, instead of two middle-aged people about to head out for a quiet drink.

He held her shoulders, leaned forward and kissed her cheek.

'You look gorgeous,' he said.

She felt suddenly shy. As she searched her brain for something to say, something low-key but vaguely amusing, her phone, in the pocket of her jeans, started buzzing.

'Sorry,' she mumbled, stepping back from him. 'I'll just get this.'

It was a number she didn't recognise. Frowning slightly, she pressed the Answer button and held the phone to her ear.

'DI Kelly? Martine Reynolds here. *Evening Star*. I'd like your reaction to a story we're running later this week. A local woman is being terrorised by her violent ex-partner. She claims the police – your team, in particular – are doing nothing to protect her. Would you like to comment?'

Martine Reynolds. Muck-raking local hack with about as much integrity as your average psychopath. Ellen hung up and turned to Jim.

'Sorry,' she said. 'I'm going to have to deal with this.'

# THREE

The meeting took place in a hotel room. The Novotel in Greenwich. They'd arranged to meet at five pm. Nathan closed the office early and drove her to Greenwich, making slow progress through the thick rush-hour traffic.

The journey from Lewisham took half an hour. Plenty of time for her to think about what she was doing and to wish she'd never agreed to it. She tried to tell Nathan how she felt but he wouldn't listen, kept telling her she had no choice. It was the only way to stop things getting any worse.

The journalist was waiting for them in the hotel foyer. Tall, thin and blonde with over-tanned skin and a hard face. Chloe didn't like her. If she'd been alone, she didn't think she'd have stayed, but Nathan was beside her, shaking hands with the journalist and saying how good it was that she was doing this for them.

Before Chloe knew it, they were in a lift, travelling up the hotel to a beige room.

'You ready to begin?' Martine asked, pulling a small digital recorder from her bag.

Chloe glanced at Nathan, who nodded. She swallowed. 'You really think this will work?'

'It's the only way,' Martine said. She spoke gently and slowly, like she was conversing with a stupid child. Chloe wasn't fooled for a second. The journalist was a cow, the sort of cold, opinionated woman that Chloe did her best to avoid most of the time.

'It's just …' Chloe could hear the wobble in her own voice and hated herself for it. Knew the other woman would hear it too, and use Chloe's weakness against her.

'I can't help thinking,' she continued. 'What if it's not Ricky?'

Nathan sat beside her. The bed sagged under his weight, the movement making her feel sick.

'We've already spoken about this,' Nathan said. 'Who else could it be? You need to show him you're not scared of him. You can do that, Chloe. I know you can.'

'We can use a false name, if you want,' Martine said. 'The focus of this piece is solely on the failings of the police. No need at all for me to mention you by name.'

Chloe wondered why she hadn't thought of that herself. She tried to remember if Nathan had already suggested it, but so much was a fog these days. Remembering anything at all was difficult. It was the stress. She knew that. Whenever she got stressed out, her mind started to misbehave. Like it was running on a low battery.

'What name would you like me to use instead?' the journalist asked.

Ivy. The name popped into her head. As a little girl, she'd always wished she was called Ivy. There was a time she'd tried to convince her parents and everyone else to use that name instead of Chloe. Funny how she'd forgotten about that.

Except that was a long time ago. She didn't want to be Ivy anymore.

'Let's use my real name,' she said. 'If I really want to send a message to Ricky, that's the best way to do it, isn't it?'

The way the journalist and Nathan smiled at her told her she'd made the right decision.

'Steve, the photographer, will be here soon,' Martine said. 'We'll get some really good shots of you to go with the piece. Make sure the police know they're dealing with someone who won't be messed around.'

'And Ricky,' Chloe said.

'Of course.' Martine nodded, but Chloe could see she wasn't paying attention. She was fiddling with the recorder, testing it worked before placing it on the table in front of Chloe. A red light on the machine flashed on and off.

Recording in progress, Chloe thought. Made her feel like she was someone special. Maybe they were both right. Maybe she had no choice.

Martine sat back in her chair and smiled at Chloe.

'Ready to begin? Let's see if we can persuade the police to do their job properly and catch this fucker before he can do any real harm.'

Chloe hated swearing, particularly in women, but she did her best to smile and not show her true feelings. Three years with Ricky had made her something of an expert at hiding how she really felt.

'Okay,' she said. 'What do you need to know?'

\* \* \*

Afterwards, Nathan drove her home. They were nearly at Hither Green when he suggested they stop off for something to eat.

'We could go to the Italian place in Lee,' he said. 'My treat. I don't know about you, but I'm starving.'

Starving was stretching it, she thought. He had enough fat across his middle to last several weeks without food. She didn't feel like going to a restaurant. The whole encounter with the journalist had left her feeling dirty. Like she'd done something she shouldn't have. Sharing such personal information with a complete stranger, it was horrible. She wanted to be at home, soaking in a deep, warm bath and pretending this evening had never happened.

Except going home meant being alone and she didn't think

she could bear that either. Briefly, she wondered about asking Nathan if she could sleep at his. Just for one night. But she was afraid he'd read it the wrong way, think she was implying something different. And if he thought that, then things would get awkward between them.

He wasn't interested. She knew that because she knew men. Knew how they acted when they liked a woman. Nathan never acted that way. Never showed the slightest bit of interest in being anything except a friend. She knew why, of course. Nathan had principles. A man like Nathan, a good and moral man, what on earth would he ever want with someone like her? Because Nathan knew the truth. Knew what sort of a woman she really was.

She'd told him the first time they'd ever met. At the little house on Nightingale Grove where she now lived. It had all come out. He'd asked about references from her previous landlord and when she started to explain, she'd found herself telling him the whole story. Words tumbling over each other as she raced through every last, sordid detail. And afterwards, when she'd finally stopped speaking and crying, he'd pulled a blue silk handkerchief from his breast pocket and handed it to her.

'Sounds like you could use a friend.' That was all he said. Never mentioned a word of what she'd told him then or any time after that.

Which was why now, when he asked if she'd like to go for a meal, she smiled and said what a good idea it was.

'But only if you let me pay,' she said. 'It's the least I can do.'

At the restaurant, she ate little and drank more wine than she would normally. They talked about everything and nothing. By the end of it she was exhausted, but also relaxed. It was a long time since she'd felt like this.

Fifteen minutes later, when Nathan pulled up outside her house and asked if she'd like him to sleep on the couch, she was able to smile and tell him truthfully, yes, that would be great.

# FOUR

The counsellor's office was in a bright glass annexe at the back of Lewisham Hospital. From the waiting room, Ellen was able to look out across Ladywell Fields. She supposed all this light and green views was meant to make the clients feel better about themselves. If that was the case, it didn't work.

She arrived early, hoping to get in and out before ten am. The big announcement at work was scheduled for ten-fifteen. Ellen didn't want to be late. Luckily, Briony Murray, Ellen's perky antipodean shrink, didn't believe in not starting on time.

At the dot of nine o'clock the door to Briony's office opened and the counsellor was there, smiling and inviting Ellen to come in. Inside, the two women sat in their usual positions, facing each other on two of the low, pale yellow sofas by the window.

'So,' Briony began. 'How have you been?'

'Good,' Ellen said. 'I think. Yes. It's been a good week. Well, work's been a pain in the backside but apart from that, everything's fine.'

'Why?'

Briony had blue eyes, the sort of blue that reminded Ellen of Japanese willow pattern. Blue eyes, clear skin and cropped blonde hair. Ellen didn't know exactly how old the counsellor was, but guessed she was somewhere in her thirties. Ellen wondered how someone that young got to be so wise.

'Well,' Ellen said slowly. 'I've been seeing quite a bit of Jim. Which is, you know, it's going well. I like him.'

She thought about last night. He'd been so good. Waited patiently while Ellen spoke on the phone. First, to Chief Superintendent Paul Nichols, then Jamala Nnamani, the station's press officer. Trying to work out what angle the story would take so the station could prepare itself to deal with the inevitable backlash.

Briony smiled. 'You've been telling me that for the past three weeks. Glad to hear it's still going well. Last week, you mentioned feeling guilty. Do you want to talk about that a little more this morning?'

Not really.

'It's normal, isn't it?' Ellen said. 'Of course I'm going to feel guilty if I start seeing someone else. Especially if I start to like them.'

'Is it normal?'

'Yes,' Ellen said. 'I mean, who wouldn't feel like that? I married Vinny. I made a promise to him and myself that I'd spend the rest of my life with him. And it's breaking that promise if I fall for someone else the minute Vinny's gone.'

'But it's not like that,' Briony said. 'Is it?'

'You mean because it's nearly five years?' Ellen asked. 'You think that makes it okay? Well it doesn't. No matter what you say, Briony, it still feels like I'm being unfaithful to him. And what about Pat and Eilish? They think I've forgotten all about Vinny and I'm going to marry Jim and have more kids with him. What sort of mother does that make me if they're going around thinking things like that? I'm selfish. There. I've said it. A selfish, stupid woman who can't wait to rip her clothes off for the first guy who comes along and shows a bit of interest in her.'

'Wow,' Briony said. 'He makes you feel like ripping your clothes off? I'd like to meet this guy. He sounds pretty hot.'

Ellen groaned. How did this happen every time? She hadn't even known that's what she thought. Well, the bit about ripping her clothes off, maybe. But the rest of it. All that self-pitying guilt. Where the hell had that come from? She knew – *knew* – the last thing – *the very last thing* – Vinny would have wanted was for her to give up on her life. He'd be happy she met someone else. Just as she would have wanted that for him. So what the bloody hell was wrong with her?

'I just seem to make everything so complicated,' she said quietly. 'Why is that?'

Briony reached across the low coffee table and patted Ellen's knee. 'Complicated makes us interesting, Ellen. It only becomes a problem if you try to suppress those feelings instead of dealing with them. That's why I'm here. To help you look deep inside yourself and not be afraid of what you see.'

It sounded reassuring. It *was* reassuring. Somewhat. Until Ellen remembered the reason she'd been referred to counselling in the first place. For killing a man. Ellen knew that if she looked too deep inside herself, she would find something that scared the living shit out of her.

* * *

It was a ten-minute walk from the hospital to Lewisham police station. Ellen walked it in five, pushing her way through the crowded street market and running the final stretch until she reached the imposing white building where she worked. Europe's largest police station, slap-bang in the middle of Lewisham, recently named the most dangerous place to live in the UK. Not a surprise to Ellen or any of her colleagues, who day by day felt they were on the losing side of the war against crime.

Instead of taking the lift to her office on the third floor, Ellen went straight to Room 1.10, the large meeting room on the first floor where Chief Superintendent Paul Nichols had scheduled his meeting.

All four of Ellen's immediate team were already there, along with a fair scattering of other officers from across CID. The chairs in the room had been laid out conference-style and Ellen's team sat in a neat row at the back. She slid in beside Abby Roberts, said hello and asked about the latest rumours on Nichols' announcement. She was interrupted by Raj Patel, leaning across Abby to get Ellen's attention.

'*Star*'s due out at eleven,' Raj said. 'I've asked Malcolm to grab a copy the moment it hits the shelves.'

Ellen nodded. 'Good. What do you think Chloe's playing at?'

'She wants to be taken seriously,' Raj said. 'Part of me doesn't blame her. The way she sees it, we've done nothing to protect her.'

'Until the other night we had nothing to go on,' Ellen said. 'The attack in her house has changed things. But she already knows that, so why speak to the press?'

Before Raj could answer, the door swung open and Nichols strode to the lectern. He stood for a moment, surveying the room with obvious disdain as he waited for the chattering to die down. His gaze moved around the room, landed on Ellen and slid across to Abby. Briefly, so brief Ellen was certain no one else saw it, Nichols' eyes dropped to Abby's chest before he lifted his head and moved on to the rest of the room.

The room grew quiet. Nichols cleared his throat – delicately – and began.

'Thank you for joining me this morning at such short notice. I know we're all busy, so I'm not planning to keep any of you longer than is necessary. However, I felt it was important to bring you together this morning to share some very exciting news. Yesterday afternoon we completed the recruitment process for a new Detective Chief Inspector.'

Nichols paused for dramatic effect, did something with his face that might have been a smile, and continued.

'As you all know, our esteemed colleague Detective Chief Inspector Edward Baxter took early retirement this year due to ill health. The task of finding a suitable replacement has taken time. It has been imperative to choose the *right* individual to lead CID through these turbulent times of spending reviews and rising crime. We received many applications' – his eyes slid back momentarily to Ellen – 'and choosing the best candidate from a selection of such high-calibre individuals was a challenge.

'But I'm delighted to announce we have made our decision and, with no further delay, let me please introduce the newest addition to our CID team...'

Nichols paused again and turned his attention to the door. Along with every other person in the room, Ellen watched in silence as a tall, blonde woman walked in and joined Nichols at the lectern.

Like Nichols, the woman looked around the room at the men and women gathered there. Unlike Nichols, when she reached Ellen, her face softened and she smiled. Ellen might have smiled back. She wasn't sure. The shock of recognising her new boss had taken over everything else.

Nichols was a tall man but, standing alongside him, the

woman was just as tall. This was partly due to the red stilettos she wore. Ellen could just see the toes peeking out beneath her immaculately cut, flared black trousers. The shoes, Ellen knew because she'd been told this before, were Vivienne Westwood.

'Hello,' the woman said. 'My name is DCI Geraldine Cox. I'm very pleased to meet you all.'

# FIVE

Nathan knew he'd never survive another night on the sofa. He ached all over, neck so stiff it was agony to move his head. It had been worth it, though. Lying there all night, knowing she was sleeping so close by. He could hear her breathing, the gentle sound of it soothing him on the lumpy, uncomfortable sofa. Besides, he was used to getting by without much sleep.

Soon after it started to get bright he had an idea. A surprise for her. A burglar alarm. He'd sort it today. No arguments. Get one of those fancy ones that connected to the police station. If that didn't show her how much he was willing to do for her, he didn't know what would.

He got up early – easy enough when he hadn't actually been sleeping – and prepared breakfast for them both. Thought about going out to the garden, looking for a flower to put on the table, but realised in time that she might misinterpret the gesture. Worse, it might make her think of the flowers that were left out for her at night. He definitely didn't want her thinking that. The whole point of him being here was to make her feel better, not worse.

He used up all the bacon in her fridge and made a cheese and onion omelette to go with it. When it was all ready, he was starving, but he didn't want to start without her. He went and knocked on her bedroom door. Pushed it open when there was no answer, stood for a moment, watching her sleep. She hadn't mentioned her head yesterday and he hoped it had stopped hurting. He hated to think of it.

'Chloe?'

She stirred, but didn't wake. He walked over to the bed, shook her shoulder gently and stepped back so she wouldn't think he was standing too close.

She looked a bit surprised to see him, but she got over that. Sat up, pulling the quilt up so it covered her entire body. Not necessary because she was wearing pyjamas, but he liked what it said about her that she'd do that.

'I've made you breakfast,' he said.

She smiled and his heart soared.

'Breakfast?' She giggled. 'I never eat breakfast, silly. There's never enough time.'

'Well there is this morning,' he said. 'We can go in late. A good breakfast sets you up for the day. That's what my mum always said and she was right.'

He left then, giving her the privacy to get dressed and ready without him in the room with her. Plenty of time for that later.

* * *

Ellen was pretty sure she liked Geraldine Cox. They'd worked together on a case not so long ago. Cox had helped Ellen track down a missing child. They'd worked well together and Ellen had come to think of Cox as a friend of sorts. Even still... she wasn't sure how she felt having Cox as her boss.

It was the surprise element that most annoyed her. Maybe once she got over that, she'd feel better about things. Or when she found out why Ger hadn't called, let her know in advance what today's big announcement was all about. Failing that, it wouldn't have killed Ger to have at least mentioned she was in the running for the job. They'd only spoken a few weeks ago. Ger had called 'for a chat'. Now, Ellen suspected the purpose of the call was less 'chat' and more fishing expedition.

Back in the open-plan office, everyone was tipping in with their first impressions of their new boss. *Arrogant. Hot. A ball-breaker. Cold bitch...*

'Enough.' Ellen held up her hand, stopping the stream of invective before it got any worse.

'She's a good copper,' Ellen said. 'And that's all that matters. Calling her a cold bitch is the sort of sexist nonsense I thought you lot had got over since you've dragged your macho arses into the twenty-first century. Malcolm.' She turned to short and chubby Malcolm McDonald. 'If I ever again hear you refer to any female officer as a cold bitch, you'll be out of here and back in uniform quicker than you can shove another one of those disgusting bloody pasties down that mouth of yours. Got that?'

Malcolm blushed, shoved the pastie under a pile of paper and muttered an apology. Ellen would have said more, but she was distracted by what was on her desk. True to his word, Raj had got his hands on an early copy of today's *Evening Star*. It sat face-up on Ellen's desk. Chloe Dunbar's frightened face staring up at her from the front page. Steeling herself against the inevitable hysterical prose, Ellen picked up the paper and started reading.

Raj pulled up a chair and sat down beside her. 'What do you think?'

Ellen looked back at the newspaper, scanning the story again.

*'It happened last Tuesday night,'* Chloe said. *'Someone was in the house. I woke up and heard him walking around downstairs. I was terrified. I knew it was him, you see.'*

*'Who?'*

*'My ex. He's been following me for months. Stalking, I suppose you'd call it.'*

*'And you've reported it to the police?'*

*When I ask this question, Chloe's eyes fill with tears.*

*'I know it's difficult,' I say. 'But it's important people know about this, Chloe. Just think how many other people are being let down by*

*those being paid to protect us.'*

*'The police won't do anything,' she says. 'Of course I've reported it but they don't take it seriously. Oh they pretended. Even sent a detective around at one point. For all the good he did.'*

*'He?'*

*'DC Patel. He was nice enough, I suppose. Just didn't really help me.'*

*For the readers' benefit, DC Raj Patel works in a team led by formerly disgraced Detective Inspector Ellen Kelly, now back in her job as if nothing ever happened.*

*'Let's go back to Tuesday night,' I say.*

*'I hid in the bathroom,' she says. 'I could hear him. Coming up the stairs. I was so scared, Martine. You have no idea.'*

*'What happened next?'*

*'I thought he was going to kill me,' Chloe whispers. 'So I ran. But he came after me. I tried to get out of the house but I couldn't get the door open.'*

*Her voice trails off and I have to encourage her to keep going. She's not finding this easy.*

*'He hit me, knocked me out and left me for dead. I don't know how long I lay there, unconscious. And I don't know what he did to me while I was lying there.'*

*She falls silent and, for a moment, I am silent too. Trying to imagine the terror she must have felt.*

*'You said your ex,' I say then. 'You're sure it was him?'*

*She nods her head. 'I've told them. But they won't do anything to stop him. That's why I'm speaking to you. I don't know what else I can do. I know he'll come back, you see. And the next time, I won't be so lucky.'*

'He didn't kill her,' Ellen said.

'Maybe killing her's not what he wants,' Raj said. 'If she's dead, it's all over. She woke up. That hasn't happened before. I think he hit her because he didn't want her to see him.'

'Which means it's someone she knows,' Ellen said. 'But not the ex?'

'We've already questioned him,' Raj said. 'He has an alibi for Tuesday night. He was out drinking with a group of friends. Pub first, then on to a club. Didn't leave there until 4am. According to the bouncers, he was too pissed to stand up at that point.'

'But Chloe doesn't believe that?' Ellen asked.

'I can understand why,' Raj said. 'If she believes it's her ex doing this, then at least she can make some sense of what's happening. It must be even more terrifying to think she's being targeted by a complete stranger.'

Ellen got that. Crime victims often wanted to find meaning in what had happened to them. The problem was, sometimes there was no meaning. Other than being in the wrong place at the wrong time.

'And we've no other suspects?' Ellen asked.

Raj shook his head. 'She works in an estate agent's. Meets a lot of different people every day. We've interviewed her two colleagues. Both male. Haven't discounted them, but there's nothing to indicate either of them are behind this. And I've gone through a list of clients she's dealt with over the last four months. We're interviewing everyone but haven't found anything so far.'

'Reynolds has been clever,' Ellen said. 'Chloe comes across as very plausible while we seem utterly incompetent. '

She ran through what she knew about Chloe Dunbar. Twenty-five-year-old single woman, living on her own in Hither Green. She'd been in several times over the last few months, complaining that someone had been breaking into her house at night-time while she slept. With no evidence of a break-in and no sign that anything had been taken from her home, the case had been a low priority. Until last week, when Chloe was attacked in her house and knocked unconscious.

'She didn't mention the other stuff,' Raj said. 'Why's that, do you think?'

'Maybe Martine left it out on purpose,' Ellen said. 'She kept it simple, easier for people to relate to Chloe that way. And easier for us to spot any potential nutters who read the story and get in touch claiming the same thing's happening to them.'

'Maybe.' Raj didn't sound convinced. 'Anyway, Chloe's coming in later. I can ask her myself, I guess.'

'Good.' Ellen looked at the paper again. 'You know this is serious, right? She could be in real danger.'

'I'll take care of it,' Raj said.

# SIX

In the early afternoon, Ellen got a call from the front desk. A woman was downstairs, asking to see Ellen; insisted no one else would do.

'Who is she?' Ellen asked.

'Says her name's Monica Telford,' the desk sergeant said.

Ellen looked regretfully at the pile of files on her desk, waiting to be dealt with. She'd cleared the next few hours to work through them and could do without this. But she recognised the name and her sense of duty wouldn't allow her to pass this to someone else.

'Tell her I'll be right down,' she said.

Unusually, there was only one person in the reception area when Ellen went downstairs. A tall, attractive woman with long dark hair wearing a navy-blue trench coat and a red silk scarf with a pretty butterfly pattern. Monica Telford. A local artist Ellen had met at an exhibition a few months ago. She'd liked Monica's work and ended up buying one of her paintings.

When Monica saw Ellen, she stood up and smiled.

'Ellen. Thank you so much for seeing me.'

At the exhibition, Ellen and Monica had only chatted briefly. Ellen couldn't even recall telling Monica she was a copper. It was flattering, she supposed, to think she'd made a lasting impression. Flattering or not, Ellen wasn't about to let this drag on for too long.

'What can I do for you?' she asked.

Monica looked around the waiting area, as if she was scared of being overheard.

'Is there somewhere more private we could go?' she asked.

Ellen nodded. 'Sure. Follow me.'

* * *

'Someone's watching me.'

Ellen waited, dreading what came next.

'I know it sounds crazy,' Monica said. 'And I probably wouldn't have come in at all, if I'm honest with you. It was only when I saw that piece in the *Star*. Maybe you haven't had a chance to see it yet? There's this woman…'

Ellen held a hand up. 'I've seen it.'

'Of course,' Monica said. 'Sorry. Oh God, and you're going to think I'm some sad sap who's making all of this up because I've read that? Shit. I should have realised that's what you'd think.'

'I don't think anything yet,' Ellen said. 'Because you haven't told me anything.'

Monica smiled. 'I haven't, have I? I'm making a right mess of this. Okay. I'll start again.'

The story she told closely echoed what Ellen already knew about Chloe Dunbar, repeated in today's paper for the rest of the world. For the last few months, Monica thought someone was watching her.

'Just a feeling at first,' she said. 'Like, I'd be walking down a street, or in the park, and I'd think someone was following me. But whenever I looked around, there was no one there. At least, not anyone I recognised.

'Then I started to notice things around the house. Stuff started moving. Oh, don't look at me like I'm a crazy woman. I don't mean moving around by themselves. *Being* moved. By someone else.'

'What sort of stuff?'

By now, Ellen was going through the motions. Monica's account was too similar to Chloe's to be taken seriously.

'The cushions in the sitting room,' Monica said. 'I arrange them in a very careful way. You haven't seen my house but if you did, you'd know what I mean. I care a lot about how things look. I've organised my house just the way I like it. Everything perfectly beautiful and exactly in its right place. When something's moved, I notice. Believe me.'

Ellen thought of her own child-friendly home, nothing where it was meant to be, and felt a pang of envy. It was a constant struggle to rein in her desire for neatness and order in the face of her children's boundless enthusiasm for chaos and mess.

'My kitchen, too,' Monica said. 'A bag of pasta put into the wrong cupboard, the salt cellar in the fridge. That sort of thing. And then this morning, something else. Something that's really, properly freaked me out.'

'Yeah?'

Monica leaned forward in her chair, making sure she had Ellen's full attention. She looked excited. Almost like she was enjoying this.

'He left me something,' Monica said. 'A cup of tea and a flower. A rose. They were on the kitchen worktop when I came downstairs this morning. The tea was still warm.' She shivered. 'Like he'd only just left.'

In her mind, Ellen was already running back through Chloe's newspaper interview, going over what she remembered word for word. Making sure she hadn't missed it. Even though she already knew.

There was one detail Martine Reynolds had left out of the piece. Something no one could possibly know about unless they'd been told about it. Chloe's stalker had a unique MO. Every morning after he'd been in the house, Chloe came downstairs to find a cup of tea on her worktop. Beside it, a single rose, wrapped in black crêpe paper.

* * *

'Why, Chloe?' Raj asked. 'It was such a stupid thing to do. I told you, don't talk to the press whatever you do. What if Ricky sees it? Do you have any idea how he'll react when he reads this? I've already told you, he wasn't the person who broke into your home and attacked you. It wasn't him.'

Raj looked more upset than angry and she felt bad about that. Everything he said made sense and she couldn't understand now why she'd agreed so easily to the interview.

'It was Nathan's idea,' she said. 'The journalist is a friend of his. He said it would make a statement to Ricky and the police.'

'It's made a statement all right,' Raj said. 'Jesus, Chloe. If I was your ex and you accused me of something like this, I wouldn't be too happy. From what you've told me about Ricky, he doesn't sound like the sort of bloke who'll take kindly to something like this.'

She wanted him to stop. If he didn't stop, she'd start crying again, and she was so tired of being upset the whole time. These last few days, she'd been feeling a bit better. There'd been no more 'incidents' since the story in the paper and she'd started to hope that maybe it was all over.

'I'm sorry.' Her voice wobbled and Raj patted her hand, told her it was okay, but she knew it wasn't. She'd been stupid. Raj was right.

They were sitting in the small kitchen at the back of the estate agency where she worked. She could see Nathan getting up from his desk – again – and waddling over.

'Everything okay?' he asked.

'Fine,' Raj said before Chloe had a chance to answer. 'Just a few more questions and then I wouldn't mind a word with you, Mr Collier.'

'Of course,' Nathan said. 'But before we do that, can I get anyone a cuppa?'

Chloe and Raj both shook their heads, then had to wait while Nathan made a big deal of getting a drink for himself.

Chloe usually made the teas and coffees and she wondered if Nathan was annoyed at having to do it himself. Or whether he was only getting the drink so he could earwig on their conversation. If that was the case, he was out of luck. Raj didn't say a word the whole time Nathan was in the kitchen. Eventually, Nathan seemed to work out he wasn't wanted and left.

'Why do you need to speak to Nathan?' Chloe asked. 'You don't think he could have anything to do with this, do you?'

'I'm sure you're right,' Raj said. 'But I have to keep an open mind. Until we find out who broke into your house last week, everyone is a potential suspect.'

'It's so hard to think straight,' Chloe said, needing to explain. 'I don't know who I can trust. You've been really kind but it's not helping, is it? If it's not Ricky doing this to me, then that's worse, in a way. Because then it could be anyone and I don't understand why someone would want to hurt me or freak me out like this.'

'We'll find them,' Raj said. 'You've got to believe that. But speaking to this journalist, that's not going to help. I don't want you doing anything like that again, okay?'

She nodded. She hadn't liked the woman anyway.

'Do you really think you'll find him?' she asked.

'Yes,' Raj said. 'Of course.'

But she didn't believe him. It had been going on too long and the police had done nothing. The only person who'd done anything to help was Nathan. Maybe Raj was right and speaking to the journalist was a mistake. But at least it made her feel like she'd done something. Which was far better than sitting back and just waiting for the next bad thing to happen.

# SEVEN

I would do anything for love.

*Never understood that. Until now.*

*Meatloaf. The fat bastard won't leave me alone. The old man's fault. The Meat's biggest fan. Back to Hell was the soundtrack to my life. Christ.*

But I won't do that.

*What wouldn't you do, Meat? Me, there's nothing I wouldn't do.*

*She was distracted last night. Easy to hate her when she's like that. Not that I could ever hate her. Wish sometimes it could be easier, more straightforward. The way these things are meant to be. Wish she didn't have to be so complicated.*

*She can't help it. I know that.*

Run right into hell and back.

*In the blink of an eye.*

*It's like she doesn't want me to know what she's thinking. Like she's hiding the best part of herself. She's scared. I understand that. Understand why, as well. We have more in common than she knows. I want to tell her that, just don't know how to do it.*

*She let me touch her last night. Would have let me do more, too. I felt her skin when I put my hand inside her shirt. The shock of it. Electricity through my body. Shock after shock. Her face close to mine, smiling, letting me know she felt it too.*

*Exquisite pain. Knowing what I wanted but holding myself back. Making sure to take it slowly. Don't want to scare her off.*

*You can go your whole life not knowing. I nearly did. If our paths hadn't crossed, maybe I'd have gone on like that. Now I know, though. And that changes everything.*

\* \* \*

'I suppose I should congratulate you,' Ellen said.

'Only if you want to.' Ger smiled. 'I can understand if this might be a bit awkward for you. Which is why I wanted to see you. I was hoping we could talk things through, iron out any potential issues before they become a problem.'

They were sitting in Ger's office. What used to be Ed Baxter's office until Ed left on long-term sick leave. So far, Ger hadn't added any personal touches and the room was almost exactly as Ed had left it. The only thing missing was the framed photo he'd kept on his desk. Ed and his missus on holiday in Costa del

Somewhere or Other.

'Can't stand clutter,' Ger explained. 'Lucky for me, Ed was the same. Nothing worse than spending your first day in a new job clearing up someone else's crap. Coffee?'

She swung off her chair and went to the Nespresso machine on the shelf behind her desk. The coffee machine the team had bought Ed as a fiftieth birthday present.

'He left this for me,' Ger said. 'Told me it belonged here, not at home with him. Truth is, Ellen, I think the chemo's left him feeling so bloody sick he can't stomach anything right now.'

'You've been in touch then?' Ellen asked.

'Of course,' Ger said. 'Haven't you?'

Not as much as she should have. Hardly at all, in fact. Her last few weeks working with Ed hadn't been easy. He'd done something she hadn't agreed with and she was finding it hard to forgive him. She knew she should put aside whatever issues she had and make the most of the little time he had left, but she was finding that hard to do. At one stage, she'd considered him a close friend. Not anymore, though, and that hurt. Because she felt that way, she'd chosen to put distance between them. A distance that, in all likelihood, probably caused her more pain than it did him.

'I see him a bit,' she lied. 'But you know how it is. Family, work...'

The excuse sounded pathetic and she trailed off, unable to finish, unable to look Ger Cox in the eye as she handed Ellen a bright yellow mug.

'Milk?'

Ellen shook her head. 'Black, no sugar. This is perfect. Thanks.'

'I've gone through the current caseload,' Ger said. 'I think I'm pretty much up to speed with your team's priorities. Biggest case at the moment is this double murder on Loampit Vale?'

'Right.'

'You've made an arrest?'

Ellen nodded. 'Charged him an hour ago. He's being held over tonight and we're at the Mag's Court first thing tomorrow.'

'Excellent,' Ger said. 'And what about this?' She pulled a copy of the *Evening Star* from her desk drawer and placed it on the table. 'Should I be worried?'

'Maybe.' Ellen had thought of little else since her interview with Monica. 'Someone else came in earlier. Claims something similar is happening to her.'

'Before or after this went out?' Ger asked.

'After,' Ellen said. 'But it's not what you think. At least, I don't think so.'

Ellen told her about the tea and the rose, explaining it was the one detail left out of the newspaper report.

'And there's no way this woman could have known about it?' Ger asked.

'Not unless she'd spoken to Chloe,' Ellen said. 'Which is possible, I suppose. Although I did ask if she knew Chloe and she claims she's never even met her.'

'Well check it out,' Ger said. 'Thoroughly. Get Patel to speak to Chloe again. Ask her if she knows this Monica Telford. And do a trawl of the local flower shops. Find out if anyone's been buying up roses lately. Check online retailers as well. See if anyone's been doing a regular delivery to SE London.'

She sounded irritated and that irritated Ellen. Of course she was going to bloody check everything out. She'd be doing it right now, in fact, if she hadn't been hauled in here to 'talk things through'.

'What about this journalist?' Ger asked. 'Martine Reynolds. Is she as bad as I think she is?'

'Worse,' Ellen said. 'More concerned with shit-stirring than actually finding the truth. She won't care what's in the best interests of the public. The only person's interests she cares about are her own.'

'I'll get someone in the press team onto it,' Ger said. 'See if there's something we can do. What else?'

'I've arranged for a car to patrol both houses at regular intervals for the next week,' Ellen said. 'Nights only. During the day, we've got the COs doing the same thing on foot. I've told both women to stay with friends or family if they're scared. I've told them to get their locks changed, get an alarm, all the usual advice you'd give. And they've both been given the leaflets on stalking and how to deal with it. Forensics have been through Chloe's house. Didn't find anything out of the ordinary. Not sure what else we can do at this stage.'

'Phone them everyday,' Ger said. 'Keep in close contact with them. And get someone across to interview Chloe's ex. Again. I know he's got an alibi, but let's make sure he didn't get someone else to break into Chloe's place.'

'Except if Monica's telling the truth, it's not him, is it?' Ellen said.

'Maybe she knows him too,' Ger said. 'Although the most likely explanation is that she's making it up. She read Chloe's story and decided to claim the same thing is happening to her. What did you think of her?'

'Difficult to tell,' Ellen said. 'Very charming, very attractive. Although, there was something a bit off.'

'Off how?'

'She didn't seem as scared as I'd expect,' Ellen said. 'At one point, I got the feeling that she was enjoying herself.'

'Speak to her again,' Ger said. 'Let her see we're taking this seriously. I know it sounds like overkill but if this Telford woman is making it up, the next thing she'll do is approach the journalist for her own exclusive. We don't want that.'

'And?' Ellen asked.

Ger frowned. 'What?'

'Mag's Court tomorrow,' Ellen said. 'I need to be there. You don't have a problem with that?'

'As long as it doesn't interfere with sorting this shit out. You can always send Raj to court if you need to. I don't want you pushing yourself too hard, Ellen. You're officially still on a thirty-hour week. Which is fine. I'm all for flexible working for parents.

Heck, I wouldn't have got this far without some flexibility over the years.'

That was a load of rubbish. No one got to DCI on part-time working. Yes, it was more than possible to be a detective and work part-time. But the moment you stopped being a full-time employee, it was as good as writing an e-mail to the senior management team telling them you had no interest in ever being promoted above your current role.

'I'll be fine,' Ellen said.

'I know.' Ger pointed to the paper. 'This worries me, though. If Chloe's telling the truth, then the attack on Friday night means he's escalating. Makes me worry about what he'll do next.'

'Nothing,' Ellen said. 'Because we'll stop him. Right?'

'Right.'

Ger didn't look up from the newspaper and Ellen stood up, sensing she'd been dismissed. She was at the door, about to open it, when Ger spoke again.

'Ellen, I'm sorry I didn't say anything.'

'About what?' Ellen asked, knowing too well what Ger was talking about.

'The job,' Ger said. 'I couldn't tell you when I called. I still had another round of interviews to get through after that. Of course, if I'd thought for a second I was even in with a chance, well, I'd definitely have said something.'

'So why did you call?' Ellen asked.

She waited, hoping Ger would explain and things between

them could go back to the way they were before this morning's announcement.

'I wanted to speak to you,' Ger said. 'I was having a bad day and I wanted to hear a friendly voice. Nothing wrong with that, is there?'

'I suppose not.'

Ger smiled. 'So I'm forgiven?'

'Nothing to forgive.'

She couldn't wait to get out of there. Ger was still smiling and Ellen did her best to smile back. It wasn't easy. She knew why Ger had phoned her. It had nothing to do with Ellen's friendly voice (let's face it, she didn't have one) and all to do with pumping Ellen for information, getting the gossip on the team at Lewisham in advance of her interviews.

Ger Cox had been using her. And that hurt more than Ellen was willing to admit. Even to herself.

# EIGHT

'That's all done for you, love. Here are your new keys. Two sets there, so you've got a spare in case you need them. And those locks are strong. No one will get through them in a hurry.'

Monica stood and stretched. She'd been sitting in the back garden with a glass of Sauvignon Blanc and a magazine, relaxing while the locksmith changed the locks on the front and back doors.

She took the keys from his outstretched hand and smiled. 'I can't tell you how grateful I am,' she said. 'It's such a relief.'

He smiled back. He was a good-looking guy. Dark hair and fantastic, greeny-blue eyes. Great shoulders, too. He most definitely worked out to get a body like that.

'So,' he said. 'Who are you so keen to lock out? An ex, is it?'

She flicked hair back from her face, maintaining eye contact with those greeny-blues.

'Something like that,' she murmured. 'Girl like me, living alone. Can't be too careful, can I?'

'Suppose not,' he said, face serious, like he wanted to show her how responsibly he took his job. 'You'll be safe as houses now. No one will be able to break through those babies.'

'Except you, of course.'

Christ, she thought, listen to yourself, Monica. Flirting with the guy who's come to change the locks. Just how desperate are you?

The locksmith started to say something else, but she cut him off.

'I'll get my cheque book,' she said. 'Then you can be on your way. Wait here.'

She wrote out the cheque in the kitchen. Two hundred quid. Sickened her to have to throw money away like that. She glanced out the window into the back garden. The locksmith was still there, standing with his back to her, hands in the pockets of his jeans.

The image stirred a memory. Summertime. The Greenwich Union beer garden. Carrying her drink outside. Coming out of the pub into the sudden brightness of the summer afternoon. Seeing him for the first time. He was leaning against the tree, eyes half-closed. Laid-back, relaxed. Like nothing in the world got to him. She decided there and then that she would get to him, though. Oh yes.

He was wearing faded jeans and a black T-shirt. It was a look that suited him. His right hand hung loosely by his side, holding a burning cigarette. As she watched, he lifted this to his mouth. At the same time, he turned his head. Their eyes met. A trail of smoke drifted from his mouth into the hot, still air around him. He smiled and right then she knew she was lost.

The memory faded, replaced by others she didn't want to think about. Suddenly, the man in the garden irritated her. The way he was standing, waiting for her to come back out. She wanted him gone.

She leaned out the window and told him to come inside. Then she handed him the cheque and dispatched him through the front door as quickly as she could. When he was gone, she breathed a sigh of relief and went back into the kitchen to get the wine. Carrying the bottle outside, she refilled her glass and sat down. She leaned back in the chair and closed her eyes, soaking up the last bit of warmth from the pale autumn sun.

Soon it wouldn't be warm enough to sit outside. She was determined to make the most of it while she still could. Her mind drifted back to that summer. As it seemed to with increasing frequency these days. Ellen Kelly had asked if she could think of anyone who might want to hurt her. *Of course not,* Monica had told her, *why would anyone want to hurt me?*

Meeting Kelly today was an interesting experience. Different from the first time. Back then, Monica had no idea how intertwined their lives would become. Truth was, the first time Monica hadn't registered anything special about Ellen Kelly at all. She'd been interested in Kelly as a potential customer but, apart from that, the woman held little appeal for her.

Today was different. Today was about getting the measure of the woman. At the end of it, Monica had to admit, Kelly had been more impressive than she remembered. Attractive for sure, although the signs of middle age were already starting to show in the crows' feet at the corners of her eyes and the start of a crease either side of her nose and mouth.

It was repulsive, really, the way white skin aged so quickly. Monica, with her mixed-race genes, was graced with her mother's smooth, flawless skin. Black don't crack, her mother used to say, and it was true. So far, at least. Her mother's beautiful face flashed before her. Still hard to believe she'd never see that face again. She shook her head, banishing the sadness. Went back to thinking about Kelly.

Apart from the skin, it was clear Kelly looked after herself. She had a good body – not as voluptuous as Monica's but not bad, either – she dressed well and her dark, bobbed hair was glossy and carefully styled. Not much of a personality, though. Monica had found her cold and charmless. Almost like Kelly couldn't be bothered making an effort. It baffled Monica how some people could go through life like that, not realising the importance of getting people to like you. Because once they liked you, it was so much easier to get them to do things for you.

She thought about pouring herself another glass of wine, but decided not to. Wine wasn't what she needed right now. The day was young and she had plans for later. The encounter with Kelly had left her with a restless energy. There was only one thing to do when she felt like this.

She went upstairs. In the bathroom, she undressed and turned on the shower. As she washed, she did a quick run through the current men in her life, wondering which one to call. There was Harry, of course. In some ways he was the easiest option. But she wasn't in the mood for all that. Not tonight. She nearly went with George, the barrister, but quickly chose excitement over predictability. George was too boring for his own good. Almost made her feel sorry for his wife.

An hour later, she was ready. She looked at her reflection in the mirror, liking what she saw. Black leather strapless dress that fit like a second skin. She turned around, admiring the high, tight curves of her backside. Rolled her shoulders, loving the way the muscles rippled under the skin. When she turned back, she lifted each arm, one by one, checking the flesh around her armpits. Not even a hint of bingo wings. All those long hours at the gym were worth it.

She smiled. The face in the mirror smiled back.

It was time.

# NINE

Carl was on the phone. Speaking in the loud, showy-off voice he used when dealing with women clients. Or punters, as he liked to call them. Even though he knew Nathan hated the word. Said it showed a lack of respect and just because they were estate agents, that didn't mean they had to live up to their reputation.

Chloe was pretending to work, but really she was on the internet. She'd done a Google search, typing in her own name. Her face stared out at her from the computer screen. The same photo they'd used for the newspaper. It was a good enough photo, although you could see the spot on her chin. She'd tried to cover that over before the interview, but obviously hadn't done a good enough job. She wished now she'd asked them to airbrush it out.

Spot aside, she looked okay. Scared, yes, but that look suited her. It was what made her attractive to a certain type of man. The sort who thought he wanted to protect her. Then turned nasty when he found out it wasn't protecting she was after. Men like Ricky. All slimy charm one minute, then – before you knew it – hands around her throat as he banged her head against a wall. Calling her a stupid bitch and other names she didn't want to think about.

She knew Carl had read the piece in the paper. It was obvious from the way he kept looking at her. Curious and shy at the same time, like he wanted to ask her about it but didn't know where to start. Different from how he usually was, with his sly smiles and cheeky remarks, whispered so that Nathan couldn't hear. Knowing Nathan wouldn't stand that sort of disrespectful behaviour.

Apart from Chloe and Carl, the office was empty. Chloe's desk was near the front and she sat facing the window. She was the receptionist; her job was to greet people as they came in, find out what they wanted and direct them to the right person – Carl for rentals, Nathan for sales.

She liked it here. Enjoyed watching people outside on the street, going about their day-to-day business. It gave her a good feeling, knowing they had no idea she was looking at them. During the summer, the heat through the glass had turned the office into a furnace. She preferred it at this time of year. Today, there was just enough sunshine for lots of natural light to stream in without the unbearable heat.

'You okay?'

Carl's phone call was over and he came over, stood right by her desk and looked at her computer screen. She shut down the browser, making her face disappear.

'I'm fine,' she said.

He folded his arms, frowning. The smell of his aftershave – a strong, herbal scent – filled the air around her. She pushed her chair back and stood up, wanting to put some distance between them.

'Coffee?'

He shook his head.

'Chloe, listen.' He sighed. 'Sorry. I'm not very good at this. I just, you know, wanted to say, I think what's happening to you, it's horrible. I know I can be a bit of a bullshit merchant at times, but I don't mean it. You know that, right? I mean, if there's anything I can do, you'd tell me, right?'

While he spoke, his face grew redder and redder. He looked like telling her this was physically hurting him. Made her feel a bit different about him, if she was honest.

She patted his arm – hard muscle through the cheap shiny suit – and smiled.

'That's really sweet of you, Carl. I appreciate it. Really I do. Now then, you sure you don't want a coffee?'

He smiled, too. A really genuine smile that she'd never seen before. For the first time, she noticed how good-looking he was. Easy to miss it under the attitude and the loud clothing. Strange, she thought, how you can think you know someone and all along you've got them completely wrong.

She waited for his answer, but he didn't say anything. Just stood there staring at her with that goofy look on his face. Made her feel a bit goofy herself. Until she remembered this was Carl. Loud-mouth Carl with an ego the size of the Shard.

That was how Nathan had described Carl the day he'd offered her the job. Difficult to believe she'd been here six months already. And in all that time, this was the first proper, genuine conversation they'd had.

Carl was still staring at her, like he'd forgotten she'd ever asked him a question. Almost, she thought, like he'd forgotten where they were. This was work, after all. Not the time or the place to be making those goofy eyes at her. No matter how nice it made her feel.

When the phone rang, they both jumped. Then laughed. Doing it all at the same time as each other. She rushed forward to answer it. Carl did the same thing and their hands brushed against each other as they both reached out to grab the handset.

The shock of contact made her jump again.

'Happy Home, Carl speaking, how can I help you?'

She watched him, slight frown on his face as he listened to the caller. Then he was nodding and smiling and handing the phone over.

'For you,' he said.

Her first thought was Ricky. He'd seen the piece in the paper and managed to track her down. She didn't want to take the phone, but Carl was pressing it into her hand and almost as if she had no control over her own body, she put the phone to her ear and said hello.

'Chloe? It's Anne.'

It wasn't Ricky. Lovely Anne instead, who'd been so kind and understanding and easy to talk to. The relief was so overwhelming, Chloe barely took notice of what Anne was saying. Something about wanting to move house and getting Chloe's opinion on where might be a good area and asking if Chloe was free to meet sometime so they could talk about it properly. Chloe said sure, whatever, she'd be happy to help.

Midway through the conversation, another phone started ringing and Carl went to answer it. By the time Chloe hung up, Carl was back in business mode, flirting crudely with whatever poor woman had been unlucky enough to get through to him.

Chloe waited to see if he'd turn and look at her, but his attention was fully focussed on the phone call. Whatever had happened between them moments earlier was a passing thing. Gone before it even started. She knew it was foolish, but she couldn't help feeling disappointed.

In the small kitchen in the back, she took a single cup from the cupboard and made a coffee for herself. If Carl changed his mind about wanting a coffee, he could darn well make it himself.

* * *

The street was quiet. And dark. Patches of pitch black broken up with tunnels of orange light from the few street lamps that were working. She walked slowly, the click-clack of her pointed heels echoing back to her as she walked.

A car drove past, slowed down as it approached. She didn't recognise it and kept walking, head averted. The driver rolled down his window, shouted something out but she didn't look around and he gave up eventually.

It was a cool night but she was warm and walked with her coat open, shrugged off around her shoulders, revealing smooth, dark skin. Under the next light, she stopped, put her hands on her hips, raised one leg so her foot was resting on the lamp-post, and waited.

Several more cars passed by. A black BMW with tinted windows slowed and stopped alongside her. A window rolled down and she saw there was more than one person inside. Intrigued, she walked over to find out more. But it wasn't anything new. Young men with too much money and not enough imagination, spouting the usual predictable bullshit. She pulled the knife from her coat pocket, shoved it in the driver's face and told him what she'd do if he didn't drive away right this second.

She watched the car screech away from the kerb and went back to waiting under the orange light. The street was quiet for a while until another car came towards her. Headlights on full so she couldn't see anything at first.

The car stopped. A grey Lexus. This was the one. The driver switched the engine off, turned off the headlights and waited. Droplets of saliva had pooled at the corners of her mouth. She swallowed – once, twice, again. Excitement. Body tingling with it. Little shots of electricity – one, two, three. She licked her lips. Swallowed a final time, forced herself to take deep breaths – one, two, three. And again. One, two, three.

Monica stepped forward, out of the orange light, into the shadowy darkness.

# TEN

In the kitchen, Ellen took a bottle of Merlot from the wine rack and looked at it. To open or not to open, that was the question. Took a full two seconds to decide. It was still early, after all. Not even nine o'clock. A long evening in front of her with nothing to do except watch TV and try not to think about work. Both of which she'd find so much easier with the help of a few glasses of wine.

She drank half of the first glass while she was still in the kitchen. Topping herself up, she went into the sitting room and switched on the TV. Flicked through the channels for a bit, but couldn't find anything to hold her attention.

Her phone was on the coffee table and she picked it up, scrolling through the messages – again – checking to see if there was anything from Jim. Nights they didn't see each other, he usually called or sent a text. So far tonight, she hadn't heard from him. No reason she couldn't call him, of course. No reason apart from her own stupid pride.

Frustrated – a combination of her stupidity and his persistent silence – she put the phone down and tried to concentrate on the TV. Kirsty and Phil were helping a wealthy couple buy a house on the Suffolk coast. The couple were relocating from London. Ellen couldn't see the sense of it herself and soon her mind was drifting, going over the arrangements for Friday night. Again.

She shivered. Lust not fear. They'd been taking things slowly. Her decision and he seemed happy enough to go along with it. Friday night would change all that. They were going to a hotel. Together. Spending the night. The prospect of it, being with him like that, was terrifying and exciting.

The front doorbell rang. She thought it was him and ran to answer it.

'Ellen! Thank goodness you're in. I'm so sorry for calling around. I didn't know what else to do.'

Monica Telford swayed in the porch. She looked drunk and Ellen resisted the urge to slam the door closed again.

'It's late,' Ellen said. 'What are you doing here?'

She would have said more, but then she noticed the bruising. And the fact that Monica seemed to be doing her best not to cry. Within seconds, a dozen different scenarios were playing out in

Ellen's head. None of them good.

'Can I come in? Please, Ellen. I've nowhere else to go.'

\* \* \*

There was someone outside, walking fast along the street, stopping outside her house. Chloe held her breath, waiting for the person to move on again. She pictured him out there, staring at the house, watching her shadow moving behind the curtains. The lights were on. Stupid, stupid! She should have turned them off.

She crept over to the light switch, keeping her body low, beneath the window frame, hoping that way he wouldn't be able to see her. At the wall, she reached up and switched off the light.

It was worse now. She couldn't see. Outside, he was moving again. Footsteps coming closer. She crouched down, body pressed against the wall, hands stuffed into her mouth, forcing back the scream. If she stayed perfectly still, he might go away. Might think she wasn't in here.

In the kitchen, on the table, the remote control for the alarm. She crawled to the door, banged her shoulder against the hard edge of the sofa but kept going. Out the door, along the hall and into the kitchen. Only then did she stand up. Dark in here too, but enough light to see where she was going.

She grabbed the control but couldn't remember how to use it. One button controlled the alarm, another put a call straight through to the police. She pressed a button but it was the wrong one and set the alarm off. The screaming, wailing noise was too loud for her small house. She tried to turn if off but whatever button she pressed, nothing worked.

She pressed her hands over her ears and ran to the back door. Had to get away from the noise but she was too scared to go out front, in case he was still there. The door was locked and she couldn't turn the key. Crying, not caring about making noise now, she tried again with sweat-slippery hands. Finally, she got it open and ran into the small back garden.

It had started to rain. Big, wet raindrops landed on her head, mixed with the tears running down her face. She didn't care. Anything was better than being trapped inside that house, waiting for him to come back and hurt her again.

# ELEVEN

'What happened?' Ellen asked.

'A bad date,' Monica said. 'I don't really want to talk about it.'

'If he hurt you,' Ellen said, 'you should report it.'

Monica shrugged. 'He's an old flame. We still meet up from time to time. Just a bit of fun. You know what fun is, right?'

Something about the way she said it set Ellen's teeth on edge. She didn't want this woman in her house. 'Why are you here?' she said.

'I'm too scared to go home,' Monica said. 'Besides, you told me to call you anytime I wanted.'

'I meant phone me,' Ellen said. 'I didn't mean call over here whenever you like. How did you get my address?'

'You gave it to me,' Monica said. 'I took your details when you bought the painting, remember?'

'What if I wasn't alone?' Ellen said. 'Did you even think about that?'

Monica smiled. 'So you do know what fun is, after all. I'm sorry, Ellen. I like you. Liked you the first time we met and like you even more after today. You were very kind to me. I wanted to see you. Nothing wrong with that, is there?'

She pointed to Ellen's wine glass, sitting empty on the table.

'Any chance I could have one of those?'

'Why me?' Ellen asked. 'You have other friends, I assume.'

'They're all men,' Monica said. 'And right now, the last thing I feel like doing is propping up some bloke's ego while he thinks he's doing me a favour. Wine? One glass and I'll be gone. I promise.'

Ellen stood up.

'I'll get you a glass of water,' she said. 'And then I'll call a cab to take you home.'

In the kitchen, Ellen took a swig of wine straight from the bottle. It didn't make her feel any better but it didn't make her feel any worse, either. The wine trickled down her throat and into her stomach. She waited for the anger and frustration to pass. Outside, it had started to rain, droplets tip-tapping against the glass doors, distorting Ellen's reflection as she moved around the kitchen.

Once she was sure she could deal with what waited for her, Ellen poured a glass of water for Monica and went back into the sitting room.

Monica was standing by the fireplace, looking at the collection of photographs on the mantelpiece.

'Your kids?' she asked. 'Cute. Who's this?'

'My husband,' Ellen said. 'Don't touch them, please. Here's your water.'

She handed the glass over and sat down, hoping Monica would do the same.

'Good-looking guy,' Monica said, refusing to take the hint. She leaned in, pushed her face against the precious image of Vinny. Ellen's hands clenched into tight fists, fingernails digging into her palms.

'He died, right?'

Ellen nodded.

'That must have been awful,' Monica said. 'When did it happen?'

'Five years ago.'

Monica pointed to the painting in an alcove beside the fireplace.

'Looks good there,' she said.

It was Monica's painting, the one Ellen had bought at the exhibition a few months back.

'It's a lovely painting,' Ellen said.

Monica sat down then. On the sofa beside Ellen. She smelled of perfume, booze and sex. Monica took a sip of water and placed the glass on the coffee table. She brushed against Ellen, the side of her breast touching Ellen's thigh as Monica leaned forward.

Ellen tried to shift sideways, out of her way, but she was already pressed into the side of the sofa and there was nowhere else to go.

Monica straightened up and smiled. She seemed oblivious to Ellen's discomfort.

'You must get lonely,' she said.

Ellen swallowed.

'You shouldn't be here. I'll call a cab.'

Monica reached forward, brushed a strand of hair back from Ellen's face.

'Poor Ellen.'

Her eyes, this close, looked huge. Deep, dark pools. The smell of her was everywhere.

'I know what loneliness is like.' Monica was whispering now, voice so low Ellen had to strain to hear. 'I've been lonely my whole life. Ever since my mother left. I was only a child, Ellen. Eight years old and she left me with that bastard. What do you think of that?'

'Can't have been easy,' Ellen said. There was a tremor in her voice and she realised she was shivering. Yet she felt so hot. Face burning, hands damp with sweat. Monica's heat, so close, like a radiator.

'She left me,' Monica said. 'Instead of protecting me, she left me to deal with him myself.'

She should stop it now. Tell Monica to finish her water and get the hell out of there. If she had any sense, that's what she'd do. But she wanted to find out. Wanted to understand who this woman was, what secrets she was hiding. Because there were certainly secrets. Until she knew what they were, she wouldn't know if Monica was someone she was meant to protect. Or be scared of.

\* \* \*

'I grew up in North Kent,' Monica said. 'Whitstable. You know it?'

'A bit,' Ellen said. 'I know that part of the world quite well, actually.'

Days passed without remembering. Then, *wham*. It was all she could think of. The scream of the brakes as the train bore down on them. The two men disappearing under it. Afterwards, Dai's brown brogue at the side of the track. Just one shoe. Later, she'd worried about it. Hoped that whoever removed his body saw the shoe and thought to put it back on. For some reason, the thought of it there without Dai was unbearable. At one point she'd even considered going back, just to check. Except she couldn't face it, so she had done nothing instead. Another thing to feel guilty about.

'It's a horrible place,' Monica said. 'At least, it was when I was growing up. I loathed every minute of living there. It might have been different if things had been better at home. But they weren't. My mother left when I was a kid. I never understood how she could do that. She knew what he was like and yet she left me there. With him. I've never stopped hating him for it.'

'Your father?' Ellen asked.

Monica nodded. 'It was his fault. She'd never have left if he was a better man. He was a pig. Oh, on the surface he was mister respectable pillar of the community. But that was all a façade. He drank a lot. When he was drunk it always went the same way. He'd start moaning on about my mother. Crying and asking me why she'd left. Like he couldn't see what a pathetic loser he was. No woman with any sense would stay with a man like that. Then he'd start on me. I was just like her. Only worse because I could see how upset he was, how lonely he was and I did nothing to help. How every time he tried to show me some love, I rejected him.'

Monica shook her head. 'I was fourteen the first time that bastard tried to show me some love.'

'Wasn't there anyone you could speak to?' Ellen asked.

'I tried,' Monica said. 'There was an art teacher who was kind to me. But when I told her what was happening at home, she didn't believe me. After that, I decided to deal with it myself.'

'How?'

'Got a job, saved some money and got the hell away from there. Moved away from home when I was seventeen and haven't looked back since.'

'He never tried to find you?' Ellen asked.

Monica shook her head. 'The night I left, I stole his car. I was reversing out of the driveway when I saw him. He was roaring at me, telling me he wouldn't let me go. Banging on the car door, trying to get in. I panicked. Swerved into him and knocked him over. After that night, I never saw him again.'

Monica lifted her glass and drained the rest of her water. When she drank, her lipstick left a red stain on the glass.

A car horn beeped outside the house.

'Your cab,' Ellen said.

At the front door, Monica embraced Ellen.

'Thank you,' she whispered. She held Ellen a moment too long, soft body pressed against Ellen's, and thrust the lower half of her body into Ellen's. The movement was so sudden and brief, Ellen couldn't be sure, afterwards, she hadn't imagined it. Just as quickly, Monica released her and was running down the path, splashing through puddles and into the waiting cab.

Ellen waited until the cab had turned the corner at the end of the road and disappeared. Only then did she let out the breath she was holding. Relief that Monica was gone. The whole encounter had been deeply uncomfortable. At the end of it all, Ellen was no closer to understanding what Monica Telford was all about. The story about her father should have triggered feelings of sympathy. Instead, she couldn't shake off the feeling that Monica had been playing with her. Why, Ellen had no idea. Not yet. The one thing she knew for certain was that tonight was the last time Monica Telford would set foot inside her house.

# TWELVE

At some point during the night, it had stopped raining. Streaks of sunlight trickled through the gaps in the curtains, drawing Monica from a deep sleep. She opened her eyes. The room was alive with little speckles of dust lit up gold, dancing. As she waited for the last traces of sleep to pass, Monica thought back over last night.

It had been easier than she'd expected. The car turning up like that had been a stroke of luck. She'd recognised it immediately. Knew the driver and knew what he was looking for. All over in less than an hour. Then across to Kelly's while the bruises were good and fresh.

She could have had Kelly there on the sofa if she'd wanted to. She'd seen it in Kelly's eyes. Another glass of wine, a few more shared intimacies and anything could have happened. Monica rolled onto her back, finger pressing her clitoris as she pictured it ...

\* \* \*

Tuesday morning, Ellen was back in Ger's office.

'Had a visitor last night,' Ellen said. 'Monica Telford. Think she was trying to imply her father is the mystery stalker.'

'You believe her?' Ger asked.

'I don't know,' Ellen said.

In truth, she still wasn't sure why Monica had called around. Several times she'd thought the artist was coming on to her. Today, without the distorting effect of wine, Ellen wasn't so sure.

'I'd like to pay him a visit,' Ellen continued. 'Would you be okay if I went to see him today? He lives in Whitstable. I could be there and back before lunchtime.'

'We've got too much on,' Ger said. 'A shitload of stuff has come in overnight. It all needs to be picked up today. And you're in court in an hour?'

'That's right.'

'Our boys were called out to Chloe's last night as well,' Ger said. 'Turned out to be a false alarm. At least, I think it was. The night guys took the call. When they got there, Chloe was in her garden, totally freaking out. No sign of a break-in, but we'll have to keep a closer eye. I'll send a couple of COs around later. Check she's okay and see if there's anything we can do. Let's leave

Monica's father out of it. For now. Apart from anything else, we still don't know if Monica's telling the truth. Until we know that, let's focus our efforts on finding who whacked Chloe.'

Back in the open-plan office Ellen shared with the rest of the team, Raj was waiting to update her on Chloe Dunbar.

'She knows talking to that journalist wasn't a good idea,' Raj said. 'Although she seems to think maybe it's helped because nothing has happened to her since the piece was published. At least, that's what she said yesterday. Before last night's incident.'

'Did she say why she did it?' Ellen asked.

'Her boss's idea,' Raj said. 'Nathan Collier. I've told you about him, right? He's sort of become Chloe's protector. Couldn't bear to see me talking to her on her own. Kept butting in every few minutes to check up on us.'

'Someone to keep an eye on?' Ellen said.

Raj frowned. 'He's definitely got a thing for Chloe. She swears they're just friends, though.'

'You think he wants more than friendship?' Ellen said.

'Hard to tell,' Raj said. 'She's way out of his league. Any idiot can see that. Plus, whenever I've spoken to him, he seems genuinely concerned about her. And he's never nervous, either. If he was trying to hide something, you'd expect him to be nervous, right?'

'Unless he's a psycho,' Ellen said. 'What about Carl Jenkins, the other guy who works with them?'

'He was on a stag do the night of the attack,' Raj said. 'Got witness statements from friends who were with him all night. We already know her ex can't have attacked her. So, for now, we're still looking.'

'Let's hope you find something soon,' Ellen said pointedly. 'Before anything else happens. What about CCTV? Any leads from that?'

'Nothing so far,' Raj said. 'There are no cameras on Nightingale Grove itself. But the road is near one of the entrances to Hither Green station. We've been going through CCTV tapes from there, but haven't found anything so far. The attack happened sometime between three-thirty and four o'clock. That side of Hither Green is pretty quiet that time in the morning. Chances are, whoever broke into Chloe's house didn't come through the station, anyway. We'll keep looking, but I'm not hopeful.'

'Did you ask her if she knows Monica Telford?' Ellen said.

'Says she's never heard of her,' Raj said. 'You know, I can sort of understand where Collier's coming from. There's something vulnerable about Chloe, makes you want to protect her. If I feel like that, why shouldn't he? I won't let anything happen to her, Ellen. I promise.'

Ellen wanted to say she believed him. The problem was, he was in no position to make that sort of promise. Without any suspects, they were no closer to finding who had attacked Chloe. And no closer to making sure she was safe from any further attacks.

* * *

Monica looked forward to these weekly visits. Knew they were building up to something and liked the way that felt. Letting it happen gradually. No need to rush. In some ways, this was the best bit: the waiting. When it was all over, it was another thing she could no longer look forward to.

She put X-FM on loud and lost herself in the music – brash, upbeat rock that suited her mood. Approaching Whitstable, the Yeah Yeah Yeahs came on. *Cheated Heart*. She turned up the volume and wound down the windows, enjoying the cool breeze on her warm face.

Her father lived in an oversized, mock-Tudor house on the coast road between Whitstable and Herne Bay. Whitstable itself was pretty enough, Monica supposed. It had certainly changed a lot since she was growing up. An influx of London cool was a vast improvement. A pity that hadn't extended to her end of town.

As a child, she'd felt the injustice of it strongly. To live in a town stuffed full of classic Victorian housing and pretty fisher-men's cottages. She'd hated it then and hated it now. The old resentment coming back each time she returned to this God-awful hole.

She drove past her house and parked near the beach, got out of the car and looked out across the still, grey sea, remembering. She'd spent so much time on this beach when she was growing up. Pretending she had a different life. Imagined herself living in one of the beautiful Victorian houses closer to town, with proper parents who loved each other and doted on their only child. The sort of life she'd have if only she wasn't restricted by her father's utter lack of imagination.

This view was one of the first things she'd painted seriously. Her art teacher, Miss Ingham, had encouraged Monica to display the painting in an exhibition in Canterbury. Thinking of Miss Ingham now, Monica smiled. The crazy old bitch had had the hots for Monica. She'd never tried anything on. Nothing like that. But Monica knew the effect she had on Miss Ingham and used it whenever it suited her.

The sea was nice enough if you liked that sort of thing. And lots of people did. The sort of people who bought her paintings and ooh-ed and ahh-ed about how fucking lovely the coast was. People like Ellen Kelly. The paintings turned out well and she could knock them out without too much bother. Didn't matter whether she liked them or not. The important thing was that she made money out of it. And she did. More than most artists could say. But then, most artists weren't as talented as she was. Or as clever at influencing the people who mattered.

She left the beach and walked back to her father's place. The house was as horrible as she remembered. Each week, driving down here, she hoped it might have improved. Fat chance. The front garden was immaculate. Gardening being one of the many tedious ways her father liked to spend his time. She pictured the inside of the house, the sterile, characterless tidiness. Bare pastel walls, tasteless, flowery curtains with matching cushions on the pale green suite. The same green as the tiles in the downstairs cloakroom. Everything spotless. Not a single speck of dirt allowed anywhere. She shuddered.

These days, the front door was black. When Monica was little, it was yellow. She had a vivid memory of her mother painting it one summer's afternoon. Monica couldn't have been more than six or seven. The red scarf was tied around her mother's head, keeping her hair from falling into her face.

Like the yellow paint, her mother was long gone. Monica could remember every moment of the day she left, although she'd done her best to push it from her mind. The betrayal still hurt, even now, all these years later. No mother should ever abandon her child. It wasn't right. Monica had never stopped hating her father for letting it happen. For not being the sort of man who could keep a woman that beautiful.

She'd been coming here every week for the last two months. Ever since Brighton. Today was different, though. Today, she was going to get out of the car and speak to him.

She knocked on the front door. No answer. She tried again, but still no one came. Stupidly, it hadn't occurred to her that he might not be home. He was always home at this time. She stepped out onto the street and scanned the area, looking for any sign of him. There was a pub down the road. Her mother's local. She supposed she could go and look for him there. At the very least, if he wasn't around, someone might be able to tell her where she could find him. Except the thought of it, being back there, chatting and flirting and making small-talk with men she despised, it turned her stomach. Skinny men with fat, beer-soaked bellies that hung over sagging trousers, all thinking they were God's gift. No thanks.

She was nearly back at the car when she saw him. Limping like a cripple, his body hunched over like he was in pain. A surge of loathing hit her. The breath left her body. She pictured herself knocking him to the ground and punching that ugly face of his. Hitting him over and over, smashing his features, turning him from man into bloody, pulpy mess. Saliva filled her mouth and she had to swallow several times.

He was on the other side of the road, head down. He didn't see her. At the front door, he paused and looked around, like he was searching for something. Like he knew she was right there, across the road, watching him. She hunkered down behind the car, waited until she heard the front door open and slam shut before she got up.

At the house, she rang the doorbell again. She pictured him inside, hearing the bell and wondering who was there. They never had visitors. Another thing that had ended when her mother left. He said he preferred it like that. Didn't like any unexpected inter-ruptions to his days.

Well he was about to get one heck of an interruption today. She smiled. Was still smiling moments later when the front door opened and there he was, mouth opening and closing as he tried – unsuccessfully – to say something.

'Hello, Adam,' she said. 'Surprised to see me? I've got a bit of news for you. Mind if I come in?'

His mouth was still moving, but there were no words. Pathetic. She stepped forward. His eyes flitted past her, like he was looking to see if there was someone who might help him. There was no one, of course. She could have told him that.

# THIRTEEN

She needed to get out of the office. Away from Nathan. He was driving her mad with his endless chat and his overly attentive questions. 'Are you okay?' 'Are you sure you wouldn't rather go home?' 'How about a nice cup of tea?'

How about you go away and give me some space to breathe, she felt like screaming at him. But she knew that wasn't fair. He was being kind and good because he was a kind and good person. It was just, sometimes, he could be a bit full on.

When lunchtime came around, she told him she needed to pop out to the chemist. It wasn't true, but she knew it was the only way to make sure he didn't offer to come with her. She made a show of putting her hand across her stomach, implying it might be her time of the month. He'd be mortified if he saw her buying a packet of tampons.

It did the trick. He smiled and told her to take her time and she was out of there before he had a chance to change his mind. Except now, walking around the shops on her own, she sort of wished she'd let him come with her.

She couldn't shake off the feeling someone was following her. Eyes watching her, burning into her back. She kept stopping and turning around suddenly, scanning the faces in the crowd, watching to see if there was anyone she recognised.

Outside, it was sunny but cold and she had wrapped up warm. Here in the shopping centre, the air-conditioning was set to high and the heat was making her feel sick. She unbuttoned her jacket and loosened her scarf, but it didn't seem to make much difference.

A big woman brushed past her, banging into the shoulder already sore from last night. Chloe swayed, but managed not to fall. Further along the row of shops, a man was standing near the entrance to Holland and Barrett. She wouldn't have noticed him at all but his jacket was familiar. A pale blue Ralph Lauren blazer. Everything shut down. Her breath caught in her throat, legs refused to move. She stood frozen to the spot.

When he smiled, her stomach folded in on itself and she couldn't stand. She tried, but there was no strength left in her body to keep her standing. The shopping centre seemed to tilt and shift sideways but she knew it wasn't the building that was moving, it was her.

As she fell, Ricky started walking towards her, still smiling.

A hand grabbed her arm, steadying her. A man's voice asked if she was all right. Carl. He held onto her, steered her across to one of the benches that formed a line down the centre of the parade of shops and sat her down gently.

She tried to speak, tried to tell him they had to get out of there, had to get away before Ricky made it across to where they were sitting. But her mouth wouldn't work. Every time she tried to speak her stomach churned so badly she had to stop.

'Chloe.' Carl's voice urgent and serious, like she'd never heard him before. Eyes looking at her with such concern. She leaned into him, let him hold her and tell her it was all okay, she was going to be okay.

Across from her, the man in the blue jacket was still there. Still smiling. He was closer now and she could see her mistake. The jacket wasn't Ralph Lauren. It was a cheap replica that fit badly. The man looked nothing like Ricky, either. Thin, balding hair and a pot belly. No way Ricky would ever let himself get a pot belly.

Carl was still talking, soft, gentle words that soothed her. She liked him being with her. For the first time since all this started, she didn't feel alone.

\* \* \*

Where was Bel?

She'd be back soon.

Only popping to Sainsbury's, she'd said.

Back any minute now. She knew how Adam hated it when she was late.

There was a crack in the ceiling. Adam had never noticed it before. Easy to miss it normally. Not so easy from this angle. A long, thin crack that ran from the light-fitting the whole way across one side of the ceiling. The crack upset him. Felt as if the house had played a trick on him. All these years, working so hard at keeping things perfect and all along, that crack up there. Mocking him.

His right hip hurt dreadfully. He moved his leg, wiggled it back and forth, making the pain worse, but if he could move his leg it meant the hip wasn't broken. He rolled onto his left side, got onto his hands and knees and crawled across to the sofa. Pushed his way in behind it and sat crouched down low. Hiding.

Where in heaven's name was Bel?

He took his phone out of his pocket, checking to see if she'd sent him a text. Even though he knew she hadn't because he'd have felt it vibrating in his pocket. He tried to text her, tell her to hurry up, but his hand was shaking so much he had to give up. Couldn't get his thumb to fix on the right letters.

*Dirty bastard.*

The words spun around his head. The dreadful things she'd accused him of.

*Pervert.*

Pushing her face into his, shouting at him. So close he could feel the spittle on his cheeks when she spoke. Bringing all her hysteria and madness with her. Messing everything up, the way she always had done.

Stop it. Stop thinking about her. She didn't mean it. She was disturbed. He'd always known that about her.

*Blow jobs.*

Good God! As if he'd ever... The other things she'd said, too. About Annie. He wouldn't – couldn't – believe it. She was making it up. Sick in the head. Adam had tried to tell her. Said he'd pay for whatever she wanted. And that's when she pushed him...

He'd imagined it for so long. Opening the door and one or other of them standing there. Now it had happened. When he first saw her, looking so beautiful, he'd thought his heart would burst. Wanted to say something but couldn't get the words out. Just so happy. Overjoyed.

And when she came inside, he'd forgotten himself for a moment and moved to hug her, wanting suddenly – desperately – to tell her how much he loved her, how badly he'd missed her. Not imagining for a second she'd come back for any other reason except she'd missed him, too.

Someone was in the sitting room. Moving around. He tensed, hand over his mouth to stop himself crying out. She was back. Maybe she'd never left. He tried to remember what had happened right after he fell.

More movement, shuffling, coming closer.

She told him he was going to prison. Started to tell him what would happen to him, what the other prisoners would do to him. She'd already made a complaint, she said. It was only a matter of time.

She was closer now. He squeezed his body as tight into the corner as he could. Felt the sofa move as she brushed against it. And then, just when he couldn't bear it a moment longer, a black nose and two brown eyes around the back of the sofa, staring right at him.

'Digger!'

His voice shook, relief, not fear. The dog moved forward and started licking his face. Normally he'd never let Digger do that but right this moment, he didn't mind.

The dog soothed him, and soon he started to feel stupid. What in heaven's name was he thinking? Hiding behind the sofa like some stupid child. He crawled out and stood up, wiping his hands together, wincing as he felt the little grains of dirt rubbing against his skin. He'd better get those washed first. And then he'd get to work. Get the house in order before Bel came back.

It wouldn't do for her to walk in and find things in disarray. Bel was like him. She needed order, everything in its right place. A mess would only upset her. And he didn't want that. Not for his Bel.

A silver-edged mirror hung on the wall over the brown marble fireplace. He barely recognised the face staring at him from the mirror. So old and scared. Pathetic. He licked his fingers and took hold of the two long pieces of hair on either side of his head, smoothing these over the bald patch at the top.

Nodding at the improvement, he bent down to rub Digger's head. Hands were already dirty so he might as well.

'Not a word, hey, Diggs?' he said. 'Our little secret. No one else's.'

The dog looked up at him, brown eyes staring into his, tail wagging hopefully. Stupid mutt. Not a clue. If Monica came back, the bloody dog would probably wag his tail and greet her like an old friend.

With a bit of luck, that was the end of it. She'd had her say, done what she came here to do – frighten the life out of him – maybe that's all she wanted. He told himself this, tried his best to believe it. But deep down, he knew his daughter, knew what she was capable of.

The knowledge offered no comfort whatsoever.

# FOURTEEN

Spending wasted hours waiting around at Camberwell Green Magistrates' Court wasn't Ellen's ideal way to spend the day. She was here for the first appearance in the case against Lewis Dayton, the man charged with a double murder on Loampit Vale two weeks ago.

Lewis shot his ex-girlfriend, Roxanne DuParc, and Jason Taylor, the man Roxanne had left Lewis for. The shooting happened on a Thursday afternoon during rush hour. Which meant plenty of witnesses for the prosecution when the case went to the Central Criminal Court. Today's hearing was the first step in the long process to get justice for Roxanne and Jason.

Roxanne's mother, Darlene, was here too. Sitting beside Ellen, bouncing Roxanne's one-year-old daughter on her lap. The hearing was scheduled for eleven o'clock but it was the afternoon now, and they were still waiting.

'There's no chance he'll get out on bail?' Darlene asked Ellen. Again.

Ellen shook her head. Again.

'No way, Darlene,' she said. 'You don't need to worry about that. After today, he'll be kept in custody until the trial. And he will be found guilty, I promise. The CPS case is strong. You'll see justice done, I promise.'

'This isn't justice,' Darlene said. 'Justice would be letting me put a gun to that man's head and do the same thing to him that he did to my little girl. That's justice, Ellen. All this? It's window-dressing. Nothing more than that.'

Ellen understood how Darlene felt. She watched Roxanne's little girl, sleepy now. Thumb in her mouth as she snuggled into her grandmother's chest.

Lewis Dayton was this girl's father. Ellen couldn't begin to understand how he could have done this to the child. She knew too well the devastation children experienced when they lost a parent. To think that anyone would deliberately inflict that pain on their own child, it was inconceivable.

She felt a sudden, sharp surge of anger and stood up, needing to move around. She went outside, saw Freddie Carr, the prosecution lawyer, smoking a cigarette and went over to him.

'Are they ready for us?' Freddie asked.

'Not yet,' Ellen said. She nodded at his cigarette. 'Got a spare by any chance?'

He passed over a packet of Marlboro Lights. She lit up and inhaled greedily.

'I can't bear it in there,' she said. 'Why do we have to drag these things out so bloody much? After today, the trial won't be for months. In the meantime, that poor woman is unable to get on with her life. It's bullshit.'

'The courts are busy,' Freddie said. 'Nothing any of us can do about that. We should consider ourselves lucky we still have a legal system. The government's cut everything back so much, it's a wonder you can find any lawyers still working.'

'The problem is,' Ellen said, 'I know sometimes cases take a long time to pull together, but this one is so clear-cut. We've got over twenty witnesses willing to step forward and confirm what Dayton did. Christ, the man himself doesn't even deny it. Why do we have to go through this farce? There should be a fast track for cases like this.'

Freddie laughed. She thought maybe he didn't realise she was being serious.

'You can't have one rule for some and another for others,' he said. 'I admit the process isn't perfect, but it's the best we can do and we all need to find a way of working with it. Unless you'd rather we just put people like Dayton in front of a firing squad.'

'Why not?' Ellen said. 'Why should he get to live when poor Roxanne and Jason don't have that luxury?'

'Because we're not animals,' Freddie said. 'No one has the right to take another person's life, Ellen. If we killed Dayton, then that makes us no better than him. Is that what you want?'

Ellen didn't answer. She thanked Freddie for the cigarette and went back inside. Darlene and her granddaughter were still on the bench where Ellen had left them. The little girl had fallen asleep, cradled in Darlene's arms. Darlene was crying quietly, tears falling onto the child's head.

Ellen sat beside her, put her arm around Darlene's shoulder and held her while she cried. She didn't care if wanting Dayton dead made her a bad person. If someone handed her a gun right now, she'd go down to the cell where he was being held and kill him herself.

# FIFTEEN

*I've had a few too many. Wouldn't be doing this otherwise. I can't help thinking she knows I'm there. Watching her. It's late, but she's still up. Moving around the house. I know this because the lights are on and the curtains are open. Almost like she wants to be seen. I'm watching her and wishing I could go over there. You'd think the drink would make that easier, right? You'd be wrong. Pissed up like this, it's not going to give the best impression, is it? Don't want her getting ideas about me. She's told me enough stories. I want her to know I'm not like that.*

*Meatloaf is thudding away inside my head. Starts off with the ballads. Slow and easy. Soft voices, comforting almost. As long as they stay separate from the memories. It's later, when the harder stuff starts up, that's when the bad shit starts.*

'You took the words right out of my mouth.'

Of course, when he goes onto that one, my mind turns back to her. Mouth opening. Slowly, like she wants it but she's scared.

And then something happens.

The lights go off downstairs. Happens so suddenly, I'm left feeling a bit hard done by. Can't help it. It's like she knows I'm watching and she's doing it on purpose. Letting me watch her for a bit, getting me so I can't think about anything except her. And then, when she's got me so fired up I swear to God I'd do anything she asked me to. Bang. Nothing.

She's playing with me and I hate her for it. A second later, I'm hating myself for being such a bastard. She's not that sort of person. She's better than that. All she wants is a bit of respect. Not a lot to ask for.

But even as I'm thinking that, my mind is picturing other stuff. Dirty stuff. I know I should stop and normally I could, I swear I could. Sometimes, though, I can't help it. I want something to happen. Want it so bad that even though part of me knows how wrong it is, my mind's already there.

Prick like a fucking rock. Her and me. Me and her. All the different things I'd like to do to her. And what I'd get her to do. And I know half of that stuff would never happen but Jesus, sometimes it's so good to let yourself imagine it.

And then something happens.

Light on upstairs. Bedroom. I step back, frightened she'll see me. She's at the window, staring out. It's like she's looking right at me.

*Even though it's dark and I don't know how she could see me, I really think she can.*

*She smiles. She's wearing a dress. Haven't seen that one before. Yellow. Wrapped tight around her body. Tied at her waist. As I watch, she unties the knot and the dress falls open. She's not wearing anything underneath.*

*Sirens screaming as the Meat ratchets it up a gear. Dress slipping off her shoulders. Hands inside my jeans, grab myself. Moving fast. Like the music ramming against the sides of my skull.*

*She steps forward. Fires howling. I can see her nipples. Big and dark. Meatloaf screaming louder. She's still smiling. I'm sure she's smiling. Hand moving faster. Pictures of her racing across my mind. Me and Meatloaf. Her between us. Screaming. Begging for it.*

*I'm there now. Roaring. No other noises now. Just my own voice. Screaming into the night. I fall forward, body doubled over, eyes closed. All of it still there but fading now.*

*When I open my eyes again, she's gone. The curtains are closed and the lights are off.*

*And it's like she was never there at all.*

# SIXTEEN

Adam drained his glass and signalled for Bel to give him a refill. There was a sour taste to the wine he didn't enjoy, but the warm buzz it gave made up for that.

Bel took his glass but hesitated. 'Are you sure, Adam? You never normally have a second one.'

'It's not like I do it every night,' he said. 'Besides, nothing like a bit of wine to get us in the mood, hey?'

He winked, irritated when she didn't smile back. What on earth was wrong with her this evening? She was always encouraging him to relax a little. And now, when he was doing just that, she acted like she disapproved. It wasn't as if he was about to get legless and go on some drunken rampage. Surely she knew him better than that? That was women for you, though. Never knew where you were with them.

'I'm just worried about you,' she said. 'You haven't been yourself all day. Are you sure there's nothing the matter?'

'Fine,' he said. 'Now go on. Get us a drink like a good girl?'

When she went to get the wine, different parts of the morning played back through his head. He wished he could tell Bel about it, ask her what she thought and if he should be worried. Or if Monica was all talk and nothing more than that.

Bel was back.

'You not having any yourself?' he asked as she handed the glass to him.

She shook her head.

He watched her, standing in front of him, waiting for her next instruction. His little servant, he called her. Meant it as a compliment, although he wasn't sure she always took it as that. But what did she expect, waiting on him hand and foot the way she did?

She wasn't the prettiest woman he'd ever met. Nose too big, eyes too close together for that. Nothing wrong with her body, though. And definitely nothing wrong with the way she used it.

He took a deep slug from the glass and smiled. Feeling a bit tipsy now. Something else too. He looked up at Bel, about to suggest it when he noticed her hair.

'You've untied it,' he said. 'I told you before, I don't like it. It's messy when it's down. Doesn't suit you at all.'

She stared at him and for a moment, from the expression on her face, it was like she hated him. But then she shrugged, lifted it back and tied it in place with the tieback she kept on her wrist. He tried to look at it, checking she'd remembered to replace it this morning. Some days, she forgot and he had to remind her.

'Not only coughs and sneezes that spread diseases,' he'd say, trying to smile but not always succeeding. Surely she knew how disgusting it was?

With her hair back her nose looked even bigger, but he didn't mind that. Besides, it wasn't like she could help it. He smiled, wanting her to know he was pleased. He held his hand out for her to take. 'Don't be like that, Bel. Let's kiss and make up, hey?'

She took his hand and rubbed it slowly along the outline of her breast.

He groaned. Ever since the accident, he'd thought this type of thing was behind him. Oh the doctor had said 'relationships of a sort' were still possible. But he never thought he'd find a woman willing to do what it took to help him reach the level of relief he craved so terribly. And then she'd come along. Poor, ugly Bel. And his life was transformed.

Gently, he reached up and traced a finger across her face. She winced and tried to pull away, but he held her head with his other hand so she couldn't move.

'You're the best thing that ever happened to me,' he said. 'I love you, Bel. You know that?'

She leaned forward, her body pressing into his, and kissed the top of the head.

'Silly boy,' she said. 'All this talk of love. You're more drunk than I thought.'

It wasn't the drink talking, though. He did love her and was determined to show her he meant it.

Behind her, on the mantelpiece, images of his ex-wife stared out at him. His beloved Annie. Could it be true what Monica told him? Best not to think about it. Maybe it was time the photos went. Without them there as a reminder, he could put it all out of his mind, once and for all. Focus on what he had here and now, not what he'd once had but lost. Monica and Annie, they were his past. Bel, lovely Bel, was what mattered now. Nothing else.

# SEVENTEEN

Katy Perry was her new role model. Katy who'd come back from a bad relationship with a roar and an attitude Chloe could only dream of. She listened to Katy every spare minute she had. Like now.

*Prism* was the best album. The one Chloe identified most closely with. She had it on now. Volume up loud. Making sure she couldn't hear anything except the music. She was halfway through her second glass of wine and the alcohol gave her the courage she needed to be here on her own.

She sang along with Katy as she got ready for her night out. Scowling and prowling in front of the mirror, shouting out the chorus to *Roar*. Imagined herself singing to Ricky, showing him she was so much tougher than he'd ever thought. After *Roar*,

*Legendary Lover*. She loved that one, too. Made her think of Carl.

Some of the lines were a bit weird and difficult to make any sense of. But when Katy got to the bit about her heart beating like a drum, Chloe was right there with her.

Since yesterday, everything felt different. The upset in the shopping centre, it felt like a turning-point. Carl had been so sweet and lovely. Completely different from how he usually was. They stayed on the bench for ages. She told him all about Ricky, the flowers and everything else. He seemed really interested. More than that, he helped her get some perspective on it.

Had anything happened since the piece in the newspaper, he'd asked. When she really thought about it, she had to admit nothing had. No flowers, no cups of tea. No waking up with the feeling that someone had been in the house. Yes, there'd been the scare the other night. But thinking about that, she knew there was a chance she'd over-reacted. She'd heard footsteps and assumed it was Ricky. But it could have just been someone walking down the street and she'd jumped to the wrong conclusion. Like she did in the shopping centre.

Plus she had the alarm and that made a difference. She might be a heavy sleeper, but even she couldn't sleep through that racket. And now here she was, getting ready to go out with her new friend. She looked at her reflection in the full-length mirror. Smiled, thinking what Ricky would say if he saw her. Hair wild and loose, not straightened the way she used to do it for him. And the dress! Tight and short. She turned around and bent over, craning her head around, making sure she couldn't see her knickers. She was going for sophisticated, not tarty.

She turned back to the mirror, examining her face. Another thing she had in common with Katy. Mostly, people didn't notice. That was because Chloe had blonde hair. But there was this one time, she'd worn a dark wig to a fancy-dress party and everyone had commented on the resemblance. She'd been flattered, at first. Until they got home and Ricky pulled the wig off and threw it in the bin, telling her she shouldn't go out dressed like a tart.

Well, Ricky wasn't here now and if she wanted to dress like a tart, she would. Even though it wasn't what she wanted. She examined the dress again, worried now that maybe it did make her look a bit cheap and easy. She tried to imagine what Anne would be wearing. Even thought about calling her, but was afraid that would make her look stupid.

She was looking forward to some girly time. It had been too long. It wasn't just her mother she'd lost touch with when she got together with Ricky. By the time she'd found the courage to leave him, there was no one left. Tonight was her first girls' night out in years. If only she could be sure about the dress...

She closed her eyes. Counted to ten, then opened them again. First impressions were important. The first impression, when she opened her eyes, was good. The dress suited her. If she was honest, she thought she looked pretty amazing. Pity Carl wasn't here to see her.

Her phone rang and she ran to answer it, thinking yes, yes, yes! Except it was Nathan, not Carl.

'Wondered if you fancied going for a drink and something to eat,' he said.

When she told him she already had arrangements, he insisted on knowing more.

'It's just a friend,' she said. 'A woman.' Why did she say that? It was none of his business. 'She's thinking of moving house. Wants my advice.'

Nathan chuckled. 'Well make sure you don't give her duff information. Tell you what, why don't you let me know where you're going and I'll try to swing by later? Give her the benefit of my wisdom. She hoping to rent or buy?'

'I don't know,' Chloe said.

The dress was too short. She could see that now as she continued looking at herself. She looked cheap. Nothing like the sort of woman she was trying so hard to become.

Nathan sighed. 'Chloe, pet, if you don't know that, how on earth will you be able to offer any advice?'

'I'll ask her,' Chloe said. 'And I don't want you to come. Thanks, Nathan, but I'll be fine by myself.'

She hung up, angry and guilty at the same time. Angry with herself for being so foolish. Angry with him for making her feel stupid. Even though she knew that's not what he was trying to do. Which was why she felt guilty. She'd been really mean to him and he was only offering to help. What was wrong with her?

She stripped off, threw her tights and the dress on the bed, put on an old pair of jeans and a long-sleeved, pale pink shirt. When she looked in the mirror again, the resemblance to Katy was gone.

In the background, Katy was still singing. A soft, sweet song about loving someone unconditionally. Chloe switched the music off and called Nathan back.

'Maybe you're right,' she said 'If Anne wants help, I'll probably say the wrong thing and make myself look stupid. Why don't you come along like you suggested? I'm sure she'd love to meet you.'

If she was honest, part of her was a little bit disappointed. She'd been looking forward to it. But another part of her – the better part – knew it was the right thing to do. Nathan had been good to her. A real friend, in fact. Turning her back on him now, just because things were starting to get better, well, it just didn't feel right.

# EIGHTEEN

Ellen was in the Vanbrugh, having a quiet drink with Jim. Trying to unwind after an unproductive day at work. The hearing had eventually gone ahead yesterday and Lewis Dayton was in Wandsworth prison, awaiting trial. Today, Ellen spent her morning ensuring all the paperwork was in order before sending it across to the CPS. In the afternoon, she'd done bits and pieces of work, but nothing that felt very substantial. The memory of Darlene crying into her granddaughter's hair was a constant distraction. She was trying not to think about it but her mind kept going back to it, no matter how hard she tried.

Jim seemed distracted tonight as well. They barely spoke to each other during the first drink. Every few seconds, he'd check his phone for new messages. It was driving Ellen nuts. After the second drink, she decided to call an end to the evening.

'We should go,' she said. 'Mum's babysitting. I promised her I wouldn't be late.'

He looked surprised. 'Okay. If that's what you want.'

'Neither of us are in form,' she said. 'I can't stop thinking about work and I can see you're miles away, too. More interested in your text messages than talking. Maybe it's better to leave and grab an early night.'

'Sorry,' he said. 'I'm waiting to hear about a possible job tomorrow. Very bad manners. Maybe you're right. We should go.'

On the short walk home, he seemed to perk up. They spoke about things they wished they'd done but never had.

'Have kids,' Jim said.

'Really?'

'Really,' he said. 'Don't sound so surprised. You said yourself it's the best thing you ever did and I can see when you're with Pat and Eilish how happy they make you and how much you love them. I'd like to know what that feels like.'

'It's not too late,' Ellen said. 'Lots of men have kids in their forties.'

'Not so many women, though,' Jim said. 'And right now, I can't imagine that I'll ever want to be with anyone except you.'

'If kids are so important,' Ellen said, 'then maybe I'm the wrong woman for you.'

He stopped walking and turned to her. Cupping her face with his hands, he kissed her – oh so softly – on the lips.

'No,' he whispered. 'You're most definitely not the wrong woman. I haven't felt this right about anything in such a long time. These past few weeks with you, it's been amazing, Ellen. You're amazing. I don't want this to end.'

'Neither do I,' she said. 'But when you get to our age, life is complicated. Things like kids. Pat and Eilish are enough for me. I don't want anymore. Besides, I'm too old. Don't fancy my chances of being a mother again at forty-two. Forty-three, even. You know, if I got pregnant right now, I'd be forty-three before the child was born? There are too many risks for women of my age. I'd spend the nine months terrified.'

She was babbling and needed to shut up. He'd think she was a loon. She certainly sounded like one. Except now she'd started, she couldn't stop.

'I get scared,' she continued, her tongue acting as if it had no connection to her brain. 'So many things can go wrong. Having children, it makes you so vulnerable. Pat and Eilish are my life. I love them so much, but all the time I'm aware how precarious it all is. At any moment, something bad could happen and if it did, I wouldn't survive it, Jim. I know that sounds mad and I'm sure it's not normal to feel like this and I know a shrink would tell me it's all to do with my mother and what happened to Vinny, but I can't help it, you see. I've tried to be different, but the fear is always there.'

She would have kept going if he hadn't leaned in right then and kissed her. Soft, at first, like before, then changing to something else. His arms wrapped around her, holding her tight. She melted into him, desire blocking out everything except the feel of his mouth on hers, his body against her, his warmth. Him. All of him.

When they pulled away from each other, she was dazed. The world had tilted. Moments ago, she hadn't been able to stop talking. Now, she couldn't think of a single thing to say. He was still holding her and she knew if he wasn't, she would fall over.

'Hey,' he said, nodding at something behind her. 'Look at that.'

She turned her head. A full moon hovered over Greenwich, against the lit-up backdrop of Docklands and the $O_2$. A bat flew across the sky, in front of the moon, its silhouette black against the white gold. Ellen started to comment on the bat but found herself kissing Jim again instead. He kissed her back, his intensity matching hers. In that instant she knew it would happen tonight. It felt right and natural.

They walked back to the house. Fast. Somehow, her shaking hands managed to get the keys from her bag and open the front door. She pulled him in after her.

'Ellen?'

Her mother. How could she have forgotten her mother was here? Putting her finger on his lips, Ellen told him to go into the kitchen and pour himself a glass of wine. Said she'd be there in a minute.

'It's not wine I want,' he whispered. 'Besides, if I don't go and say hello, your mother may never forgive me.'

Ellen groaned.

'I'll need to drive her home,' she said. 'She doesn't drive and normally insists on walking but I don't like her doing that if I can help it.'

'I'll do that,' Jim said. 'Okay if I come back after dropping her off?'

'You'd better,' Ellen said.

Her parents lived on Fingal Street, two long minutes the other side of Trafalgar Road. While she waited for Jim, Ellen paced around, unsure what to do. She went to put a CD on, but couldn't choose one that suited her mood. Everything reminded her of Vinny. She needed something new. Jim music. Stupid. What was she thinking? She wasn't. That was the problem. Only it wasn't a problem. It felt good to follow her heart for once. Do something without over-thinking it first. Still the problem of the music, though. She pulled out a Nick Drake album then put it back. Too depressing. Grabbed something at random without reading the spine. A compilation. The Tommy Dorsey orchestra with Frank Sinatra. Perfect.

Trombone, then the rest of the orchestra, followed by Frank's pure, pure voice. *I'll be seeing you.* When he hit the line about looking at the moon, Ellen smiled. She swayed out of the sitting room into the kitchen where she poured a glass of wine for Jim and water for herself.

A knock on the front door. He was back. In the hallway, she paused to check her face in the mirror. In the dim light, she looked fine and she made a note to keep out of the unforgiving light of the kitchen. She wiped her damp hands down the front of her jeans and opened the door. Grinning like a bloody fool, ready to throw herself into his arms.

He was leaning against the doorframe, like he'd walked straight out of the album she was listening to. In the background, a new song. *That Face*. Something about lips and eyes. Jim spoke. She didn't hear him. Mesmerised by his face. The tug of desire so strong it scared her. No turning back.

He walked in and scooped her into his arms. Something buzzed in her pocket. Her phone's ring-tone blocked out Frank's voice. Apologising, she pulled away. Took her phone out and saw Monica's number on the display.

'Leave it,' Jim said.

'I'll only be a minute.' She put the phone to her ear. 'DI Kelly.'

Jim rolled his eyes but he smiled and she was relieved he wasn't really upset.

'I've poured you a glass of wine,' she said. 'In the kitchen. I'll be with you in a minute.'

'There's someone outside my house,' Monica said. 'I'm scared, Ellen. Can you come over?'

Ellen glanced into the kitchen. Jim had his glass in his hand and seemed quite content browsing through her cookbooks. Vinny's books, not that it mattered.

'You have the emergency number,' Ellen said. 'You should call that instead.'

'Sorry,' Monica said. 'I couldn't find it. Please, Ellen. I'm really freaking out here.'

Her voice was slurring. Not a lot, but enough to tell Ellen that Monica had been drinking. Not that she blamed her.

'I'll get a car out to you,' Ellen said. 'I can't come over myself. I can't leave my children alone in the house.'

When Monica started crying, Ellen told her to hang up and wait by the front door. Ellen would organise a car and call her back, stay on the phone until the car arrived.

Through the glass doors that separated the sitting room from the kitchen, Ellen saw Jim. The thrill of him being here had gone, replaced by a gnawing uncertainty. He needed to go. She couldn't deal with Monica while he was here. He was too much of a delicious distraction.

He had a cookbook open in front of him and was flicking through the pages. As Ellen watched, he looked up, caught her starting at him and smiled. Ellen tried to smile back but couldn't get her mouth to work.

When she told him what had happened, he couldn't have been more understanding. Part of her wished he wouldn't be so damn nice about it. Wished he'd plead with her to change her mind. He didn't, of course. Simply kissed her on the forehead and said of course, he understood. Which he couldn't because she didn't understand herself, but she supposed it was good of him to say it. She stood by the front door and watched as he climbed into his battered green Saab and drove off.

And just like that, he was gone.

A cloud floated across the sky. It blocked out the moon and plunged the street into sudden darkness. Ellen waited for it to pass. Gradually, the moon came back – a sliver of white light that grew until it was a round whole once more. She went back inside and pulled the front door closed. It shut with a click. The sound echoed through the silent house, taunting her.

# NINETEEN

Chloe liked working in Lewisham. She could walk to work and not have to bother with public transport. She felt good this morning. Her night out with Anne had been fun, although it would have been a lot better without Nathan. He'd insisted on picking her up and driving her across. Then he'd stayed for the whole evening and driven her home afterwards. She knew he was only being kind, but sometimes she felt a bit stifled by him.

Anne's eyes nearly popped out of her head when Chloe showed up with Nathan tagging along beside her. Anne was nice enough to him, but Chloe could see her trying not to laugh a few times. Like when Nathan's big belly nearly knocked the table over.

But she shouldn't be cruel. It was thanks to Nathan that she had the alarm and it was making a big difference. She was more relaxed in the house. The remote was brilliant. She'd got used to using it now and kept it with her all the time. She turned the alarm on each time she left the house. If anyone tried to break in, the alarm would go off and the police would be straight over there.

It was a twenty-minute walk from her house to the office. She walked fast, checking every now and then, making sure no one was following her. Before all this started, she used to walk along the back streets, taking the footbridge over the railway track and into Lewisham that way. These days, she kept to the busy main roads: up Ennersdale Road and down Hither Green Lane. It was a busier, noisier route, the air thick with exhaust fumes. But there were enough people around to stop her feeling scared.

She was earlier than usual, hoping to get to the office first so that she would be sitting at her desk, calm and relaxed, when Carl arrived. She knew Nathan had an appointment first thing. With a bit of luck, it would be just her and Carl for a while.

Thinking about Carl, her attention wandered, which was why she didn't notice the man standing by the bus stop wearing the light blue jacket until it was too late. She'd just reached the office, had her key in the door ready to open it when he jumped forward, grabbed her wrist and shoved her against the door. Hard.

His smell was the first thing she recognised. Even before she looked up and saw his face. Ralph Lauren *Polo*. The only cologne he ever wore. The smell of it filled the air around her, suffocating and sick-making.

He twisted her wrist and she whimpered, begging him not to break it. He smiled.

'Aren't you going to invite me in?'

He took the key from her useless fingers, fitted it into the lock, opened the door and pushed her inside. She fell to the ground and started crawling, desperate to get away, as far away from him as she could.

The blinds were down, covering the windows, blocking out the light and making it impossible for anyone to see inside. Behind her, she heard Ricky turn the key in the door, locking it. Then his footsteps, steady and certain as he crossed the small space that separated them.

\* \* \*

Thursday morning, Ellen drove to Monica's before work. The two officers who'd responded to Ellen's call last night had found no sign of an intruder. One of them later remarked to Ellen that Monica had seemed 'tired and emotional'.

This morning, the Monica who answered the door to Ellen was calm and composed.

'Come in,' Monica said, smiling. 'Although I don't have too much time. Thought I'd go to the studio this morning. Try to get back into doing some work. How are you, Ellen? You look tired, if you don't mind me saying so.'

Tired because I was up half the night on your behalf, Ellen was tempted to reply. She was tired, but there was nothing new about that. She was always tired. Monica, on the other hand, looked like she'd had at least twelve hours' decent kip. If she was hungover, there was no outward sign of it.

'I won't stay,' Ellen said. 'Just wanted to check you're okay. You sounded in a bad way last night.'

'I'm fine,' Monica said. 'Maybe I over-reacted. It's hard to know, isn't it? When this starts happening to you, it's easy to become paranoid. You were very kind to me, Ellen. I don't take that for granted. I hope I didn't interrupt anything?'

'Like what?' Ellen asked.

Monica laughed. 'Don't be so coy, Ellen. I know you have a boyfriend. You let it slip the night I called over. Don't you remember?'

Ellen shook her head. 'Too much wine and my mouth goes all loose. Sorry. Listen, if you're sure you're okay, then I'll be out of your hair. Have a good day.'

As she left, she turned back, looked at the outside of the house.

'I thought you said you'd got an alarm fitted,' she said. 'Don't they normally put a box up so people know the place is alarmed?'

'It fell down,' Monica said. 'Someone's coming over later to fix it. Don't worry, Ellen, I'm doing everything you've told me to.'

'Which system did you go with?' Ellen asked.

Monica frowned. 'What do you mean?'

Ellen knew Monica knew exactly what she meant. She shook her head. 'Doesn't matter. Have a good day, okay?'

As she drove off, she wondered why Monica would lie about

getting an alarm fitted when she clearly hadn't. Only one reason came to mind. Monica had lied about the alarm because she didn't feel scared enough to get one. A fact Ellen found very interesting indeed.

* * *

The stink of his cologne filled her mouth and nose, making her gag. He was lying on top of her, the weight of his body pressing down, his face so close she could see the tiny pores on his nose, feel his breath, warm and damp on her face, when he spoke.

'What the fuck were you playing at?'

His hand was between her legs, pulling her pants to the side. His breathing was loud and fast and his erection pressed against her thigh. She shook her head, begging him. Not that, please not that.

'I have a business to run,' he said. 'How do you think I can do that with everyone reading those fucking *lies* you've written about me?' he shouted, voice high and angry just like she remembered.

'I'm sorry.' She was crying now, couldn't help it even though she knew he hated it when she cried. 'I'm so sorry, Ricky. Please don't hurt me. Please.'

But it was too late for that. She should never have spoken to the journalist. Should never, for a single moment, have thought she could fight him and win. She'd never won when she was with him. So stupid to let herself believe it might be any different after she left.

# TWENTY

Ellen spent a frustrating morning trying to find something that linked Chloe Dunbar and Monica Telford. Both women claimed not to know each other. So there had to be another connection. Monica was lying. This bare fact underpinned all the work Ellen was doing. She had no proof, but was basing the assumption on a feeling she had. The sort of gut feeling she'd learned to trust over the years.

The question was, why? Why was she lying?

Ellen stood up from her computer, frustrated. She needed to talk about it, sort through the different, conflicting ideas racing around inside her head. Apart from Abby, the office was empty.

'Fancy a coffee?' Ellen asked.

Abby looked around from her computer and smiled.

'I'd kill for one,' she said. 'I'm trying to update the outstanding cases on the system and each time I try to save it, another part of me dies.'

They went out of the station and across the road to Danilo's, the little coffee shop that was second home for many of the people working in Lewisham station. On principle, Ellen refused to drink the liquid served in the staff canteen that pretended to be coffee but tasted like burnt mud.

Once they'd found a table and settled with their mugs, Ellen told Abby how she'd spent her morning so far.

'There has to be something that connects the two women,' she said. 'They both swear not to know each other.'

'You think they're both telling the truth?' Abby asked.

'Hard to tell,' Ellen said. 'More to the point, why would either one lie about it?'

'Monica might lie,' Abby said. 'She only made a complaint after Chloe's story was printed. If she's some sort of delusional nutter, isn't it possible that she read Chloe's story and decided to report that the same thing had happened to her?'

It was the most likely explanation. Ellen had seen enough attention-seeking delusionists over the years. People turning up at the station to report non-existent crimes. Wasting valuable police time that would be better spent helping real victims.

'It makes sense apart from one thing,' Ellen said. 'The news story doesn't mention the flowers or the mugs of tea. Monica couldn't know about that unless Chloe told her.'

'Or unless the same thing had happened to her,' Abby countered. 'Isn't it possible Monica's telling the truth?'

'If she's telling the truth,' Ellen said, 'then both women are being harassed by the same person.'

'Who could be anyone,' Abby said. 'Maybe they shop in the same supermarket or drink in the same pub occasionally. Or go to the same park or cinema or restaurant. There could be any number of ways they're connected without either of them knowing about it.'

'And the alternative?' Ellen asked.

'The alternative is that Monica's making it up,' Abby said. 'And if she is, then you're right. Chloe must have told her the bits that weren't in the news story.'

'There is another explanation,' Ellen said, only thinking it now. 'Maybe Monica knows whoever attacked Chloe and that's how she found out.'

'Or maybe Monica herself is the attacker,' Abby added. 'Do you think that's an option?'

'At this stage,' Ellen said. 'Everything's an option, isn't it?'

The bruises on Monica's neck the other night were something else to think about. Why had Monica turned up at Ellen's house right after it happened? What message was she trying to give that night? Ellen didn't know, but she intended to find out.

* * *

Back at the station, Alastair, the junior detective in the team, was waiting for her. Ellen liked Alastair, liked how methodical he was. She had marked him out early as someone who wanted to work hard and ascend the ladder. She wouldn't let go of him too quickly though, it was important to have someone like him at her back – thorough, a good lateral thinker and reliable.

'I've got the info you wanted,' Alastair said.

Ellen sat at her desk, pulled out a spare chair and motioned for him to sit down.

'What is it?' she asked.

'Nothing yet that connects the two women,' Alastair said. 'But something interesting on Monica. Might be something, might be nothing.'

'Well I won't know until you tell me,' Ellen said.

Alastair nodded.

'Some stuff you already know. She grew up in Whitstable. Raised by her father mainly. Mother left when Monica was a kid. Husband reported her missing at the time, but our boys tracked her down easily enough. The MisPer file was closed. There's a statement in it to the effect that she'd been found but didn't want any further contact with her husband or daughter.

'Adam Telford's a respected businessman. Independent financial advisor. The guy I spoke to in Canterbury seems to think Telford dealt well with what happened. Brought the daughter up on his own, kept working. Made a good life for them both.'

'Anything on the accident?' Ellen asked.

Monica had told her she'd hit her father in the car she was driving the night she left home.

'That's where it gets interesting,' Alastair said. 'Incident was recorded as a hit and run. Driver was never found and Telford always claimed he didn't know who took his car that night. Detective in charge of the case at the time tried to pin it on the daughter, but Telford swore she didn't do it.'

'Maybe he couldn't bear to think of his own daughter doing something like that to him,' Ellen said.

Alastair shrugged. 'Maybe. There's more, though.'

'Go on.'

'The accident resulted in significant injury to Telford's pelvis,' Alastair said. 'He had a number of operations on it in the following years. I managed to track down the surgeon who'd dealt with it. Had a quick chat with him just now. Seems a common problem in men following pelvic injury is penile dysfunction.'

'You mean it left him impotent?' Ellen asked.

'Apparently so.'

That changed things. Maybe. It wouldn't be easy to forgive someone for doing that to you. It was possible that Adam Telford had spent the years since the injury plotting his revenge. But even if he had, it still went no way to explaining who had attacked Chloe in her house last week.

\* \* \*

'She's lying.'

Ricky Lezard plucked an invisible hair from the lapel of his blue jacket and smiled, making Raj want to slam a fist into his face.

'Detective Patel.' Lezard's lawyer sat forward, hands folded neatly under his chin. 'My client has already told you what happened. You have no evidence whatsoever to back up Ms Dunbar's allegations. Allegations which are – quite frankly – potentially libellous. If you've got no further questions for my client, perhaps we could go? Mr Lezard is a busy man. He has been most accommodating already. If you're not going to charge him, then you really must let him go.'

Raj glanced at Abby, who shrugged. They had no choice. The solicitor was right. There wasn't a shred of evidence that Ricky Lezard had done anything wrong. Nothing except the fear and panic Raj saw in Chloe's face when she'd come in earlier.

She'd barely been able to speak and when she was finally able to tell Raj what had happened, she was shaking so badly and crying so much it was difficult to understand her. She said Lezard grabbed her as she was going into work. Forced her inside and locked the door. When they were alone, he threatened her. Told her if she ever, ever accused him of being some lowlife stalker, he would kill her.

'How did you find her?' Raj asked.

'The journalist,' Lezard said. 'Martine. I took her out for a drink, asked how I could find Chloe. She told me where she worked so I came over. As I've already told you, I read the piece in the *Star* and I was worried. I wanted to make sure Chloe was okay. We lived together for three years and she still means a lot to me.'

'You've just accused her of lying,' Abby said. 'Why would you care about someone who says those things about you?'

Lezard sighed. 'Poor Chloe. She has all sorts of problems. She's delusional, you know. Likes to make things up. When I read the paper, I realised she'd got even worse than when we were together. It's the reason we broke up, you know. I couldn't take the lies anymore. Doesn't mean I don't care for her, though. What sort of animal do you think I am? The poor girl needs help, anyone can see that.'

The lawyer made a show of tidying his papers and preparing to leave. He looked at Raj over the rim of his half-moon glasses.

'Will that be all?'

Raj nodded, sick of it suddenly. He believed Chloe and knew this designer-clad wanker was lying. The fact there was sod-all he could do about that depressed him beyond belief.

* * *

*The Evening Star* offices were on the top floor of a red-brick industrial building behind Catford Bridge station. Ellen came straight over after speaking with Raj. She flashed her warrant card at the receptionist, demanded to see Martine Reynolds. Now. The receptionist lifted the phone in front of her and whispered something Ellen couldn't hear. When she finished speaking, she asked Ellen to take a seat, said Ms Reynolds would be right out.

Ms Reynolds left Ellen waiting for twenty minutes, her mood darkening as each minute passed. When the journalist finally appeared, all fake smile and cold eyes, Ellen got straight to the point.

'You told Ricky Lezard how he could find Chloe Dunbar,' Ellen said.

The smile slipped.

'I don't know what you're talking about.'

'You told him,' Ellen said.

Martine frowned. She looked confused. A good act, but Ellen wasn't buying it.

'There's no point denying it,' Ellen said. 'He's already dropped you in it.'

'If you already know,' Martine said, 'what are you doing here? Surely you've got better things to do with your time than harass innocent members of the public, Detective Kelly?'

'Detective Inspector,' Ellen said. 'And there's nothing innocent here. I want to know why you did it. You know what a scumbag he is. You know how scared of him she is. And yet you led him straight to her. Why?'

There was a tremor at one corner of Martine's mouth.

'It's none of your business,' she said.

'I can make it my business,' Ellen said. She took a step forward and the journalist jumped back, like she'd been hit.

'He got to you,' Ellen said. 'Didn't he? Like he gets to everyone. What did he do, Martine? If you tell me, I can do something about it. Arrest him and make sure he doesn't hurt any more women. Tell me what he did to scare you so much that you were willing to give Chloe up like that.'

The journalist looked like she might cry.

'Go away,' she said. 'You don't know what you're talking about.'

She turned, ready to go, but Ellen wasn't finished.

'He hurt her too,' Ellen said. 'Attacked her on her way into work this morning. She's too scared to make a complaint about him. If no one complains, he'll be free to do the same again. What's to say he won't come back and hurt you like he's already hurt her?'

'He won't.'

'How can you be so sure?' Ellen asked.

Reynolds shook her head but didn't say anything. She looked angry, little patches of red on both cheeks, her mouth drawn into a tight, straight line. For a moment, Ellen thought the anger was directed at her. Then she realised.

'Oh you stupid woman,' she said.

'Don't you dare say that.'

'What did he do?' Ellen asked. 'How far did he have to go to make you think he was interested in you? I bet you haven't heard a word from him since you told him what you wanted, have you?'

Martine drew herself up, looked Ellen in the eye and told her to leave. Ellen stood her ground, stared at Martine until the other woman was forced to look away.

Ellen smiled.

'I doubt you'll be hearing from him again,' she said. 'I can't promise the same thing. From now on, I'm watching you, Reynolds. You'd do well not to forget it.'

She waited, half hoping Reynolds would rise to the threat, but she was too clever for that. After a moment, Ellen left.

At the door she turned and looked back. The journalist was still standing in the same spot. The red patches had gone from her face. She looked old and tired and desperately unhappy.

# TWENTY-ONE

'An injunction.'

Raj was smiling at her, like he was giving her good news. Chloe didn't understand, and told him.

'We can get an emergency injunction out against Ricky,' Raj said. 'I've just spoken to my boss. We can get it sorted today. Drive across to the Magistrates' Court and get one there and then. It will keep you safe, Chloe.'

Safe. She closed her eyes, repeated the word to herself. Was it really that easy? When she opened her eyes, Raj was crouched down in front of her.

'Chloe, listen to me. Before today, we had no proof that Ricky even knew where you were. He made a big mistake today coming to where you work. If we take this to a judge, we can get an emergency non-molestation order. It means Ricky will be forbidden from approaching you or communicating with you in any way. If he even tries to speak to you, he'll be locked up.'

She could still smell his cologne. Couldn't wait to go home and have a bath, scrub away every last trace of him. Between her legs still hurt. Just his hand. He didn't do anything else. Knew if he did that they'd find traces of him inside her. So he'd used his hand instead.

'Chloe?' Raj put his hand on her arm, making her jump.

'Sorry.' He backed away. 'I'm so sorry, Chloe. Are you okay?'

She'd been so scared. Thought he was going to kill her. He kicked her instead. Twice in the stomach. Then he'd left. She was still lying there half an hour later when Carl came in and found her.

If it wasn't for Carl, she'd never have gone to the police. Too scared to even do that. But Carl insisted. And maybe he was right. Maybe this injunction thing would put a stop to it all.

'Will it work?' she asked.

'Yes,' Raj said. 'I think it will.'

* * *

It was only a short-term measure. Raj explained that on the drive to the Magistrates' Court. They applied for this today and later, they would have to go back to court once Ricky had been served notice of the order. But that was a formality, Raj assured her. Nothing to worry about.

The court was nothing like she'd expected. From TV, she thought judges wore wigs and black cloaks, but this judge wore a grey suit and no wig. He sat at a table across from her and was really kind. When she started crying, he gave her his own handkerchief to dry her tears.

Raj had warned her there might be a delay, but it was all over very quickly. The judge granted the order, told her she didn't need to be scared anymore and that was it.

Outside afterwards, Raj explained that Ricky would be served with the order straightaway. A special courier would be despatched to deliver it, making sure Ricky couldn't miss it or pretend he hadn't seen it.

'And if he tries to make any sort of contact,' Raj said. 'Even a phone call, he'll be banged up.'

'I don't know what to say,' Chloe said.

'Feels good to do something positive,' Raj said. 'Come on. I'll drive you home. Is there anyone you can call? You shouldn't be alone this evening.'

She wanted Carl. But he hadn't called and she was too shy to call him. Seeing her in that state earlier, it had probably scared him off for good. There was always Nathan, of course, but she didn't think she could bear the thought of him right now. The smell and the size of him, he seemed to take up the whole house when he was there.

Then she thought of Anne.

'There is someone,' she said. 'Let me give her a ring and see if she's free.'

She pulled out her phone and dialled Anne's number. When Chloe told her what happened, Anne promised she'd come straight over.

'I'll bring wine and nibbles,' Anne said. 'We can have a proper girlie night in. How does that sound?'

It sounded just fine to Chloe. As she put her phone back into her bag, it beeped with a text. Carl, asking how she was. She typed a quick reply, ended it with two 'XX' kisses. She put her phone away and smiled at Raj. The first time she'd smiled all day. Things were definitely starting to get better.

# TWENTY-TWO

Friday morning, Chloe's doorbell rang as she was getting ready for work. She went to the window and peered out, terrified she'd see Ricky standing on the doorstep. When she saw Carl instead, her stomach flip-flopped. He was standing in the doorway, sheltering from the rain. Checking herself quickly in the mirror, she ran downstairs to let him in.

'Thought you might like a lift,' he said. 'I practically drive past your house on the way in. Seems silly not to stop.'

He looked embarrassed, like he wasn't sure he was doing the right thing or not. She had to stop herself grabbing him and hugging him.

'That's really sweet of you,' she said. 'Come in. I just need to finish putting my make-up on.'

'You look lovely to me,' he said, cheeky again, now he knew it was okay to be here.

She tried to think of something clever to say back to him but nothing came to her. Instead, she said thanks before running back up the stairs. When she came back down, he was standing in the kitchen.

'Nice place,' he said. 'You've got it looking really pretty. You like it here?'

'I don't know,' she said. 'I did to begin with. But after every-thing that's happened, I'm thinking I might move out. Make a fresh start somewhere else.'

He nodded. 'Can't say as I blame you. But it'll be better now, won't it? This injunction thingy you told me about, he'll have to stay away now?'

'If it works,' Chloe said. 'But Raj – that's the detective – he seems to think it will. Says Ricky would be mad to try anything. If he does, he'll go straight to prison.'

'Should be there already,' Carl said.

She didn't want to talk about all that now. She'd woken up this morning in a good mood. Anne had stayed late last night and drank too much wine. She was funny and interesting and they'd had a good time. When Anne left, Chloe switched the alarm on and slept right through the night.

She thought she'd be nervous seeing Carl again but now he was here, it felt like the most natural thing in the world.

'Shouldn't we get going?' she asked.

'Yeah,' Carl said. 'Listen, Chloe, I want to ask you something, but you can say no. I understand if you're not ready.'

'What is it?'

'Do you fancy going for a drink after work tonight?' he said. 'Just the two of us. If you don't want to, it's fine. I mean, I know you've had a horrible time of it and maybe you want to keep well away from all men for a while.'

'I'd love to,' she said.

He was still babbling and she had to talk over him. He stopped talking and stared at her.

'You sure?'

'I'm sure,' she said.

He smiled and again she thought what a lovely smile he had.

'Well then,' he said. 'That's great. Yeah. Really great. Cheers.'

She stepped forward, reached up on her tip-toes and kissed his cheek.

'You're welcome,' she said. 'Now come on. Let's get to work.'

When she stepped back down, she noticed he was blushing, a red flush that crept along his neck and up his cheeks. It made him look seriously cute.

\* \* \*

Ellen was nervous. The sort of nerves she hadn't experienced since... well, since forever.

Jim was nervous too. He hid it well enough, but little things gave it away. The way his leg kept jigging under the table. And the shake in his hand when he lifted his champagne flute to touch it against hers.

'To you,' he said.

To us, she almost said but decided, just in time, that was way too corny. She stayed silent instead, sipped the champagne and wished she could taste it.

They were in the bar at the top of the Shard, Europe's new highest building by London Bridge station. Their plan was to have a drink here, eat in a restaurant Jim knew under the railway arches in Borough Market, and then back to their hotel in south London.

Except food was the last thing on Ellen's mind. She couldn't stop thinking about later. She'd pictured it hundreds of times. Wanted it more than she'd let herself admit. One night. Tomorrow it was back to the daily grind of juggling work and family. Doing it alone was so bloody difficult. Her mind fast-forwarded six months from now. Not alone anymore. Sharing the responsibilities with Jim. Waking up in the morning beside him. Weekends spent lazing about with the kids. Nights given over to hot, steamy sex.

For a long time, she'd thought that part of her – the sexual part – had died with Vinny. She'd been wrong.

'Ready to go?'

Jim reached out to touch her wrist. Shocks of electricity shot up her arm. Waves of desire made her light-headed. Champagne and lust – the best legal high there was. Drunk with desire. She giggled. Couldn't help it. She was happy. Tipsy. Carefree. Horny.

Jim said something else but she didn't hear him. The thunderstorm of blood pumping through her head blocked out everything else. He was smiling now and she wondered, vaguely, what he was smiling at. When he smiled, a dimple appeared under his left eye. It was the very first thing she'd noticed about him all those years ago in primary school. Too young then to know anything about sex or longing. It was damn sexy, though, that dimple.

'Do we have to go to the restaurant?'

Her voice. Didn't know how she got the words out. Didn't care, either. Her nerves had steadied, disappeared, replaced with a startling clarity. This was it. He was it. The person she'd been waiting for. Felt like she'd been waiting her whole life, even though she knew that wasn't true. Right now, nothing mattered. Nothing made sense. At the same time, she'd never been more certain about anything.

The smile disappeared.

'You've changed your mind?' he asked.

'Only about eating,' she said. 'Not about anything else. I don't think I can wait any longer, that's all. Can we skip dinner and go straight to the hotel?'

\* \* \*

She was laughing. Real, proper belly laughs. Carl was laughing too. The best bit about it was that she couldn't remember what they'd both found so funny. Then Carl puffed his cheeks out and started again: *'The first duty of an estate agent is to stuff his face with bread and pasta and chocolates until his stomach is so HUGE he starts looking like he's got a tyre wrapped around his middle.'*

He had Nathan's voice down to a T. And when he moved, waddling around the way Nathan did – that strange, dainty way he had of walking – she couldn't help herself. It was cruel, she knew that, but there was something about Nathan that invited it.

Nathan had been out of the office on viewings all afternoon. Which made it easy enough for them to sneak off for a drink when they closed the office. Nathan had already invited her to a quiz night at his church. Said it would be fun and a great way to meet some new people. She'd half-promised to be there, but the drink with Carl had turned into an early dinner at Nandos. After that, when he'd offered to drive her home, it had seemed rude not to invite him in.

And now here they were in the sitting room, larking about like a pair of giddy teenagers. When he'd finished his Nathan impression, and she'd managed to stop her giggles, Carl held up the empty bottle of wine.

'Any more where this came from?' he asked.

She shook her head, good mood evaporating in an instant. What sort of person was she, not thinking what he might like? She thought she'd done okay, making sure she only drank a tiny bit, leaving the rest of it for him.

He pulled a sad face and sat beside her on the sofa. He sat

close, his thigh pressed against hers. She tensed, waiting. He put his hand on her cheek – his touch was gentle and nothing like she'd expected.

'I had a great night, Chloe.'

She dared to look at him then, trying to work out if this was some sort of trick. But what she saw in his face surprised her. He looked soft and sweet and was smiling at her, like he was delighted by her.

His hand was still on her face, thumb stroking her cheek, softly, gently. She didn't want him to stop. And when he leaned into her and kissed her, his lips were soft too. She didn't respond at first. Just let him kiss her, still waiting to see what way it would go.

He pulled back, blue eyes looking into hers. He had the loveliest eyes.

'Are you okay with this?' he asked.

'Of course,' she said. 'Well, I think so. Yes.'

Suddenly she was smiling, too. All the tension disappeared, replaced with a sort of happy lightness she'd almost forgotten it was possible to feel.

And when he kissed her a second time, she wrapped her arms around his neck, pulled him closer and kissed him right back.

# TWENTY-THREE

The first time was quick and desperate and over too quickly. The second time they took things more slowly, getting used to each other. Sometime later, they ordered room service. Toasted sandwiches and chips. They sat side by side in the bed, eating and talking over each other. Talking about everything and nothing. Ellen's children, Frank Sinatra, Almodóvar movies, Jim's family, crap TV programmes, Bruce Springsteen, Ellen's memories of her birth mother, the best unusual food combinations (Ellen: vinegar and strawberries; Jim: cheese and marmalade).

The hotel was a beautiful Art Deco building in Deptford. Their room was on the top floor with a view along the river to Greenwich. After eating, they wrapped themselves in sheets and moved across to the window. Jim dragged an armchair over and sat down, pulling Ellen onto his lap.

'The river looks beautiful at night,' Ellen said. 'Especially now the rain has stopped. Even better than during the day.'

'I don't know about better,' Jim said. 'Different, yes. Beautiful, definitely. But it's pretty impressive all the time if you ask me. One of the few good things about living in London.'

'One of the many, you mean,' Ellen said, elbowing his stomach.

'Ouch,' Jim said. No. I know you love London, but I'm not sure I feel the same way. Half the time I wish I lived somewhere else. London's too busy for me.'

'If you don't like it,' Ellen said, 'why did you come back?'

'Family, I suppose. My dad wasn't an easy man but after he died, there was only Ray and my mum. And poor Ray, he's not the easiest. I couldn't bear to think of Mum having to deal with that on her own.'

'The dual curse of the Irish,' Ellen said. 'Alcoholism and mental illness. I'm pretty sure my birth father was an alcoholic.'

Jim's arms, already wrapped around her, tightened.

'I thought you couldn't remember him.'

'I don't,' Ellen said. 'Not really. It's more of a feeling than anything else. Vague memories of him coming home drunk. I remember never feeling safe when he was around. It was always better when he wasn't there. Except that last night, of course. I used to think, you know, maybe if he'd been there, he'd have tried to stop her.'

Her mind flickered back to the single sheet of white paper

folded over on her bedside table. She still hadn't told him. Hadn't told anyone.

'Poor woman,' Jim said.

'Poor Eilish, you mean,' Ellen said, referring to her dead sister. 'Murdered by her own mother.'

'Eilish, too,' Jim said. 'But it must have been so awful for your mother.'

An animal screaming in pain. The worst sound Ellen had ever heard. She remembered so little of that night but that sound, coming from her mother as she held her dead baby in her arms, was seared into Ellen's brain. And yet… Ray, Jim's brother, had a breakdown some years earlier. A complete mental collapse, according to Jim. Ray's illness meant he had to give up his job and his home. He'd never killed anyone, though.

She lay back, her head resting against Jim's shoulder. It was late and she was tired. She should sleep. Jim's hand ran up and down her bare arm, sending little shivers through her body. His hand moved up, across her shoulder and along her chest, moving lower and lower, pushing the sheet out of the way.

Ellen leaned back, pressing her body against his. She took his hand, guided it along her stomach. His fingers skimmed the top of her pubic hair and she groaned.

Plenty of time for sleep later.

She stood up and led him back to the bed. This was all she wanted. To feel the weight of his body on her, to open her legs and give herself up to this. She wanted to be consumed, for every other thought and memory and feeling to disappear until there was nothing left except him and her and this cascading crescendo of desire.

* * *

In the kitchen, Monica pulled a bottle of wine from the rack and opened it. Resisting the urge to drink it straight from the bottle, she poured a healthy serving into a balloon-sized wine glass and drank from that instead. As soon as she was able to, she took another slug and stood with her eyes closed, waiting for the booze to kick in.

Her mouth ached from the effort of smiling when all she'd really wanted to do was scream with the boredom of it all. Her head hurt – actually hurt – from having to work so hard making meaningless small-talk. The amount of thick people she was forced to deal with on a daily basis was an unbearable burden at times.

But she carried it off. With aplomb. She drank more wine, silently toasting herself on a stellar performance. She was good. No one better. Almost made her feel sorry for people like Ellen Kelly, who had no idea – not a fucking clue – what they were dealing with.

She refilled her glass and carried it into the sitting room. The curtains were open and she stood at the window, looking out at the quiet street, as she tried to decide how to spend the rest of her evening. It was only ten o'clock. Too early to be stuck at home alone on a Friday night.

She'd been with prospective clients. A group representing local businesses that bought art and displayed it on their office walls. An easy and lucrative way of making money. She'd spent two hours with them and knew they'd wanted her to stay longer. But the thought of spending another second in their tedious company was more than she could have endured. So she'd made her move, smiling apologetically and saying she had a busy day tomorrow and needed her beauty sleep. Played all coy when they'd both told her how fantastic she looked. As if she didn't know it herself.

On the way home, she took a detour. Had a drink in a bar she sometimes went to in New Cross. The sort of place you could sometimes find guys into something a bit different. No joy tonight, though. One bloke coming on to her but his breath stank of dead animals and she was nowhere near drunk enough to consider that.

So she'd come home. And now she was wishing she hadn't.

The lights in the house across the road were switched off. A pity. She could do with a distraction and Harry would have been just perfect. She wondered where he was and who he was with. Getting it away with someone his own age for a change. Cheeky git. She'd have to teach him a lesson. Remind him what he could get with her that no prim little bitch his own age was likely to do for him.

Tonight had been a mistake. She should have cancelled. Should have realised a night out with a collection of the world's most boring people wasn't going to give her the sort of thrill she needed right now.

She'd been consumed by a restless energy ever since the trip to Whitstable. She had to think of something to make the time pass. Her mind switched from her father to Ellen Kelly. Still no phone call. Kelly was probably too busy getting on with her perfect life to spend time worrying about the people she was paid to protect. Monica would bet any money Kelly wasn't wasting her Friday night sitting around feeling sorry for herself.

Things weren't moving fast enough. Something needed to happen to make Kelly sit up and take notice. Monica thought getting the police out the other night might have made a difference. Fat chance. No one was taking her half as seriously as they ought to.

She looked at her reflection in the mirror that hung over the fireplace. Stroked the yellow bruises on her neck, thinking. And then it came to her. She knew exactly what she had to do. Her mood improved instantly. She carried her glass over to the big armchair by the window, sat down and started planning.

# TWENTY-FOUR

After breakfast, they went for a walk through Deptford market. It was a clear, sunny day that made everything vivid. Or maybe that was just her. She had to stop herself skipping as they crossed the road outside the hotel.

Jim reached out, took her hand in his. It felt good there.

'Remember this bloke Jerome I was telling you about?' he asked.

Ellen nodded. The young apprentice who'd been working with Jim for the last four months.

'He's really good,' Jim said. 'As soon as he's trained up, I'm planning to cut down my hours. Means we'd be able to spend a bit more time together.'

'What? You mean during the day and stuff?'

Jim grinned. 'Your enthusiasm never fails to bowl me over. Yes, during the day and stuff. I like you. I like being with you. Hey, we could take up a hobby together.'

'A hobby.'

'Yeah, you know, like bridge or tennis or golf. What do you say?'

'I say you'd better be joking.'

'What?' He feigned disappointment. 'You don't *want* us to have a hobby together?'

'Most definitely not.'

'And the bit about seeing a bit more of each other?' he asked. 'Would you rather I was joking about that too?'

She thought about it. Not for long.

'No,' she said. 'I'm glad you're not joking about that.'

Ahead of them, Ellen could see the market, crowding out the bottom of Deptford High Street onto the New Cross Road. Her father used to bring her here when she was a kid. They'd come on Saturday mornings and buy a whole salmon from the Cod Father fish shop. These days, when she wanted fresh fish, she bought it from the fish counter in Drings on Royal Hill.

'There's a brilliant fish stall down there,' Jim said. 'The Cod Father. You can get a whole salmon there for under a tenner.'

It was unnerving. She would be thinking about something and, right at the same moment, he'd start talking about it. Unnerving but kind of cute, too. If you were the sort of person who did cute. Which she certainly was not.

Two miles along the river from Greenwich, Deptford High Street was a different world. Down-at-heel, edgy, diverse, bursting with life. Pushing their way through the Saturday morning crowds, taking in the variety of things you could buy – everything from bathroom appliances to fresh lobster – was invigorating. Ellen felt like a child with a pocketful of money. She couldn't decide what to buy first. She wanted all of it. At a stall selling fake designer jeans, she had to stop herself grabbing a selection there and then. Before she could indulge her desire for useless tat, Jim grabbed her hand and steered her off the high street, down a quiet street leading off to the east.

'Where are we going?' she asked.

'Here.' He pointed in front of them.

Ellen stopped, delighted. Right in front of her, at the end of the street, stood a white stone church. At the front of the building there was a circular tower with a steeple rising from the centre. Four giant columns enclosed the tower, making Ellen think the church would sit better in a rural Italian village rather than here, in the heart of urban Deptford.

'It's beautiful,' she said. 'I've seen the spire, of course, whenever I've driven past. But I've never taken the time to come and see it.'

'St Paul's, Deptford,' Jim said. 'Baroque. Designed by Thomas Archer and built in the early eighteenth century.'

'Can we go inside?' Ellen asked.

'Not now,' Jim said. 'But we can come back another time.

Bring the kids. You have to phone ahead to make an appointment. Better still, the church has its own chamber orchestra. We should come some evening and see a concert.'

'I'd like that,' Ellen said.

Inside the churchyard, they sat on the church steps looking back towards the market. Ellen wondered if Sean had ever been here. It was the sort of place he'd love. She'd never heard him mention it, but that didn't mean anything. These days, they lived such separate lives.

'Are you and Ray close?' she asked. She'd often wondered what it was like for other siblings. Whether they felt that fierce, protective love she had for her twin brother.

'Not like you and Sean,' Jim said, doing that thing again. Cute, she decided.

'And not as much as we used to be. I idolised him when I was a kid. He was my big brother. We never had that competitive thing that some brothers do. He looked after me, I guess. Our dad wasn't an easy man so Ray was sort of my role model. I didn't want to be better than him, I just wanted to *be* him. Does that make any sense?'

'Perfect sense,' Ellen said.

'By the time I went away, we'd already grown apart,' Jim said. 'My fault. I'd realised there was something different about him. My parents tried to ignore it. Well, my mother did. I don't think my father even noticed, if I'm honest. My mother acted as if all the messed-up things Ray did were just minor setbacks. She didn't get it. She couldn't see that Ray's just… he's not… normal's the wrong word but he's not equipped to deal with day-to-day life the way most people are. His head's not wired that way. He can't cope. And because he can't cope, he cracked up. Couldn't take the strain.

'The first time he lost it, I was sixteen. Ray was twenty. Still living at home. Poor Mum thought he was working, but he'd been fired from whatever job he had. Again. He still got up every morning, let my mother make him breakfast before he headed off. Except instead of going to work, he'd go and sit on his own for the day. Then this one day, he went to the pub. And stayed there. Didn't come home for three days. Police eventually found him near London Bridge, drunk and confused.

'At the time, I was angry with him. Hated him for putting my poor mother through it. She had enough on her plate with my father, believe me. I thought, stupidly, that he had some choice about the way he behaved.'

'You don't think that now?' Ellen asked.

Jim shook his head. 'He can't help who he is. I didn't understand that back then. It's because of him I left home and went travelling. I wanted to get away. From all of them. From Ray and his problems and my parents and their inability to see him for what he really was.'

Except he came back. And now here he was, sitting beside her, brown hair hanging down over a greeny-blue eye. Brown hair speckled with sparkles of golden sunlight. Eyes the colour of the sea on a summer's day. Their arms were touching. She could feel the outline of hard muscle through the fabric of his shirt. She remembered what his body looked like naked. The memory made her shiver.

'What made you think about me and Ray?' Jim asked.

'Sean, I guess,' Ellen said. 'I miss him sometimes. We're not as close as we used to be. Which is normal, of course. Except I've done something and haven't told him about it and I feel guilty.'

'Why?'

'Because I should have spoken to him first.'

The folded sheet of white paper on the table by her bed. Folded over to cover up the writing she knew by heart. Each word branded onto her brain.

*Noreen McGrath, Hope House, Middle Road, Shilbottle, Alnwick, Northumberland, NE66 2TH.*

'I've found our mother,' Ellen said. 'Noreen. I've got an address and a telephone number. I'm going to contact her.'

'And Sean won't like that?' Jim asked.

'He wants to forget all about her,' Ellen said. 'I can't do that. I thought I could. I tried, really tried, but it's no good. I need to know why she did it.'

Jim's silence irritated her.

'What?' she asked. 'You think I should leave it?'

'Sorry,' Jim said. 'I was just thinking… it must have been so terrible for her. Bad enough losing one child, but then to lose the other two as well. Being locked up all that time, knowing you and Sean were out there somewhere, without her. She must have felt so helpless.'

Ellen had to swallow the lump in her throat before she was able to speak.

'So you think it's the right thing?' she asked.

He squeezed her arm. 'Of course I do.'

'Only I can't help thinking,' Ellen said. 'If she'd wanted to find me, she'd have done something about it herself.'

His phone started ringing. He jumped up, pulled it from his pocket, checked the caller's number and diverted the call.

'Take it if you need to,' Ellen said.

He shook his head.

'Your mother was convicted of murdering your sister,' he said. 'She spent time in prison. Even if Eilish's death was an accident – and you don't know that it wasn't – the guilt she must have felt, can you imagine what that would do to a person? Just being on trial... And for the death of your own daughter.' He shook his head. 'She might not want to talk about it. Will you be okay with that?'

Standing there like that in front of the church, hands held out, he reminded Ellen of Christ on the cross. Except hotter than that. A lot hotter. He wore a white linen shirt. The top buttons were open, revealing a patch of tanned skin and the silver chain he wore around his neck. The sun reflected off the small medallion hanging off the chain so that it seemed to glow with its own light. The chain had belonged to his father and he once told her that he never took it off. Ellen pictured herself walking over to him, running her hand up inside the shirt, along his flat stomach.

'I don't want to talk about it,' she said. 'Not anymore. Do you mind?'

'Fine by me,' he said. 'Come on. Let's go back to the market and spend some money. There must be something we can pick up for Pat and Eilish.'

They walked away from the church and into the throng of Deptford Market. The noise and bustle was just what she needed right now. It helped block out the dark thoughts she didn't want.

# TWENTY-FIVE

'We're going out again tonight.'

'Who?'

'Me and Carl, of course.' Chloe frowned. 'The guy from work. I've just been telling you about him. Haven't you been listening?'

'I'm confused,' Anne said. 'I thought you worked with Nathan.'

Anne sounded groggy, like she'd just woken up. But it was nearly midday.

'I work with both of them,' Chloe said. 'But you've met Nathan. Surely you don't think… I mean, I know he's lovely and everything, but not in *that* way.'

'Sorry,' Anne said. 'Of course. Right then. Where are you going and what are you going to wear?'

'He's taking me for dinner. Some new restaurant in Blackheath he says is lovely,' Chloe said. 'And that's the problem, I don't know what to wear. What do you think?'

Anne laughed. 'Chloe, darling, I have no idea what your wardrobe looks like.'

Of course. Stupid, stupid. What was she thinking?

'Sorry,' Chloe said. 'I'd better go. I'm still at work and Nathan will be back soon. I don't want him to know about me and Carl. He wouldn't approve.'

'Whoa,' Anne said. 'You can't leave it there. I'll tell you what, Chloe, I'll come over later. Help you get ready. I'll bring a bottle of something fizzy. Get you in the mood. How does that sound?'

'Are you sure?' Chloe asked.

'Absolutely,' Anne said. 'Isn't that what friends are for?'

It was only when she hung up that Chloe noticed Nathan had come back in at some point. He was standing in the kitchen doorway, staring at her. She wanted to ask how long he'd been there, but something about the look on his face stopped her. It was a look she'd never seen before: disappointment mixed with anger. Or maybe she was just imagining it.

She smiled brightly and turned to her computer, pretending to get on with her work. Even though she was so excited about later, work was the very last thing on her mind right now.

When she looked back again, Nathan was still standing in the same spot.

'Are you okay?' she asked.

His face cleared and he smiled, transforming him from an ogre to the friend she knew and trusted.

'I'm fine,' he said. 'You?'

She nodded, tension draining from her body, glad it had only been her imagination.

'I'm fine, too,' she said. 'Thanks.'

# TWENTY-SIX

It was early afternoon by the time Ellen collected the children from their sleepover. They'd spent the night with their friends, Rufus and Izzy. Their mother, Kirstie, insisted on dragging Ellen in for a coffee and a 'date debrief'.

'You've got that glow,' Kirstie said. 'The one you only see on women who've been having too much good sex.'

'Can you have too much good sex?' Ellen asked.

Kirstie looked glum. 'How would I know? The last time I had a good shag was in my late twenties. In that rare time when things were actually good between Phil and me. Before I found out I wasn't the only person he was having great sex with. So come on, gory details please. I've no love life of my own so I have to share yours. What was it like?'

'We had a great time,' Ellen said. 'I like him. A lot, I think. At the risk of tempting fate, I'd say things are going pretty well right now.'

Better than that. After checking out of the hotel, he'd driven her home and they'd gone straight to bed. Again. She'd thought it might feel strange, having sex in the bed she'd once shared with Vinny. But it wasn't. Everything about being with Jim felt right.

'Are you seeing him later?' Kirstie asked.

'Tomorrow,' Ellen said. 'I wanted to spend some time with the kids this evening. Not that they seem bothered one way or the other.'

In fact, when she'd come to collect them, both children had been disappointed to see her, begging her to let them spend another night at their friends' house.

'They're welcome to stay,' Kirstie said.

Ellen shook her head. No matter how brilliant Jim was, being with her children was more important. She'd promised them a movie and pizza night and that's what she was going to give them. Whether they liked it or not.

Besides, Jim hadn't asked to see her tonight. Which was fine with Ellen. Things were great right now and she hoped they'd continue that way, but she wasn't going to rush things. And she certainly wasn't going to let him take priority over being with her children. They would always come first.

\* \* \*

They ordered pizzas from Geronimo's Pizza House on Trafalgar Road ('the crack cocaine of pizzas' was how Vinny used to describe them) and watched *The Princess Bride*, Ellen's all-time favourite children's movie.

When the film ended, she took Eilish to bed then stayed up chatting with Pat, the two of them snuggled on the sofa together. His latest obsession was Minecraft and he spoke compulsively about his kingdom, his favourite Minecraft videos on YouTube and the pros and cons of Minecraft PC versus Minecraft for tablets. Midway through a lengthy explanation about the Minecraft game, Pat suddenly asked about Jim.

'If he's a plumber,' Pat said, 'does that mean he has to stick his hand inside people's toilets when they're broken?'

'Sometimes, I suppose,' Ellen said. 'Why don't you ask him when we see him tomorrow?'

'What's happening tomorrow?' Pat asked.

'Jim's coming with us to Sean and Terry's for lunch,' Ellen said. 'Is that okay?'

Pat shrugged. 'Suppose so. I don't care, really. He's okay, Jim. He's funny. But I don't want to live in his house, Mum. I like living here. He lives miles away and it's really far from my school and where my friends live.'

'We're not moving into Jim's house,' Ellen said, making her voice sound as firm as she possibly could. 'This is your home, Pat, and I have no intention of moving out. Not now, not anytime in the future either.'

'Yeah but what if you and Jim get married?'

'I've only been seeing him a few weeks,' Ellen said.

'Eight weeks and four days,' Pat interrupted.

'Okay. Eight weeks and four days. Way too early to think about anything long-term.'

'So you might stop seeing him and get a different boyfriend instead?'

'No!' Ellen nudged him with her elbow. 'Pat, I don't know what's going to happen with Jim. I like him and I think he likes me. Who knows what will happen in the future? For now, all I can do is take things one day at a time.'

Pat yawned and Ellen took that as her cue to suggest it was bedtime. For once, he didn't protest. A few minutes later, he was tucked up in bed, eyes already closing as sleep swept down and claimed him. Ellen kissed him on the forehead, lingering for a moment as she always did, before she switched off his light and went to go. She was just closing the door when he said something.

'Sorry,' she said. 'What was that? I didn't catch it.'

'I said I hope you don't get a new boyfriend,' Pat said. 'I like Jim. He's nice and you smile more when you're with him.'

'I'll bear that in mind,' Ellen said. 'Goodnight.'

'Night, Mum. Love you.'

'Love you too, darling.'

Downstairs, Ellen went into the kitchen and poured herself a healthy measure of Merlot. She wanted Jim. Had barely stopped thinking about him all day. Worse than a besotted teenager. She stood in the kitchen, leaning against the island, drinking wine and going back over every detail of last night, wishing he was here now and they could do it all over again.

She finished her wine, poured another glass, went into the sitting room, put on a CD and sat down. The CD was from Jim. Elbow. A band she knew only because they'd played at the closing ceremony of the London 2012 Games. She loved every song on the CD, even the over-played *One Day Like This*. When it came on, she cranked up the volume, letting the soaring orchestral extravaganza fill the room.

Her phone was on the table. She picked it up and sent Jim a text: *Home alone with Guy Garvey. What you up to?*

He'd told her what he was doing but she couldn't remember. Meeting his brother? Maybe. She wondered how late he'd stay out and if he'd think about dropping this way later. If he replied to her text, she would send him another text, suggesting just that.

But he didn't reply. She drank more wine and listened to more music. At some point, unable to keep her eyes open, she drifted into an uneasy sleep, dreaming of a stranger in the house, creeping around upstairs, trying to steal the children from their beds.

She woke with a start, convinced at first it was more than a dream, that there really was someone there. It was only gradually, as she became more awake, that she realised she was okay.

A bad dream, nothing more than that. The children were safe and so was she.

# TWENTY-SEVEN

Monica knew, the moment she woke up, it was going to be a bad day. Too much wine the night before and not enough food. Turned her dreams into nightmares that were still with her. Her mother's voice screaming at her, saying things a mother should never, ever say to her own child. This followed by something worse. The crying. Her mother bawling like a fucking baby and saying she was sorry, hadn't meant a word of it. Liar. Repeating it over and over and over until Monica couldn't bear it a single second longer.

In the kitchen, she washed down three Ibuprofen with two cups of strong black coffee. Her mother was still there but fading now, the voice getting quieter, replaced by other, normal noises, like the traffic on the road outside and the sound of the TV blaring through the wall from the house next door where deaf Mrs Mallet lived. Mrs Mallet who had two daughters who visited every Sunday without fail and a son who came most Wednesday afternoons with bags of shopping for his dear old mum. Mrs Mallet who probably never had a single exciting thing happen in her entire boring, suburban life lived utterly without purpose or meaning. Monica hated Mrs fucking Mallet and her bland, sycophantic offspring.

Products of their mother's loins. The thought of it made her want to throw up. She'd never met Mr Mallet, who had 'passed over to the other side' some years before Monica moved here, but she felt sorry for him, having to spend his life with an ugly cow like that. She hoped he'd at least had a mistress, someone to add a bit of spice to a life that must have otherwise been unbearable.

How very different deaf Mrs Mallet was from her own mother...

It was difficult to remember the details of that afternoon. Her memories were fuzzy, almost as if she'd dreamed the whole thing. Or maybe she felt like that because part of her wished that was true.

Fuck it. Nothing to be gained by standing here thinking about what might have been. She threw her cup in the sink and called Kelly. When she'd finished on the phone, she went upstairs to get ready.

She was applying the final touches to her make-up when the doorbell rang. She stopped what she was doing, waited for whoever it was to go away. When the bell rang a second time, she went to the window and looked down, taking care to stay well hidden behind the curtain.

Part of her had hoped to see Ellen Kelly. When she recognised Harry's dark, messy curls she bit her lip, disappointed. It was like Kelly had forgotten all about her already.

She checked her reflection in the mirror, taking her time. Added a touch more lipstick, opened another button on her shirt, making sure the curve of her breast and the black, lace bra could be easily seen. The bruises on her neck were still there but she'd covered them with make-up. If he asked about them, she'd think of something plausible. But she doubted it was her neck he'd be looking at. She shook out her hair, winked at herself and went downstairs.

Time to teach someone a lesson.

'Got some really good skunk.' Harry held out his hand, showing her the small plastic bag filled with dried-out leaves. 'Want to get wasted with me?'

She leaned forward, pretending to examine the package, making sure she rubbed against him, just gently enough so he wouldn't know it was deliberate.

'I'm meant to be meeting a friend,' she said. 'Maybe another time.'

He looked so disappointed, her mood lifted instantly. It was difficult to stay angry with him.

'Good time the other night?' she asked.

He frowned. 'What do you mean?'

'I called over,' she said. 'Friday night, I was feeling a bit bored. But you weren't there. I assumed you were out with your girlfriend.'

His face flushed red, making him look even younger than he was.

'I don't have a girlfriend,' he mumbled. 'You know that, Mon.'

Anyone else, she wouldn't let them get away with calling her that. The way he said it, though, there was something sweet about it. She'd better watch it or she'd start getting soft on this boy.

'What do you mean you don't have a girlfriend?' she asked. She ran a finger along his cheek, feeling the heat. 'A good-looking bloke like you. Girls must be falling over themselves.'

'Not interested,' he said. 'Girls my age, they're just so boring, you know?'

Poor sap was too transparent for words. If he wasn't such a honey, she'd be tempted to slap his face, tell him to man up a bit. Hadn't he ever heard of playing hard to get?

She moved forward until the tips of her breasts were touching his chest. His face turned even redder, his breathing was fast and shallow, pupils dilated so big the blue iris was barely there. She dropped her hand, let her fingers trail along the front of his trousers, touching the outline of his erection through the soft denim.

'We can't get too close,' she whispered. 'I'm not ready for that yet. You do understand, don't you?'

When he nodded, he reminded her of a dog. Mouth hanging

open, eyes looking at her with a mix of longing and adoration. There were worse ways to spend her Sunday. A couple of spliffs to take the edge off; add in a bit of playing around with young Harry and she might even be able to switch off some of the sounds and images in her head.

Besides, her plans for Harry extended well beyond this afternoon. It was worth sparing a few hours reminding him what he had to look forward to if he did what she needed him to. And if she managed to have a bit of fun along the way, well then, all the better.

# TWENTY-EIGHT

Sunday morning, Ellen woke early. There was a pattern to Sundays: a late breakfast and the Sunday papers before picking her parents up, driving to Mass and, after that, back in the car and across the river for lunch at her brother's. Not this Sunday morning. Monica's phone call changed that. Ellen got the children up early and drove them across to her parents' house.

'Something's come up at work,' Ellen explained to her mother. 'There's nothing I can do about it, Mum. I'm sorry.'

'You'll be back in time for lunch?' her mother asked.

'Of course,' she said. 'I'll ask Sean to pick you up and I'll go straight to his. I'll be there by one thirty at the latest. I promise.'

Twenty minutes later, she was on the A2, driving east on her way to see Adam Telford, Monica's father. Ger had told her not to, but she wasn't doing it during work time so Ellen couldn't see the harm.

Inevitably, this route brought back unwelcome memories. The last time she'd been out this way was to find a young girl who'd been abducted. She'd found the child but, in the process, lost her old partner and mentor, Dai Davies.

The closer she got to Higham, the village where it happened, the faster the memories came until she had to pull in to the side of the road and wait for them to pass.

She'd planned on going straight to Whitstable. Instead, she turned early off the A2 and drove north towards Higham. At the end of the village, she followed a narrow road for a half mile or so. Somewhere near here, there was a laneway leading off to the left. Yes. There it was. She drove down the lane to the ramshackle house at the end, stopped the car and climbed out. A cold wind blew across the flat fields, making her shiver.

It was a desolate place. Even if Ellen hadn't known all the terrible things that had happened here, she would feel the loneliness, the sense that out here, with the flat countryside stretching away on all sides, you were as close as you could get to the end of the world.

There was a series of books she'd loved as a child. She couldn't remember much about them except they involved a group of children living in a house called World's End. This house reminded her of those books.

The door was ajar. She pushed it open and peered into the

kitchen. Saw the filth, the decay and the trails of mouse droppings on the floor and table. Particles of dust hung in dazzling stripes across the room, trapped in rays of sunlight that poked through the filthy window.

The last time she'd been here, there was a pile of old-fashioned videos on the table beside a box of cupcakes. Or were they donuts? It hardly mattered now. No sign of either today. A tune played through her head as she turned and walked back outside. The theme tune from *The Rainbow Parade*, a children's programme she used to watch with Sean when they were kids. The tinkle of the piano, light notes, like raindrops.

In the distance, a train rumbled past. Ellen looked across the fields, towards the railway. In her memories, the distance from the house to the track was vast. Today, it seemed much shorter. A short jog to the tattered barbed-wire fencing, under that and on to the end of the field where the ground dropped away to the track below.

She didn't go down there. Couldn't do it. Her body froze, refused to let her get any closer. A sharp wind rose from the east, swept across the open countryside, cut through her on its way towards the city. She wrapped her arms tightly around her body and thought of Dai.

'*Survivors, Ellen. That's what we are, you and me. It's not ideal but we've got no choice, see?*'

He'd proved himself wrong, in the end. Turned out he was no more of a survivor than anyone else.

Grief slammed into her. So sudden and sharp, she doubled over, struggling to catch her breath. They were there now, in front of her, Dai Davies and Brian Fletcher. The train bearing down on them.

And then they were gone.

She didn't want to stay here a moment longer. She ran through the wind to the car. When she put the key in the ignition, her hand was shaking so bad she had to try several times before the key finally slotted into place. She switched the engine on and drove off, knowing this was the last time she would visit this desolate place.

* * *

Adam turned up the water pressure and stepped into the shower, letting the hot water beat into him, washing away all traces of Bel and what they'd done. It was like this every time. The moment it was over, he could barely wait to get in here and make himself clean again.

*Cleanliness is next to Godliness.*

Sister Theresa. Mean little face and strong arms.

*Pull your pants down and bend over.*

He washed, soaping down every inch of skin, making sure he missed nothing. When he'd finished, and all the soap had rinsed away, he switched off the hot tap but remained under the water.

*THIS is what happens to boys who come to school looking like that.*

177

When he couldn't stand it any longer, he got out, grabbed his towel and started drying. As he lifted his arms to dry underneath, he caught the slightest smell of something that wasn't soap. The lingering traces of stale sweat. He threw the towel down, angry with himself for being so careless. How had he missed that?

Back in the shower, he took the nailbrush and used it to scrub both armpits. He scrubbed until the skin broke and the water turned pale pink, tainted with his blood.

*DON'T EVER let me see you sticking that finger up your nose again.*

This time, when he thought he was clean enough, he left on the hot tap but turned off the cold. He lifted both his arms, pushing each armpit under the scalding water, biting down on his lip to stop himself crying out with the pain of it.

*Dirty, disgusting child.*

Water pooled around his feet as it ran down the plughole, changing from pale to dark pink and then to red. Sister Theresa's words in his head, the cane in her hand, striking down on his bare buttocks, again and again and again.

# TWENTY-NINE

Ellen and her kids were regular visitors to Whitstable. She liked the town and the seafront was lovely, especially in summertime. They liked to come early on Saturday mornings, have a wander around the market and spend the rest of the day down on the beach.

Adam Telford lived on the east side of town, by the sea. The house was a modern, mock-Tudor affair in a row of identical modern, mock-Tudor homes. The sort of houses bought by people with lots of money and no taste.

Ellen rang the doorbell. As she waited, she looked around. The neighbourhood was affluent with upwardly mobile pretensions and no sense of aesthetic. Each house had a big car parked in the driveway: a line-up of Saabs, Mercs, Volvos and Beemers.

Adam Telford's house was the exception with a yellow VW Beetle parked out front.

She was about to ring the doorbell again when the door was opened by a petite woman with long dark hair, an unfortunately large nose and an even more unfortunate lack of charm.

'What do you want?'

Ellen gave her name and showed her warrant card.

'I'm looking for Adam Telford,' she said. 'Is he in?'

'He won't want to speak to you,' the woman said.

'He doesn't have a choice,' Ellen said. 'I can come in and speak to him here or I can take him in for questioning. What's it to be?'

'Is this to do with his ex-wife?' the woman asked.

'That's none of your business,' Ellen said. If the unfriendly cow thought Ellen might tell her the real reason for the visit, she could think again. 'Can I come in? Or do you want to go and get him and I'll question him here on the doorstep. I'll speak to his neighbours, too. I'm sure they'd be interested to know that Telford is part of an ongoing criminal investigation.'

That worked. The woman stepped back and motioned for Ellen to follow. Inside, she took Ellen through a large, airy hall and into a spotlessly tidy sitting room. Ellen wondered if the pastel colours and floral patterns reflected Adam Telford's lack of taste or the woman's. The whole place smelled of disinfectant and air freshener; a chemical, unpleasant stink that made Ellen feel sick.

A tall, thin man was sitting on a high-backed wooden chair

reading a copy of the *Sunday Telegraph*. He put the paper down when he saw the two women. It was only then Ellen noticed he was wearing thin, plastic gloves. A skin infection, OCD or extreme eccentricity? she wondered. From the stink of chemical cleaners and the sterile tidiness, she'd have put her money on OCD.

'Police to see you,' the woman said.

Ellen introduced herself and he stood up, frowning as he limped across the room and held out his hand.

'Adam Telford,' he said. 'How can I help you?'

She shook his hand, repressing a shiver when she felt the plastic.

He wasn't a handsome man. Thin white hair brushed across a bald head, a high forehead and deep brown eyes. Immaculately dressed in navy-blue corduroys, a pale pink shirt and a silk cravat.

'It's about your daughter,' Ellen said.

He looked quickly at the woman, then back at Ellen.

'Monica?' he asked. 'What about her?'

'Maybe we should sit down first,' Ellen said.

'Of course. Please, take a seat. Bel, love. Give us a moment, would you?'

The woman nodded and left the room, glaring at Ellen as she went. Ellen wondered if the woman might be some sort of nurse. Surely a girlfriend would want to stay and find out what the hell the police wanted?

'What's this about?' Adam asked. He looked scared and Ellen found that interesting. She watched him as he sat down, adjusted his trousers carefully before crossing his legs.

'When was the last time you saw your daughter?' Ellen asked.

'Monica left home many years ago,' he said. 'I haven't seen her or heard from her since.'

'That's not what she told me,' Ellen said.

He licked his lips. 'What did she say?'

Ellen thought back to the phone call earlier. 'She said she came to visit you a few days ago. But you kicked her out. Told her you wanted nothing more to do with her.'

'Sorry,' he said. 'I forgot. She did call to the house recently. And yes, I asked her to leave. She said some terrible things, you know. Not just about me. About my wife, too.'

'You forgot?'

He shook his head, eyes sliding away to the side, refusing to look at her.

'I didn't forget,' he said. 'I don't want to talk about it, that's all. The visit was unpleasant. I rather wish I could forget about it. She was… she's not well, is she? In the head, I mean.'

'Monica says you threatened her,' Ellen said. 'She says she came out here and told you she was going to report you. When you heard that, you warned her off. Your exact words, I think, were: *'I've sorted your mother and I'll sort you as well if you're not careful.'*

'She's disturbed,' Telford said. 'I'd never hurt Monica. Or my ex-wife. You shouldn't listen to her, you know. She says all sorts. Always has done. Can't believe a word she says.'

He stopped abruptly. Like he realised – too late – he'd said too much.

Ellen's hands clenched into fists, fingers dug into the palms of her hands, hurting.

'You're calling her a liar?' Ellen said.

'I'm saying she makes stuff up,' Telford said. 'Like her mother that way.'

'What happened to Monica's mother?' Ellen asked.

'She walked out on us,' Telford said. 'Never gave her daughter a second thought. I was the one who took care of Monica. Fed her and clothed her and gave her a roof over her head. Wouldn't have killed her to show a bit of gratitude occasionally.'

'Is that what you call it?' Ellen asked. 'She was only a child. Your job was to protect her. Not to molest her.'

'Please.' He put his hands over his ears, and when he looked at Ellen, his eyes were wet with tears.

'No more,' he said. 'I would never do anything like that. Why do you find that so difficult to believe?'

'Your wife walked out, then your daughter did the same thing as soon as she was old enough. Want to tell me what they were running away from, Mr Telford?' Ellen said.

'I think I bored them,' he said. 'Sorry, Detective, I'm sure you wanted a more exciting answer, but that's the truth of it. Monica and her mother, well, they like excitement, adventure. That doesn't appeal to me. I prefer a quiet, ordered life. Just like my Bel. Peace and quiet, that's what we like.'

My Bel. His girlfriend, then. Young enough to be his daughter.

*I was fourteen the first time that bastard tried to show me some love.*

'I heard you were in an accident the night Monica left,' Ellen said.

Telford dropped his eyes and patted his leg. 'Left me with a limp.'

'Is that all?' Ellen asked.

'I think you probably know about my other injuries,' he said. 'Don't you?'

Framed photos stood in a neat line along the mantelpiece. Each one showed different images of the same person – a dark-haired, dark-skinned woman so strikingly beautiful it was difficult not to stare at her. Annie Telford. Monica's mother and Adam's wife. The resemblance with her daughter was obvious, although Monica – despite her own striking looks – was nowhere near as perfectly pretty as her mother.

One photo caught Ellen's attention. Annie again. Holding a small child. The woman was gazing directly at the camera, her arms holding the child loosely, as if she was about to drop it. A red scarf, wrapped around her dark curls, was the only bright thing in the photo. The expression on her face was one of utter misery.

Ellen nodded at the photo. 'Your wife?'

'Yes.'

'It can't have been easy for you,' Ellen said. 'When she left, I mean.'

'Wasn't easy for either of us,' Telford said. 'But I did my best.'

The door opened and the little dark-haired woman came back in.

'Are you nearly finished?' she asked. 'Only we're going out to lunch later and we need to head off soon.'

Ellen had a list of dates from the nights Chloe and Monica claimed there'd been someone in their house. She went through these quickly, knowing it was pointless. As predicted, Bel claimed she'd been with Adam on each occasion. Not that it mattered much. Ellen was already pretty sure it wasn't Adam Telford who'd broken into Chloe's house, chased her down the stairs and whacked her over the head. The man could barely walk.

Bel had moved across the room and was sitting on Adam's lap, smiling at Ellen like she'd got one over on her. Ellen knew she'd got as much out of Telford as she was likely to. She pulled a card from her wallet and handed it to him.

'Call me if you'd like to chat,' she said. 'Or if you think you'd like to get in touch with your daughter. I'll see what I can do.'

It was a lie, of course. She had no intention of letting him anywhere near Monica. But she hoped the promise of a reunion might tempt him to pick up the phone sometime.

They both insisted on walking her out, obviously wanting to make sure she left. At the door, she paused and turned around.

'One last question. Do either of you know a woman called Chloe Dunbar?'

The blank looks on their faces was all she needed.

'Ricky Lezard?'

Another blank look before they both shook their heads.

Pointless. She left them to get on with their Sunday and walked back to her car.

She was about to drive off when the girlfriend came running out.

'Please,' she said, panting as she skidded to a stop by Ellen's car. 'What was all that about? He won't tell me anything and I'm worried about him. He looks scared, like something really bad has happened. What did you say to him?'

Ellen looked at this fierce little woman. How old was she? Thirty, at most. She figured Adam Telford to be somewhere north of sixty.

'Why are you with him?' she said.

'I like him,' the woman said. 'You got a problem with that?'

Several problems, but none of them Ellen wanted to discuss right at this moment.

'He must be – what – thirty years older than you?' Ellen asked. 'Twenty-five, at least. I don't get it.'

'Nothing to get,' Bel said. 'Adam takes care of me. I like that.'

Ellen took this to mean Bel liked Adam's money, but maybe she was wrong about that. Although why else would a young woman stay with an impotent man old enough to be her father?

'You can call me too,' Ellen said. She took out another card but the woman refused to take it.

'I know what I'm doing,' Bel said. 'You don't need to worry

about me, copper. Not for a second.'

On the drive back to London, Ellen remembered the photos in the sitting room, particularly the one with Annie Telford looking so miserable. She recalled her own early days of motherhood. The numbing nothingness she'd felt after Pat was born. Followed rapidly by euphoria and infinite love. With Eilish, the euphoria and love had been instant. Never once did she remember feeling miserable. But she'd been lucky. Baby blues had never really affected her. Was that what she saw in this photo? Or did the problem go deeper than that?

In the days and weeks that followed, the image would stay with Ellen. She would think about it, and wonder if Annie's misery following the birth of her daughter might go some way to explaining what Monica did. Or if, on the other hand, the sort of twisted person Monica was had nothing at all to do with her mother and everything to do with the fact that some people were just born that way and there was nothing Ellen – or anyone else – could do but accept that.

# THIRTY

Chloe woke late. Pale grey light sneaked into the room through the gaps in the curtain. No sign of yesterday's sunshine. She didn't care.

Last night with Carl. He'd treated her like a princess. Really took care of her. Insisted on buying all the drinks and later, in the restaurant, refused to let her pay her half of the bill.

It felt different from their first night together. Both of them more nervous. Which was strange, when you thought about it, because of what they'd done the first time. And then, at the end of the night, he'd driven her home but nothing else had happened. A kiss on the doorstep, but she didn't invite him in and he said he understood. Told her this felt special and he didn't want to rush things, either.

She could hardly believe this was happening. A week earlier, she was living in fear of her life, literally terrified that Ricky was going to turn up on her doorstep any moment and really hurt her. But all that had stopped now.

He'd called last night. She hadn't called back yet, but she would. Later. She'd sort of half promised Nathan she'd go to church with him this morning. She checked the time on her phone. Ten-thirty! Way too late for church.

There was a text waiting for her. Carl.

*Gr8 time last nite. Hope you ok. Fancy a quick drink 2nite? Xx*

Two kisses! She hugged the phone to her chest, thinking about Carl and his lovely blue eyes and the way he made her feel. Special. Sort of how Ricky had made her feel, at first, but different too. With Ricky, he always made it clear, right from the beginning, that he was the one in charge. It was one of the things she'd liked about him to start with.

Carl wasn't like that. He pretended to be this real lad but actually, when it was just the two of them, he was really shy and always wanting to know what she wanted and was this wine okay and was she sure she liked the restaurant and ...

She replied to his text. Quickly, before she changed her mind and got chicken about it.

*Gr8 time 2. Wd luv drink. Call me? Xxxxx*

She pressed Send, little tremors of excitement running through her.

She rolled over onto her side, blinking away the bits of daylight that broke into the room.

The curtains! She sat up in bed, panic stripping away the last, lingering effects of sleep.

They were only partially drawn, a big gap down the centre that was letting the light in. Ever since this business with Ricky, she'd been so careful every night. Double locking the front and back doors, making sure the bolts on the front door were pulled across. And making sure there wasn't a single gap in the curtains where someone could peer in from outside.

She tried to remember going to bed last night. The details were a bit hazy. She didn't think she'd drunk that much but come to think of it, her head did feel a bit thick and she never usually slept in this late.

She thought she'd closed them properly, was pretty sure she had, in fact. But, if she was being honest, she couldn't swear by it a hundred percent. In her hand, her phone buzzed. Another text from Carl: *Xxxxx*.

She was being silly. Worrying about the curtains, of all things!

She reached out for the alarm remote control and pressed the button that switched off the alarm. Her mouth was dry, another sign she'd had too much wine. Even though she'd drank lots of water when she came home. She did remember that. She had a water purifier in the kitchen and always drank a pint before bedtime, knowing it was the best way to keep her skin looking fresh.

She looked around for the glass she'd brought up with her, but it was empty. She sent a quick *xxx* and a smiley face back to Carl then got out of bed. Putting on her fluffy dressing-gown and matching slippers, she went downstairs.

Midway down the stairs, she stopped, scared suddenly of what she'd find down there. She'd left her phone up by the bed and wished she hadn't. Part of her wanted to call Carl and ask him to come over straight away. Another part of her knew she was being stupid. She had her injunction. Ricky couldn't come near her, couldn't do a single thing to hurt her. It was over. Carl said it was only natural to feel like this from time to time. She'd spoken about it last night. Said that even though she didn't think Ricky would come back, she couldn't help feeling scared. He'd offered to sleep on her sofa but she'd said no, that wasn't right. She had to get used to being on her own.

When she'd said that, he'd looked at her like he was really proud of her and it made her feel special all over again. She didn't think he'd be proud if he saw her now, standing on the stairs like a ninny, too scared to go into her own kitchen. That got her moving again. She ran down the last few steps and straight into the kitchen.

Later, she'd try to work out when she knew something was wrong. She would tell Raj she felt it the moment she opened the kitchen door. In truth, it was a second or two before that. Possibly when she felt the gush of cold air across her legs while she was still in the hallway.

Or when she glanced behind her, right before going into the kitchen, and noticed that the bolt on the front door was pulled back. And even if she knew then, it didn't stop her. She pulled open the kitchen door and went inside. Moving fast because she knew now what she was going to find.

The door that led from the kitchen into the tiny back garden was open. Swinging gently in the wind that blew through the open door and wrapping itself around her legs and body, making her shiver.

And on the kitchen worktop, her favourite mug, the one Nathan had given her as a moving-in present. Pink with little bunny rabbits painted onto it. The flower lying alongside it, just like she knew it would be. She lifted the mug, felt how warm it was, saw the steam rising from the freshly made tea inside. The mug slipped from her hand, crashed onto the cheap lino and broke, little shards of china and hot splashes of tea, bouncing against her legs.

She didn't even notice. All she could think of was how stupid she'd been. Ricky had told her what would happen. How he would make her life a misery if she ever dared walk out on him. He was only doing what he'd said he would. Her big mistake was that she hadn't taken his threats seriously enough.

# THIRTY-ONE

'I dropped it,' Chloe said. 'I know you said I wasn't to touch it, but I was so freaked…'

She looked freaked. Raj didn't think she was making it up. He tried to think what Ellen would do. She was always telling him to follow his gut. If you felt something, chances were that feeling was right.

'And you're certain you locked both doors?' he asked.

'As certain as I can be,' Chloe said. 'I mean, I make sure to lock them every night. Why would I forget to do it last night?'

'You told me you'd been out,' Raj said. 'Maybe you had a bit too much to drink and forgot?'

'Even if I did,' Chloe said. 'And I'm not saying that's what happened, but even if I did, it still doesn't explain this.' She pointed at the broken mug still scattered on the floor.

The call had come when he was still at Aidan's. There'd been some talk of spending the day together but when Chloe called, Raj had used work as an excuse to get out of there. Spent the drive over here hating himself for being such a coward. For being relieved when Chloe's call had come through. He'd sent a text, saying how sorry he was and promising to make up for it later. So far, Aidan hadn't replied.

Chloe refilled the water filter and poured herself another glass. Her third since Raj arrived. And he'd only been here half an hour. Which made him think that Chloe might have had more to drink than she was letting on. Her movements were slow and sluggish too, like she hadn't woken up properly.

'I thought it was over,' Chloe said.

Poor kid. Raj wished there was something more he could do. Times like this he hated his job. He'd joined the police because he wanted to help people. Half the time – more than that – he ended up feeling useless. The force was changing. Lack of resources and funding, combined with Superintendent Paul Nichols' sociopathic need to prove that crime in Lewisham was falling made it increasingly difficult for decent coppers to get on with their day job. Instead, Raj was spending more and more time on paperwork – either justifying his existence or tweaking crime reports so that Nichols' monthly reporting figures pleased whatever shiny-faced bureaucrats he was accountable to.

'I'll take the pieces of the mug,' Raj said. 'And the flower. Get them dusted down for prints and any traces of DNA.' Chances of finding something were close to zero, but at least it would reassure Chloe that he was doing something.

'Chloe, I know I've already asked you this. Are you sure you don't know a woman called Monica Telford? She's an artist. Lives in Lee. Ring any bells?'

Chloe frowned. 'Monica? I don't know anyone called Monica. Why?'

'No reason,' Raj said.

Alastair had already cross-checked both women and found nothing to connect them. Didn't mean the connection wasn't there, though. It was possible Raj just hadn't found it yet. Or else there was nothing to find.

'I'll speak to my colleagues in Hammersmith,' he said. 'Get them to have another chat with Ricky. Although I'm not sure that will do any good. His alibis so far have been watertight.'

'Well then he's getting someone to do it for him,' Chloe said.

'I need some other names,' Raj said. 'Is there anyone else you can think of who might want to scare you like this? You must meet all sorts in your job, I imagine. Always thought being an estate agent's a bit like being with the police. You get to see the full range of humanity – good and bad. And you'll need to think about staying somewhere else for a few days. What about your mum? Have you called her yet?'

Chloe shook her head. 'I want to, but I'm afraid she'll put the phone down on me. That's what she did the last time I called.'

'She knows you're not with Ricky any longer, though?' Raj asked.

'She knows. But she said that doesn't change anything. The way she sees it, I only moved in with Ricky to spite her. When I told her I'd left him, I thought she'd be happy.'

'Why wasn't she?'

'She thought it meant I'd move back to Spain,' Chloe said. 'When she heard I was staying in London, she lost it.'

'There must be someone else,' Raj said.

A pink flush brightened Chloe's pale cheeks.

'I could ask Carl,' she said. 'But I'm not ready for that. *We're* not ready. We're trying to take things slowly, you see. If I suddenly ask to move into his, it'll change things. I don't want that.'

'Carl from the office? What's this got to do with him?'

'We're seeing each other,' Chloe said. 'Why?'

* * *

Chloe had Carl's telephone number but no address for him. Raj sat in his car and called Malcolm, told him what he needed. While he waited for Malcolm to call him back, Raj phoned Ellen.

'So she's dating this bloke she knows absolutely nothing about,' Raj said. 'Doesn't even know where he bloody lives.'

'Why would she know that?' Ellen said. 'I don't know where you live and I've been working with you for the last five years.'

'Yeah, but we're not dating,' Raj said.

'You asking me out, Patel?'

Raj smiled. 'In your dreams, Ma'am. Listen, I've got to go. Malcolm's calling me.'

Hanging up from Ellen, he took Malcolm's call.

'What have you got?'

'Carl Jenkins,' Malcolm said. 'Twenty-three-year-old estate agent. Lives on Ardmore Crescent in a two-bed flat with his mum, Gloria. You want the address?'

Ardmore Crescent was a short drive from Chloe's house in Hither Green. When Raj knocked on the door, it was opened by a tall, elegant woman with grey hair pulled back into a neat bun. She was clearly concerned when Raj produced his warrant card and asked to speak to Carl.

'He's not in any trouble, I hope?' Mrs Jenkins said.

'Just a routine enquiry,' Raj said. 'Shouldn't take up any time at all, Mrs Jenkins.'

He followed her into the small flat, down a dark corridor to a clean, modern kitchen at the back.

'Carl's still in bed,' she said. 'He likes a lie-in on a Sunday. Only chance he gets. I'll go and get him for you.'

She disappeared and Raj could hear her, knocking on her son's bedroom door then the muffled sound of their voices. A few minutes later, Carl himself appeared, looking like he'd just got up. Tousled dark hair, eyes heavy with sleep, dressed in a pair of faded denims and a crumpled T-shirt.

Raj already knew Carl. He'd met him a handful of times in the estate agent's office where Chloe worked and had the impression that Carl was a decent enough bloke.

'Sorry,' Carl said. 'Mind if I make a coffee first? Can't function right without caffeine. You want one?'

Raj watched as Carl moved about the kitchen, turning the kettle on and spooning instant coffee into a matching pair of patterned mugs. Raj could think of worse ways to spend his morning. The guy was seriously something. Blue eyes, dark skin, thick dark hair and a body that looked like it had walked straight off the pages of one of Aidan's fitness magazines. The only imperfection Raj could see was Carl's nose, which had obviously been broken at some point. In Raj's opinion, the flatness across the bridge of the nose added character to a face that would otherwise be too pretty.

Coffee made, Carl sat down across from Raj and smiled. Raj found himself smiling right back as he lifted the bitter-smelling coffee to his mouth. Blue eyes that reminded him of Aidan. He was a sucker for blue eyes.

'Is this about Chloe?' Carl said. 'Nothing's happened, has it?'

'Why would you think something's happened?' Raj asked.

'This business with her ex,' Carl said. 'I know she's been a bit freaked. But I thought all that was finished.'

'Chloe says you and her have been seeing a bit of each other,' Raj said.

Carl smiled again. Less cheeky this time, a bit shy.

'Yeah.'

'How long have you worked together?' Raj asked.

'Me and Chloe? Since she started,' Carl said. 'About six months, something like that. I've been there a year now. My mum wanted me to go to uni but I couldn't see the point. Want to work with property. I'll make more money out of that than doing some stupid degree and spending the next ten years paying off a big loan.'

'So you've worked with her for six months but the first time you asked her out was last week?' Raj said.

'Yeah, well.' Carl shifted in his seat and started again. 'Truth is, she was a bit stand-offish at first. I got her wrong, thought she was a bit stuck-up. And she's so pally with Nathan, I thought she had her eye on him. I mean, I know he's a fat bastard but I reckoned maybe it was his money she was after. He's rolling in it, after all.'

'What changed your mind?'

'The newspaper,' Carl said. 'Moment I read it, I knew I'd got her all wrong. Felt terrible about it. I wasn't planning on, you know, jumping her or whatever. I just wanted to chat. Tell her I was sorry she was having such a shitty time. We went for a drink and one thing led to another.'

He smiled. He had a great smile. Face lit up like he was the happiest bloke you'd ever meet. Difficult not to smile right back at him, even though Raj was here to question him, not grin at him.

'I'm seeing her tonight,' Carl said. 'Going to take her to the Catford Conservative Club. Do you know it? New pub where the old Con Club used to be. Dead cool. She'll love it. Hang on, though. You still haven't told me what all this is about. Has something else happened to her?'

When Raj told him, Carl seemed genuinely upset and concerned for Chloe. The bloke was either a really good liar or he had nothing to do with what happened last night. Raj asked him a few more questions but, by now, it all felt a bit pointless. A few minutes later, he thanked Carl for his time and left.

Back in his car, he checked his phone. A text from Aidan.

*Make it up to me how exactly?*

Raj replied quickly – and graphically – even added a smiley face before he pressed Send.

Then he switched on the engine and drove away, smiling.

# THIRTY-TWO

Greenwich Market on a Sunday. The place was buzzing. Monica wandered around the stalls, pausing every so often to chat to one of the stallholders. She loved this place. Loved that she lived close enough to walk over here on a Sunday morning. Loved that this was something she was part of. Somewhere she belonged.

She'd dressed carefully: black woollen dress – fitted – high boots and a scarlet-red silk and cashmere wrap. The boho-glamour look suited her and she worked it to perfection this morning.

She stopped at a stall selling designer T-shirts. The T-shirts themselves were awful – punk-inspired patterns so unoriginal she could barely bother to pretend. But the guy selling them was divine. White-blonde hair, chiselled cheekbones and eyes the colour of bluebells.

She got his attention pretty quickly and the T-shirt chit-chat quickly turned to other things. He'd asked her out within ten minutes. She gave him her number and left without buying anything. Sometimes it was almost too easy.

Later, she wandered into the park and immediately wished she hadn't. Sunday had to be the worst day to come here. Full of happy, smiling couples with their adorable brats on scooters and bicycles and bloody rollerblades. Not seeming to notice that the day was grey and cold and totally unsuited for family outings to the park. Ahead of her, a young girl came towards her, wobbling dangerously on her rollerblades. Only a matter of time before she fell. Monica considered not stepping out of the way but the father was cute. At the last minute, she jumped sideways, accidentally on purpose falling into him.

A flurry of apologies and – was it her imagination or did he hold on to her a fraction longer than he needed to? – she was on her way again. She walked up to the top of the park, keeping an eye out, but the one family she wanted to see wasn't about.

She left the park at the first exit and walked down Vanbrugh Hill, turning right into Annandale Road. There was no car outside Kelly's house but she stood outside for a while, watching.

When she grew bored with this, she walked down to Woolwich Road, crossed over and onto Fingal Street. She wasn't sure which house she wanted, but it was fun trying to guess. In truth, it could have been any one of the identical Victorian terraces but, if she was betting on it, she'd have chosen either: the end-of-terrace house with the red front door and collection of grotesque garden gnomes in the front, or the freshly painted semi-detached house with the yellow front door and a window-box planted with blue crocuses and a yellow flower she didn't recognise.

As it turned out, she didn't have to wait long to find out whether she was right or not. She hadn't even reached the end of the street when a car turned in and stopped outside the house with the window-boxes. She watched a tall, good-looking man get out of the driver's seat and approach the house. Moments later, a flurry of activity as people spilled out of the house, all heading towards the car.

Forcing herself not to move too quickly, Monica turned and walked towards the group. As she drew closer, she was able to work out who each person was. The elderly couple were the parents, the boy and girl obviously Kelly's kids. The guy, same dark hair and blue eyes, had to be Kelly's brother.

A little closer and she dropped her bag, contents scattering onto the pavement. The brother and the old man rushed forward together. She bent down, started picking things up as they did the same.

'I'm so sorry,' she said. 'So clumsy. I don't know what happened.'

'Clumsy happens to all of us,' the old man said.

He spoke with a strong Irish accent. For a moment, she wondered if she'd got it wrong. Tried to recall if Kelly had mentioned Irish parents. She'd assumed – wrongly, it seemed – that the Kelly had come from her husband. Now, she thought Kelly was probably one of those right-on feminist types who would refuse to change her name when she got married. Boringly predictable.

'Now then,' the man was saying. 'I think that's everything. Are you okay, love?'

Monica smiled. 'I'm fine, Mr Kelly. Thanks ever so.'

To her surprise he laughed.

'It's Flanagan,' he said. 'I don't know where you got the Kelly from.'

She forced the smile to stay where it was.

'I'm so sorry. You're Ellen's dad, I know, so I just assumed…'

'Ah you're a friend of Ellen's.' The woman was here now, face smiling up at Monica. *Any friend of Ellen's…* Monica half expected to hear her say it. Not that she needed to. The smile said it for her. Her own face was hurting now from the effort of smiling back, but she kept it up.

'I saw you with Ellen a while back in the park,' she said. 'But I don't think we were ever introduced. I'm Monica.'

They all shook hands with her – the mother, the father, the brother. She tried to recall the brother's name, but it kept eluding her. She was tempted to guess, but in the end she didn't have to. He offered it all by himself.

'Sean,' he said. 'We haven't met, have we?'

She pretended to think for a moment, then shook her head.

'I think I'd have remembered,' she said.

He smiled, but didn't seem to get that she was flirting with him. She thought maybe he was a bit thick. Or gay. She wondered what the trad Irish parents would think of that. Helped keep the smile in place a little longer as she pictured it.

'Going anywhere nice?' she asked.

'We're having lunch at Sean's,' the mother said. 'It's a bit of a family tradition. Sean and his… partner. They do a great Sunday roast.'

The slightest hesitation was a surprise. They obviously knew and accepted it. Or pretended to.

'Ellen not joining you?'

'She's working,' Sean said. 'Good to meet you, Monica. Sorry to rush off but my partner,' he winked when he said this and she liked his cheekiness, 'won't be happy with me if we're late. See you around.'

She said goodbye and watched as they all piled into the silver BMW and drove off. She watched until the car turned left into Woolwich Road and disappeared around the corner. Then she pushed open the gate of Number 12 and walked into the front garden.

A door to the side of the house led into the back. This opened easily and she walked through into a small, courtyard-style garden. A high wall ran along the back of the garden, making it impossible for anyone to see over and notice she was in here. The only way she could be seen was by someone inside the house. And there was no one home. All over at Sean's playing happy fucking families.

As she'd hoped, there were more flowers back here. Strange to see so many blooms this late in the year. Whoever looked after the garden obviously knew what they were doing. A flowerbed ran along one side of the garden, alive with more blues and yellows. Another flower, too – startlingly pretty with long, thin, cerise pink petals.

Monica walked over to the flowers, crouched down and started pulling them, one by one, from the bed. When she'd removed each one, making sure she got them out at the roots, she tore the petals into tiny pieces and sprinkled these across the garden, watching them float in the air then drift slowly to the ground. Satisfied that was enough to wipe the incessant smiles off their smug Irish faces, she stood up, rubbed her palms together to dislodge the little bits of clay, and left.

All things considered, it had been quite a good morning.

# THIRTY-THREE

Sunday lunch at Sean and Terry's was a regular event. Ellen's family were already sitting around the table, waiting, when she arrived. Closer to two than one thirty, but at least she'd made it. Unlike Jim, who'd sent her a text earlier saying an emergency job had come up and he wouldn't be here for lunch. She'd tried calling him back, but he didn't answer. His absence left her with a sense of unease she didn't like.

'Father Barry was asking after you,' her mother announced before Ellen even sat down. 'Said he hadn't seen you for a while and wondered if you were okay.'

'I hope you told him how busy I've been,' Ellen said, wondering why she bothered. In the world according to her mother, being busy was a poor excuse for not attending Sunday Mass.

'I told him you'd be there next Sunday,' her mother said. 'So you'd better not let me down. I'd hate poor Father to be disappointed.'

'And what about Sean?' Ellen asked. 'Was he asking about him as well? Or does his sense of Christianity not extend that far?'

Mrs Flanagan looked across at her son and smiled. 'It's different for Sean, Ellen. I can't be asking him to come along. He still has a lot of issues with the Church. And I can't say that I blame him, if I'm honest. The Church isn't very accepting of some things. Sean, you see, he'd feel uncomfortable if I pushed him. It'd only cause problems between himself and Terry.'

Ellen winked at Sean. 'So what you're saying is if I was gay, it'd be okay for me to skip Mass, but because I'm straight it's not?'

'She has a point, Bridget,' Ellen's father said. 'You shouldn't keep going on at her. I can't say I blame her for not wanting to go, anyway. Half the time I have no idea what that priest is on about. Did you understand a word of the sermon today?'

'Of course,' Mrs Flanagan said.

'Go on, so,' her husband said. 'Enlighten me.'

Ellen's mother clamped her lips shut and looked down at her plate, refusing to speak. Ellen's father rubbed his hands together, grinning widely. Delighted, Ellen knew, that he'd got one over on his wife. It was a rare enough occurrence, after all.

'Will we have lunch now?' he asked. 'I don't know about anyone else, but I'm starving.'

Sean and Terry lived in a modern, riverside apartment in

Limehouse, across the river from Greenwich. Lunch was the usual feast. As they sat around the table after pudding, Ellen truly believed she'd never be able to eat again.

She sat back in her chair, doing her best to focus on nothing else except enjoying this precious family time. Around her, conversation drifted and she caught snatches of it, content to listen rather than take part. Her father, Terry and Eilish were discussing some obscure TV programme Eilish adored but Ellen, to her shame, had never heard of. Luckily, Terry seemed to know all about it and they were in a heated discussion over whether or not the central character had done the right thing ditching her boyfriend. At the other end of the table, her mother and Sean were gossiping about old friends and acquaintances. Ellen had heard it all before and had no desire to hear it again.

She looked around for Pat and saw him standing outside on the balcony. She pushed her chair back and went out to join him.

'They have them in Switzerland,' Pat said, pointing to the cable cars that ran across the river, linking the $O_2$ on the south bank of the Thames with the Excel centre on the north. 'Jim told me about them. Can we go there sometime, Mum?'

'Switzerland?' Ellen said. 'Maybe. In the meantime, we can go on those. How about next weekend? Sean and Terry are away, so we'll go on Sunday.'

'Can Jim come too?' Pat asked.

'If you'd like that,' Ellen said.

Pat shrugged. There was something self-consciously grown-up

about the gesture. Ellen hugged him, squeezing tight and wishing she could hold him this way forever. He endured it for a moment, then pulled away.

'You're squashing me,' he said. But he was smiling and she knew he was secretly glad. They didn't hug each other enough these days. When had all that stopped?

'I'd like Jim to come,' Pat said. 'Sometimes it's a bit boring when it's just me, you and Eilish. No offence, Mum.'

No offence. The latest phrase amongst Pat and his gang of lovely friends.

'None taken,' Ellen said. Pat lunged then, wrapping his arms around her middle and burying his head in her shoulder.

'Thanks, Mum,' he whispered. 'You're the best.'

* * *

Everything was moving too quickly. Chloe wasn't ready for this. She'd tried to explain that to Carl, but he didn't get it. Or wouldn't get it. Made her wonder if he was any better than Ricky. Just another bloke who wanted to control her. They were all the same. Stupid to have thought he'd be any different. The only man she knew who wasn't like that was poor old Nathan. And only because he didn't think of her like that. Because he was more interested in God than in living, breathing humans.

She'd barely heard from him these past few days and guessed he was sulking because she hadn't turned up at his church yet. Well that was his problem, not hers. Except if he wasn't sulking, maybe she'd call and ask him to come over. She was scared on her own and didn't know what to do about that.

She was tired. Legs trembling, body shaking. She'd been walking all afternoon. Ever since the argument with Carl. He'd called over, all full of himself. Told her he'd spoken with his mother and it was all arranged. She could move in straight away. Stay as long as she liked. His mum was fine with it.

His mum! She hadn't even known that about him. Made her wonder what else she didn't know. She couldn't move in with someone she hardly knew. But when she'd tried to tell him all this, he got so angry. Told her she was being stupid and she couldn't stay in the house alone, it was madness. And when he'd started saying that, it reminded her so much of Ricky, she'd told him to go and then she'd pushed him out the door herself, slamming it hard.

After he left, she'd grabbed her coat and gone straight out. Walked up through Blackheath, down through Greenwich Park as far as the river. Then she'd kept on walking, following the river west until she reached Deptford. Now she was somewhere near New Cross, tired and cold, with no idea what to do or who she could turn to.

She didn't even know where she was. She looked around, trying to get her bearings, but it wasn't easy. At some point, it had grown dark and she wasn't yet familiar enough with this part of London. She tried to think back, remember which route she'd walked to get here, but she'd been so preoccupied she hadn't taken any notice of where she was going.

She was in a quiet residential street of flat-fronted Victorian cottages. There was no one else about. Lights had come on in several of the houses, offering the promise of comfort and safety. She pictured people – families – inside those houses, gathered together for Sunday dinner or in front of their TVs, cocooned and safe.

Unlike her, out here alone.

A noise behind her made her jump. She swung around, hand over her mouth. Saw a shadow flit under the streetlight then disappear.

'Hello?'

Nothing.

She turned in the opposite direction and started walking, fast. Her footsteps echoed across the empty street. Or were they someone else's footsteps? She looked behind, didn't see anyone, but couldn't shake off the feeling she wasn't alone. She walked on, faster, footsteps slap-slapping, heart thud-thudding. Up ahead, another street, busier than this one, orange streetlights, the rumble of traffic moving along the road. People.

She started running. He was there. Behind her. She couldn't see him or hear him but she knew he was there. She ran until her body couldn't take it. Heart pounding, lungs aching, legs weak and barely able to hold her up. She was out on the big busy street now. People walked past, cars drove up and down. No one paid her the slightest bit of attention.

Tears turned everything into a blur. Orange and yellow haze of car lights, flashes of colour as people passed in and out under the streetlights. Face wet from sweat and tears. Body shaking. Throat sore from trying to drag air down it. Air that tasted of car fumes and dirt and all the stink of the city.

And somewhere nearby, *he* was there. Watching and waiting. And there wasn't a single thing she could do to stop him.

# THIRTY-FOUR

*I don't like this. She needs to make her mind up. It's not fair to keep me hanging on. Does she want this or not? One minute, she can't stay away from me. The next, she's so cold it's like she hates me.*

*If she's not careful, she'll be sorry. She'll come looking for me one day and I won't be there. I'll have found someone else. But there isn't anyone else. Sometimes, when I'm not doing so well, I swear to God, I nearly hate her for it.*

*Is that possible? Can you hate someone and love them all at the same time?*

*Yes. Right now, right this second, I swear that it's exactly how I feel. Part of me wanting to love her and protect her and make sure nothing bad ever happens to her again. The other part — the bad, evil part of me — wants to punish her for making me feel this way.*

*I don't like it. She knows that and she does nothing to make it any better. Sometimes, I even think she's doing it on purpose.*

\* \* \*

Too scared to get a taxi, not knowing who might be driving the car, she jumped on a bus as far as Lewisham. There, she waited ages for a bus, but none came and she had to walk the final stage. She went the long way around, along the high street, up Hither Green Lane and down Ennersdale Road.

At the house, all she'd have to do was go inside, grab a few things. Then she'd jump on a train to Greenwich. She'd booked a room in the Holiday Inn Express. One night there, then she was on a plane to Spain. She should have done it earlier instead of wasting all this time trying to make a go of things herself. Mum had been so happy to hear from her. Offered to pay her ticket and everything. Promised things would be just the way they used to be. Before Ricky came into their lives and ruined everything. Mum was right. She'd never been able to stand on her own two feet, so why on earth did she want to start doing it now?

*Just you and me, Chloe. Like we used to be.*

There was a time, not so long ago, it was the last thing she wanted. How stupid she'd been. Mum had always looked out for her, been her best friend as well as her mother. People used to mistake them for sisters, not mother and daughter. Chloe had hated it for reasons that now seemed so silly. They'd have fun together. Like they used to before she grew up and decided she wanted a life of her own.

Some sort of life it had turned out to be.

Ennersdale Road was quiet. When she turned into Nightingale Grove, it was quieter again. There was someone behind her. Not her imagination this time. She had to keep going. Nearly home.

Footsteps. Walking when she walked, stopping suddenly when she stopped. She swung around, eyes scanning the road, peering through the darkness. Couldn't see anyone, but she knew he was there.

'Hello?'

A figure stepped out of the shadows, walked towards her. She should move. Run. Get as far away as she could. But she was frozen to the spot, watching it happen like she was far away and not even inside her own body. And then, right when she thought the fear would consume her, when she thought this was it and she would die right here, right now, the person moved under a streetlight and she saw who it was.

She laughed, shaky, hysterical laughter. Laughing so hard, her eyes watered and her stomach hurt.

'I'm sorry,' she gasped. 'I just wasn't expecting… I thought it was someone else. But it's only you.'

\* \* \*

'Will you be my best friend forever?' Eilish asked as Ellen tucked her into bed.

'I'll be your mum forever,' Ellen said. 'And your best friend if you want me. But you'll have so many friends, Eilish.'

'Even more than now?'

Ellen smiled. 'Even more.'

Eilish had her father's personality. All lightness and sociability. Poor Pat took after Ellen: dark and difficult. She bent down and kissed Eilish on the forehead, inhaling her daughter's soft, sweet smell.

'I love you, Mummy.'

'I love you too, darling. Sleep tight and don't let the bed bugs bite.'

Pat was reading a book when she went in. The latest *Alex Rider* book. Ellen loved Anthony Horowitz for getting her son into reading.

'Another few minutes, Mummy? Please?'

'It's nearly eight,' Ellen said. 'How about I let you read until eight-fifteen, then turn the light off?'

When he smiled, it transformed his face, the darkness banished, reminding her of what he was like as a toddler. He'd been happy then. Happier, at least. Not that he was unhappy now. It was more that he lacked Eilish's innate ability for happiness. For his sake, Ellen wished he was less like her and more like his father.

'Will you read it to me?'

He held the book out. She sat down, took it from him and started reading.

At twenty past eight, his eyes were closing. Ellen shut the

book, switched the light off and gave him a kiss goodnight.

'I dreamt last night that you got shot,' Pat said. 'We were on a walk and a man came along and shot you. He didn't shoot me, but I couldn't stop crying because you were dead and I wasn't. I don't want to live without you, Mummy.'

Ellen sat down again, wishing she could lie beside him, not talk anymore and just go to sleep. She was suddenly so very tired.

'Pat,' she said. 'You know if you have a bad dream and you tell someone, it means you never get that dream again and that the dream can't ever come true.'

'Really?' His voice told her he didn't believe that. Not for a single second.

She smiled. 'Cross my heart.'

'Yeah, yeah. Love you, Mum. You can go now. I'm tired.'

At his bedroom door, she hovered, wondering if she should say something else. Hoping he was okay.

'Night, Mum.'

'Night, darling.'

She left, taking care to leave the door open so the light from the hall shone into his room. Just the way he liked it.

As she came downstairs, the front doorbell rang. She ran to answer it, saw Jim's outline through the glass panels.

'Hey.' She opened the door and they hugged. He was warm, his T-shirt damp with sweat, like he'd come straight from the gym.

'Sorry.' He patted his T-shirt. 'I've just finished work. Probably should have gone home and changed first but I wanted to see you. Thought maybe I'd catch the kids before they were asleep?'

'They're in bed,' she said. 'But Pat's still awake. Just. If you run up now, you'll catch him before he nods off.'

She listened as he went upstairs. She could hear the rumble of his voice and Pat's and wondered what they were talking about. Strange to think her children were building their own relationships with him, separate from her and him.

It struck her that she was happy. Right here, in this moment, perfectly content with her lot. She considered this revelation, checking it over, doubting it and half expecting to find something that would dispel the feeling.

But she didn't find anything. Work was going well, her family were healthy and happy. And there was Jim. All things considered, life could be a lot worse. She was lucky, and she knew it.

# THIRTY-FIVE

*Hush little baby…*

Her eyes are open. She thinks her eyes are open. In the darkness, it's difficult to tell. She tries to remember what she's doing here, but the place where her memories used to be is empty. Or missing. She knows her name. Chloe.

Cold Chloe. Teeth chitter-chattering. Body shaking. Ice cold. Tries to move but nothing happens. Her name is Chloe. Was Chloe. Pictures – faded, hard to focus – drift around inside her head. Things that don't make sense. A man with blue eyes and dark hair. A name. Ricky. She thinks she knows Ricky but she's not sure.

A flash of focus then. A moment's clarity… Shock. She'd got it all wrong. Why? She can't remember. Nothing in her head now, nothing anywhere except pain. Oh God, the pain.

*Don't say a word…*

A face. Kind face. Smiling. Arms wrapped around her, hugging her. Singing her to sleep.

*Mama's gonna buy you a mocking bird…*

Mummy. She's crying.

*Mummy loves you, my darling…*

Sweet soft voice.

Crying. Holding her tighter now, telling her she loved her, begging her to stay.

*And if that cart and horse fall down…*

She has to go. She's floating. Drifting away. Moving from the pain. Better like this. Because the pain, it's bad now. Really bad. She can't take it.

*You'll still be the sweetest little baby in town.*

The pain fades. And everything else with it. No cold now. No anything. Drifting, floating. Gone.

# THIRTY-SIX

It was the sound of someone moving around downstairs that woke Monica. She opened her eyes, the dream fading as she tried to work out if the person downstairs had been part of the dream too. Or if there really was someone there.

Her shoulders ached and the muscles in her arms were stiff. It happened sometimes if she'd spent too long in the gym. She rolled her shoulders, flexed and unflexed the muscles along each arm, waiting for worst of the pain to pass.

Sometimes when she woke, it took a while to work things out. Where she was and who she was. The strength of the dreams made it difficult to escape them in those first few moments between sleep and wakefulness. Ever since Brighton, the dreams had been more frequent, more vivid than ever. This had been one of the worst. Her mother was there, of course. As present in her dreams as she'd been absent from her life. Saying those things to her, half-smiling, like it was funny. Like she didn't know it was wrong, all wrong. Lying – because of course it was lies, they both knew that – and never shutting up. Just going on and on and on until she couldn't bear it a moment longer. Until…

Whistling.

She sat up in the bed, heart racing. What if she'd been followed?

At the same time as she thought this, she noticed other things. The stale smell of a body that wasn't hers. The indent on the spare pillow. And then she remembered. Her world spun 360 degrees until everything was in place and she was fully awake. The tread of feet on the stairs, the bedroom door opened and there he was.

'Harry.'

He smiled. He really did have the loveliest smile.

He was carrying a tray. The smell of fresh coffee and buttered toast invaded the room, blocking out the other smells.

She patted the side of the bed, beckoned him over.

He placed the tray on the table beside the bed and sat down where she'd told him to.

'Breakfast in bed,' he said. 'Hope it's okay?'

He gave her that puppy dog look, eyes all big and watery, mouth half open. Made him look like a retard. He was sitting too close. She shifted across to give herself more room, but he just moved with her. Like he was attached to her with Velcro.

And still staring at her. Jesus Almighty, is that what love looked like? If it was, she could do without it, thank you very much.

But she remembered why he was here and she smiled and thanked him. Although she couldn't quite bring herself to let him feed her the slivers of toast when he tried to. That really was a step too far.

Later, they went to the park. Her idea. She'd reached the point where she couldn't take anymore. It wasn't just Harry, although he didn't help. It was everything. The lingering effects of the dream, the unbearable build-up of tension, the feeling that something was about to happen and if it didn't soon, she would explode from the waiting for it. The desperate, claustrophobic sense that the house was closing in on her and if she didn't get out, her body would close down, simply stop working and everything she was would disappear.

How did you explain that to someone? You couldn't. Not without sounding like a nutter. And she wasn't mad. Furthest thing from crazy there was. All this, the planning, the thinking through every single piece of it, having to go back over things time and again to make sure she hadn't missed anything. That was the problem. Her mind was burning up from the effort of it all.

Another reason to be grateful to Harry. If she could just switch her mind off for a bit, let herself relax, then being with him wasn't such hard work. Yes, she had to be careful, make sure she didn't reveal too much of herself. But she could hardly call that hard work. She'd had a lifetime's practice.

He yabbered on a bit, but that was mostly okay. She was happy to let him talk while she pretended to listen. And he didn't need much back. Seemed more than happy just being with her. They strolled through the park hand in hand – okay, that was an effort, but she had to make allowances – while he talked at her and she zoned out.

After a bit, he went quiet. She waited a few minutes, pretending she was still lost in her own thoughts or the loveliness of the moment or whatever. Then she squeezed his hand, still clinging on to hers like a child's.

'I've wanted to talk to you about something,' she began. 'But I haven't known where to start.'

He returned the pressure on her hand.

'What is it?' he asked. 'You know you can talk to me about anything, Mon.'

'I know,' she said. 'It's just, well, you know I don't find it easy. Trusting people, I mean.'

'You and me both,' he said.

He stopped, took her face in both of his hands and stared hard.

'Listen,' he said, voice all urgent now, getting ready to communicate something of great importance. She had to fight the urge to giggle.

'We've both been through a lot, right?' he continued. 'I understand, Mon. At least, I want to. If you'll let me? Look, I never told you this, but I really admire you. Because you're so open about it. Talking about that shit, it can't be easy for you. You're amazing, you know that?'

She reached up and stroked his face, fingers tracing the tickly overnight stubble.

'So good-looking,' she said. 'You've no idea, have you?'

He blushed and it made him even cuter. She smiled.

'I know I can trust you, Harry.'

He nodded.

'The thing is,' she said. 'I'm scared. There's this woman. A detective with the police.'

'What's her name?'

'Ellen,' Monica said. 'Ellen Kelly. If I tell you about her, do you swear not to breathe a word to anyone?'

'No one,' he said.

She smiled, knowing she had him. And then she started talking.

# THIRTY-SEVEN

He'd messed up. Sick – shaky sick – standing outside her house trying to light a cigarette. Tremor in his hands so bad he couldn't do it. Ellen stepped in, took the lighter from his hand and did it for him.

'This isn't your fault, Raj.'

He sucked on the cigarette, holding in the breath until his head started to spin.

'Raj?'

He turned away, unable to bear the sympathy in her face. Didn't deserve that. Closed his eyes and there she was again. Poor Chloe. Lying on the cheap sitting-room carpet. Thrown to the ground after her killer garrotted her. The line of the wire cutting a red necklace into her delicate skin. His stomach twisted, reflux vomit burnt his throat, turned his mouth bitter. He swallowed it back down.

'Raj.'

Ellen was speaking to him, asking if he was okay.

'I'm fine.'

Did he say that? Lying bastard. Kept going back over yesterday morning. He'd been distracted. Thinking too much about Aidan and not enough about the job. Stupid, selfish piece of shit.

'The boss wants us working together on this,' Ellen said. 'But only if you're up to it. If you're not, if you're too upset by what's happened, I'll completely understand.'

'I'm fine,' he repeated. His voice sounded okay, that was a start. No way he was letting anyone else take this from him. His mess, his job to sort it out.

'Really,' he said. 'I'm okay. Let's do this.'

An hour later, he wasn't feeling any better but at least it had started. Ellen had taken control, imposing order on the chaos. Making it feel like there was a way through this. Maybe.

The street was cordoned off, SOCOs inside the house and all along the road, searching for clues. Two teams of uniforms assigned to the door-to-doors. And Raj was sat in the back of a police car with Nathan Collier, who'd finally stopped crying.

'I need you to go over it again,' Raj said. 'Tell me how you found her. Don't miss anything out.'

'She didn't show for work this morning,' Nathan said. 'At ten o'clock I phoned to see where she was. When she didn't answer,

I got worried. After everything that's happened, it's only natural, isn't it? I couldn't shake off the feeling that she was in some sort of trouble. I tried her mobile a few more times and when she still didn't answer, I drove over here.'

His voice trailed off.

'And then?'

'She didn't answer when I rang the doorbell, so I let myself in.'

Outside, a red Porsche pulled up at the edge of the police cordon. Raj watched Mark Pritchard unfold himself from the tiny vehicle and walk towards Ellen, who was standing nearby briefing two uniformed officers. Mark leaned down, gave Ellen a kiss on the cheek and a hug. Something about the way he held her made them look – for a moment – like a couple.

Raj switched his attention back to Nathan.

'How did you do that?'

'Do what?' Nathan asked.

'Let yourself in,' Raj said.

'The front door wasn't locked,' Nathan said. 'All I had to do was push it and it opened.'

Something not right there but Raj let it pass. For now. He wanted to hear the rest of it.

'I went into the sitting room and there she was. Just lying there. I didn't recognise her at first.'

Raj knew what he meant. The strangulation had bloated her face.

'I tried to resuscitate her,' Nathan said. 'Did everything I could, but none of it made any difference.'

And in the meantime, Raj thought, that big fat body of yours was mucking up the crime scene.

Nathan started crying again, making the whole car shake as he rocked back and forth. Raj tried to picture the same man standing behind Chloe, wrapping a piece of wire around her throat and pulling on it until she stopped breathing. He couldn't see it, but that didn't mean anything.

It was hot inside the car. Nathan, dressed in a thick winter coat, was sweating. The smell of him, combined with the rocking of the car, made Raj want to throw up. He got out of the car and leaned against the bonnet, letting the air cool him down, waiting for the nausea to pass.

At the end of the road, Ellen had extricated herself from Pritchard and was coming towards him. He knew what came next, knew the different pieces of work they'd need to cover as the investigation got underway. And he was ready for it.

He pushed himself away from the car.

Carl Jenkins, Ricky Lezard and Nathan Collier. All three men would be brought in for questioning. Raj wanted to make bloody sure he got to sit in on each interview. Ellen might think she was leading on this, and maybe that's how it seemed on paper, but this investigation was his. And if Ellen Kelly or Ger Cox didn't like it, that was their problem.

* * *

Ellen pulled up outside Monica's house on Brightfield Road and switched off the engine. Abby sat in the passenger seat. Ellen had picked her up from the station and they'd driven over here together.

'Are you okay?' Abby asked.

Ellen closed her eyes, saw Chloe's body.

'I will be,' she said.

What sort of person could do that to someone? To have the physical and mental strength needed to pull the wire tight and keep holding it while the person you were killing struggled and fought for their life.

'It scares me,' she said. 'What if he does it again before we find him?'

She looked out at Monica's house. Imagined the killer watching this house too, planning his next move. Finished with Chloe and moving on to his next victim. Ellen opened the door and got out.

Brightfield Road was a quiet street of terraced Victorian cottages in up-and-coming Lee Green, South-East London. Monica lived midway along the street. Her house, with its exposed brickwork, window baskets and original shutters, was postcard pretty.

A few years ago, before she'd been promoted to DI, Ellen had dealt with a burglary on this street. The victims, a brash married couple who both worked in banking, had gutted the inside of their house, whipping out all the character and replacing it with lots of glass and plastic.

Monica hadn't attempted anything like that. Inside, the house was all rich colours, dark corners and stripped floorboards. Ellen thought of Adam Telford's house – the clinical cleanliness and the muted shades of pastel – and guessed Monica's choices were another way of distancing herself from that life.

'I thought I'd been forgotten,' Monica said, as she led Ellen and Abby into the cosy sitting room.

'We've been busy,' Ellen said.

There was someone else in the sitting room, a young man with thick curly hair, an intense face and a serious attitude. Monica introduced him as Harry but gave no further explanation of who he was or what he was doing in her house. As for Harry himself, he said nothing when Ellen said hello, simply stared at her with a look that she translated as 'fuck you'.

'Harry,' Monica said, 'could you give us a few minutes alone?'

'You sure about that?' The question was for Monica but he didn't take his eyes from Ellen.

'Certain, darling,' Monica said. 'I'll be fine. Tell you what, why don't you head home for a bit and I'll call you later?'

That got his attention. He turned to Monica, looking confused.

'I thought we were going to hang out for the day.'

'Later,' she said. 'I've got things to do first. Please, Harry?'

Eventually she coaxed him out the door.

'Is he her son or her boyfriend?' Abby asked, as Monica said goodbye to Harry at the front door.

'God knows,' Ellen said. 'But please don't ask her that when she comes back. We're not here to antagonise her, remember?'

She stopped speaking as Monica reappeared, all smiles, like she'd completely forgotten about Sunday morning's phone call.

'Sorry about that,' she cooed. 'Harry's a sweetheart, just a bit too keen, if you know what I mean.'

Ellen glanced at Abby, who raised her eyebrows. Question answered.

'What can I do for you?' Monica asked.

Ellen had put Raj in charge of pulling in suspects. They'd be brought into Lewisham and held for questioning. Put in a custody room until the police were ready for them. Which could take some time, but that was all part of how it worked. Bring them in, let them sweat for a bit, then question them. If you did it too soon, they didn't have enough time to consider the consequences of being questioned as part of a murder investigation.

Meanwhile, Chloe's body had been taken to the morgue, a call had been put through to the station in Valencia, Spain, where her mother lived, and the crime scene was still cordoned off while SOCO continued their investigations. Ger Cox had organised a team briefing for an hour's time. Before that, Ellen had wanted to come across and see Monica. Chloe's murder had caught them off-guard. They weren't about to let the same thing happen again. As FLO, and therefore someone better equipped at dealing with hysterical members of the public, Ellen had brought Abby with her.

'Something's happened,' Ellen said. 'Can we sit down?'

Ellen kept it brief, left out most of the detail; simply said that Chloe had been found dead in her house earlier that morning.

'We still don't know how she died,' Ellen said. 'But I really didn't want you to hear this from anyone else. It'll be all over the news by this evening.'

Monica said nothing at first. Her face was blank and it was impossible to guess what she might be thinking.

'I can't believe it,' she said eventually. 'That poor girl. What happened? You must have some idea. I mean, you'd know if it was a heart attack or a suicide or if someone killed her, right?'

'We really won't know for sure until we get the post-mortem results.' In her mind, Ellen saw the body again. Chloe's bloated head and the red line around her neck. 'But it wasn't a heart attack or a suicide.'

Monica was silent while she seemed to take this in.

'Okay,' she said. 'So should I be scared? I mean, what should I do? What are you going to do? How can you be certain this won't happen to me? Oh Jesus. I thought it was my father, remember? But he doesn't know Chloe. So if it's not him, then…'

'Listen to me,' Ellen said. 'There could be all sorts of explanations and there's every chance this has nothing to do with what she said had been happening to her.'

'What she *said*?' Monica shouted. 'You're saying you still don't believe her? Even after this? Jesus, Ellen. Do you think I'm making it up as well?'

Abby sat beside Monica and started speaking to her in that soothing voice that mostly worked on members of the public but never failed to set Ellen's teeth on edge.

'Monica,' Abby said. 'You've got to try and stay calm. You're a strong woman, I can see that, and you need to stay strong now, okay? No one thinks you've made anything up. We're simply saying we don't know how Chloe died. Not yet. Of course, it's only natural to jump to conclusions and assume there's a connection with the complaints she made, but we can't do that. Our job is to investigate all angles. And that's what we're going to do. Okay?'

Monica pulled her hand away and stood up, pacing the small space between the chairs as she spoke.

'It's not okay,' she said. 'Don't either of you get it? I thought this was my father. But it can't be. He doesn't know Chloe. I'd bet my life on it. I should have worked that out before now. But I was scared and I wasn't thinking straight. Well I'm thinking straight now. And you want to know what exactly is going through my head right now?'

'What?' Ellen said, not sure she really wanted to know.

'This is some sort of serial stalker,' Monica said. 'He's targeting local women and he's scaring the shit out of us. And once he's done scaring us half to death, he kills us.'

It was one theory. If she was in Monica's place, Ellen guessed she might think something similar. She was pretty sure the press would jump to the same conclusion. It was a shit storm waiting to happen. With poor Raj Patel right in the middle of it.

Ellen stood up. 'I've got to get back to the station,' she said. 'Abby will stay for a bit. She can answer any other questions you have and hopefully reassure you we're doing everything we can.'

Monica shook her head. 'That won't be necessary. I'm a strong woman, remember?'

Abby's face went red. Anger or embarrassment or some mixture of the two. Ellen couldn't be sure and didn't care, either.

'Abby will stay,' Ellen said, ignoring the scowl on Abby's face. 'Make sure you're okay. And Monica, whatever you do, don't speak to any journalists. It won't help. We'll brief the press and we'll decide the best way to manage that relationship. The last thing we want is any hysterical press coverage. It will only make things worse.'

On the way out, Ellen paused at a small photo on a low table in the corner by the window. It was a copy of one of the photos she'd seen on Adam Telford's mantelpiece. Annie Telford, holding a baby Monica in her arms and looking utterly miserable. If it was her mother, Ellen thought she'd probably have chosen a better photo to remember her by.

'Did you ever try to find her?' she asked.

'How did you know it's her?' Monica asked.

'I went to see your father yesterday,' Ellen said.

'You saw him?' Monica said. 'That must have been fun.'

'He has a girlfriend,' Ellen said. 'Did you know that?'

Monica snorted. 'Poor cow. Hope she gets sense and leaves

before he sucks the life from her too.'

As she walked to her car, Ellen couldn't shake off the feeling someone was watching her. She stopped and turned around, half-expecting to see someone following her. There was no one there.

A chilly wind started up, gusting down the street and wrapping itself around Ellen's body. She ran to the car and climbed inside, shutting the door, blocking out the wind and the strange sense that she was being watched.

# THIRTY-EIGHT

The start of a murder investigation. Depressing and exhilarating. Not many coppers would admit to the second bit. Not sober, at least.

The incident room had been set up around a central focus. A whiteboard with Chloe Dunbar's photo in the middle. Suspects' names written on the board, with arrows connecting each name to the photo. Ger Cox, magnificent in her tailored suit and heels, stood beside the whiteboard issuing orders. Malcolm, already in Office Manager mode, was taking notes, making lists and building an online directory for the investigation.

Tension was building. Sizzling and crackling and adding to the general sense that this was a big one. Jamala Nnamani, the station's Communications Manager, was seated alongside the detectives, preparing the media line. The first press statement had already been issued in preparation for the evening's TV and tomorrow morning's newspapers. Superintendent Nichols was on standby for the press conference at ten o'clock tomorrow morning.

'Alastair.' Ger pointed at Alastair Dillon, head and shoulders taller than the rest of the team, even sitting down. 'I want you going through every bit of the forensics as it comes through to us. Blood splatters, footprints, DNA, fingerprints, the lot. That's your number one job until I tell you otherwise.'

'Yes, Ma'am.'

Ellen wondered if he ever got bored with it. Being the details man. He was good at it, better than anyone else she'd ever worked with. Even still. There must be times he wished he was given a different role. Something that got him out of the office from time to time. Something with a bit more edge to it.

'Ellen, can you pull together a report on stalking, please? I want information on the sort of person who typically stalks someone, the frequency of stalking victims who are hurt and killed by their stalkers. When a stalker kills, is he more likely to go on and kill again? Do we potentially have a serial killer on our hands?'

'Sure,' Ellen said.

'Chloe's mother has been informed,' Ger continued. 'She's flying back from Spain later today. Ellen, I want you to meet her at the airport. Malcolm, will get you the flight details. Poor woman. Losing a child is the worst thing, isn't it?'

'I left Monica with her boyfriend,' Abby said. 'He's very protective and she said he'll stay with her every night, make sure she's okay.'

'Did she seem okay?' Ger said.

'She was upset,' Abby said. 'Obviously. But all things considered, I'd say she was a good sight finer than I'd have expected.'

'Bring the boyfriend in,' Ger said. 'Give him a grilling and make sure he's not hiding anything.'

'I've already spoken to him,' Abby said.

'I want him in here,' Ger said. 'A bit of a scare won't do him any harm. If he's not hiding anything, he'll be out again quickly. We still haven't found anything connecting the two women?'

'Chloe didn't know Monica,' Raj said. 'I asked her the other day. I'm keen to start the interviews, Ma'am. Nathan Collier and Ricky Lezard are both downstairs, waiting to be interviewed. Carl Jenkins is top of my list, though. It's taken me a bit longer to track him down. He's showing someone around a flat in Blackheath. Thought I'd head over there, speak to him, then come back and deal with the other two. Collier first, then Lezard. Let him sweat it out for as long as possible.'

Ger scanned the laptop, open on the desk in front of her, frowning.

'According to this,' she said, 'Lezard was at a conference in Woking yesterday and last night. We had to send someone down there this morning to bring him here?'

'Staying in a hotel,' Raj said. 'Alone. Could have slipped out unnoticed, driven to London and back without anyone knowing about it.'

Ger shook her head. 'Start with Lezard. Find out if he has an alibi for last night. Malcolm can check that out. No point keeping him in if it turns out he couldn't have done it.'

'What if he got someone else to do it?' Raj asked.

'If you think that's a possibility after you've questioned him,' Ger said, 'then we'll deal with it at that point. Ellen, how about you take Lezard while Raj goes across and breaks the news to Jenkins. And remember, he was her boyfriend. Be gentle with him. At first. Abby, you go with Raj. I'd like your take on how Jenkins reacts when Raj tells him what's happened. And while you're all doing that, I'll go downstairs and start with Nathan Collier. Out of the three, he's the one who most interests me.'

'Collier?' Raj said. 'With all respect, Ma'am, the bloke was in bits when I spoke to him earlier.'

'Maybe he was putting it on,' Ger said. 'Or maybe he really is heartbroken she's dead. Either way, doesn't mean he's not guilty.'

'But he was her boss,' Raj said. 'Fifty-one percent of all female murder victims are killed by their partner or ex-partner. We all know the most likely explanation is that either Jenkins or Lezard is behind this.'

'We know no such thing,' Ger said. 'I know you want this case solved, Patel. We all do. But don't let that cloud your judgement. And remember who's in charge. Now go. And take Abby with you.'

Ellen willed Raj to keep his mouth shut. Obviously deciding he'd pushed it as far as he could, he shoved his chair back and stood up.

'I'll get to it then. Ma'am.'

Ger nodded, turned her attention to the others.

'The same applies to the rest of you. Keep your heads clear. We go where the evidence takes us. That's the only thing that works. Now get going. We've got a lot to do.'

\* \* \*

Over the past few days, Ellen had done her own reading on Ricky Lezard. Hadn't found much she liked. A self-made businessman with a reputation for turning nasty when things didn't go his way. In business and in his personal life.

Four separate domestic abuse complaints against him: Chloe and other women he'd dated before her. None of the complaints had ever got as far as Court; each victim retracted her statement at the last moment. He was a nasty bastard and Ellen would have loved an excuse to lock him up. There was only one problem. It was obvious within the first ten minutes that he couldn't have done it.

The conference in Woking had ended with a gala dinner that went on until after midnight. Eighty-nine witnesses could testify that Lezard had attended the dinner and also given an engaging post-dinner speech on the business benefits of Britain's withdrawal from the EU and forging stronger links with the emerging economies of South America and South-East Asia.

Ellen let him go, frustrated by the time she'd wasted. Raj could easily have found out about the speech. A quick phone call to the hotel would have done it. Ger was right. Raj's desperation to catch the killer could cause problems for all of them if they weren't careful.

Upstairs at her desk, Ellen's mother called on the landline. She'd called earlier; Ellen had let the call go to voicemail and forgotten all about it.

'Mum?'

'Oh Ellen, I'm sorry to bother you at work, love. Is there any chance you could come over?'

'What is it?' Ellen said.

'It's difficult to explain over the phone,' her mother said. 'Can you just come? Please, Ellen.'

She didn't have to ask again. Promising she'd be right there, Ellen hung up and ran.

# THIRTY-NINE

Carl Jenkins was showing a prospective tenant around an apartment in Blackheath. The apartment was in a tall, Georgian building midway between The Clarendon Hotel and The Princess of Wales pub.

When Raj pulled up outside the house, Carl was standing outside the building, smiling and shaking hands with a man wearing a pinstripe suit who didn't look young enough to be living alone. The smile slid from Carl's face when he saw Raj and Abby walking towards him.

'Sorry,' he said to the boy in the suit. 'I've got to deal with this.' Then, to Raj: 'Something's happened. I knew it. She hasn't answered my calls. I thought she was still angry but it's not that, is it?'

'Haven't you been at the office this morning?' Raj asked.

Carl shook his head. 'Monday mornings are always busy. Why? Is that where she is?'

Raj remembered what Ger said about being gentle but his head was too full of Chloe's ruined face.

'Chloe's dead.'

He heard Abby's sharp intake of breath, knew she'd have something to say later about doing it this way. That was Abby, though. She would take the boss's line, no matter what that line was. Abby's number one priority was herself. If the boss said jump, Abby would be the first to ask where and how high.

'Can we go inside?' Abby was holding Jenkins by the arm. With her free hand, she'd taken the bunch of keys he'd been holding.

'This one?'

Jenkins nodded and Abby put the key in the lock, turned it and opened the door. Gently, she led Jenkins into the house, treating him like he was the bloody victim. Raj understood. Or thought he did. Abby hadn't seen the body. And she didn't know Chloe.

He remembered the first time Chloe came in. She'd been upset, but held it together well. There was a sort of fragile strength about her he'd admired. He asked about her ex, Ricky Lezard, wanting to understand their relationship, thinking it would help him work out whether she was telling the truth or not.

'We met in a Soho bar,' Chloe said. 'I was a waitress.' She

laughed. He could hear it now. A soft, breathy Marilyn Monroe laugh. 'Just like that Human League song. You know the one?' She started to sing. *I was working as a waitress in a cocktail bar, when he found me-e-e-e-e. He picked me up, he shook me up, he turned me around. He turned me into someone ne-e-e-ew.'*

He'd held his hand up, unable to take anymore. He shouldn't have done that. Should have let her sing for as long as she wanted and applauded her when she'd finished.

The apartment was on the top floor with huge windows, high ceilings and sweeping views across the heath to Lewisham. Raj thought again about the young man in the pinstripe suit and wondered what sort of job you'd need to be able to afford rent on a place like this.

'How did it happen?' Carl was crying. Tears rolling down his cheeks. 'Sorry.' He wiped his face with the sleeve of his jacket and took a deep, shaky breath. 'Can I sit down?'

'You said something about Chloe being angry,' Abby said.

Carl shook his head, frowning. 'Yeah, but... please, can you tell me what happened? She was scared.' He looked at Raj. 'You know how scared she was. We argued, see. I wanted her to stay with me for a few days. Cleared it with my mum and everything. I thought she'd be happy. But when I said it to her, she went off on one. Started accusing me of trying to control her and that's not what I was doing. I told her that, but she wouldn't listen. Said I was just like her ex and that's when I lost it.'

'Lost it how, exactly?' Raj said.

'Nah,' Carl said. 'Not like that. I mean, I told her it was over. Said if that's what she thought of me, I didn't want nothing to do with her.'

'So you had a row,' Raj said. He saw Abby's face and shifted slightly, so she was out of his line of vision. 'Can't say I blame you for losing it. I'm not sure how I'd react if someone compared me to an animal like that. And all you were doing was trying to do what was right. What anyone would do under the circumstances.'

Carl shrugged. 'I was stupid. Soon as I calmed down, I knew that. I called her, wanted to tell her how sorry I was, but she wouldn't answer my calls.'

'You went over there?' Raj said.

'Yeah, just to see if she was okay, you know. Didn't like to think of her in there alone being all scared.'

This time he did look at Abby. Saw she felt it too. The sudden buzz when you knew you were on to something. The boss's words in his head again. *We go where the evidence takes us.* Well right now the evidence was taking them straight to Carl Jenkins.

'Is that what happened?' Raj said. 'You got there, all ready to give it a second chance and she started on at you again. Comparing you to her ex and making all sorts of crazy accusations. I'm right, aren't I?'

When Carl shook his head, Raj wanted to slap him. Why drag it out? They all knew where this was leading. Raj rubbed his hands along the tops of his legs, taking slow, deep breaths.

'Must have been a shock,' Raj said. 'You turn up, all good

intentioned, hoping for a happy reunion, a bit of thanks even. I mean, here you were, giving up your Sunday night for her. Driving across to Hither Green when you'd much rather be down the pub with your mates. And when you get there, all that good intention, she just throws it right back in your face. I wouldn't blame you for losing it, mate, seriously. Putting up with that shit? Give me a break.'

And then something he hadn't expected. Carl was on his feet and running at him, screaming at Raj to shut up. Shut his fucking face because he didn't know what he was talking about. Other stuff too that got lost as Raj lunged, Chloe's breathy little laugh, her out-of-tune voice and her poor, swollen face all whirling around inside his head as he shoved his fist into Carl Jenkins's stomach and drove him to the ground. Lashing out a second time, ignoring Abby's voice shouting at him to stop. The crunch of bone, warm blood splashing onto his hand and arm, little drops of it landing on his face as his fist connected with Carl Jenkins's nose, breaking it a second time.

# FORTY

'It must have been during the night,' Ellen's father said. 'Or I suppose it could have been done yesterday afternoon when we were out. It was dark by the time we got home and I never went outside. Why, Ellen? Who would do such a thing?'

All sorts of people, unfortunately, Ellen thought. She'd already got a constable across to take a statement. For all the good it would do. The chances of catching the little bastards were slim to zero.

'I'm so sorry, Dad.'

He patted her arm.

'Would you stop saying that, Ellen. It's not your fault.'

She knew that and that's not why she was apologising. She was saying sorry for being part of a police force so understaffed and overstretched that crimes like this barely got a look-in. The constable who'd taken her parents' statement would feed it into the system, her parents would be assigned a crime number and after that, not much else would happen. It made her depressed and angry.

The garden was her father's pride and joy. He spent so much time out here, planting and weeding and cleaning and doing whatever people did with their gardens. Ellen's mother joked that her father cared more about his garden than he did about her. Now some low-life had destroyed it. For what?

Ellen was in the kitchen with her father, standing at the window looking out at the devastation. Every single flower had been pulled from the bed and ripped apart. The work of a psycho. A psycho who was clever enough not to do the same out front in case anyone saw them. Who had waited until her parents were out of the house or in bed asleep before going out there and wreaking havoc.

It didn't make sense, but neither did so much of what she saw in her job. Something about this felt personal, though. In a way she couldn't quite put her finger on. Not yet.

'It's only a garden,' her father said. 'I know that. So why do I feel so upset? They were my autumn blooms, Ellen. Crocuses, sternbergias and nerines. What a waste of time, hey?'

He was leaning on the worktop, back bent slightly, the way it had got in recent years. Sometimes, it was like she didn't see him properly, she thought. Like when she looked at him, all she saw was a younger, more vibrant version of the man he'd become. She saw him as she remembered him. Or as she wished him to be.

Not today. Now she saw the curve in his back, the shake in his hands, the sagging in the skin at his jaws. When had he become so old?

'It's natural to be upset,' Ellen said. 'Any mindless act like that, it upsets us because we don't understand it. It's worse because they've destroyed something you really care about. But you can replant it, can't you? Get it back to the way it was?'

He shook his head, still looking out the window.

'We'll all help,' she said. 'Me and the kids. Sean and Terry, too. We'll come over and have a planting party. Set aside a Saturday and get stuck in. What do you think?'

Her father didn't answer. She was about to say something else, but he put his hand on her arm.

'Shh,' he said. 'Not now, Ellen. I need a moment alone. Do you mind, love?'

She didn't mind, but in her entire life she didn't ever recall a time where he'd shut her out.

'Please,' he said. 'Go and find your mother. She's upstairs putting clothes away. Give her a hand with that. I'd be better off on my own.'

She left quietly, closing the door behind her. She knew it was natural for him to be upset and natural he might want to deal with that alone. But knowing didn't make it any easier. As she went upstairs to find her mother, she couldn't help thinking it felt like the end of something.

* * *

Nathan was sweating. Streams of it running down his back, pooling in the seat of his boxer shorts, tickling his buttocks and the bit between them. The woman in front of him was firing questions at him, trying to catch him off-guard, get him to say something he shouldn't. He was too clever for that, though.

'Mr Collier,' she said. 'How long had Chloe worked at Happy Homes?'

'Six months,' he said. 'Thereabouts. Maybe closer to seven. I'm not sure.'

Six months, five days to be exact. Not that he was about to tell *her* that. She had spikey blonde hair that reminded him of Chloe's. Except Chloe's was longer and not as thick. Chloe had fine, silky hair. Like a princess in a fairytale.

The shock of it kept hitting him. He'd start to think he was getting used to it and then – *wham!* – it whacked him again and he was right back there in the flat, kneeling on the floor and holding her little body.

He'd prayed for her, begged God to treat her kindly. Take her soul and make her happy. Even though he wasn't sure she deserved happiness. Not the way she'd behaved this past week. The pain of it had almost been too much to bear. Or so he'd thought. It was nothing compared to this.

'Mr Collier? Nathan?'

The detective's voice jerked him back. Asking more questions. How they'd met, why he'd offered Chloe a job, what their relationship was like. On and on. All questions she'd already asked and he'd already answered. Telling her everything and nothing.

'We met when she was looking to rent a flat,' Nathan said.

The detective checked something on the piece of paper in front of her, frowning. 'I thought you looked after the sales side of the business and your colleague…'

'Employee,' Nathan said. 'Carl works *for* me, not *with* me.'

And not for much longer. Judas wasn't a patch on Carl Jenkins when it came to betrayal. He still found it hard to believe. The way she'd opened her arms and let him… Like some sort of cheap prostitute.

He hadn't been able to think of anything else. Picturing them together. Like that. How could she? The thought of it – Chloe and Carl – it disgusted him. Literally made him want to get sick. He tried so hard not to think about it but it filled his mind, until he couldn't think about else. Image after filthy image. Worse at nights, when he lay in bed trying to sleep. Closing his eyes and seeing it all play out. Chloe taking her clothes off, stripping naked for Carl, lying on the bed and opening her legs. Letting him do that. Making the pure impure. Ruining her.

'Go on.'

Focus. He couldn't mess this up.

'Carl was out of the office,' he said. They were still there, in his head, Carl on top of her, grunting as he shoved himself inside her.

'I knew the place on Nightingale Grove had just come on the market, so I offered to drive her across.'

Standing in the doorway, framed in sunlight that turned her hair golden, like a halo. Mesmerising him. He'd never seen anything so beautiful in his entire life.

He hadn't done it to scare her. That had never been his intention. He'd never meant to hurt her, either. The night he'd hit her, he hadn't planned that. It was only to stop her seeing it was him. He'd only ever wanted to take care of her. Was that so hard to understand?

'You let her have the house at a very reduced rent,' the detective said.

His bottom was itchy. He shifted in the chair, clenching and unclenching his buttocks. It didn't help.

'I felt sorry for her,' he said. 'She told me a little about what she'd been through. Enough for me to know she needed help.'

The detective nodded. Hard face. He didn't like her one bit. Women didn't suit certain jobs. A detective's job wasn't easy. You had to be hard to do that and women weren't naturally hard. Women were soft and pure and beautiful. It was men who ruined them. Men with their disgusting urges that they couldn't control no matter how hard they tried.

It was difficult. He knew that as well as anyone. But just because something was difficult, it didn't mean you shouldn't try.

Look at Father John. Forty-three years a priest. A life of prayer and celibacy and *not* giving in to those base instincts that made us no better than any other animal.

'So,' the detective said.

A sudden flash of what he'd like to do to her. Blocked out almost as quickly as he thought it. Focus. He couldn't let that side of himself take over.

'You gave Chloe a home and a job. It makes me wonder what you expected in return, Mr Collier?'

Bitch.

Stop it! No call for that.

'Nothing,' he said. 'I expected nothing in return. You don't understand, do you? I just wanted to help. There's nothing wrong with that, is there?'

She wouldn't understand. He wasn't like other men. He'd never have asked for that. Wouldn't have wanted it for her. All he wanted, everything he'd done, it was all for her.

# FORTY-ONE

The envelopes lay spread out on the bed. Monica arranged them until they were in date order, earliest on the left, moving across to the most recent – from a few months ago – on the right. The same handwriting on each envelope, the same person's name on each one. Different addresses. Seven envelopes. Seven addresses. A small number of all letters she'd written over the years.

As a child, she'd written letters that never got sent. Those ones, she'd binned long ago. They were an unpleasant reminder of her own weakness. The letters on the bed were from the last ten years. They were the ones that had been sent back to her, RETURN TO SENDER scrawled on them. There were more, but she didn't know what had happened to them.

Until Brighton, she'd let herself believe her mother had

received the other letters. She used to picture her mother's joy opening each one and knowing Monica hadn't forgotten her. Proud, maybe, that her little girl was all grown up and had made such a success of her life.

Stupid.

She grabbed one at random, ripped it in two, ripped the two halves again. She carried on ripping until there were no letters or envelopes left. Just white flakes of paper, scattered across the white cotton sheets. Like the flowers in the old couple's back garden.

Through the wall, she could hear the TV in Mrs Mallet's bedroom. One of her daughters had popped round but the stupid cow had forgotten to turn down the volume on the TV. Monica pictured the old crone and her ugly daughter, sitting on matching armchairs in the sitting room, talking about things that didn't matter and pretending their relationship meant something.

She needed to go to Whitstable again. She had things she wanted from the house. Valuable things. On her last visit, she'd taken a front door key from a rack of keys in the hall. She would use this the next time. Pick a moment when he'd be out of the house so she could sneak in and take what she needed. He had so much crap, like the ugly Aynsley ornaments he collected. They were worth money. She didn't see why he should get to keep them all.

Downstairs, she picked up the photo that had caught Kelly's attention. The original photo used to sit on the mantelpiece in the sitting room. This was a copy she'd badgered her father to get for her room. The only photo she had of her with her mother. Poor cow looked properly miserable in it. And who could blame her? Married to that useless heap of shit.

A pulse was throbbing at the front of her neck. She put her finger against it. The steady *thu-dum, thu-dum* was background to the white noise in her head. Her father. Hunched up in that fucking armchair, head in his hands, body shaking as he cried. Little Monica, trying to pull his hands away from his face, not understanding.

And all he could do was cry.

*Thu-dum, thu-dum.*

Monica was crying too, pulling at him and begging him to tell her where Mummy was and why was he crying. And then the stupid bastard pushed her away, walked out of the room and up the stairs. She ran after him, every bit as pathetic as he was.

He locked himself in the bathroom. She stood outside, banging on the door, screaming at him to let her in.

*Thu-dum, thu-dum.*

Useless heap of shit.

Her mother's miserable face, looking up at her.

Stupid, lying bitch.

It was all his fault. Why couldn't her mother have admitted that? Why'd she have to say all that other stuff? When she started that, Monica had shouted at her. Like she was shouting at her now. She'd lifted the bottle, lying on its side on the dirty table.

Lifted it like she was lifting the photo now. Over her head and smashed it down. The photo hit the ground, glass shattering. Just like the bottle when she smashed it into that stupid, lying face.

Two months, a week and two days. Her mother.

Two months, a week and one day. Ellen Kelly.

Two different women. Two different days. Two different betrayals. First her mother, then – a day later – Ellen Kelly.

*Thu-dum, thu-dum, thu-dum.*

Two stupid, lying bitches.

# FORTY-TWO

Ellen found Raj in the second pub she tried. Sitting in the small beer garden at the side of The Duke, wrapped in a black wool coat and chain-smoking his way through a packet of Marlboro Lights.

'Didn't think this was your sort of pub,' Ellen said, sitting across from him. She'd left her coat in the car and regretted that now. She hoped this wouldn't take too long.

'What's that supposed to mean?'

'I thought you'd go for somewhere a bit more classy,' she said. Or with a rainbow flag hanging outside, she thought, but didn't say. Raj's sexuality was none of her business. Although she hoped he had someone to go home to later.

She tapped the packet of cigarettes. 'Spare me one of these?'

'If you're here to counsel me,' he said, as she took a cigarette and lit it, 'you can go now. I'm not in the mood.'

'Stop feeling sorry for yourself,' she said. 'You messed up. Big deal. We all mess up from time to time. Besides, the way I heard it, he went for you first. You were only defending yourself.'

'Fuck off, Ellen.'

She wanted to slap him. Or hug him. Carl Jenkins was in custody. Charged with assaulting an officer. Raj, meanwhile, had been suspended pending an investigation into exactly what had happened at the apartment in Blackheath. The story going around the station was that Jenkins got what he deserved. Jenkins' attack on Raj, combined with the fact that he had no alibi for Sunday night, also moved him to number one place on their list of suspects. A fact which added to the general – unspoken – consensus that Raj had done the right thing.

'Just listen to yourself,' Raj said. 'Defending myself? I broke the poor fucker's nose, for Christ's sake. I thought the Met was trying to clean up its act. I mean, I know *back in the day* when people like you first started out that this sort of thing was par for the course. Copper whacks some poor sod and the force all get behind him and cover it up. I don't want this covered up, Ellen. I lost control, couldn't stop myself. My bad. No one else's.'

Definitely a slap.

'Don't be so naive,' she said. 'Nothing we do is that black or white and you know it. You lost control. So what? The way you're beating yourself up about it now tells me it won't happen again.

It's not like you're some thug who laid into someone just for the hell of it. You're right, we did have coppers who did that sort of stuff. All the time. But things *have* changed, Raj. The Met's a very different place today. Different, and better for it. That's because we have people like you. Good, decent people who care about what they do and go about their jobs the way they're meant to. No back-handers, no false convictions or jumped-up charges. Just honest to God coppers working their arses off to make the world a better place. You can't let this one thing ruin everything. I won't let you.'

'Is that what you did?' he asked.

'What do you mean?' she said.

'You know exactly what I mean.'

Billy Dunston.

Ellen pulled on the cigarette but it made no difference. It was all there, inside her head. Always there. The heat from the gun, the smell, his face – what was left of it. And that split-second decision when she lifted the gun and pulled the trigger a second time.

She threw the cigarette to the ground, stubbed the burning tip out with her foot and stood up.

'I'm still here,' she said. 'And that's better than not being here. Especially now you've been suspended. Maybe one day, when I've caught the person who killed Chloe and they're behind bars, maybe then you'll realise what I'm talking about. In the meantime, you stay here, drinking and feeling sorry for yourself while

I go and do your job for you.'

She walked away without looking back. Later, as she drove past the pub with Abby on their way to collect Chloe's mother from the airport, she glanced over and saw he was still sitting there. A full pint of lager in front of him, smoking another cigarette.

\* \* \*

'Bless me, Father, for I have sinned. It's two months since my last confession.'

He'd skipped a month. Told himself he was too busy, but that wasn't true.

'I'm sorry,' he said. 'I've done something wrong and I don't know what to do about it.'

'Start by talking about it,' Father John said. 'Let the Lord help.'

Father John's words were a balm. He shouldn't have left it so long. This was what he needed. Confession followed by absolution.

'There was this woman, Father.' And so it began. Words pouring forth out of his mouth. A torrent. Couldn't have stopped if he'd tried. The relief, the knowledge that he wasn't alone. That his holy Father was here beside him.

He'd felt so lonely. These past few days, particularly. So busy focussed on Chloe, he'd almost forgotten. She was nothing. A distraction, that was all. Turning his head, making him forget what really mattered.

When he'd finished speaking, there was silence. He could hear

Father, breath heavy through the wooden grille that separated them. He waited, suddenly scared. What if…? But he needn't have worried. Should never for a second have doubted his Lord.

'God the Father of mercies, through the death and resurrection of your son, you have reconciled the world to yourself and sent the Holy Spirit among us for the forgiveness of sins. Through the ministry of the Church, may God grant you pardon and peace. And I absolve you of your sins, in the name of the Father, and of the Son and of the Holy Spirit. Amen.'

His soul soared. Father John's words filled the small space, giving the comfort he craved. Like a heavy weight being lifted, everything was good again.

He was forgiven.

# FORTY-THREE

Sinatra and a hefty glass of Merlot. Self-medicating her way through the evening, knowing sleep wouldn't come easy. After leaving Raj, she'd driven with Abby to London City airport where they'd met Patricia Dunbar, Chloe's mother. The meeting had been as gruelling as Ellen had expected. By the time she'd taken Mrs Dunbar to the morgue and comforted her afterwards, Ellen was fit for nothing.

Chloe's mother was an older version of her daughter. The same wispy blonde hair and elfin features, the same lispy, little girl voice. Ravaged with grief, Patricia focussed obsessively on one thing: the arrangements for Chloe's funeral. Ellen had seen this before. Families and loved ones of murder victims often became overly concerned with the details of the funeral. It was a way of imposing control over an incomprehensible situation. Unfortunately, this – along with everything else – was something that was also taken away from them until the long and arduous process of the murder investigation reached some sort of conclusion.

*Losing a child is the worst thing, isn't it?*

Ellen remembered Vinny's parents, Brendan and Aisling, the day of the funeral. Even in the depth of her own pain she'd seen how badly they were affected. And chose to ignore it because she didn't have the strength to deal with their grief as well as her own. She regretted that now. Whatever else happened, she must make sure Pat and Eilish never lost touch with Vinny's side of the family.

She finished her wine and poured herself another glass. In the sitting room, *Songs for Swinging Lovers* was on the music system. Ellen sat down with her Blackberry, flicking between e-mails and the internet, reading the latest new reports on Chloe's murder. Nothing from Martine Reynolds yet, but that was only a matter of time. Ellen expected she'd see the journalist's orange face amongst the crowd of hacks at tomorrow morning's press conference.

She'd invited Jim for dinner tonight, had to cancel when she realised she'd be working late. Now, she wished she hadn't. She didn't want to be alone. She called him but it went to voicemail and she hung up without leaving a message. Tried Raj, but got his voicemail too. This time, she left a message, asking him to call and let her know he was okay. Then she put down her

Blackberry, closed her eyes and let Frank take her to a better place.

* * *

The doorbell rang, making Monica jump. Red wine spilled down her hand, onto her wrist, soaking the cuff of her white shirt. Made it look like she'd slashed her wrists. She smiled. Suicide was for losers. She drank the wine, burped some of it back up. It stank, but there was no one here to care about that.

He was banging on the door now, calling her name. Stupid bastard couldn't take a hint. Sober, she might have let him in. But she'd had too much wine for that. Couldn't stick the thought of putting up with all that gooey-eyed mooning.

Kelly's fault she was drunk. Wouldn't have hit the *vino* if Kelly hadn't dragged all those memories to the surface. She went across to the window, looked outside. Just in time to see Harry's back retreating across the road. Getting the message. Finally.

She flicked the curtain closed and went back to the wine bottle. Empty. She pulled a fresh bottle from the wine rack, found the corkscrew and tried to insert it into the top of the bottle. It wouldn't go in. Screw-top. Stupid. She should have noticed. She threw down the corkscrew, opened the bottle and sloshed more wine into her glass.

The day had started out well enough. Good to see them finally treating her with a bit of respect. Went downhill fast after Kelly's visit. Dark memories dragging her down, taking her places she didn't want to go.

Regrets, she had a few.

She was in the sitting room now. Music playing. She looked around, confused. Didn't remember coming in here. Must have drunk more than she realised. Frank Sinatra. Why Frank?

Ellen Kelly liked Frank. She'd said so the first time Monica met her. Maybe Kelly was the reason she'd put Frank on. Trying to get inside Kelly's head. Frank's voice drifted over her, singing of a love deep in the heart of him. Under his skin. She remembered what that felt like. Knew what Frank meant when he promised to never give in. Singing the words aloud strengthened her resolve. She wanted to call him. Hear his voice. Except she was drunk and he'd probably hang up on her. Again.

Different song in the room now. *Strangers in the Night*. She liked that one. That's what he'd been at first. Dark, hot nights. Pretending to love him was easy. His passion had excited her. His passion for her. Possessive passion. Hot words whispered in her ear. Hands all over her all the time. Like he couldn't get enough of her. No man ever could.

Pretending she felt the same way. By the time she realised she wasn't just pretending, it was too late.

The great pretender. Was that Frank, too? Maybe not. She needed more wine. Freddie Mercury. Stupid. Should have known that.

Her glass was empty. She looked for the bottle. Couldn't see it. Found it in the fridge in the kitchen. Chilled red wine. On the sleeves of her white shirt. Like blood.

She drank the cool wine. Disgusting. Better than nothing, though. Her mobile was on the kitchen table. She picked it up. Never drink and text. She scrolled through the address book, trying to find someone she could call. At Kelly's name, she paused. Then changed her mind. Thought of something better.

She made some coffee, sat at the laptop and opened her e-mails. Kelly had given her a business card and one of the first things Monica had done was memorise the e-mail address and phone number.

She took her time over the e-mail, making sure she got the tone quite right: a little bit timid, a touch uncertain whether she was doing the right thing. It took twenty-five minutes. When she was finished, she read it twice, making sure the wine hadn't affected the writing. Satisfied it was as good as it could be, she pressed Send.

That done, she shut down the laptop, cranked up the volume, drank some more wine and started dancing.

\* \* \*

The thudding drum of techno-punk vibrated through the dance-floor, making Raj seasick. Bodies heaved all around him, dancing to the beat. The air smelled of sweat and poppers. He needed a drink. Looked around, couldn't see the bar. Tripped, nearly fell, but someone caught him. Blue eyes and shoulders. Nice smile. He was a sucker for blue eyes.

'You okay?' Face up close, shouting at him through the music.

'More than okay.'

Words lost in the *thud-thud* of the music. Stomach moved, vomit rose up his throat. He pulled away, pushed his way through the throng, aiming for the exit. Didn't make it. Puke burst from his mouth, splattering some bloke's shiny brogues and the bottoms of his tight, white jeans.

Two bouncers grabbed him and dragged him outside. One of them punched him in the face and he fell down, groaning. Tried to get back up but got kicked in the stomach and rolled over, arms up, protecting his head.

Nothing else happened, though. The bouncers moved back inside, laughing. He heard the door slam shut and everything went silent. He was in an alleyway at the back of the club. From far away, he could still hear the music, a steady heartbeat through the concrete walls.

The ground was wet, soaking his trousers and shirt, making him cold. In his pocket, his phone started ringing. Aidan again. He'd been calling all evening. They were meant to be going out tonight. A new bistro on Frith Street. Drinks afterwards with some of Aidan's mates.

By the time he'd got the phone out of his pocket the ringing had stopped. Probably just as well. He rolled onto his back. A black sky scattered with a sprinkling of stars. A silver slice of a crescent moon. A half-remembered line from somewhere. Something about lying in the gutter, looking at the stars.

He was tired. Eyes closing, the stars and the moon disappearing. He should get up. Go home. But he couldn't find the energy to drag himself off the ground. His phone slipped from his hand, landed on the wet ground. He barely noticed.

Stars gone, moon gone. Only darkness now. Finally.

\* \* \*

Ellen was in bed, drifting towards sleep, when her Blackberry beeped, notifying her of an incoming e-mail. She nearly ignored it; too sleepy, at first, to care what it was about. But the memories of the day were too strong. The e-mail could be important. She rolled over and pulled the Blackberry from her bag.

One new message. From Monica Telford. Ellen checked the time. After midnight. Instantly, the sleepiness was gone. She opened the e-mail and started reading.

It was a strange e-mail, with a tentative tone that didn't sound like Monica. Almost, Ellen thought, as if someone else had written it. She read it once, not understanding at first what Monica was telling her. It was only when she read it again that it hit her. And when that happened, the careful, cautious happiness Ellen had let herself feel these past few weeks shattered.

# FORTY-FOUR

Bel had been gone three days. Adam was missing her. Funny that. He'd grown used to being on his own. Settled, he supposed. The thought of sharing his life again, all the messiness and unpleasantness of it. If anyone had asked him if he was ready for that, he'd have said no thank you very much. But that was before Bel.

She got to him in ways no one else had ever come close. Not that there'd been others. Annie and Bel. The full sum of his sexual and romantic experiences. He'd made a mistake with Annie. Fooled himself into thinking the beauty on the outside would be matched by what was inside. She changed though. Couldn't cope. Tried to blame him for what happened, even though it was no one's fault. In the end, she turned out to be no different from his mother. Dirty and mean and incapable of loving anyone apart from herself.

He tried calling, but Bel's phone went to voicemail without even ringing. She must have switched it off. She'd promised to call him and he wondered why she hadn't done that. Wondered if he should worry about her. He thought about calling again, leaving a message this time, but she wouldn't like that. She'd tell him he was being too possessive and maybe he was. It was difficult to know what to do.

Part of him knew this anxiety wasn't normal. She'd only be gone for five or six days. However long it lasted. He wasn't even sure. At least she was regular. Made it easier to predict when she'd be away and how long for.

He'd worried, at first, about asking her. Thought she mightn't understand. Or might feel rejected or something stupid like that. Because this wasn't about rejection. He missed her like crazy when she wasn't here. And if he could have it any other way, he would.

He picked up his phone again, then put it down. Moved around the sitting room, plumping cushions and straightening the rug in front of the fireplace. Last night, he'd removed all the photos of Annie, stacked them neatly into a box which he carried into the spare bedroom. This morning, he could see little dust tracks along the mantelpiece and he hurried to wipe these away, wondering – again – where all the dust came from.

With the sitting room in order, he felt calmer. Started into the rest of the house, humming to himself, the tension gradually easing as he moved from room to room, imposing cleanliness and order.

The washing machine finished its cycle and he emptied it, placed the clothes into the plastic basket and carried this outside into the sunshine. Nothing like the smell of freshly laundered clothes. The trick was not to leave them out for too long or they started to smell funny. Two hours thirty-five minutes was about right on a chilly day like today. Then, when they were still damp, he'd bring them back inside and iron them dry.

Midway through hanging them, he came across a pair of Bel's panties. White cotton edged with white lace. He pictured her moving towards him, wearing these and nothing else. He lifted them up, about to press his face against the soft, clean cotton when he saw the faint trace of a brown line down the centre.

*You dirty little pig.*

He threw the pants down, wanting to stop the memory, but it was already too late.

Sister Theresa pulling him by the arm to the top of the class. He was trying really hard not to cry. She was shouting at him. His hands and face were dirty and she'd told him – Lord God above, hadn't she told him every morning since he'd started? – that he had to be clean coming to school. He tried to tell her it wasn't his fault. The water had been cut off and they weren't able to wash. His clothes were dirty, too. And the toilet, he couldn't tell her about the toilet, stuffed with poo and toilet paper and the thick white pads covered in blood.

But Sister Theresa wasn't listening. She had the cane and was shouting at him to pull down his trousers. He couldn't do that. His underpants were dirty. Streaked with three-day-old poo but he'd had to wear them because there were no clean clothes, no clean anything because they didn't have any water.

Sister Theresa didn't care about that. She pushed him towards the desk, pressed his face down on the rough wood and pulled his trousers down. He was screaming and kicking out but nothing was going to stop her and when she finally got them down there was this God awful, deadly silence that seemed to go on and on and he couldn't take it anymore, couldn't bear the waiting and he felt it, knew it was going to happen even though it was his body and he should be able to control it. But it was coming now. Warm, wet wee running down his legs, forming a little pool on the ground, soaking through the hole in the bottom of his shoe.

The smell of it, so strong in the clean, lovely classroom. When she'd started beating him, he'd cried and begged her to stop. Even though he knew he deserved it. She was right.

*Dirty, disgusting little pig.*

# FORTY-FIVE

Ellen passed the e-mail across to Ger first thing in the morning. There was nothing else she could have done. Now, an hour before the press conference, she was sitting behind a glass wall, watching Ger and Alastair interrogate Jim O'Dwyer.

'Where were you on Sunday night between the hours of seven pm and midnight?' Ger asked.

She already knew the answer to that question because Ellen had told her.

'I was working until about seven,' Jim said. 'A house in Lewisham. After that, I went over to friend's house.'

'Who?'

He hesitated. 'Ellen Kelly.'

Alastair shifted in his chair and looked uncomfortable. Ellen prayed he wouldn't want to talk to her about it later. As Ger continued asking questions, Ellen took out her Blackberry and re-read Monica's e-mail.

*Dear DI Kelly*

*I promised to send you the names of anyone I could think of who might want to hurt me. Until now, I've believed the person doing these terrible things was my father. I've already told you what an unpleasant man he is. In fact, I withheld much of the worst details from you.*

*Chloe's death changes things.*

*The person you're looking for is clever, as well as cruel. My father isn't clever. Far from it. His stupidity and ignorance contributed in no small way to my mother's decision to leave him. Unlike him, she was an intelligent woman with a zest for life that a man like my father is incapable of grasping.*

*So who else is there?*

*A year and a half ago, I was in a serious relationship. It went wrong, as these things sometimes do. We went our separate ways but, recently, we re-established contact. His name is Jim O'Dwyer. He lives in Greenwich and works as a plumber. He was keen to rekindle our relationship but I turned him down. I believe, you see, that the past is another country. What Jim and I shared was special, of course, but we have to move on. I'm sure this is a sentiment you would approve of. You strike me as the sensible sort.*

*Sadly, Jim hasn't taken kindly to my rejection. He seemed to think we could pick up where we left off. He has always been a hot-headed, angry sort of man. When we first met, I took this as a sign of a passionate soul. Now, I'm not so sure. In fact, that hot head of his has got him into a lot of trouble. It was the reason our relationship broke down.*

*You've been looking for something that connects me with Chloe. In the past, Jim has done work for several estate agencies in Lewisham and Greenwich. Isn't it just possible that, through this, Jim might have met Chloe and become as obsessed with her as he obviously is with me?*

*I apologise for putting all of this in an e-mail. I realise the last thing you want is for me to pour my heart out to you in this manner. But I feel I have no choice. Please contact me when you can and I will come to the station to make a formal statement, backing up what I've said here and adding additional information you will find useful.*

*Yours in anticipation, Monica.*

None of it was true. At least, not the important bits. Jim was with Ellen on Sunday night. He couldn't have killed Chloe. The relief when she'd realised that still made Ellen uncomfortable. Because it meant that at one point, right after reading the e-mail, she'd believed maybe he had.

In the interview room, Ger was asking Jim if he'd ever done work for Happy Homes estate agency. He shook his head. Never even heard of them. He looked calm and had declined the offer of a duty solicitor. At first, Ellen thought that was a mistake. Now, she realised the only mistake was believing anything Monica had ever told her.

Everything about the e-mail irritated Ellen. From the crawly tone to the faux-intimate way Monica implied she was sharing secrets with Ellen. The line that got her most, though, was the one describing Ellen as 'the sensible sort'. Made Ellen want to storm over there and punch Monica Telford's smug face.

Maybe she'd do just that.

* * *

At Brightfield Road the curtains were still drawn. Ellen jumped out of the car and banged on the front door until a sleepy-looking Monica opened it. She had a red towel wrapped around her body and looked like she'd just dragged herself out of bed.

She smiled. 'Ellen. So early. What a service.'

'Cut the crap.' Ellen pushed passed her into the house. Caught the stink of stale wine and wrinkled her nose in disgust.

'Coffee?' Monica asked.

She closed the door. The hallway grew dark and Ellen tensed. She swung around, saw Monica looking at her, still smiling. How she wanted to slap that smile away.

'What are you playing at, Monica?'

Monica held her hands up. The towel stayed in place, something Ellen could never master.

'I don't know what you're talking about,' Monica said.

'Like hell you don't.'

'Oh my,' Monica said. 'This is about the e-mail, isn't it? Do you want me to come down the station and make a formal statement?'

'No thanks,' Ellen said. 'Tell me about you and Jim. You know, don't you? It's why you sent that e-mail instead of calling me like any normal person would do. I don't know what your game is but I want no part of it. Neither does Jim.'

Monica laughed. 'Oh Ellen. You should hear yourself. So prim and proper. *I want no part of it. And neither does Jim.* What do you know about Jim and what he wants?'

'He told me,' Ellen said. 'And I believe him.'

A lie, but so what? Lies were something Monica was obviously well used to.

Monica and Jim. She couldn't get her head around it. Couldn't, if she was honest, imagine him with anyone else.

'I felt sorry for you,' Ellen said. 'That story you spun me about your father abusing you and some mad stalker out to get you. None of it's true, is it? You invented it all as a way of getting to Jim through me.'

'Of course I didn't make it up,' Monica said. 'I contacted you because I was scared. After Chloe was killed, well, I realised it wasn't my father. I tried to think who else it could be and Jim was the only person I could think of. There's nothing wrong with that, is there?'

'Bullshit.'

They were still standing in the hallway. Facing each other. Monica closest to the door.

'Out of my way,' Ellen said, pushing past Monica. She couldn't stand to be here a moment longer.

'You won't win, you know.'

Ellen knew she shouldn't rise to it. Knew she should ignore Monica and get the hell out of there.

'He was here last night,' Monica continued. 'Begging me to take him back. He can't stay away from me.'

Ellen ran through a list of possible things she could say. In the end, she chose none of them. Instead, she pulled open the front door and stepped outside.

Across the street, Monica's toy boy – what was his name? – peered through an upstairs window. He appeared to be staring straight down at Ellen.

She was tempted to go over there and warn him. Give him a few friendly words of advice on the woman he'd got involved with. He wouldn't listen, of course. Men rarely did.

She slammed the door shut and walked away. Fast.

\* \* \*

A hot shower, a couple of painkillers and too many cups of coffee to count. Nothing made Raj feel better. Not that he deserved to feel good. He'd been a complete twat last night. Lucky a hangover was all he had to deal with. Falling asleep in the alleyway, anything could have happened to him.

He lived alone in a flat on the top floor of a converted police station in Lee. He'd laughed when the estate agent suggested it. Then he'd seen the apartment, fallen in love and put an offer in on the spot. And now it was home.

His real home was the three-bed suburban house in Hounslow where he'd grown up. Mother and two younger sisters still living there. Father dead almost five years now, although Raj still felt his presence every time he went back there. Which probably explained why he didn't visit as often as he should.

He lay on the sofa, waiting for the worst of the hangover to pass, wallowing in self-hatred. Missed calls and two messages from Aidan. The first angry, the second worried. A vague feeling he'd done something he shouldn't. Couldn't remember anyone from the club, but that didn't mean nothing had happened. Wouldn't be the first time he'd forgotten. There'd been a bloke with blue eyes but he didn't think that was it. Then he remembered. He went back over every detail, his feelings of self-loathing intensifying by the second.

He checked his phone, hoping maybe Ellen had sent a text. Apart from the messages from Aidan, nothing. He sat up, unable to bear the inertia, needing to do something. Anything.

His laptop was on a desk by the window, overlooking the courtyard at the centre of the building. He powered up the laptop and opened the browser. Typed in Chloe Dunbar's name and got to work.

He might be off the case, but that didn't stop him from looking into things himself. It mightn't make him feel any better but he was pretty sure it couldn't make him feel any worse, either.

# FORTY-SIX

Kelly's visit left Monica feeling exhilarated. She got dressed, taking extra special care over her appearance, replaying the interaction over and over. Kelly's face when Monica told her he'd been here last night… Hilarious! Righteous anger rapidly replaced by uncertainty. Kelly didn't know what the hell to think. Served her right.

As she applied her make-up, Monica noted the grey tinge to her skin. Too much drinking these last few weeks. She frowned at her reflection in the mirror. She was a weak fool to have let things get this far. She pinched her cheeks, trying to put some colour into them. Time to knock the drinking on the head. Her looks were a commodity. She needed to take better care of herself.

She flexed her arms, watched the hard lift of her muscles. Not bad, but a trip to the gym was overdue. Another thing to add to her 'to do' list.

When the doorbell rang, she knew who it was. Harry. Velcro man. She went downstairs to see what he wanted this time.

'Sorry,' he said when she opened the door. 'Just wanted to make sure you were okay. Couldn't help noticing you had a visitor.'

Of course you could help it, she felt like saying. Little creep. Nothing better to do than sit inside that horrible house, staring at her while he played with himself.

'I was just about to go out,' she said.

'Oh.'

She smiled. 'But actually I'm glad you called. I could do with a friend right now.'

She stepped back to let him into the house. As he passed, she reached out and touched his arm. He jumped.

'Hold me?' she whispered. 'I don't want to be alone.'

* * *

Jim was released. For now. The owners of the Lewisham house confirmed he'd come out to deal with a boiler emergency Sunday afternoon. They were unable to confirm what time he'd left, but Ellen was certain he'd arrived at hers by half-eight. Which meant, in theory, he might have had time to kill Chloe before driving across to Ellen's. But the lack of any motive or anything that connected him with Chloe meant he was free to leave. For now.

In the early afternoon, Ellen drove over to his house. He lived in a modern townhouse on the Peninsula, the last in a row of white, terraced houses on the waterfront. He didn't seem pleased to see her.

'I was just heading out,' he said. 'Got a load of jobs on and I'm running late. What is it?'

He was wearing work clothes. Faded jeans and an old sweater that had seen better days. He looked great.

'Can we go inside?' she asked.

He frowned, anger or annoyance she couldn't tell, then turned and went into the house, holding the door open for her. She walked past him, along the narrow corridor into the kitchen.

'Coffee?'

'Thanks.'

She watched him move around the kitchen, turning the kettle on, spooning coffee into the cafetière, taking white mugs from a cupboard and placing them on the table in front of her. He didn't speak while he did this and she was grateful for that.

Finally, the coffee was poured and he sat opposite her, waiting.

'You want to know why you were brought in for questioning?' she said.

He nodded. 'And why you couldn't tell me if I was a suspect in a bloody murder investigation.'

'I couldn't do that,' she said. 'I got an e-mail with information about you and the victim. I had to pass that on to my boss.'

'Me and Chloe Dunbar? I'm sorry, Ellen. You've lost me.

You're saying you received an e-mail saying that I knew her? That's bullshit. Who sent it?'

She couldn't tell him. Even if she knew, in her heart of hearts, that Monica was making it all up, she couldn't risk it. Which meant she couldn't ask him about his relationship with Monica, either.

She stood up. 'I shouldn't have come. Sorry.'

'Is that it?' he said. 'I get dragged in and questioned about a murder and you can't even tell me why?'

'There are things you haven't told me,' she said. 'Makes me wonder what else there is that I don't know about.'

Jim frowned. 'What the hell are you talking about?'

'It doesn't matter,' she said. 'I need to go.'

'Where does that leave us?' he asked.

'I can't see you,' Ellen said. 'Not until this case is over. After that, I can explain everything.'

'And what?' he asked. 'In the meantime I just hang around not knowing what's going on or why I'm suddenly number one suspect in a case you're working on? That's bullshit, Ellen.'

He reached across the table and took her hand.

'Don't do this,' he said. 'Please.'

She pulled her hand away and stood up.

'Thanks for the coffee,' she said. 'I'll see myself out.'

'Wait.' He came after her and grabbed her arm, pulling her around so she was facing him. 'Don't leave. Not like this.'

She looked down at his hand, kept looking until he removed it.

'I need time out,' she said. 'We both do. Let's get this case behind us and then we can talk properly. I'll call you.'

'Ellen!'

When she didn't answer, he swung around and punched the wall. Hard. A dent appeared in the smooth surface. The moment of rage was brief, but enough to tell her she was right. She barely knew this man. Until she did, she wasn't letting him get any closer.

Ellen pulled open the front door and stepped outside. Jim made no effort to stop her. As she drove away, she glanced back once in the rear-view mirror. Saw him standing in the doorway looking towards her, cradling his damaged right hand in the palm of his left hand.

When she turned onto the main road, he disappeared from the mirror but the image of him, framed in the doorway, lodged in her brain, refusing to budge, no matter how hard she tried to get rid of it.

* * *

By the time she'd finished with him, Harry was in a loved-up daze of satisfaction.

They hadn't even made it as far as the bedroom, tumbling onto the floor in the hall, ripping the clothes off each other. A nuisance because it meant her earlier work, getting herself ready, had all been wasted. She went upstairs and started over again, left him lying on the hall floor, smoking a roll-up.

He was still there when she came back down, twenty minutes later. It took all her will power not to kick him and tell him to get the hell out. Instead, she knelt beside him and kissed him gently.

'I need to be somewhere,' she said. 'Meeting a potential customer. I can't afford to be late.'

She stepped back, giving him space to pull his boxers and trousers up. It irritated her he didn't do that while she was upstairs. What did he think – that it was attractive to see him like that? Withered little penis drooping against a thigh that was too hairy and too skinny. The memory of what they'd done made her shudder.

At the door, he took her in his arms and started to kiss her. She pushed him away, forcing a laugh.

'Don't make me have to go upstairs again,' she said. 'I don't have time!'

He let her go, patches of red appearing on each cheek.

'Sorry,' she said. 'I'm still a little tense, to be honest. It's all been too much, Harry.'

'We'll sort it,' he said. 'I'll sort it. You don't need to worry anymore.'

'You promise?'

He smiled.

'I promise.'

She watched him leave, waited until he was back inside his own house before stepping outside.

An autumn sun made the day seem warm. Monica lifted her

face up to the sky and smiled. A good day so far, no doubt about it. Harry was like a puppy, so young and so very eager to please. Like any good little puppy, he was a quick learner. She didn't even have to spell it out for him, just a hint of what she wanted and he was on it in a flash.

The revulsion she'd felt earlier was gone, replaced by something else. A sort of fondness for the boy. Strange. All that devotion was rubbing off on her. She wondered what it would take to twist him, turn the devotion around and make him hate her instead.

It was something to consider when he started to bore her. Not yet, though. Not while he was still useful.

# FORTY-SEVEN

Ellen stood in the viewing area, watching Mark slice a straight line down the centre of Chloe's body. He put his hand inside the girl and removed her organs, one by one, weighing them and making comments into a hand-held voice recorder.

Ellen hated post-mortems. It wasn't the body bits that got to her. Nor the butchery. She was generally okay with the blood and guts and smells that some of her colleagues couldn't stomach. No, what Ellen couldn't stand was the sense of invasion. Standing here now, watching Mark cut open Chloe's body, she felt like a voyeur watching something forbidden.

'She hadn't eaten in a while,' Mark said. 'Had her last meal almost twenty-four hours before she was killed. Any idea why?'

'She was scared,' Ellen said. 'Too terrified to eat would be my guess. Poor thing.'

She remembered seeing Chloe at the station once. She'd come in to report another suspected break-in at her house and Ellen had been looking for Raj, found him in an interview room taking yet another statement from Chloe. At the time, Ellen had warned Raj not to spend too much time on this. Showed just how wrong she could be.

The body in front of her bore no resemblance to the pretty woman she'd seen that day. The essence of Chloe – what she'd thought and felt and loved and hated – was gone. It would be lovely to imagine that Chloe's soul was somewhere safe and happy, but Ellen didn't believe that. When someone died, that was it. Nothing left except the memories others kept.

The thought depressed her and she willed Mark to hurry up, get the job over and done with so Chloe's broken body could be closed up and left in peace.

\* \* \*

'I need some fresh air.' Ellen turned to Abby. 'Fancy a walk?'

Abby lifted her hands over her head, stretching.

'Great idea,' she said. 'Twice round the heath then back?'

Outside, night was suffusing the sky, claiming the city. Ellen glanced around, checking there was no sign of Martine Reynolds. As predicted, the journalist had turned up at this morning's press meeting, asking questions all aimed at making the police seem incompetent. Since then, she'd been spotted hanging around the building, stopping officers at random, trying to get quotes from them. Ellen knew what she'd give Martine Reynolds if she saw her.

'I saw her drive off earlier,' Abby said, when Ellen asked about the journalist. 'Obviously got what she needed, now she's gone back to write it up and turn it into a pack of lies.'

The heath was a brisk ten-minute walk from Lewisham Station. As she turned into Mounts Park Road and saw the open space stretching out in front of her, the tension across Ellen's chest eased up. Across the heath, the purple sky dipped down to embrace the jagged outline of the city.

They walked all the way to Greenwich Park and continued east, walking a loop around the heath and back towards Lewisham. Ellen's house was nearby. Empty now. Both children were having tea at their grandparents. Ellen had another two hours work in front of her before she got to see them.

'What's wrong?' Abby asked.

'Why do you think there's something wrong?'

Abby smiled. 'You've been in foul form all day. Snapping at anyone who dares speak to you and hitting your keyboard so hard I'm surprised it hasn't broken yet. Plus, you never, ever suggest going for a walk when we're in the middle of something. So come on. Spit it out.'

'It's this investigation,' Ellen said. 'We've got all these different strands that should come together but nothing's connecting. We've got Nathan Collier, Carl Jenkins, Ricky Lezard. All linked with Chloe but sod-all else.'

'What about the guy they brought in earlier?' Abby said. 'O'Dwyer. Where does he fit in?'

'That's the problem,' Ellen said.

It felt good to talk about it. She hadn't expected that. Especially Abby, of all people. They were hardly the best of buddies. And yet, here she was, pouring her heart out about Jim like they were intimate confidantes.

'Wow,' Abby said when Ellen finally stopped talking. 'That's a lot to take in.'

'So what should I do?' Ellen asked.

'Okay,' Abby said after a moment. 'Here's what we know. Carl Jenkins and Nathan Collier are still suspects. Jenkins' only alibi for Sunday night is his mother. Collier doesn't have any. Discounting Lezard for now, that leaves us with three suspects: Jim, Jenkins and Collier. We know Jim didn't kill Chloe because he was with you. But it's possible he's connected to this somehow, right?'

'So our priority is to find something connecting one of these men with both women,' Ellen said.

'And to find out if Monica is telling the truth or not,' Abby said. 'What about Jim? How well do you know him?'

She'd known him almost her whole life. The memory of it came rushing back, pushing away Abby, the heath and everything else.

*Her first day of primary school. She and Sean had joined the class* mid-term. The upheaval of the past year had thrown everything off course, including school. They were both nervous. She tried to hide her nerves by pretending she didn't care. School was stupid and the kids in it even more so. She had resolved, beforehand, to have as little to do with them as possible.

Sean, on the other hand, was inconsolable. Clung to their new mother, begging her not to make him go in. And when the teacher came and gently prised him away, he started screaming. Ellen hated the teacher from that moment onward and continued to do so for the rest of her time in primary school.

Inside, the classroom was horrible; a million times worse than she could ever have imagined – full of cruel-looking children and stupid pictures on the walls and another woman who seemed to do nothing but order the children around. The teacher put Sean sitting on her knee and talked to him in a low voice, trying to calm him down.

The other woman – a teaching assistant, Ellen learned later – told Ellen to sit in the empty seat near the back, 'beside Jim, that's a good girl'. Ellen stood at the front of the class, looking along the sea of hostile faces, trying to find 'Jim, that's a good girl'.

She felt sick, like she might vomit. The only thing that stopped her was the thought of vomiting in front of all these kids and them laughing at her. She took a step forward, willing the boy called Jim to show himself. Another step. Still no sign of a chair she could sit on.

Then a face. A boy with plump, rosy cheeks and brown eyes was standing up. He smiled and a dimple appeared under his left eye. It made him look kind. Despite herself, Ellen found herself smiling *back. There was something about him.*

*'Over here,' he said.*

*And then she saw it. The empty seat. He beckoned her forward and she walked, confident now, knowing where she was going and why. She slipped into the seat beside him and he sat back down. He nudged her with his elbow. She turned to see what he wanted and he was grinning at her and pointing to the teacher.*

*'That's Mrs Flynn,' he whispered. 'She's a right cow.'*

*Right then, Ellen knew school wasn't going to be quite as bad as she'd expected it to be.*

'I thought I knew him,' she said. 'But how well can you really know someone?'

'Not my place to say,' Abby said. 'But you're no idiot, Ellen. If you like him enough to let him into your life, then I'm sure you're right about him. Maybe you should do what you're always telling us to. Trust your gut. I bet that's telling you he's not part of this. Am I right?'

The sky had changed colour, deep purple faded to black tinged with the orange glow from the lights coming on across the city. Around the park, windows twinkling in the grand Georgian townhouses, offering the false promise of security and comfort. In truth, Ellen knew that the lives of the people living in those houses were every bit as messy and complicated as her own. Money offered the illusion of difference. But that's all it was. An illusion.

# FORTY-EIGHT

Nathan stayed in the shower until the water turned cold. When he got out, the mirror had steamed over. He dried himself quickly and ran along the corridor to his bedroom. In here, there was no escaping his reflection in the sliding mirrored doors of the built-in wardrobe.

He'd had the wardrobe fitted three months earlier. Part of a project to modernise the house he'd lived in his entire life. When his mother died two years ago, he didn't have the heart to start the work, even though the estate agent part of him could see the place needed a serious overhaul.

When she was alive, he'd been desperate to do the work but she'd always resisted. Her home and she'd have it the way she liked it, and there's the end of it. He'd resented her for it. Evening after evening spent looking at the flock wallpaper and thick blue carpet, imagining how much better it would be if she'd only let him do it.

And then, suddenly, she was gone. There hadn't been a single thing wrong with her. Hail and hearty at seventy, he'd thought she had a good twenty years left, at least.

A peaceful death. That's how the paramedics described it. He'd been so angry at first. With the doctors who couldn't save her, with God for taking her, with everyone. Two angry months of hating before he'd found his way back. There was a sort of peace after that. Acceptance of God's will was part of the healing process. Even then, he wasn't ready to make the changes he'd wanted to do for so long. To touch one part of the house felt like a betrayal. Until that day, six months and six days ago.

He came home that evening, saw the house as she would and knew it was time. He started with the upstairs. New bathroom and new bedroom. Left Mum's room untouched, though. Thought he'd leave that until last. In his weaker moments, when the lust and pride were at their strongest, he imagined them deciding it together. Choosing new curtains and wallpaper. A new bed that they would share.

Chloe.

The pain was physical. A tightness across his chest and heart that was worst at moments like this. Alone and exhausted, the need for pretence gone because there was no one else here.

Mum wouldn't have liked it. Always said he was too good for

most women. A nice, kind, decent boy, what did he need with women, anyway? Didn't he have her and wasn't she enough for him? And for a while she was. But then she'd left him and what did she expect? For him to be alone forever?

Lust and pride.

Two of the seven deadly sins.

He prayed and prayed not to feel the way he did and sometimes he was able to keep a lid on it. But then she'd do something, a little thing like a smile. Or she'd smooth her skirt along her thighs after crossing her legs, and all the resolve, all the praying and will power was useless in the face of it.

*Silly boy.*

If Mum was here, she'd tell him straight.

*It's what's inside that matters. Not what's on the outside.*

She used to say that after a bad day at school. Boys – and girls – pulling and poking and punching. Mocking the fat boy all part of their daily entertainment. Not caring how it made him feel.

He'd had a good chat with Martine earlier. She'd called for a quote and he'd filled her in on a few things. Told her who the real culprit was. He hoped Martine would do Chloe justice.

He'd wrapped a towel around himself after the shower. A navy-blue towel around his middle. In the mirror, he looked like a big blue football with a small head on top and two fat arms sticking out either side of it.

*Beauty is as beauty does.*

He unwrapped the towel, let it drop to the floor. Rolls of fat bulged out at his sides, hung down low so you could barely see his man bits. Eyes like little raisins buried into the fat of his face.

He grabbed a piece of stomach fat, jiggled it. Watched how the flesh wobbled, little waves of wobbling fat.

Man boobs. Moobs.

In school, they'd called them tits. Titty Collier. Boys used to grab hold of them and twist them, laughing when he cried out with the pain of it.

Here comes Titty Collier. Chanting at him, in the corridor, the playground, on the way home from school. And then he'd get inside and Mum would be waiting with his tea, ready to sit and listen and tell him not to pay any attention to silly boys and girls who couldn't see beyond his appearance to the lovely, lovely boy he really was.

*And have another helping of pasta, Nate, and there's treacle pudding for afters. Your favourite.*

He thought of Carl, flat stomach, muscled shoulders and clear, clean skin. Felt a surge of loathing so strong it made him light-headed, like he might fall over if he wasn't careful.

*Beauty is as beauty does.*

Any time they'd gone to a restaurant he'd been really careful, making sure not to eat too much so she wouldn't think he was a greedy pig. There was always food at home for later. He preferred eating alone, anyway.

Carl ate a bacon butty at his desk most mornings. Stuffed it down his throat with no consideration for the other people in the office. Not realising how galling it was to watch him eat that rubbish and not put on a single ounce.

Said he worked out so he didn't have to be careful about what he ate. Easy to work out if you looked like that. Wasn't like Nathan hadn't thought about it. But every time he did, he saw himself, Titty Collier, turning up at a gym full of people like Carl and he knew it would never happen.

He'd only wanted to be friends. Made that clear from the start. Told himself it would be enough. And when it wasn't enough, when he knew he wanted more than that, well, he tried. No one could say he didn't try.

# FORTY-NINE

Monica wanted to scream until the sound of her voice blew the whole place apart, leaving her with enough space to breathe properly. She'd been in the city too long. It got to her after a while. She needed to get away from all this bloody congestion. Today, the feeling of oppression was worse than ever.

She'd expected Jim to call. There was nothing to stop him now Kelly knew the truth. At least, as much of the truth as Monica chose to share with her. She had deliberately held some of it back, resorting to that childhood habit of saving the best for last. It was better to let the mind linger over it, that delicious build-up of anticipation. If she revealed it all in one go, she'd have nothing left to look forward to.

She remembered the first time she'd seen them together. The

day after Brighton. Still recovering from all of that, she'd gone to the park hoping to clear her head. When she saw Jim, she thought it was a sign. Until she saw who was with him.

The shock, her second in twenty-four hours, shook her very core. She stood, frozen, unable to move, waiting for him to see her as they passed. But his head was turned away from her, listening to what that bitch was saying. He walked right past and didn't even see her. Playing happy fucking families with someone else's wife and kids.

Monica recognised Kelly straight away. She'd met her at an exhibition. Kelly had spent ages mooning over the Kent paintings. Keen for a sale, Monica asked what it was about the paintings Kelly was so taken with.

'It's the landscape,' Kelly replied. 'So bleak it should be ugly but it's not. Do you know what I mean?'

Monica said of course she did, added a few meaningless insights of her own and clocked Kelly as a bit of a fruitcake. Eventually, after a decision that took way too long, Kelly went with one of Monica's favourites. The flat, North Kent landscape stretching across the canvas in muted shades. In the middle, a child. A boy, Kelly said. Monica didn't disagree although when she'd painted it, she had a girl in mind.

What the hell was he doing with someone like that?

She had to get out. Now.

Outside, the street was quiet. Like always. Such a stupid, dead-end place she'd chosen to live. She couldn't remember now, what on earth had drawn her to this middle-of-nowhere corner of London. Apart from the proximity to Greenwich, it really had nothing going for it. A street full of smug, smiley parents with irritating children who all had stupid names like Molly or Theo.

No sign of Harry, which was a relief. The house across the road stood silent and empty. She thought about their conversation this morning, wondered if he was doing anything useful about it. Decided he was most likely out with his mates, getting off his head on 'gear' and listening to that awful music he was so into.

She walked along Lee Road, up to Blackheath. Today, even the heath wasn't enough. That was the problem growing up by the sea. It spoiled you. Even if you hated every inch of the place and hoped you never saw it again as long as you lived, it left you with a need for uncluttered landscapes and open spaces. Probably explained why she painted it so obsessively. Almost like she was reconnecting with something inside her that might die otherwise.

She jumped on a bus to Greenwich. The latest Hollywood rom-com was due to start in just under an hour at the Picture-house. It would do. She bought her ticket and sat in the bar upstairs where she tried to numb the tension inside her with a large glass of Rioja.

The film was crap and she didn't even bother trying to follow the predictable plot. The other members of the audience were couples or groups of women. She seemed to be the only person who'd come to see the film alone. The observation did nothing to improve her mood.

Afterwards, she considered trawling a few local bars, looking for a bit of fun. She got as far as Xanadu, a trendy new place across from the Picturehouse, but inside it was too bright, too packed, too noisy and she couldn't face it. Pulling her jacket tight around her body, she turned away from the prospect of pleasure and waited for a bus back to Lee.

The wine made her woozy and when she jumped off the bus at the end of her road, she walked slowly. There was a strange car parked outside her house. A battered old crock that had clearly seen better days. A loser's car. Some bloke trying to prove he was cool enough to drive a piece of shit and not be bothered about what it said about him.

At the front door, she rooted around in her bag, found the keys and pulled them out. She was putting them in the lock when she heard something behind her. She turned and saw someone climbing out of the car and coming towards her.

The moment of recognition was a celebration. Her heart galloped as her breathing grew ragged. She could do nothing to stop the smile that spread across her face, so wide it hurt.

'Hey stranger.'

Exhilarated, she stepped forward, body swaying in anticipation, remembering how it had been between them. How it had always been better with him than anyone else.

'Glad you could make it. It's been a while.'

\* \* \*

Ellen found the CD she wanted. The Righteous Brothers, *One for the Road*. She scrolled through to her favourite track, sat back and closed her eyes as the brothers, Bill Medley and Bobby Hatfield, sang about lost love to a background of joyful, soaring instrumentals. They sang as if their hearts were breaking. Voices so sweet and soft, it felt like her heart might break too.

When that ended, she poured the rest of the wine into her glass and switched to Nick Cave, *The Boatman's Call*. Music to match her mood. The first track on the album reminded her – painfully – of her wedding day. She skipped that and went straight to *Lime-Tree Arbour*. Haunting piano melodies filled the room.

She walked across to the window and looked out. In the house directly opposite, a single light shone from a room upstairs. Nick's voice wrapped around her, singing of suffering and a hand that protects. Across the street, a shadow appeared at the window and closed the curtains. As Nick sang the last line of the song, the light behind the curtains was switched off. The final piano chords faded away, replaced by nothing but darkness and silence.

# FIFTY

*Hands shaking like a bastard. Practically shitting myself I'm so scared. Something else too. Excitement. Feeling like if I can do this, I can do anything. I get the key into the lock, turn it and I'm inside, standing in a big, modern kitchen. An island the size of my own kitchen in the middle of the room.*

*Behind me, the door swings shut. The click of the lock makes me jump. It sounds loud in the quiet house and I stand still – too scared to breathe – waiting to hear if the noise has been heard upstairs. But there's nothing and after a minute I relax.*

*I'm wearing my trainers, soft soles so I don't make any noise. Even though it's dark outside, the glare of the streetlights through the sliding glass doors make it easy for me to see where I'm going.*

*I shift around the kitchen, touching things every now and then.*

*Empty wine glass by the sink, little pool of red wine at the bottom. I lift it and drink the last few drops. Knowing she was drinking from the same glass a few hours earlier, knowing I'm down here, doing this while she's sleeping a few feet away, it's a turn-on. Feel myself getting hard and let myself enjoy it, just for a moment.*

*Pictures stuck to the fridge with little magnets. The kids. He's dark, just like his mother. The girl has freckles and red hair and looks nothing like them. Other stuff gets my attention. A school newsletter. St Joseph's. I clock the address and am about to leave it at that when I see something else. There's a photo of the boy on the newsletter. Holding a football and smiling. Caption underneath says his name is Pat Kelly and he's just been made captain of the school football team. There's a list of football matches – times, dates, locations – alongside the photo. I take the newsletter, fold it up and put it in my pocket.*

*It's a big house. As well as the kitchen, there's a sitting room and a separate dining room. A downstairs loo as well. I didn't plan on going upstairs, but now I'm here I can't help it.*

*I go slowly, stopping at each step, listening out for any sign that someone's awake. But there's nothing at all. Just the in-out, deep breathing that gets louder the higher I go. Four rooms up here and a big bathroom with one of those fancy Victorian baths.*

*They sleep with their bedroom doors open, each one of them in their own room. I can't help thinking how lucky those kids are to grow up in a house as big and lovely as this. Think about the shithole I grew up in and nearly laugh at how different it was to this.*

*I really didn't plan to go into her room. Didn't think for a second*

*I'd be brave enough for something like that. But she's snoring. Loud, steady snores that make me brave. My father used to snore like that. One of the few times you'd feel safe because you knew, when the snoring started, he was gone and nothing in the world would wake him up.*

*She's lying on her back, mouth open. On one side of the bed, the quilt has slipped away and she's not wearing any clothes. I imagine all the things I could do to her, right here and now, and she wouldn't stand a chance in hell.*

*I take the phone out of my pocket and creep forward into the room. My heart is louder than a fucking drum and my breathing is too fast. I do what I need to do and get out of there, lean against a wall and force myself to calm down. Angry now. Acting like some fucking idiot who's never seen a woman naked before.*

*When I'm in control again, I go back, stepping just inside the door. The stink of the wine she's been drinking. Stupid bitch. Two kids to look after and she's so fucking out of it she doesn't even notice there's someone in her house.*

*I hated her before tonight and I hate her even more now. I've had enough, need to get out of here. Don't even stop to look in on the children. Thinking I can do that another time.*

*The snoring and the smell follow me out of the house and down the road. Mixed in with all the stuff I don't want to think about. I start running, thinking if I run fast enough, I'll be able to get away.*

*Except there's no getting away from any of it. Everything that happened, it's so long ago now, you'd think — wouldn't you? — I'd be able to forget it. Doesn't work like that. Shit sticks. And even though I'm running, I know it's pointless. I can run and run but it won't do any good. When I stop running, he'll still be there with his stinking breath and his dirty moods and his big hands, like fucking table-tennis bats, banging on the table in time to Bat Out of Hell, music blaring out of the stereo through the thin walls until it feels like the whole house is vibrating with the beat of it.*

# FIFTY-ONE

'Where are we with CCTV?' Ger asked.

'Still going through it,' Alastair said. 'I started with the camera that's on the corner of Nightingale Grove and the station. Haven't found anything yet. There's another camera that's positioned at the other entrance to the station, near the main parade of shops in Hither Green. I'm going to cross-check all the people and cars with Sunday night and the dates Chloe stated there was someone in her house.'

'How long?' Ger said.

Alastair shrugged. 'Could take a few hours, could take the whole day. I'll go as quickly as I can but…'

They'd agreed Ellen could remain on the case. For now. As long as she had no more involvement with Monica Telford.

Which suited Ellen just fine. Jim's name had been added to the list on the whiteboard, a double-ended arrow connecting him to Monica. Another line, with a questionmark, between his name and Chloe's photo.

'Forensics found something interesting,' Malcolm said. 'Chloe has a water filter in her kitchen. One of those jugs that filters the water for you. They ran a tox test and found traces of benzodiazepine. According to the tox guys, that's a psychoactive drug commonly used to treat anxiety and extreme pain. Diazepam by any other word. Too mild to be conclusive, but might be worth asking the doc to run a toxicology report. What do you think?'

Goosebumps spread out across Ellen's arms and back. The room suddenly felt very cold. There was silence as the team digested this new piece of information. Ger was the first to speak.

'You said the traces were mild. How mild?'

'The water we drink is shit. Pardon me, Ma'am. But tap water, it's full of all sorts of crap. Tiny traces of benzodiazepine aren't that uncommon. Lots of other things in there too. I can give you a list if you want.'

'No thanks,' Ger said. 'Isn't that what the filter's for? To filter out all the crap.'

'Exactly,' Malcolm said. 'Which is why it's unusual.'

'That would explain why the poor kid never woke up the nights she claimed someone was in her house,' Ger said. 'Anything else?'

'Nothing we don't already know,' Malcolm said. 'No sign of a break-in, no sign of a struggle before Chloe died. The killer caught her completely unawares. They've picked up several different sets of prints from the house and we've got matches for Jenkins and Collier. Nothing surprising about that, though. Both men admit being in the house at different times.'

'Any other prints?' Ellen asked.

Malcolm nodded. 'Chloe's, of course. Several others too. No matches, though. Oh, and that includes no match for Ricky Lezard. If he was ever in the house, there's no trace of it.'

'What about Monica?' Ellen asked.

'Chloe said they didn't know each other,' Abby said. 'Why would she lie about that?'

Something niggled at the back of Ellen's mind, but she couldn't nail it down. Chloe and Monica. There was a connection somewhere. If only she could find it.

'I still think it's worth a try,' she said. 'Can we get a DNA sample from Monica? Prints, too. We can cross-check these with what we've picked up from the house.'

'That's not your call,' Ger said. 'For the record, everyone, Ellen won't be dealing with Monica Telford anymore. If Monica calls or tries to speak with Ellen, you're to put her straight through to me. Got that?'

Ellen saw the glances passed between her colleagues but knew no one would be stupid enough to say anything. She'd asked Abby to keep her mouth shut and sincerely hoped she could be trusted to do that. She already knew she could trust Alastair. The last thing she needed right now was everyone commenting on her love life and what a mess she'd made of it. She was more than capable of doing that herself, without anyone else's input.

* * *

When Nathan got into work on Wednesday, Carl was already there. Sitting at his desk like nothing in the world had changed. Carl stood up when Nathan walked in, approached him with his arms open, like he wanted to embrace him. The sheer, barefaced cheek!

'Nathan.' Carl's eyes were red-rimmed, like he'd been crying. Nathan wasn't about to fall for that one. He'd seen, first-hand and too many times, what Carl's attitude was where women were concerned. Treated them as if they were no better than common prostitutes. Swaggering about the place after each dirty encounter, winking at Nathan, making him complicit, somehow, in his disgusting behaviour.

'You can gather up your things,' Nathan said, brushing past him.

'Huh?'

Nathan looked at him. Grey skin, red eyes, shoulders stooped over like an old man's. If only Chloe could see him.

'You can't stay,' Nathan said. 'I'd have thought that much was obvious.'

Stupid, brash fool didn't get it.

'What you doing, Nathan? You can't think I had anything to do with it? Listen to me, man. Whatever the police told you, me and Chloe, it was the start of something special. I liked her. Really liked her.'

'You *liked* her?' Ice in his heart, ice in his voice. Let this horrible creature know just what he thought of him. 'She deserved something better. Now go on. Clear your stuff and get the hell out of here.'

'And that's it?' Incredulity made Carl's voice shrill. 'All the work I've done for you, all the extra hours I've put in, all the fucking money I've made and you just stand there and tell me to leave? You can't do that.'

'I'll pay you till the end of next week,' Nathan said. 'You're on a week's notice, anyway. Check your contract. You'll see I'm not doing anything I'm not supposed to.'

Unlike you, he thought. Seducing a poor girl, getting her into bed and then what? In all the time he'd been here, Carl had never stuck with any woman beyond a few dates. Even if Chloe hadn't died, Nathan wouldn't have put up with it. Carl had to go. No two ways about that.

He'd expected Carl to have another go. Wasn't expecting what Carl said next, even though he ought to have known it would come to this eventually.

'I get it,' Carl said. 'It's nothing to do with her being dead, is it? You're getting rid of me because you're jealous.'

Carl stepped closer, so close Nathan could see the little pores on his nose, smell the sour, metally stink of last night's beer on Carl's breath.

'You wanted her for yourself, didn't you? No point denying it, mate. You were about as obvious as it was possible to be. Perving all over her any chance you got. Touching her, standing too close. She noticed it all, you know. We had a right laugh about it. A right laugh about you. Jesus, mate. You looked in a mirror lately? Chloe was class. She'd never have looked twice at a fat fucker like you. She was way out of your league. You're pathetic, you know that? A pathetic fucking loser.'

'Stop it!' Nathan put his hands over his ears, trying not to hear. But Carl kept going until he couldn't – wouldn't – stand it. He charged forward, head down, body slamming into Carl's. The two men flew back, crashed into Carl's desk. Carl shouting. Fist out of nowhere smacked into his cheek. Flashes of pain. On the ground now. Face pressed against the slate-grey carpet tiles he'd got fitted five months earlier. He'd let Chloe choose them. Told her the place needed a woman's touch.

He tried to get up, but Carl was on top of him. Grabbed Nathan's hair, jerked his head back and slammed it into the ground. Blood in his mouth. Taste of metal. White, bright pain. Screams. Stop it. Please. Carl had his arm, twisting it behind and up his back, pulling hard.

'No!' Screaming louder now. Made no difference. Arm yanked higher. Any further it would break. Nose still bleeding. Crying. Snot, tears, blood.

And then nothing.

His arm was free and the pressure of Carl's weight on his body was gone. Carl's shadow, standing over him. He tensed, waiting for more.

'You're not fucking worth it, mate.'

Shadow moved away. Electronic ring trilled across the office as the door opened. Gust of cold air, then the door closed again and Carl was gone. Nathan curled over on his side, cradling his damaged arm with the good one, crying like the pathetic loser he was.

# FIFTY-TWO

'We made the front page again.' Abby smacked the latest copy of *The Evening Star* on Ellen's desk. A black-and-white photo of Carl Jenkins took up the top half of the front page. Underneath the potentially libellous headline, *Police incompetence lets killer walk*.

Ellen knew she shouldn't take it personally but found it difficult not to. It was a classic Martine Reynolds piece of lazy journalism. Full of unfounded accusations of police incompetence. The journalist also made it pretty clear Carl Jenkins was their main suspect. Lezard and Collier were mentioned too, but only in passing.

'Glad to see I get a mention,' Ellen said. 'Wouldn't want Raj getting all the credit.'

'Where does she get this shit?' Abby asked.

On the last big case Ellen had worked on, Reynolds had a source inside the station. Ellen's ex-boss, Ed Baxter. With Baxter out of the picture, she wondered who else might have leaked this information. The most obvious answer, of course, was one of the voluntary Community Support Officers doing the legwork the paid detectives didn't have the time or the inclination for. There was someone else, too, but she dismissed that idea almost as soon as she thought it. He might be angry, but he'd never stoop this low.

'Could be anyone. Disgruntled CSO more than likely,' Ellen said. 'Chances are we'll never know who. Listen, have you heard anything from Raj?'

'You think this is him?' Abby asked.

'Course not,' Ellen said. 'Just wondering how he is, that's all.'

'I haven't spoken to him,' Abby said. 'Left a few messages but he hasn't got back to me. I imagine he's feeling pretty low.'

'Let's pay Jenkins another visit,' Ellen said. 'Nathan Collier, too. Their office is just down the road. I'll treat you to a coffee in Danilo's along the way.'

* * *

'Carl Jenkins no longer works here.'

'Since when?' Ellen asked.

'This morning,' Collier said. 'I expect certain standards from my staff, Detective Inspector. Carl behaved in a manner I found unacceptable. I had to let him go. I had no choice.'

Ellen and Abby were sitting across from Nathan Collier in his estate agency office on Lewisham High Street. When he'd seen the two detectives coming in, Nathan had switched the sign on the front door to Closed before taking a seat behind his desk and inviting them to sit down as well.

'Unacceptable?' Ellen said.

'Fraternising with another member of the team,' he said. 'I won't tolerate that sort of thing.'

When he spoke, he looked at her face but avoided eye contact, eyes sliding away to a spot just above her head. She wondered if this was because he was lying or just nervous.

'Are you talking about his relationship with Chloe?' Abby asked.

'Relationship!' Collier's voice rose several pitches, his round face glowing. 'Carl Jenkins wouldn't know the first thing about relationships. He's only interested in one thing when it comes to women.'

'What's that?' Ellen asked.

'Sex.' He spat the word out like it hurt his mouth. 'Women are simply objects for men like that. Treat them mean, keep them keen. He used to say that, you know. As if it was something to be proud of. As if poor Chloe hadn't endured enough already. She was making such progress.' He smiled. 'She would have been coming to church with me this weekend, you know. We were so close.'

'So close to what?' Abby said.

'To saving her,' Nathan said.

Ellen shifted on her chair. She needed to move around. It helped her think. She stood up and walked to the window, looked out at the street. The market, all the people going about their daily lives. For some of them, this day could be their last. And they had no idea.

She turned back to Nathan and Abby, both looking at her, waiting. Nathan's desk was at the back of the office, a big, ugly teak affair that was too large for the place. Two smaller desks near the front. Chloe's and Carl's, Ellen guessed.

'How did Carl take the news that he was out of a job?' Ellen asked.

'He wasn't happy about it,' Nathan said, rubbing the bruise under his right eye.

'Did he do that to you?' Abby asked.

Nathan shook his head, but Ellen was certain he was lying.

'What are you going to do?' Ellen said. 'You can't run the business single-handedly, can you?'

Collier shrugged. 'I'll get new people. Property market's booming right now, while the job centres are full of people who can't find jobs. One phone call and I'll have them lining up to be interviewed. To tell the truth, a change is overdue. Carl stopped pulling his weight a while back. I was planning to get rid of him, anyway. As for Chloe, well, I offered her the job out of the kindness of my heart. Thought she could do with a helping hand. As you can see, it wasn't a helping hand she wanted, was it? Turns out she wasn't the person I thought she was. In many ways, I think the business is better off without both of them.'

'So you're saying Chloe's death is good for business?' Abby asked.

Nathan flushed. Again. 'That's not what I said, Detective. You weren't paying attention. I cared deeply for Chloe. Unfortunately, she wasn't very good at her job. She made simple mistakes and was incapable of prioritising. I tried my best to make excuses for her. She was stressed and worried and that can have a terrible effect on a person's work. Of course, I realise now the true reason for her distraction. She was too busy making eyes at a fellow worker. And that saddens me, Detective. As I've already said, it's not the sort of behaviour I expect from my employees.'

Outside, Ellen breathed thick mouthfuls of dirty Lewisham air, relieved to be away from the sweaty, prissy company of Nathan Collier.

'He did it,' Abby said. 'Carl Jenkins isn't our man. It's that sociopath we've just been speaking to.'

'Why do you say that?' Ellen asked.

'Serious?' Abby said. 'Didn't you hear him? All that stuff about correct behaviour and standards and bloody *saving* her. He's a creep. A religious creep, too. The worst kind. Saving her. There's a euphemism if ever I heard one.'

'Get hold of his medical records,' Ellen said. 'See if he's been prescribed Diazepam anytime recently.'

Abby nodded and started to say something else but it got lost as Ellen's phone started ringing. Alastair. Calling to say he'd found something on the CCTV footage at Hither Green station. Any chance Ellen could get back right away to take a look? Every chance, Ellen told him.

'Got to get back,' Ellen said after she'd hung up. 'See if you can track down Jenkins. Let's get his side of the story. See how it compares to Collier's version. You okay to do that?'

After she'd left Abby, Ellen practically skipped back to the station. They were getting close to something. She could feel it. Abby was right. Nathan Collier had guilt written all over him.

# FIFTY-THREE

This was the evidence she'd been waiting for. Ellen knew it the moment Alastair sat her in front of the screen and played the clip.

'This is Thursday, the second of September, the first night Chloe claims someone had been in her house. Here's the car, parking outside the pub and then someone getting out.'

'We can't see the driver?'

'The camera angle's wrong,' Alastair said. 'We can see the left side of the car quite clearly, but the right side is out of the camera range. But that might not matter. Look. Here's footage from the other two nights Chloe reported a break-in.' More video, the same car parking in the same place. 'And here's the night she was killed. Check the time here at the bottom of the screen. 19:35. What did Pritchard say about time of death?'

'Between 19:30 and 21:00,' Ellen said. 'This image isn't great. What can you tell me about the car?'

'Red Fiat Punto,' Alastair said. 'Red or possibly purple. Difficult to see in the dark. Can't make out the registration but I've already spoken with Rui in the lab. He thinks he might be able to do something with that.'

There it was again. The flutter of excitement. They were getting close.

'How soon?' Ellen asked.

'A day,' Alastair said. 'Maybe a little longer, but he's already working on it. There's something else too.'

'Go on.'

Alastair smiled. It transformed his face and Ellen made a note to remind him he should smile more often. If he did, he might have a better chance of finding a girlfriend.

'Want to know who drives a red Fiat Punto?' he said.

She didn't want to say, scared of jinxing it. On the other hand, it was too good a chance to pass up.

'Nathan Collier?'

The smile widened until Alastair was positively grinning.

'Got it in one, Ma'am.'

\* \* \*

Raj created a new folder on his hard drive: Chloe. Here, he stored everything he'd been able to find out about her, adding the new information to what he already knew from working the case.

Before being suspended for whacking Carl Jenkins.

So far, he hadn't broadened his search much beyond Jenkins. He knew Jenkins had killed her. All he had to do was prove it. And in doing so, prove everyone else wrong. The only problem was, so far he hadn't found anything.

Jenkins' online profile was unsurprising. Facebook and Twitter accounts, both of which he used frequently. His Facebook page was full of photos of lads' nights out, all the usual nonsense you'd expect to see from an average twenty-something bloke out to enjoy himself. The Twitter account seemed to be used mainly to follow – and comment on – Crystal Palace's performance in the League. A 3-1 victory against Liverpool last Saturday provoked much comment and excitement from Jenkins and those he followed.

Which was when Raj felt the first flicker of doubt. On Saturday afternoon, Crystal Palace played a match that, according to Jenkins himself on Twitter, was 'historic'. And yet, after the match, Jenkins chose to take Chloe out to a fancy restaurant instead of spending the night celebrating with his mates. Which backed up what he'd told Raj on Sunday morning. He was mad about the girl.

Further investigations led Raj to doubt himself even further. Carl Jenkins just didn't fit the profile of some sad, obsessed stalker. Judging by Twitter and Facebook, Jenkins was funny and popular. Lots of his Facebook friends were attractive young women who commented freely on his wall. If Jenkins was hiding some dark side of his personality, he was doing a damn good job of it.

Frustrated, Raj pushed his chair away from his computer and stood up. His shoulders hurt from too long hunched over a keyboard. He was finding it hard to concentrate. Thoughts darting all over the place, searching for that elusive something he'd been so certain he'd find with Carl Jenkins.

He checked his phone. Still no message from Aidan. He'd called twice, left messages both times, but nothing in return. He wondered if this was it. If he'd finally pushed Aidan so far, his lover had given up on him. He took a cigarette, lit it up and stood at the open window, smoking and trying not to think about Aidan. Thought about the case instead, wondered how they were coping without him and whether they'd made any progress.

He'd gone out earlier to stock up on cigarettes and milk. In the shop, he'd seen the latest edition of *The Evening Star* and picked it up with the rest of his supplies. He read the article on the walk back home. The fact that Martine Reynolds shared his view of Carl Jenkins offered no comfort. When he'd finished the cigarette, he picked up the newspaper and read the article again. Reynolds had been at yesterday's press conference. In the piece, she quoted Cox, saying the police were still exploring all avenues. *Police talk for 'we've got nothing better to tell you'.* Towards the end, Reynolds added a quote from Collier:

*Nathan Collier, Chloe's good friend and colleague, expressed his genuine grief and anger at the police's failure to protect the woman he described as 'a truly beautiful human being who deserved to be cherished. If she'd stayed away from Carl Jenkins, I believe she'd still be alive today.'*

Raj imagined Reynolds had a hard time getting that quote through the *Star's* in-house legal team.

*Deserved to be cherished.*

What sort of person spoke like that? Raj didn't know much about hetero relationships, but he imagined most enlightened twenty-first-century women wanted something a bit more substantial. Like sex, for starters. If someone ever told him they'd like to cherish him, he'd run a mile.

He remembered his early misgivings about Collier. Quite simply, the bloke was always there. The very first time Chloe had come in, complaining that someone had broken into her house, Nathan Collier was with her. And every time since, come to think of it.

Two ideas came to him simultaneously. The first: it was Nathan Collier who'd fed all of this nonsense to Reynolds. The second: there was something off about the relationship – or whatever it was – between Chloe Dunbar and Nathan Collier.

Throwing the newspaper aside, Raj sat back down at the computer and typed Nathan Collier's name into the search engine. Over 5,000,000 results came back. Easy enough to sift through them and find the Nathan Collier he was looking for. Lewisham estate agent, beneficiary of Lewisham Council's 2010 Entrepreneur of the Year award. On this page, a brief bio of Collier. Local boy, Thomas Tallis educated, living in the house he'd grown up in, vital member of the local Lewisham business community. A photo of Collier receiving his award: shiny face, shiny suit, shiny pleased-with-himself smile. Brief mention of the award ceremony in *The Evening Star*. Written by – surprise, surprise – award-winning muck-racker Martine Reynolds. Which explained the connection. Two local cronies cosying up to each other, mutually scratching each other's backs. A few more glowing pieces by Reynolds, one listing Collier as a key 'mover and shaker' in SE London.

Something about Collier's reaction on Monday morning had bothered Raj. At the time, he'd put it to one side, thinking he'd come back to it later. When events took over, he'd forgotten all about it. Until now.

He went back over it, tried to recall exactly what Collier had said and what it was that bothered him at the time. And then – *wham!* – there it was. So obvious he wondered what on earth could have possessed him to overlook the blindingly obvious until now.

He went back over everything Collier had said, that morning outside Chloe's house and later in the station as well, cross-checking everything he thought he knew. The more he went through it, the more it made sense.

There was only one person he really trusted, so he called her.

'Ellen, it's me. I need to talk to you. Any chance you could come over?'

'I'll be right there,' she said. 'Give me your address and put the kettle on.'

And that was it. No cold shoulder, no recriminations or snide comments about what a dick he'd been. Put the bloody kettle on. He hung up, smiling.

Twenty minutes later, the downstairs bell went. Raj pressed the button that released the main front door, opened the door to his apartment, lit a cigarette and waited.

# FIFTY-FOUR

Monica opened a bottle of Merlot, knowing it was a bad idea. She needed to steer clear of the *vino*. But given the circumstances, what the hell was she supposed to do? Christ. Being that close to him. The surge of longing she'd felt for him; it scared her.

So why was he being such a complete bastard? Last night he'd acted like he hated her. There was no reason for him to be like that.

They'd been so good together. Made for each other. He'd felt it too. She saw it in his eyes when he turned and saw her that very first time. Face changing, soft at first, then focused and determined when she played hard to get. Someone like that, you had to make them do a bit of running. All part of the game.

Wasn't her fault if he'd never seen it that way. All that bullshit he'd fed her at the time, about them getting too close too quickly. That wasn't him speaking. It was that bitch he'd been working with, putting words into his mouth, making him say things he didn't feel. Making him break Monica's heart.

She'd tried to get him to see it last night. If he'd only let his defences down, let himself relax long enough to feel it too. They were meant to be together. But he refused to listen.

It was why she threw her wine over him. To stop him ripping their past apart. It did the trick. At first. Until anger replaced the shock on his face. She thought he was going to hit her. He took a step towards her, face like thunder, and that old feeling of power surged through her. It was a turn-on, knowing she could provoke such a reaction. Knowing there was passion behind the thunder, as well as anger.

She wanted more of that passion. Memories of their time together swirled a whirlwind inside her head. Most of them good. The bad stuff was there too, of course, but she could avoid thinking about that. There were enough good times to focus on.

This was difficult. *He* was difficult. Maybe that was part of the attraction. She went upstairs. She was going to see him. Right now. Give him one last chance. If he refused, she'd make sure he regretted it for the rest of his life.

In the bedroom, she switched the light on and sat at the dressing table. She examined her face, wondering what he saw when he looked at her. Her hair was tied back. She released it, shaking it so it fell around her face and shoulders, remembering how he used to love running his hands through it. She thought of Ellen Kelly's short, straight bob and smirked.

Her skin was taut and blemish-free. No need for anything except a few strokes of blusher. Then black eyeliner, mascara and her favourite red lipstick. A dab of *Jo Malone* on her wrists, the nape of her neck, cleavage and she was ready. She stood up and took a look in the full-length mirror, liking what she saw. Tight jeans emphasised the length and slenderness of her thighs. A white shirt, tucked into the jeans, top buttons left open, revealing black bra and full breasts. No wonder Harry had it so bad.

Outside, the garden gate creaked open. A moment later, the doorbell rang. Harry. Little creep. Never gave her a moment's peace. She stayed still, thinking he'd go away, but he persisted. Pressing down on the bloody bell until she couldn't stick it any longer. She ran down the stairs, ready to give him a piece of her mind. It was all very well getting together every now and then, but surely even he wasn't so thick that he really believed this meant anything. She was so far out of his league it was laughable.

She pulled the door open, the tirade dying in her mouth when she realised it wasn't him. Instead, standing on her doorstep was a pretty young woman with dark skin, dark eyes and dark, shiny hair tied back in a neat ponytail.

Monica recognised the face but couldn't place it. Whoever this woman was, she'd been assigned to the 'insignificant' list in Monica's mind.

'DC Roberts,' the woman said.

Monica groaned. Couldn't help it. All fired up, ready for some serious action and this bloody cliché-talking nobody turns up wanting a cosy chat? Not bloody likely.

'I was on my way out,' Monica said. 'Whatever it is, you'll have to come back.'

The woman smiled. 'Not a problem. Why don't I come with you? We can speak on the way.'

'Not likely,' Monica said. 'The place I'm going, it's not suitable for a pretty little thing like you. You'd get eaten alive.'

When the woman blushed, Monica started to shut the door.

Instead of crawling back under whatever rock she'd come from, the stupid cow stuck her foot in the doorway, preventing the door from closing.

'In that case,' the woman said. 'I'd better come inside.'

And before Monica could stop her, she'd pushed the door open, was brushing past her and walking straight into Monica's sitting room.

\* \* \*

'Nathan Collier was Chloe's estate agent,' Raj said.

'So?' Ellen said.

'Isn't it obvious?' Raj said. 'As the estate agent, he had to have had keys to her house. Yes, she got the locks changed, but they worked in the same office. It would have been easy for him to get his hands on the new set and make a copy. All he had to do was sneak the keys from her bag when she wasn't looking.'

He was right. It had been staring them in the face all this time and they'd missed it.

'The morning he found Chloe,' Raj continued. 'He told me the front door was open, but he was lying. He used his key to let himself into the house.'

'How do you know he was lying?' Ellen asked.

'He said he pushed it and it just opened,' Raj said. 'It's not that sort of door. The spring is broken. I remember from an earlier visit. If the door's left unlocked, it swings wide open.'

'You think he killed her?'

'I can see how it played out,' Raj said. 'He gives Chloe a job and somewhere to live. Because he has the hots for her. But he's smart enough to realise a woman like Chloe wouldn't look twice at someone like him. Not unless he shakes things up a bit. So he starts scaring her. Or maybe that was never what it was about. Maybe he just wanted to be close to her. Whatever.

'And it works. For a while. She freaks out and because she's got no one else, she turns to good old Nathan. She starts relying on him more and more.'

'What about the interview with Martine Reynolds?' Ellen asked. 'What was that about?'

'Nathan and Martine are mates,' Raj said. 'Mutual appreciation society that goes back years. So when Chloe starts to get properly scared, Nathan steps in, says the police aren't doing their jobs right but he knows someone that will help.'

A lot of what Raj said made sense, but most of it was

circumstantial. Unless the video footage came through, there was nothing concrete they had on Nathan Collier.

'She mentioned a friend,' Raj said. 'I remember her saying something about meeting a friend for drinks. Can't remember her name but might be worth trying to track her down. Ask if Chloe ever spoke about Collier?'

'Chloe's face has been all over the news,' Ellen said. 'Surely this friend would come forward if she knew something?'

'Maybe she's away,' Raj said. 'I don't know. But we should try to find her, at least.'

By the time Ellen left Raj's apartment, it had grown dark outside. She decided to walk home, giving her a chance to clear her head. She walked up Lee Road, the houses on either side gradually becoming grander the closer she got to Blackheath village.

Nathan Collier. Lots of different parts of the investigation were coming together now. She took out her phone and called Abby. Got voicemail, left a message.

'Abby, Mark ran a tox report on Chloe. Results came back late this afternoon. Traces of Diazepam in her blood, just as we suspected. Have you checked Collier's medical records yet? We need to find out if he's been prescribed Diazepam anytime over the last few years.'

Abby was up to something. Earlier, Ellen had tried to speak to her when Abby had come back from seeing Carl Jenkins. Except as Ellen walked over to Abby's desk, Abby had slammed her laptop shut and walked off. If Ellen was a paranoid sort of person, she'd think Abby was trying to ignore her.

Whether she was or not, Ellen needed to speak to her. She was over the heath now, across Charlton Way, under the shadow of the high wall of Greenwich Park and round the corner onto Maze Hill. Nearly home. She put her phone away and covered the last stretch quickly. It was late and she didn't want to think about work any longer. Quality time with the children followed by food and a bottle of wine. There were worse ways to spend an evening.

# FIFTY-FIVE

Nathan's stomach hurt. Trousers too tight, digging into the soft flesh. He shouldn't have had that last bit of ice cream. Not on top of the chips. Mum's special chips, made the way she used to in her old-style deep-fat fryer. She loved cooking for her special boy.

He had *The Evening Star* in front of him. Read the story again, the tingle of excitement quickly replacing the sense of failure he always felt when dinner ended. Carl's face and that headline – did it for him each time he read it.

He stood up, a restless giddiness making it impossible to stay sitting down. At the very corners of his mind, there lurked some doubt. He pushed it away, refusing to think about that. What Carl had done was very wrong and when people did wrong things, there were consequences. That was Carl's problem, he'd never had to deal with the consequences before.

Not like Nathan. Consequences, confession, forgiveness. Nathan knew – forced himself to do it each week at confession – what consequences were. Knew that it wasn't enough to say sorry. You had to mean it, too. And wasn't that what he'd done? He'd confessed. Opened his heart to the Lord and begged forgiveness. And the Lord, in his merciful goodness, had granted that forgiveness.

All men are sinners.

Nathan knew that was true and accepted it, even though it was a difficult truth to live with. But that was infinitely better than living in ignorance the way a man like Carl did.

Of course, that didn't mean he should be vindictive. He'd thought about this. Even considered going around to Carl's house, offering the olive branch of friendship. Thought maybe if Carl saw that Nathan forgave him, it might help Carl forgive himself. But Carl wasn't ready for that...

And if he really thought about it, Nathan didn't think he was ready, either. Not yet. Needed a bit more time first. Time, prayer and patience. Rome wasn't built in a day and Nathan couldn't expect all those old feelings to disappear overnight.

In the sitting room, he switched the TV on, flicked through some channels, paused, briefly, at the menu for the adult channels.

'Lord grant me the strength to do the right thing.'

He closed his eyes, repeating the words out loud, blocking the images his foul body told him it needed, ignoring the tightness in his groin, the desperate longing that he tried so hard to control, but sometimes it got the better of him no matter what he did.

'God my Father, merciful God, Almighty Father, be with me now. Guide me to do the right thing.'

It was this place. The house so cramped and claustrophobic. Every room full of the memory of his mother. All their happy times together. This distraction was his mind's way of coping. Get away from the house and the images would disappear. It was no life, this. Coming home to an empty house, night after night after night.

He threw the remote down, grabbed the car keys and ran from the house. He didn't know where he was going but right now, anywhere was better than here.

* * *

Monica wasn't happy. Another row with Jim. Their last. She promised herself that. Enough was enough. She walked fast down the quiet street, mind racing back over the evening, giving herself over to the anger, letting it drive her, guide her, knowing the only way she'd be able to sleep tonight is if she acted on it.

He hadn't even let her into the house. Stood in the doorway and acted like he didn't want her there. Bastard.

She'd gone home but couldn't settle, so she was out walking the streets, looking for action. Rage made her reckless. When the first car pulled up, she approached the driver, ready to get in without giving it a second thought. It was only when she saw his face, something inside her recoiled and she drew back.

He didn't like it. Started shouting at her, calling her a cunt and other words like that. She turned and looked at him, willing him to get out, ready for anything. But he must have seen the rage in her face and decided against it. He pulled away from the kerb and drove off.

Jim would pay for the way he'd treated her. Him and her father both. Two lowlife bastards who'd done their best to ruin the only little slivers of happiness she'd ever known.

Another car drove down the street, slowed as it approached and pulled up alongside her. A grey Lexus. The window rolled down and the driver leaned across, eyes running up and down her body. She looked at his hands, resting on the steering wheel, remembered what they'd done to her the last time.

'You looking for something?' he asked.

She walked towards him, smiling, climbed into the car and strapped herself in. As he drove away, she reached into her bag and ran her thumb along the sharp edge of the knife she'd brought with her.

\* \* \*

Ellen woke with a start. She'd been dreaming, but the dream was gone by the time she opened her eyes. At first she thought one of the children must have woken her. She lay in bed, heart beating faster than it should do, listening for the pitter-patter of feet as one of them went to the toilet or ran down the corridor to her bedroom.

Instead of that, she heard the creak of a door being slowly opened. The sitting-room door. It had creaked like that for the longest time. She'd kept meaning to ask her father to take a look at it.

She sat bolt upright, panic rising as she reached for her phone. Was midway through calling it in when she paused. First, she needed to be sure. She slipped out of bed, looked around for something she could use as a weapon. A pair of crutches in the wardrobe, left over from the time – six years ago – when Vinny had broken his foot. She found one crutch hidden behind clothes she no longer wore, pulled it out and decided it was better than nothing.

In the corridor she paused, listening for sounds of someone moving around down there. Couldn't hear anything and was starting to think maybe she'd imagined it. Then she heard it again. The door creaking. And something else. A shuffling sound, like someone trying to move without being heard.

'Who's there?'

Her voice was too loud. Seemed to echo back at her. She swung around, checking both children's rooms. They couldn't wake up. If they did… In one hand she had the crutch. Her phone was in the other hand. She didn't think twice this time, lifted it to her ear and dialled the station's emergency line.

At the same time, she started moving, down the stairs and

into the hall, crutch held high, ready for the attack. Hall empty. She threw open the sitting-room door, pressed down on the light switch. Blinded by the sudden brightness, she faltered. Felt something behind her, turned, but it was too late. No one there.

The back door slammed shut.

She moved into the kitchen, phone still pressed to her ear, giving her name and warrant number to the duty sergeant. The kitchen was empty. Nothing left of the intruder except a vague, familiar smell that she recognised but couldn't place.

She scanned the room, searching for any sign that he was still here, but found nothing. She checked the back door. It wasn't locked and she was certain she'd locked it before going to bed. She always did. The key wasn't in the door, either. When she looked for it, she saw it lying on the floor nearby.

As she locked the door, a sudden thought struck her. She swung around, scanning the kitchen, looking carefully at all the worktops. Only started breathing again when she was certain there was no cup of tea or flower anywhere to be seen.

# FIFTY-SIX

Monica waited until after the rush hour before getting on the road. As a result, the drive to Whitstable passed quickly, despite the rain that had been falling ever since she woke up. Driving into the town at midday exactly, she caught the main news on the radio. The body of a man had been found in his car early this morning. She turned up the volume and listened.

*'The man has been identified as German banker Wilhelm Bretz. Mr Bretz's body was discovered early this morning. He had been stabbed several times and a police spokesman said his body had been 'mutilated' although he refused to give any further details. Mr Bretz is survived by his wife, Hilde, and their two young children.'*

Monica turned into her father's road and switched the radio off. Wilhelm Bretz. Always good to put a name to a face.

Even a dead one.

Out of the car, she ran through the rain towards the house. She opened the front door, using the key she'd taken the last time she was here. Making sure not to wipe her feet on the mat, she stepped inside the house that had once been her home.

She thought she'd have the place to herself. Didn't like it one bit when she heard someone moving around in the kitchen. She'd watched him leave ten minutes ago. Out for his daily constitutional, which always took exactly twenty-five minutes. More than enough time to get what she wanted and get the hell out of there. Except now it seemed someone else had got here first.

A little black dog ran into the hallway, tail wagging as it approached her feet and started sniffing her shoes. She took a step back, repulsed. For a moment she wondered if she'd somehow stepped inside the wrong house. The Adam she remembered would never tolerate a dog. Something smelly and dirty and *real* that might mess up the perfect order and cleanliness of his house? No way.

She lifted her foot, about to kick the beast, when someone screamed at her to stop. A small, skinny woman was standing at the kitchen door, screaming like some sort of witch.

'Touch the dog and you'll be sorry.'

'Who the hell are you?' Monica asked.

'Shouldn't I be asking you that?' the woman said. 'Except I already know the answer to that. Recognise you from the photos. Monica, isn't it?'

'And you are…?'

The answer was obvious, of course. The very fact of it made her rethink the image she had of her father as a pathetic loser. Not that this woman was anything special. Nondescript was about the kindest thing you could say about her. Apart from the nose, of course. A massive protrusion from a face that was otherwise excruciatingly ordinary.

'Bel,' the woman said, not moving or showing any sign of friendliness.

Bitch.

'Adam's girlfriend. Monica.' The way she said Monica's name, like it was something dirty. 'I've heard all about you. Nothing good, in case you're wondering. Adam's not here. You'll have to come back another time.'

'I can wait,' Monica said.

'I don't think so,' Bel said. 'How did you get in, anyway? We got the locks changed a while back. No way you could have a key.'

Monica smiled. 'Unless Adam gave me one, of course.'

Bel frowned. 'The spare? I've been looking for that. Bastard told me he'd lost it.'

Monica walked further into the hall, letting the front door glide gently closed. Bel stood her ground, even when Monica got right up close.

'So he hasn't told you?' Monica said.

'Told me what?'

She was several inches shorter than Monica and scrawny with it. But there was a hardness about her that made Monica think twice about starting anything physical. She never did that unless she was certain of the outcome.

'About my little visits.'

Monica dangled the key under that honking great nose.

'Daddy gave me this last week,' she said. Not strictly true, but no need to share that with Bel. What sort of stupid name was that, anyway?

'Gave it or you took it?' Bel said. 'We leave all the keys hanging on the rack over there,' she nodded to the rack Monica had lifted the key from during her last visit. 'Easy enough to take it without Adam noticing.'

'His girlfriend.' Monica let the word hang in the air between them. Hoping her face told Bel just what she thought of that set-up.

'Yeah, that's right. Been with him these past few years, if you must know. Not easy, either. But you'd know that. He can be a bit of a handful, your old man. Suppose that's why you left?'

'Something like that,' Monica said. She stepped away from the smaller woman, bored now. 'All right if I go upstairs?'

Bel ran across, stood at the bottom of the stairs, arms stretched out either side.

'Don't even think about it. I want you to leave. Now. Or else I call the police.'

'Like they'll care,' Monica said. 'This is my house.'

'Not for much longer.'

That caught her short.

'What do you mean?'

'Me and your dad,' Bel said. 'We're getting married. Tying the knot as soon as we sort out all the paperwork. Soon as we're married, he's going to sign everything over to me. And there's not a single thing you can do about it.'

'I don't believe you.'

Bel shrugged. 'Like I care. Now, out. Three seconds or I'm calling the pigs.'

Monica took a step closer, changed her mind.

'Fuck you.'

She turned and left. Quickly, before she did something stupid.

Back at the car, Monica threw the bag onto the passenger seat and climbed in. It was the final betrayal. Her mother, Jim, Adam. She wasn't having it. That house and everything in it belonged to her.

She wouldn't let him do this.

She adjusted the rear-view mirror until it was positioned so she could see her face. Pupils dilated, cheeks flushed red, eyes glowing bright. She'd never looked as good as she looked right now.

Hate suited her.

# FIFTY-SEVEN

'You can't cancel a session just like that.'

'I'm sorry,' Ellen said. 'The situation's unavoidable, I'm afraid.'

'You rearranged Monday's meeting to today,' the woman on the other end of the phone said. 'You need to keep the appointment. It's one of Dr O'Keefe's rules. Can't you come in later? Dr O'Keefe has a free slot at midday.'

'I don't think that will be possible,' Ellen said. 'But I'll book another session as soon as I can.'

'Your next appointment will be next Monday as normal,' the woman said. 'If you miss that one, Dr O'Keefe may well refuse to continue with you.'

Resisting the urge to flick her middle finger at the phone, Ellen apologised – again – and ended the call. Cancelling one of her counselling sessions made her feel like a naughty schoolgirl. Which was ridiculous. She was a grown woman, after all, and had every right to cancel a session if she didn't feel like attending.

She hadn't slept.

Her call had triggered a blue light response. Two cars roared down Annandale Road, sirens wailing, lights flashing. Both children woke and it took an age to settle them again. Four uniforms up and down the street and across gardens, torches scanning the area. The officer in charge, Paul Keane, was someone she knew from around the station. Decent enough bloke, but she could see the doubt creeping across his face when the uniforms reported back. No intruder sighted.

Fresh footprints on the soft ground at the back of the house indicated that maybe she hadn't imagined the whole thing.

'A burglar,' Keane concluded. 'You need to turn your intruder alarm on at nights, Ma'am.'

'It doesn't work,' she'd replied. 'Keeps going off for no reason.'

'Get it fixed,' Keane said. 'In the meantime, count yourself lucky you woke up and caught the bastard before he stole anything.'

But there was something missing.

Last night, she'd checked all the obvious things: computers, TV, the jewellery she kept in the little safe in her bedroom. Who would think to check the fridge door? And who in their right mind would believe her?

She couldn't work out where the line was between suspicion

and paranoia. The latest school newsletter had disappeared. Big deal. In a house with two young children, things went missing all the time. She'd asked Pat and Eilish this morning when she'd first noticed. They'd both denied taking it. Pat even tried to convince her the newsletter had been missing for days. Maybe he was right. Most likely he was. Which got her thinking, what if last night wasn't the first time?

And when she started thinking like that, she knew she had to stop. Knew that going down that path wouldn't lead her to a good place. So why did she keep trying to get there? Because her head was all messed up and the last thing – the very last thing in the world – that she wanted or needed was to have to sit and talk all this through with someone younger and infinitely wiser. Easier by far to cancel the appointment and live with the guilt instead.

She was sitting in her car outside the school, listening to the drumbeat of rain falling on the roof. Late getting the children ready this morning, now late for work. Guilt piled on guilt in the best Catholic tradition. Her mother would be so proud.

\* \* \*

*Foo Fighters on the iPod. Music blasting through the headphones, Dave Grohl's voice, all that energy and intensity. Volume up high. The Pretender. I'm the enemy. The song dips in places, going slow and low, then Grohl cranks it up again – louder, faster – a rhythm beating through my body. And then it ends. I play it again from the beginning.*

*Half a roach on the ashtray by the bed. I light it up and let the music rip my head off as the skunk works its way through me.*

*Still buzzing. Haven't slept yet. Headphones on, steady supply of blow and I'm flying, man. Bag over in the corner. Last night's booty. Great word. I'm laughing now. Mind moved on from last night to Nicki Minaj. Go figure. Booty. That's what did it.*

*Laughing so bad I have to sit up or I'll get sick. Can't breathe. Face wet with tears. Take another pull on the roach, anyway. Last thing I need but what the fuck. I deserve it. Pulled a blinder last night.*

*Running down the street, holding onto the bag like I'm carrying the crown fucking jewels. And before I know it, I'm down on the Trafalgar Road, walking west. And even at this time of night, there are people out and about, students walking in groups, drink making them loud. I pass a group of girls. The sort I normally try to avoid, scared of all that hair and confidence. This time, I look them straight in the eye and when one of them – blonde and tanned and fucking lovely – smiles, I grin right back at her. And for a moment, I feel like I'm really someone.*

*The mood's with me the whole way home so I'm still hyped when I get inside. Have a few beers but that doesn't do much to calm me down. I know what I need, but it's late and doesn't seem right, somehow. Plenty of time for that later.*

*So that's how I've ended up like this. Mind drifting here, there, everywhere. Headphones on because that's the only way I can block out the other sounds, the ones from my life before this.*

*I'm tired now. Coming down a bit. Eyes getting heavy. Not sure I* want to sleep but it's coming at me like a juggernaut, rolling in and over, until I've disappeared altogether.

And when it comes, I can't tell you if it's a dream or a memory. All I know is that the music's stopped. And the Meat is back. Ramming his brand of fucking shite around inside my head. I'm trying to shut him out but the only way I can do that is if I switch the iPod back on. But my arms won't move. Body stuck to the bed, like a weight's on top of me. Like I'm drowning.

I was six. I know that because it was three days after my sixth birthday. Wanted a party but the old bastard wouldn't hear of it. Took the strap to me instead. Then three days later, he must have felt bad about that.

We were by the sea back then. Beach a ten-minute walk from the house. My mother didn't want us to go. Six years old and I could sense her anxiety. I was too excited to care about that.

He held my hand the whole way there. I don't think I'd ever felt so special. So grown up. Hot summer's day. Waves of heat shimmering along the silver-grey stones on the beach. Water icy cold when we got over the stones onto the sandy bit. So quiet. No one else about. Like he was a king and this was our own private beach.

He'd brought a few cans. Course he had. I didn't mind, though. He was in a good mood and I knew that was the beer working. Drink making him happy.

We had a net and were fishing for the little crabs that lived in amongst the rocks at the edge of the water. We could see a crab, a bit further out, too far for me to reach. He took my net, leaned out and *fell, crashing into the water with an almighty splash. The shock of it – his yell as he realised he'd lost his balance, the sudden splatter of cold water on my face. I couldn't help it. Felt the laughter bubbling up and it burst out of me. The more I tried to stop, the more I laughed. He got up and when I realised he was okay, I laughed again, relief this time. Then I saw the expression on his face and knew that laughing was the very last thing I should have done.*

*Christ!*

*I want it to stop. Know what's coming. I try again to move my arms but I know it's pointless. I'm right back there now, he's grabbed me by the neck and he's dragging me into the water. I'm kicking and crying and screaming, water everywhere, splashing all around us. And he's shoving me forward. Water fills my mouth, my lungs, can't breathe, can't scream for help. His hand on my neck, pushing me down. And I know. Right there and then I know. I'm going to die.*

# FIFTY-EIGHT

At the café, Ellen stopped under the shelter of the porch and peered through the glass door. Sean was there already. Sitting at a table near the back. He had his back to her and didn't turn around until she ordered her coffee at the counter.

He smiled when he saw her and she smiled back, ridiculously pleased to see him. She'd nearly cancelled this too. Thought she mightn't be able to face the inevitable questions about Jim. Now she was here, she knew how stupid she'd been to even consider it.

'I'm amazed you could make it,' he said. 'You're usually so busy.'

'Couldn't wait to get away,' Ellen said. 'Thanks. This place is lovely, by the way. Don't think I've been here before.'

He'd called earlier and suggested lunch at You Don't Bring

Me Flowers, a flower shop and café beside Hither Green station. He was working on a house in the area. So close to Lewisham it seemed foolish not to make the effort. She hadn't told him about the break-in and didn't intend to. She'd have to tell her parents at some point because the children wouldn't be able to keep it quiet. Until that happened, she didn't want to talk about it.

The waitress brought Ellen's coffee, along with a sandwich for Sean.

'Goat's cheese and onion marmalade,' he said. 'Delicious. You not eating?'

Ellen shook her head. 'Coffee's all I feel like.'

Sean put his sandwich down. 'What's up?'

The loss of appetite was the first thing that always happened. The mere thought of food made her want to throw up. After that, the shadows would start closing in. Over the years, she'd developed different strategies for dealing with them. Mostly, she could manage the dark moods she refused to call depression. Right now, though, she was so knackered she didn't have the energy.

'I miss you, El. Don't see enough of you anymore.'

Inside her head, a flicker of light. She managed a smile. 'You know what?' she said. 'That sandwich looks bloody good. Maybe I'll have one as well.'

While they ate, they chatted about inconsequential things. Midway through his sandwich, he brought up the one subject she'd been dreading.

'How's Jim?'

'Fine,' Ellen said. 'Well, you know.'

'Do I?'

'I like him,' she said. 'I just want to take things slow. Nothing wrong with that, is there?'

'Nothing wrong except it's not true,' Sean said. 'Something's happened. One minute you're all loved up and he's coming over for lunch, the next, anytime anyone asks about him, you do your best to change the subject. I'm not the only one who's noticed it, either. Mum and Dad are worried too. Mum called last night. Asked me to speak to you. She thinks you're working too hard and you're doing that to avoid dealing with whatever's going on in your personal life.'

Ellen looked down at her plate so he wouldn't see her face.

'That's why you called,' she said. 'Because Mum told you to.'

'I called because I wanted to see you,' he said. 'Jesus, Ellen.'

'Jesus yourself,' she muttered.

'You sound just like Pat when you do that,' Sean said.

She kicked his ankle, making him yelp. He kicked her back. Harder.

They smiled at each other. For a moment, everything felt as it should. Until Sean had to ruin the moment by talking about Jim again.

'Jim's called too,' Sean said. 'Wanted to know how you were doing.'

'I hope you told him it's none of his business,' Ellen said.

'I asked him what had happened,' Sean said. 'He said I'd have to ask you that. Said it wasn't his place to tell me about it.'

'He doesn't seem to think it's his place to talk about anything,' Ellen said. 'Anyway, I don't want to talk about it, okay? Jesus, Sean. I've only been seeing him a few months and the whole family has a bloody conference about us the moment things ease up a bit? Give me a break, would you? Tell me about next weekend instead. Make me jealous. Come on.'

Sean relented and started describing the hotel he and Terry would be staying in for their weekend mini-break to Sitges on Spain's east coast. While Sean spoke, Ellen started to relax, enjoying the simple pleasure of hearing him speak and watching the different expressions that shimmered across his face.

When they left the café, the rain had stopped and Sean walked Ellen back to her car.

'Tell the kids I said hello,' he said. 'I'll miss seeing them this weekend.'

'They'll miss you too,' Ellen said. 'Pat's been playing up a bit recently. I'm hoping it's just a phase.'

'I'm sure it is,' Sean said. 'He's a good lad. I'll catch up with him next week. Take him out somewhere. See if I can work out what's going on.'

'Maybe you'll have more luck than I've had,' Ellen said.

'You're a good mother, El. Whatever's going on with Pat, he'll talk to you eventually. He always does.'

At her car, Sean leaned forward and kissed her cheek. Too

quickly he let her go. She watched as he walked to the end of the street, crossed the road, turned the corner and disappeared out of sight.

She remembered a day in the park when they were both kids. They'd had a row and he'd run off. She ran after him, trying to catch him and make amends, but he was too fast. She couldn't remember what the fight was about, or even which park they were in. All she had was the memory of running after him, down a grassy hill. His back in front of her, the space between them gradually increasing as he got further and further away from her.

Sometime later, she'd promised him she'd never do anything to upset him ever again as long as she lived. Like most childish promises, it wasn't one she kept. Standing in Hither Green that afternoon, she wished with all her heart that she had.

# FIFTY-NINE

'Why didn't you tell me?'

'Didn't want to worry you,' Adam said. 'Did I?'

'Well, I'm worried now,' Bel said. 'And you still haven't explained how she got the bloody key.'

The memories of that afternoon were all muddled up in his mind. When he tried to put them into some sort of order, it was too difficult.

'It's not easy for me,' he said. 'When I think about Annie and Monica, it makes my head go funny.'

They were standing in the kitchen, facing each other. He wanted to push past her, get to the sink and wash his hands, clean them until his head cleared and he could think straight. He stuffed his hands into his trouser pockets, curled them into fists and tried not to let his mind think about the germs he must have picked up when he was out. Bel was still talking, jabber, jabber, jabber. She had a high-pitched voice that he found hard to take at times. He squeezed his fists tighter, tried to focus on what she was saying.

'You need to forget about them,' Bel said. 'They left you, Adam. Get over it. I'm here now. You don't need anyone else. I told her, you know. Told her we were getting married.'

'Jesus, Bel, what you have to go and do that for?'

Wrong thing to say. She crossed the space between them, coming so close he could feel her breath on his face when she spoke. Faint smell of toothpaste and coffee.

'Because I knew you'd never get around to telling her,' Bel said. 'What's wrong, Adam?' She moved closer, her groin pushing against his. She took his hand, slipped it inside the top of her blouse.

'I thought it was what you wanted.' She leaned into him. 'It is what you want, isn't it?'

He felt the lacy fabric of her bra and squeezed hard.

She threw her head back, so she was gazing up at him, face flushed, eyes bright. Her pupils big and dark, the way they always went when she was in the mood. The top of her blouse was open, giving him a clear view of her small round breasts.

*Pervert.*

He pulled his hand away, the memory of his daughter's voice ruining it.

'Adam?'

Bel, lovely Bel. He'd already lost so much. Couldn't bear to lose her as well. She was all he had left.

He trailed his finger down her neck and onto the smooth, soft skin outside her bra. He forced himself to do it slowly, knowing how much she hated it when he rushed things.

'Let's do it,' he said. 'I'll speak to the registrar tomorrow. First thing.'

He pushed the bra to one side, giving his hand free rein with her tit. He rubbed his thumb across her big brown nipple, feeling it harden. She moved in closer, hot breath against his ear.

Christ, she was a good girl.

'Promise?' she said.

She grabbed his hand, pushed it down her stomach until his fingers were touching the lining of her lace panties.

'Promise.'

He'd missed her. Missed this, more to the point. Six days every month he had to go without. He'd tried talking to her about it. Even offered to pay for the operation. She took it the wrong way, though, got the hump and wouldn't let him touch her for days after that. He'd been too scared to raise the subject again but once they were married, maybe she'd reconsider.

She pushed his hand down further and he groaned. She said something else about the house and his will, but her voice was lost in the rush of blood roaring through his head. If she wanted the house after he was gone, she could bloody have it. She did things for him that no other woman ever had. Things he'd never thought possible after the accident. He'd get her as many houses as she wanted if that's what it took to make her carry on doing these things for him.

* * *

The board in the incident room was filling up. Names added as witnesses came forward and more suspects were identified. Ellen was looking at Nathan Collier's name when Abby came into the room.

'Do we know anything about a woman Chloe was friendly with?' Ellen said.

'Why?' Abby asked. 'Is she important?'

'I don't know,' Ellen said. 'I spoke to Raj yesterday, he mentioned it.'

'What about her mum?' Abby said. 'She might know who Chloe was friends with. Want me to ask her?'

'Good idea,' Ellen said. 'How's she doing, anyway?'

'How do you think?' Abby said. 'She's in bits. Keeps asking when Chloe's body will be released so she can organise the funeral properly. How did you get on with Collier earlier?'

First thing this morning, Ellen had paid Nathan Collier a visit. She'd wanted to follow up the information Raj gave her.

'He swears he doesn't have a set of keys to Chloe's place,' Ellen said. 'Says the front door was on the latch and that's how he was able to get in. I've checked the door myself. Raj is right about the hinge. It's broken. But it's also possible Collier was telling the truth about the latch.'

'You don't believe him, though?'

'Not for a second,' Ellen said. 'I'm just waiting for Alastair to confirm one more thing. As soon as we've got that, we'll be taking Collier in.'

'I need to speak to you about something,' Abby said. 'Is this a good time or…?'

'Now is fine,' Ellen said. 'How'd it go with Jenkins, by the way?'

'Odd,' Abby said. 'He didn't seem to care about the piece in the paper. More concerned with telling me what he thought of his ex-boss. Didn't tell me anything we don't already know. Nathan Collier had the hots for Chloe but she wasn't interested. Then again, he's hardly likely to say anything else, is he?'

The office door burst open, making both women jump.

'Ellen!' Alastair came out, looking jubilant. 'Just been on the phone to Rui. He's managed to get a partial registration from the CCTV image. I've already cross-checked it against Collier's car. It's a match.'

Seconds earlier, she'd felt her energy levels dwindling. The sudden breakthrough was just the hit she needed.

'Let's go,' she said. 'Across to the lab first, take a look at what Rui's got for us. Alastair, you come with me. Abby, go see the boss, tell her what we've got. Check she's happy for us to bring Collier in.'

Abby nodded and Ellen followed Alastair, already heading down the corridor to the lift at the end.

As the lift doors swung open, Ellen remembered something. She turned back.

'Abby!'

'Yeah?'

'You said you wanted to talk to me,' Ellen said. 'What was it?'

'It can wait,' Abby said.

In the lift, Alastair pressed the button for the ground floor, the doors closed and the lift started moving. Ellen watched the numbers on the digital display counting down to the ground floor. The breakthrough they'd been waiting for. All going well, Nathan Collier would be charged by the end of the day.

# SIXTY

This wasn't happening. A week ago, his life had been as good as it had ever been. The Chloe effect. Secretly, that's what he called it. She seemed to add magic wherever she went. Business booming since she'd come on board. Doing so well he'd been looking to open a new office in Downham. The connection between them had felt so real. And then she'd opened her legs for Carl Jenkins and all of it was ruined. He would have forgiven her. She wouldn't even have had to ask. But now, before he had a chance to make things right, she was gone.

They'd turned up at the office. Told him they were arresting him. He'd tried to run. Stupid, stupid. A fat bastard like him, he didn't stand a chance. They were on him in seconds, stronger than they looked. Got his hands behind his back, cuffed him and here he was.

How much longer?

They did it to freak you out. So the important thing was not to get freaked out. Stay calm. He tried to think what they could have on him. Nothing. They couldn't have anything because, if they had, they'd have arrested him before today.

*Arresting you for the murder of Chloe Dunbar.*

Murder.

Fear clawed his insides, made it difficult to breathe. Chest so tight he thought maybe this was a heart attack. Mind full of Chloe. Standing in the doorway, lit up from the sun, blonde hair like a halo. Her smile. The way it made him feel when she smiled at him, like he was the most important person in the entire world. The laundry-fresh smell of her underwear. Opening the drawer and lifting things out, pressing his face into them, the gentle sound of her breathing while she slept in the bed just inches from where he stood. Moving across the room to watch her, so close he could reach out, touch the soft skin on her face. Not daring to do anything else in case she woke up.

Diazepam. Prescribed in the weeks after Mum passed away. Easy enough to crush into tiny pieces that he could slip into the water filter she drank from every night before going to bed. Worked like a dream. It was difficult not to tell anyone what he'd done. Not to show people just how clever Titty Collier could be when he put his mind to it.

The Diazepam was the one thing he'd omitted from the

confession box. God knew he was sorry and that was enough for Nathan. No point involving poor Father John in all of this. It wouldn't be fair on him. At the time, he'd felt guilty about that. Now, he was glad. Meant he knew for sure there was no way Father John could have told the police. He'd had the foresight to empty the filter that morning. Which meant, apart from God, there was no chance anyone else could possibly know what he'd done.

He tried to focus on that, but he couldn't. Mind kept wandering back over the last six months. Always coming back to Monday morning. The smell of it. The mess she'd made – did that happen before or after you died? – so disgusting it didn't seem like it was his Chloe. He'd gone to her anyway, held her and kissed that beautiful, ruined face. Blood on his hands afterwards. Warm, sticky blood. Retching into the sink as he tried to wash it off. Watching the water turn red, still not believing it.

He couldn't stand this. Brain too full of it all, as if the weight of it was pressing down on him. He stood up, pushed his chair back, breathing deeply, unable to get in as much air as he needed. Staggered over to the door, black shadows closing in on either side, reducing his vision to two single pinpoints of light. Somewhere, deep inside his mind, he knew what was happening. His own fault. He'd stopped the medication a few weeks ago. Thought he didn't need it any longer. He needed it now. Thought he might die without it.

He threw himself against the door, tried to scream, but only a wheezy whistle came out. He was dying. Heart attack, stroke, something terrible happening and no one here to help him. He fell to the ground, hands clawing at the collar of his shirt, ripping it open. Cold air on his chest. Cooled him down but still couldn't breathe.

Pin pricks of light disappeared.

# SIXTY-ONE

They had arrested Nathan Collier, but Ger wouldn't let Ellen sit in on the interview. Ellen's ex was a suspect in the same case. If Ellen was involved in the interview, Collier's lawyer would have a field day. Ellen knew it was the right decision, but that didn't mean she had to be happy about it.

She left the station in a bad mood that didn't improve on the walk from Lewisham to Greenwich. The children were at her parents. She was due there for her tea. Which gave her an hour to get some clothes in the washing machine and do a general tidy-up beforehand.

A man was standing outside her house. For a brief moment she thought it was Jim. She stumbled on a crack in the pavement. By the time she'd steadied herself, she'd realised it wasn't him.

This man was shorter and wider. His dark hair was starting to recede and when he walked towards her, it was with an awkward shuffling movement that was nothing like the elegant way Jim moved his body.

'I rang the doorbell but there was no one there,' he said. 'I didn't know what else to do, so I waited. I need to talk to you.'

She didn't have the time or the energy for this. But he looked so vulnerable, shuffling from foot to foot, avoiding eye contact while he waited for her to say something. No time, no energy and – damn it all – not the heart to send him away.

'Would you like to come in for a coffee?' she asked.

'Okay,' Ray O'Dwyer said. 'Why not?'

She'd only met Jim's brother a handful of times. Shy and socially awkward, he wasn't easy company, although she found his vulnerability endearing. Like a little boy who needed taking care of. A boy in a man's big, bulky body, Ellen thought as she watched him settle awkwardly on one of the stools by the island in the centre of her kitchen.

'We can go into the sitting room if you like,' she said. 'Those stools are bloody uncomfortable.'

'I'm fine here,' Ray said. 'Do you have any biscuits to go with the coffee? I get a bit hyper if I don't have something to soak it up.'

'Sugar doesn't make you more hyper?' Ellen asked.

Ray blushed. 'Maybe. I think I just like the way a biscuit takes away the bitter taste, you know?'

Her phone rang. Abby. Excusing herself, Ellen went into the

garden so she could talk without being overheard.

'What's happening?' she asked.

'Collier's been taken to hospital,' Abby said. 'He was in a cell, waiting for counsel to show. Duty officer heard him banging around, went in and found Collier unconscious.'

'Any idea what it is?'

'Not yet,' Abby said. 'But that's not why I'm calling. I wondered if I could call around for a quick chat?'

'Not right now,' Ellen said. 'Maybe later. I'll call once I know what I'm doing.'

When she hung up, she spent a pointless moment trying to second guess what Abby wanted to talk to her about. She gave up quickly enough and went back inside. The kitchen was empty.

'Ray?'

A shuffling sound as the door that separated the kitchen from the sitting room opened and there he was.

'I was looking at your music collection,' he said. 'You don't mind, do you?'

She did, but decided not to tell him that. Instead, she finished making the coffee and placed the cafetière on the granite worktop alongside two mugs and a packet of biscuits. She watched Ray open the biscuits uninvited and help himself.

He took a large bite of biscuit and started to speak. The mouthful of biscuit made it difficult to understand what he was saying.

'Why won't you speak to him?' Ray asked. 'He's really stressed out and worried. I know how much he likes you, Ellen. What's happened to make you suddenly start ignoring him?'

This was a mistake. She should never have let him into the house. And now he was here, she had no idea how to get him out again without upsetting him further.

'It's complicated,' she said, churning out the same old nonsense she'd fed Sean earlier. '*I'm* complicated, Ray. The truth is, I like to be in control. Things with Jim, they took a turn for the worse and it made me feel like I was losing that control. When that happens, I shut down. I can't help it. I'm sorry. It's not Jim's fault. Or maybe it is. I don't know.'

She stopped speaking, embarrassed at having revealed so much of herself. This was the problem, of course. Once the control was gone, anything could happen. Here she was, babbling like an idiot to some bloke who didn't give a damn one way or another about what went on inside her head.

Then she realised he was smiling. The smile sat oddly on his face, like it was something he wasn't used to doing. It was a nice smile, nonetheless.

'I'd love to know what that's like,' he said.

'What do you mean?'

'Feeling in control,' he said. 'My whole life, I don't think I've ever felt in control of anything.'

'What about with your music?' Ellen asked. She knew Ray was a talented pianist. She had a vague memory of hearing him play once, years ago, and being touched by the skill and passion of his performance.

'No,' he said. 'In fact, that's almost the opposite of control. Oh, when I'm practising or learning something new there's an element of control, I suppose. But when I'm playing a piece, playing it properly, not just learning it, something happens. My fingers move and play all the right notes but it's almost as if it's someone else doing it, not me. It's difficult to explain.'

'You mean the music controls you, not the other way around?' Ellen asked, intrigued by the idea.

This time the smile was less awkward. 'Yes, that's exactly what it's like.'

'Well I don't have that,' Ellen said. 'You're lucky.'

'Isn't it exhausting?' Ray asked. 'Having to be in control the whole time?'

'I don't know any other way to be,' Ellen said. 'Anyway, you're not here to talk about me, are you?'

If they carried on like this, the next thing she knew she'd be sharing stories of her early life and the death of her baby sister. Telling him how that single event triggered a lifetime of insecurity that she was only able to overcome through obsessively trying to put order on a world that rarely made sense. She might tell him that order and control were her protection, her way of making sure bad things didn't happen to those she cared most about. And if she started on that, she'd probably end up telling him that when someone breaks through all those carefully constructed walls of order and kills her husband, then she was capable of things even she – in her darkest moments – didn't care to dwell on. Because then she'd have to tell him the one thing she'd swore she'd never tell anyone: that the moment she pulled the trigger and blew Billy Dunston's head off his body, right at that moment she had never felt more in control of anything in her entire life.

'Will you call him?' Ray asked. 'Just talk to him, see if you can find a way through this. He really likes you and you should at least speak to him. Please?'

She wanted to say no. To tell him that until she'd worked out how she felt about it all, it was better – for her, the kids, everyone – that she kept well away from his brother. Instead, when she opened her mouth to say just that, she found herself reaching out for Ray's hand instead and squeezing it tight.

'I'll speak to Jim,' she said. 'Of course I will.'

# SIXTY-TWO

A panic attack. He could have told them that. When he opened his eyes, a middle-aged nurse was kneeling beside him, checking his pulse.

'I'm Jackie,' she said. 'Don't try to move, Nathan. We've called an ambulance. It'll be here in a few minutes.'

She had a kind face and a nice voice. He asked her to stay with him until the ambulance came. He wanted her to come with him to the hospital too, but she said she couldn't do that.

'But you don't need to worry,' she said. 'You're in good hands now.'

He had to be handcuffed to a policeman. In the ambulance and at the hospital. By the time they'd reached the hospital, he was hot and sweaty. Body giving off the sour odour he'd grown used to. When the doctor examined him, the cuffs came off but the man stayed in the room with them. Watching Nathan the whole time. Nathan could see the disgust in the man's face when he took off his top so the doctor could listen to his heart.

'I haven't done anything wrong.' He said this to the doctor, thinking maybe the doctor would help. But the doctor didn't seem to care about that. Wanted to know about his 'history' instead. Had he ever had a panic attack before (yes), when did they start (after my mother died), was he on any medication (yes).

He thought they'd keep him overnight, at least. Told the doctor if he was taken back to the station the same thing would happen again. The doctor said that wasn't his problem and told Nathan to take the medication he'd prescribed. Said it would help him sleep.

The tablet sat on the green plastic tray alongside his dinner. Plastic food on a plastic plate. Some sort of meat in a thin, brown sauce. The smell of it, synthetic and salty, mingled in the air with the bleachy smell of the room and the sweaty smell from his armpits and the folds of flesh across his middle.

He ate quickly, shovelling it into him, barely bothering to chew before swallowing the chunks of meat and morsels of artificial mash. It gave no comfort and was gone too quickly. When he'd finished, he swallowed the small pink tablet, lay back on the hard bed and waited.

* * *

Something was wrong. Ellen was in the sitting room. Sitting at the small table in the alcove, going through e-mails on her laptop. Tidying up loose ends before tea at her mother's house. She stopped typing and turned around in the chair, scanning the room slowly.

What was it?

Along one wall, Vinny's extensive collection of CDs, a handful of Ellen's mixed in amongst them. The TV in the corner, curtains still open, even though it had got dark at some point. She stood up to close them, not liking how exposed she felt with them open like that. Midway across the room, just past the fireplace, it hit her.

The mantelpiece. A series of framed photos of her family: the children, her parents, Sean and Terry. And a gap where the photo of Vinny should be.

She looked around, checking to see if it could have fallen, somehow. Knowing that wasn't what had happened but looking for it anyway. When she couldn't find it, she ran up to her bedroom. The photo of him she kept beside her bed was still there. Of course it was. Where else would it be?

She checked the children's rooms, trying to see if anything was missing. They had so much crap it was difficult to tell, but she couldn't see anything out of place. Downstairs, she ran through the CD collection, checking the ones that meant the most to her.

All there. She tried to think when was the last time she'd seen that photo. She'd have noticed straightaway if it was gone. Wouldn't she? Maybe not.

Ray. He was the last person in this room. No reason for him to take it. And she couldn't remember seeing him trying to conceal anything when he'd come back into the kitchen. Maybe he'd hidden it. She started looking for it – again – when she realised how pointless it was. The photo was gone. Only two people could have taken it. Ray O'Dwyer or whoever was in her house last night. It crossed her mind – briefly – that Ray and her intruder could potentially be the same person.

Paranoia. She didn't know what was real and what wasn't. This was what Chloe's life had been like. Weeks of it. Not knowing what to believe and not being believed when she tried to tell people what was happening. No wonder she turned to Nathan Collier. The one person who'd seemed to believe everything she said. Because he was the person doing it to her.

What if they'd got it wrong about Collier? Not possible. All the evidence pointed to him. His car parked down the road from her house each night she claimed there'd been an intruder. Same car there the night she was killed.

Collier was the killer.

She knew that. But she couldn't shake off the feeling that all this – last night's break-in, the missing photo – that it was connected, somehow, with what had happened to Chloe Dunbar. Maybe it was paranoid to think it, but some part of her was certain the link was there. And if there was a link, she would find it. First, though, she had to make sure her children were safe.

She called her mother, asked if the children could stay the night with her.

'Of course,' her mother said. 'But we're expecting you for tea, Ellen. Don't tell me you can't make it.'

She looked at the list of unread e-mails, remembering that she had to find time to call Abby as well.

'I'll be there,' she said. 'Of course I will. I'm really looking forward to it.'

She hung up, switched the laptop into sleep mode and went upstairs to pack overnight bags for the children.

# SIXTY-THREE

Thursday night and The Trafalgar was rocking. Ellen pushed her way through the crowds, wondering why she'd agreed to meet here. The Vanbrugh, her local, was a lovely pub which served good food and decent wine at a reasonable price, didn't play loud music and you could always find a seat.

'Ellen!'

Miraculously, Abby had found a small table by the huge, curved window that hung over the river like a pregnant belly.

'Isn't it just beautiful here?' Abby gushed. 'I've already ordered you a glass of wine. Here.'

Ellen hung her coat over the back of the chair and sat down. Abby was right. If you ignored the jabbering from the mix of students and Hooray Henries, this was indeed a beautiful spot.

She took a healthy slug of wine, hoping it would kick in quickly. The short walk from her house to the pub had left her on edge. She couldn't shake off the feeling she was being watched. Turned around every few seconds, scanning the street, but there was no sign anyone was following her. She knew it was just her imagination, told herself she was being foolish. It didn't help.

'Are you okay?' Abby asked.

Ellen nodded. 'Sure.'

She looked at the water, treacling past beneath the window. Lights from the riverside apartments on the Isle of Dogs lit up the far side of the river and reflected in the water like dozens of tiny stars.

'Nathan Collier's back in the cells,' Abby said. 'Turns out it was a panic attack. Nothing more serious.'

'Is that what the Diazepam's for?' Ellen asked.

Abby nodded. 'Apparently so. Long history of extreme anxiety, which got worse after his mother died last year.'

'This won't help our case,' Ellen said.

'What do you mean?'

'History of mental illness,' Ellen explained. 'Bet you anything his brief uses it to try to prove he's not of sound mind.'

'Yeah but if he has got a mental illness,' Abby said, 'shouldn't that be taken into account?'

'He bloody killed her,' Ellen said. 'Wrapped a piece of wire around her throat and pulled it tight, kept on pulling until it had cut through her skin, ripped her trachea and cut off her air supply. Mental illness or no mental illness, he knew what he was doing.'

'Sorry.'

Ellen felt guilty. She could be such a bitch at times.

'Don't be,' she said. 'I'm the one who should apologise. I didn't get much sleep last night so I'm tired. And grumpy.' She smiled. 'What was it you wanted to see me about?'

'I'm not sure this is a good time,' Abby said.

'Why not?'

'Well, if you're grumpy now, what I've got to tell you isn't going to make you feel any better.'

'Can't make me feel any worse,' Ellen said. 'Okay. Come on then. Whatever it is, just get it over and done with. I'm a big girl, Abby. I can take it.'

'It's about Jim O'Dwyer,' Abby said.

* * *

Harry was sprawled on the sofa, feet resting on her lap. They smelled. Not badly, but enough to put her off the wine she was trying to drink as she flicked through the TV channels, looking for something decent to watch.

They'd shared a spliff earlier and the dope had left her relaxed, lazy and more than a little horny. She shifted forward slightly until his feet were lying on her crotch. She glanced over, pleased when she saw he was watching her. When she felt the heel of his foot, pressing down, she smiled. Half the time he drove her mad, but tonight a bit of Harry was just what the doctor ordered. That, and the fact that he deserved it. He'd done well; this was payback.

The familiar theme tune for the ten o'clock news trilled out of the TV. A man's voice read the headlines. Chloe's name got a mention, but Monica had already caught up with that. The fat boss was under arrest. No surprises there.

She put her head back and closed her eyes. His foot ground into her until she moaned. She lifted her skirt, heard the breath catch in his throat when she pulled it high enough so he could see she wasn't wearing anything underneath.

*A woman's body discovered in a flat in the London Road area of Brighton.*

Her eyes shot open, she sat up, pushed his feet out of the way. A female reporter stood outside an ugly grey building with dirty net curtains behind dirty glass.

*'Police have confirmed that earlier today a woman's body was found in this house here on Calvert Lane. Neighbours called the police when they noticed an increase in the number of flies in the property over the past weeks. So far, the woman's identity remains unknown. Police have appealed for anyone with information about the deceased to call this number...'*

'What is it, Mon? What's the matter?'

Ignoring him, she grabbed the remote and pressed the Rewind button. Played the piece a second time. And a third. When she'd finished, she paused the TV and turned to Harry.

'Sorry about that,' she said. 'Thought it might be important.'

'Was it?'

She shook her head. 'Not a bit. Now where were we?'

He leaned forward, ran his hand along her thigh. It felt hot and heavy and she resisted the urge to push it away. It wouldn't do to upset him. Especially now. The hand on her leg squeezed. She tried not to wince. His pupils were huge. He smiled and she did her best to smile back. Hoped it was enough then realised, of course it was. All she had to do was open her legs and pretend to go along with it.

His hand moved higher, fingers digging, probing, pushing her legs apart. His face moved towards hers. She looked past him, across the room at the image frozen on the TV screen, remembering.

\* \* \*

Ellen said goodnight to Abby outside the pub and walked home. Fast. She couldn't feel the two glasses of wine and by the time she'd turned into Annandale Road, any sense of relaxation was gone.

The suburban streets were quiet, felt like she was the only person out and about. Behind her, something moved and she swung around quickly. If someone was following her, they'd picked the wrong night. Abby's news had stirred something dark in Ellen and she was in the mood for a fight.

A fox walked out of a garden, stopped when it saw Ellen and stared at her. She stared back. Obviously deciding there was nothing interesting about her, the fox turned and walked away. Leaving Ellen alone once again.

By the time she reached the house, she was hot from walking so quickly. She rooted around in her bag, found her keys, unlocked the door and stepped inside. The house felt unnaturally quiet. She stood in the hallway, listening for any noises. Nothing.

She took her shoes off and moved around downstairs, turning lights on. In the kitchen, she paused by the fridge, looking at the empty space where the newsletter had been.

She knew she should go to bed. She also knew she wouldn't be able to sleep. She poured herself a glass of wine and sat down at the laptop. Entered the name Louise Jamieson into the search engine and started reading.

Everything she found confirmed what Abby had told her in the pub earlier. Louise Jamieson was a former plumbing apprentice and the victim of a hit and run. The incident left her with a broken back and an injury she'd never recovered from.

After the accident, Louise accused her boss of running her over. Said he'd been coming on to her for months, following her and leaving abusive messages for her. She claimed he ran her over after she confronted him and told him to stop. The boss in question? Jim O'Dwyer.

Ellen drank more wine and went back over the four stories

she'd found about the incident. It happened eighteen months ago, around the time Jim was seeing Monica. Ellen thought maybe that meant something, although she didn't know what.

Upstairs, a floorboard creaked. At first, she thought it was one of the children moving around. Until she remembered they weren't here. She told herself it was probably nothing. The house was old and the floorboards creaked all the time.

She strained her ears, listening for other sounds, but couldn't hear anything. She'd forgotten to get the alarm fixed and regretted that now. She vowed to make it a priority tomorrow morning. Someone walked past the house, footsteps loud and fast. Suddenly they stopped. Ellen ran across to the window and looked out. Saw a young bloke she didn't recognise, sending a text from his phone. She waited until he'd moved on down the road before letting the curtain drop back down.

In the kitchen, she refilled her glass. Across the room, something moved. Someone was there. She jumped and the glass fell from her hand, wine and shards of shattered crystal scattered across the floor. Then she realised. There was no one there except her own reflection in the French windows.

This was ridiculous. *She* was ridiculous. Chloe Dunbar had endured months of torment and here Ellen was, freaking out after one small incident where nothing had actually happened. She needed to get a grip.

After she'd finished sweeping up the broken glass and mopping up the rest of the wine, Ellen went upstairs, got her quilt and pillow and carried them down to the living room. She took a crutch as well.

Tonight, if anyone tried to break into her home, she would be ready for them.

# SIXTY-FOUR

The duty solicitor was a stout, middle-aged woman with frizzy grey hair dressed in some horrible, brightly coloured flowing dress that made her look like a hippy instead of a professional. Nathan hated her instantly.

Hated her more when she asked him – right out – whether he'd killed Chloe. Whatever happened to innocent until proven guilty? And this was the person being paid to protect him!

She asked him to call her Sarah but he refused, insisting on Miss Welsh (no rings on her fingers so no need to embarrass them both by asking if it was Miss or Mrs). He wondered what sort of woman would choose a job like this, working in prisons and police stations, representing the worst of society?

The two detectives interviewing him were women, too. Almost

made him wonder if it was some sort of conspiracy. Maybe this is what they did whenever the murder victim was a woman and the suspect was a man. They tried to intimidate the man by surrounding him with the sort of women no right-minded man would ever want to be around.

He'd lost track of how long they'd been asking him questions. Going back over the same thing again and again, trying to trip him up, get him to admit he'd killed her. Then a sudden change of direction that threw him off-guard.

'Did you believe her?'

The blonde detective with the blue eyes like ice.

'What do you mean?' he asked.

'Did you believe Chloe when she said someone had been in her house?' the blonde said.

'Yes, of course,' he said. 'Why wouldn't I?'

'She must have been very scared.'

'She was,' he said. 'Especially when you lot refused to take her seriously. She was lucky to have me, I can tell you. The only person who believed her.'

'Because you knew she was telling the truth,' the detective said.

'That's right.'

'And you knew she was telling the truth because it was you, wasn't it?' the detective said. 'You were the person Chloe was scared of. Only the poor girl didn't realise it.'

He glanced at Miss Welsh but she remained stony-faced, not giving any indication of what he should say. As if she didn't realise that's what she was being paid to do. Useless.

'Of course I wasn't,' he said. 'That's ridiculous.'

They couldn't know. He'd gone over every detail, never once left any trace of himself in the flat. Yes, they'd probably pick up traces of DNA if they looked hard enough. But Chloe was his friend. He was in and out of her flat all the time, helping her with stuff, dropping around for chats and cups of tea. Normal things that normal people did when they were friends.

He was about to explain this when the other detective, the pretty dark-haired one, opened the envelope on the table in front of her and pulled out a sheet of paper.

'Could you explain this?' she asked.

'Please tell my client what you're showing him,' Miss Welsh said.

But he already knew. His car. Parked outside Hither Green station. The same place he parked it every time he went over there at night-time. Far enough away from her house so no one would make the connection.

Except now someone had.

'Mr Collier?'

The tightness started across his chest, throat closing. He grabbed the edge of the table in front of him, tried to remember the techniques the doctor had spoken to him about. Deep, slow breathing, counting numbers – one, two, three, close your eyes and focus.

'And these other images. All taken from a CCTV camera

outside Hither Green station. If you'd care to open your eyes and look at the date and time in the bottom right-hand corner of each image, you'll see it correlates with the different nights Chloe reported that someone had broken into her house.'

One, two, three. Focus.

All he'd ever wanted was for her to notice him. To see beyond the fat to the person inside. The lovely person he knew was in there, just waiting for someone like her. Waiting his whole life and hadn't even known it until she'd turned up that afternoon. Standing in the doorway like an angel.

'And this one here from Sunday, twenty-fourth October. The night Chloe was killed.'

One, two, three.

'I didn't do it.' Shouting too loud. Couldn't help himself. 'I loved her. I'd never do a single thing to hurt her. It was Carl Jenkins. He's who should be sitting here, not me.'

The tension eased. Suddenly, he could breathe again.

'I didn't kill her. I swear to you.'

'So how do you explain these?' the pretty one asked.

'I was keeping her safe,' he said. 'Sometimes I drove over there, went past the house just to check she was okay. She was scared and no one else wanted to know about it.'

'You're lying,' the blonde one said.

'DCI Cox,' Miss Welsh spoke up. About time. 'Can I please have a few minutes to confer with my client?'

The blonde nodded, spoke into the tape recorder and switched it off. A moment later, the two detectives left.

Miss Welsh cleared her throat before speaking.

'Nathan,' she said. 'I think it's time you told me the truth.'

# SIXTY-FIVE

Ellen spent the night on the sofa. She woke early, showered, got dressed and went across to her parents' house for breakfast with the children. Managed to endure her mother's running commentary on how tired Ellen looked and how she had to stop pushing herself too hard, before finally ushering the children out the door to school. Right after that, she got into her car and drove to Bromley, six miles south of Greenwich.

The house she wanted was on a quiet road behind North Bromley train station. A standard, three-bed Victorian terrace midway down a row of identical houses. Ellen found a space nearby and parked up.

The house was well-maintained with a pretty front garden full of plants Ellen didn't recognise. A young woman in a wheelchair was in the garden as Ellen approached, pulling weeds from a bed underneath the front window.

'Louise?'

The woman swung her chair around and looked up at Ellen, using her hand to shield her eyes from the sun.

'DI Kelly?' she said. 'Bang on time. Come in.'

Ellen followed the woman up a ramp into the house.

'It's divided into two flats,' Louise explained. 'I get the whole lower floor. Which is as much as I need, quite frankly. Coffee?'

'Yes please.'

Inside, the flat was every bit as pretty as the outside: vintage furniture, stripped wooden floorboards and lots of colour. The living area was all open-plan, kitchen and dining table at one end, living area at the front of the house. Ellen sat on what she thought was a Parker Knoll straight-backed armchair and watched Louise move around the kitchen, preparing the coffee.

'I'd almost given up on you lot,' Louise said, coming across the room with a tray balanced on her lap.

'Want me to take that?' When Louise nodded, Ellen took the tray and put it on the big square wooden coffee table.

'So,' Louise said once the coffees were sorted. 'What have you got for me?'

'It's like I explained on the phone last night,' Ellen said. 'I think I might have found a link between what happened to you and another case I'm investigating. I don't want to say too much just yet. But would you mind if I asked you a few questions about what happened?'

She watched Louise take a sip of her coffee as she seemed to consider what Ellen had said. She was a pretty girl. Blonde, like Chloe, but with more substance to her. A steeliness that told you she wasn't someone to be messed around with. Ellen wondered if she'd always been like that or if it was something she'd had to develop to deal with everything she'd been through.

'I don't mind answering questions,' Louise said. 'But I do mind being lied to. If there's a connection, or even a possible connection, can't you just tell me what that is?'

'Jim O'Dwyer's name has come up in connection with a stalking case,' Ellen said. 'I can't say more than that. I'm sorry.'

'I don't understand,' Louise said. 'I was so sure I'd got it wrong.'

'What do you mean?' Ellen asked.

'I don't think – at least, I didn't think – Jim did this to me,' Louise said. 'I told your lot that at the time. They wouldn't believe me, though. Made him out to be a right psycho. Made me out to be some poor little victim being terrorised by her big bad boss. It wasn't like that. I don't think so. If that's why you're here, I'm afraid you're wasting your time. And mine.'

The relief was huge but short-lived.

'I read your statement,' Ellen said, remembering everything she'd read late last night. The witness statement, signed by Louise Jamieson, in which she'd stated that she believed her boss, Jim O'Dwyer, was the person who'd driven into her.

'I was doped up when I signed that,' Louise said. 'Doped up

and probably suffering PTSD. I'd just found out my bloody back was broken, for Christ's sake. That detective, right? All he cared about was getting a conviction. Didn't give a shit about actually trying to find out who really did this.'

'I'm sorry,' Ellen said. 'Some detectives can get like that. I'm not one of those. Jim's name came up in an investigation that, right now, isn't making a lot of sense. I'm trying to work out if he's really a suspect or if we've been given his name because someone has a grudge against him.'

'I was so excited when I got the job with Jim,' Louise said. 'I'm sure it sounds weird to you, but I really wanted to be a plumber. I saw it as a chance to work for myself. I'm not academic, always knew uni wasn't an option. Plumbing, it's a career, isn't it? I know you don't see many women plumbers but I thought I could turn that to my advantage. And I did at first. I was good at it. It was fun and Jim was a great boss. He's a pretty cool guy. Except I was only with him about four months when it all started going wrong.'

'What happened?'

'Weird things,' Louise said. 'Someone scratched my car. But that happens. It was nasty, though. Whoever did it scratched the word 'bitch'. I was upset but more angry than anything else. My front headlights were smashed and I started to wonder if it was personal. Then the e-mails started. Nasty notes, calling me a bitch and other stuff too. I kept them all, showed them to the police. They only really did something about it after I was hit.

'Why were they so sure it was Jim?'

'My fault,' Louise said. 'When stuff like that happens, you become paranoid. I'd already been to the police, you see. I gave them his name. I couldn't think of anyone else and it seemed too much of a coincidence that it only started after we were working together. And the police seemed so sure. It was the e-mails, you see.'

'What about them?' Ellen asked.

They were sent from a Gmail account,' Louise said. '<u>Jimbo@gmail.com</u>. I remember showing it to Jim and both of us thinking it was a bit freaky. You know, that someone had used his name. The thing is, when the police looked into it, turned out whoever set up the account hadn't just stolen Jim's name. The account was actually registered to him. Name, address and date of birth. All there.'

'So when you heard that, you assumed it was him too?'

Louise frowned. 'I didn't know what to think. I thought I knew him pretty well. It was never like that between us. I'm gay, for starters. Jim knew that, never seemed bothered by that. Besides, I wasn't his type.'

'How did you know that?'

'I just did,' Louise said. 'I mean, you get a vibe, don't you, when a guy's interested. I never got that vibe from Jim. Not a single hint that he felt that way about me.

'And when he came to see me in the hospital, he was so genuinely upset. He wasn't faking that. Unless he's a complete psycho.

Look, I've really thought about this. Think about little else, if I'm honest. At first, yes, I thought it was Jim. But you know what? The more I think about it, the more certain I am that he didn't do this to me. If you really want to prove you're different from your colleagues, then find the person who did.'

Outside, Ellen sat in her car for a long time, self-loathing washing over her in waves. Louise Jamieson. Pretty, level-headed Louise. Unwilling to take the easy option and lay the blame for her tragedy on someone who didn't do it.

Ellen knew what she had to do. She couldn't put it off any longer. She took her phone from her bag, found Jim's number and called him. Doing it now, before she found another reason to put it off.

# SIXTY-SIX

*'Hush little baby don't say a word,*
*Mama's gonna buy you a mocking bird.'*

She's lit up by the white light. It surrounds her, like a halo. And she's singing the song her mother used to sing to her. The same song she sang for him once. When she told him about her mother. How close they'd once been.

'Like me and my mum,' he murmurs.

She smiles.

'Exactly the same.'

She looks so happy. He doesn't think he's ever seen her so happy. He wants to be with her. To step out of wherever he is into that bright, white, shining light. He puts his hand out but even though she's there, right in front of him, he can't reach her.

*And suddenly she's fading.*

'No! Don't go. Please, Chloe. Don't leave me.'

*She's still singing but her voice, along with everything else, is moving, drifting further away.*

'Collier!'

Hand on his shoulder, shaking him. Paul Herring's little ratty face in front of him. Chloe gone. The medication made it difficult to wake up. But Herring was there and the fear of what he'd do to him gave Nathan the strength needed to focus.

'Sorry.'

'Second time tonight you've woken me,' Herring said. He was still holding Nathan's shoulder. Face pushed up close, his breath sour when he spoke.

'Don't let it happen again.' The pressure on his shoulder increased until he cried out. That seemed to please Herring, who smiled. 'Fucking wake me again and you'll be sorry.'

He let go then, bunk-bed rattling as he climbed up onto his own bed. Nathan lay still, barely daring to breathe, listening to Herring shift around until settled. When Herring finally stopped moving, Nathan stayed on his back, even though the position was becoming uncomfortable. He was so big that whenever he moved, the bunk-beds shook, causing the metal frame to rattle loudly. Herring didn't like that.

The need to go back to sleep was strong, the drugs fooling his body it was okay to relax. His eyelids were heavy, kept drifting closed. It took everything he had to force them open each time that happened.

Somewhere, a man started screaming. Nathan wondered if it was the same man as last night or someone else. From his limited experience so far, all men sounded the same when they screamed.

Above him, Herring shouted at the screamer, called him a fucking pansy and told him to shut the fuck up. Some of the other prisoners started up as well, until it seemed as though the whole place was alive with the noise of it all.

He couldn't bear it. Put his hands over his ears, trying to block out the noise, but it made no difference. And even as he did this, and listened to the pitch in Herring's voice rising the more he shouted, even while all this was happening, his eyelids still started to droop.

His bladder was full. Tight and aching from the pressure of what was inside it. Thinking what Herring would do to him if he wet the bed made it worse. He put his hands between his legs, pressing against his penis, praying for the control he'd need to get through the night.

And when that didn't work, when he felt the first trickle of damp through his pyjama bottoms, the moment of blissful relief when his bladder relaxed and the damp turned to a warm puddle as the liquid burst forth, and over him, when he felt the bunks shifting, saw Herring's feet hanging down as the room filled with the smell of it, Nathan Collier opened his mouth and started screaming too.

# SIXTY-SEVEN

They arranged to meet outside the Cutty Sark pub. The grey, overcast afternoon suited Ellen's mood. When she arrived at the river, Jim was already there, leaning over the wall, looking across the murky stretch of water towards the sprawling development of modern apartments along the northern edge of the riverbank. He looked lonely.

'Hello.'

He turned and smiled. No dimple, so she knew the smile was insincere.

'Ellen.'

She'd wanted to see him but now he was here in front of her, she felt awkward. She tried to think if things with Vinny had ever been this difficult. Hand on heart, she didn't think so. Her mother accused her once of looking at the past through rose-tinted glasses. Said Ellen had never been very good at appreciating what she had.

'Always wanting more. Even when you were a little girl. Nothing was ever good enough.'

That wasn't true. Not when it came to Vinny.

'Thanks for coming,' she said. 'I wanted to say sorry.'

He raised his eyebrows, waiting. He wasn't making this easy. Part of her respected that. Another part of her hated him for it.

And then he smiled again. Properly this time, with the dimple under his eye. The smile was what she'd remember when all this was over. It would trigger other memories, make her regret the way she'd behaved. She knew this, even while knowing – at the same time – it was already too late for regrets.

'Walk?' He tilted his head west and she nodded. Talking was easier when they didn't have to look at each other.

They walked in silence at first. Passed the Naval College and were the other side of Greenwich when she started speaking.

'I can't tell you how your name came up in the investigation,' she said. 'You understand that, don't you?'

'You don't need to,' he said. 'I worked it out myself. It was Monica.'

Ellen stopped walking and stared at him. 'How?'

Jim sighed. 'You'd mentioned someone called Monica. I didn't think anything of it at first. It was only after I was questioned that I started to think about who might have done that to me.

It had to be her.'

'How could you be so sure?' Ellen asked.

'She's dangerous,' Jim said. 'We went out with each other a few times. It was nothing special, but she seemed to think it was. She became obsessed. When it was obvious I didn't feel the same way, she turned really nasty.'

'Why didn't you tell me about her?'

Jim shrugged. 'Nothing to tell. Or so I thought. We dated a few times and then I finished it. End of. She still calls and sends texts, but I ignore her. She'll get the message eventually.'

'You know we've charged someone,' Ellen said. 'So you're officially off our list of suspects for now.'

'Is that why you went to see Louise?' he asked. 'Is it something to do with what happened to her?'

'How do you know about that?' Ellen asked.

'She called me,' Jim said. 'Right after you left. What did you expect her to do?'

'You didn't tell me about that, either,' Ellen said 'Why not?'

'I wasn't ready,' he said. 'What happened with Lou was so horrible. I was gutted when I heard about it. Then to be accused of doing that myself. It's not something I like to talk about.'

'I thought I knew you,' Ellen said. 'I can see now part of it was my fault. I'm not used to being with someone. I'd been with Vinny so long, maybe part of me thought that's how a relationship should be. I think I forgot, you know, that getting to know someone, it takes time.'

'We've got time,' Jim said.

'Are you serious?' she asked. 'After everything that's happened, you still think we should give it another try?'

'If I'm honest,' he said, 'I don't know what to think.'

'Well I do,' Ellen said. 'I need a break from all this. It's too complicated and I don't have the energy for it.'

'Relationships *are* complicated,' Jim said.

'Which is why I don't want one,' Ellen replied.

'So that's it?' he said. 'You're ending it because I'm complicated. Jesus, Ellen, have you looked at yourself recently? You raise complicated to a whole new level. Don't worry. I get it. It's fine for things to be complicated when it's your shit we're dealing with. As soon as the tables are turned and I need a bit of support, you don't want to know.'

'It's not like that,' she said.

'It's exactly like that. I'm sorry I couldn't be the person you wanted me to be. I really am.'

He turned and walked away without looking back. The further he moved from her, the less clear he became until eventually he was nothing more than a dark outline against the relentless grey of the cold morning. And then he was gone entirely, following the bend in the river as it curved left, towards the white, domed roof of the O$_2$.

A misty rain had started to fall. Ellen could feel it now, cold and damp against her face, seeping through her jacket, soaking into her clothes. She waited another moment, half-hoping he would change his mind and come back to her. He didn't.

A flash of white crossed the sky. A single white swan. It dipped down, skimmed the river and landed smoothly on its dappled surface. The world around felt oddly silent, as if time itself had stopped and the only two living things left were Ellen and the white swan, floating along the Thames in the quiet chill of autumn.

# SIXTY-EIGHT

The dog was dreaming, making little doggy noises every now and then. Dreaming of rabbits, no doubt. Adam leaned down and patted the dog's head.

'At least you catch them in your dreams, Digger.'

Bel had washed Digger earlier so he didn't smell too bad. Adam wanted her to wash him every day but she'd refused, saying it wasn't good for the dog's skin. Adam knew he should have put his foot down at the very beginning, refused to let the dog inside the house at all. Too late to do anything about it now. Besides, he'd sort of got used to the stupid mutt.

The dog was asleep on the floor of Adam's study. A small room on the ground floor at the front of the house. Adam was sitting at his desk, going through the silver business card-holder he kept, looking for the card the police woman had left him.

He'd promised Bel he would call the police and tell them everything.

'She scared me,' Bel said. 'Properly scared me, Adam. Tell the police what she's done or I'm not staying.'

His desk was by the window. From where he sat, he had a clear view across the garden to the road that separated the house from the sea. He scanned the road now, looking for Bel's yellow car. She'd gone to the shops, made him promise he'd have made the phone call by the time she came back. Which, judging by how long she'd been gone, was any minute now.

He found the detective's card, placed it on the blotter in front of him and read the details. DI Ellen Kelly. A landline number and a mobile. He picked up the desk phone and tried the mobile number first. He listened as the connection was made and the phone at the other end started ringing. On the road, a car appeared. A red Alfa Romeo that slowed down as it passed the house, then sped up again. No one he knew.

On the phone, Ellen Kelly's voice asked him to leave a message.

'This is Adam Telford,' he said. 'You came to see me recently. I need to speak to you urgently. Can you call me back? Please. It's important.'

He hung up, gave a final glance out the window, just in time the see the red car turn at the end of the road and come back. Another bloody teenager using the street like a driving track. They all came out here when they were learning to drive. He was sick of it.

Turning from the window, he saw the dog was awake, looking at him. Bloody creature followed him about the place like a shadow when Bel wasn't here. Sure enough, when he left the room, the dog stood up and padded after him. As he closed the door, Adam caught a glimpse of the red car, slowing down again. He should report them and all, but that would have to wait. Right now, he had bigger things to worry about.

\* \* \*

Ellen had been on her way to work when the call came. Because she was driving, she'd been unable to answer it and had to let it go to voicemail. When she parked in the station car park, she listened to the message. Adam Telford sounded desperate. She'd tried calling him back, but he wasn't answering. On a whim, she'd changed her mind about going into the station and had driven out here instead.

Just past Sittingbourne, the sky cleared. The clouds, so grey and oppressive when she'd woken up, had floated away. By the time Ellen pulled up outside Telford's house, the sky was a bright piercing blue that offered the false promise of warmth.

As she stepped from the car, Ellen's phone beeped with a text message. It was from a number she didn't recognise. Someone had sent her a photo. The sun made it difficult to see the picture clearly. She couldn't work out at first what it was. She shielded the phone with her free hand and the image gradually became clearer. Even then, when she could see it properly, she didn't understand it. Suddenly, like a punch to the stomach, it hit her. A wave of revulsion washed over her. She couldn't stop staring at the image, mind churning as she ran through all the different possibilities.

The image was dark, like the photo had been taken in a room with the lights off. There was a woman in the photo, lying on a bed, a white leg – the only flash of colour – protruding from under the quilt. It was too dark to see the colour of the quilt, but Ellen knew it was a dusty blue. Just as she knew that the person she could just make out in the photo on the bedside table was her dead husband. She was the woman lying in the bed, fast asleep, with no idea that someone was standing over her taking a photo. The sense of invasion was debilitating. Ellen felt violated. Knowing this was how Chloe must have felt in the weeks leading up to her death did nothing to help. She was standing outside Adam Telford's house, the phone in her hand as she worked out what to do. She had no idea how long she'd been here. The initial shock passed, rapidly replaced by a burning anger. She focussed on this now, feeling it creep across her stomach, into her veins and around her heart.

She wanted to deal with this immediately. Was tempted to leave now without bothering with Adam Telford, knowing her attention wouldn't be on him. The only thing that stopped her from driving away was the possibility that whatever he had to tell her might somehow be connected with the bastard who'd sent the photo.

She walked quickly to his house, an icy wind cutting across her, so sharp and cold it stung her face. She was about to press the doorbell when she noticed the door was slightly open. She pushed it open a little wider and leaned in.

'Hello, Mr Telford. Adam? Is anyone home?'

Something about the way his voice had wavered in the phone message told her whatever he wanted to tell her, it couldn't wait.

She called his name again.

Nothing. Ahead of her, the house was still, with the sort of deadly silence that chilled her far more than the wind outside. She called his name again. Fear crawled its way through her stomach and across her chest, clogging in her throat, making it difficult to breathe.

Her mind flashed back to a different time. Standing on a different doorstep, breathing in rose-scented air, not knowing a killer was waiting for her on the other side of the door. That door had been open, too. Ellen had walked through the doorway and into a nightmare.

She jerked back, away from the house. Her mouth opened, lungs desperate for air that couldn't get through her fear-clogged throat. And then she was breathing again. Despite the time of year and lack of anything resembling a flowerbed, the cold October air seemed to carry the smell of roses with it.

Her heart pounded, hard and loud. She pressed her hand against her chest, feeling the strong, steady drumming. She looked up at the crisp, clear sky and waited for the drumbeat to subside and the images in her mind to go back into the dark, inaccessible corner where they belonged. She needed to calm down. Breathe and think. No reason to believe anything was wrong. Chances were he'd gone out and forgotten to close the door behind him.

Nothing to worry about. She kept telling herself this as she walked back to the house. She knocked loudly on the door and called his name again. Silence. She pushed the door wide open and stepped inside.

'Mr Telford?'

The silence was complete. As if the house itself had died. Or someone in it.

The sitting-room door was closed. She moved towards it, put her hand on the handle ready to push it open, when she heard something. A rustling sound, so faint she almost missed it, coming from the other side of the door.

She froze. Slowly, slowly, she craned her head forward so that she could press her ear against the closed door. There it was again. Reminded her of her father. He liked to read the broadsheets over breakfast. Each morning, he would spend most of the meal shaking out the paper, straightening it and folding it into shape, as he moved from story to story. This sounded just like the paper when he shook it, right before folding it.

She didn't want to open the door and face whatever was in there. She knew it wouldn't be good. Knew even though there was no reason to think it. Even though there were a thousand rational reasons she could find to explain why no one replied when she called out. Why, if the house was empty, someone – or something – was clearly in there. The desire to flee was strong.

She ground her teeth together, pressed down on the handle and pushed open the door.

The curtains were closed, making it difficult to see through the gloom. She stood in the doorway, scanning the shapes in the darkness. The rustling sound was louder now, and came from somewhere over by the armchair near the fireplace.

There was a dark shape, barely visible against the other shades of darkness. Slowly, she started to make sense of it. There was a head and a body. She thought at first the head had been separated from the body but, as she moved towards it, she realised that wasn't the case. It was just hard to imagine how, with all that blood and a cut so deep, the head had managed to stay attached. It was even harder to imagine how the poor creature could still be alive.

The body was moving in regular, jerking spasms. Like it was repeatedly being given electric shocks. With each jerk, its legs brushed against the pages of a newspaper lying near it on the ground.

The closer she got, the stronger the smell became. Dog faeces and blood mingled with the pervasive stink of chemical air freshener. The stench caught in her throat, causing her to gag. She put a hand across her nose and mouth. A pointless attempt to block it out.

She didn't know what compelled her to cross the room to the dying dog. If she'd been thinking straight – thinking, at all – she would have turned and run. Got as far away from that dreadful scene as quickly as she could. But the way the dog stared – eyes pleading with her to end the pain, to make it stop – meant she couldn't just walk away.

She crouched down beside him and put her hand on his stomach. He flinched once, then stopped. Was still for a moment then gave another, mighty spasm. His legs jerked forward, rustled against the newspaper and were still. Ellen reached out to stroke his face. The dog whimpered, briefly. Ellen's hand touched something beside the dog's head. Soft material. Like corduroy.

A sudden image. Adam Telford sitting in a chair in this room, reading the *Sunday Telegraph*. Dressed in a pale pink jumper and navy-blue corduroy trousers.

'Hello?'

He didn't answer. She knew now he was here. In this room. Sitting in the same chair he'd sat in the last time she was here. She hadn't seen him before. In the dark, his body was nothing more than another dark shape in a room full of them. Her attention had been so focussed on the dog, she hadn't thought to look for anything else.

She went to the window and pulled open the heavy curtains. Light seeped into the room, bringing colour and focus. Ellen blinked as her eyes adjusted. On the floor, the dog was still twitching, although the gaps between each spasm seemed longer.

Behind the dog, Adam Telford sat on the straight-backed arm-chair. His head was thrown back and he stared at Ellen, mouth hanging open like he was midway through telling her something.

She stared back at him, noticing the grey film that had settled over the iris of his eyes, changing their colour from brown to a milky grey. Her stomach contracted. Bile burned the back of her throat. She swallowed it down, determined not to throw up.

A slice of sunshine reflected off a piece of metal on the ground beside the dead dog. Ellen leaned forward, hand across her mouth and nose to block the smell. It was a silver metal chain with a small, round medallion hanging on it. Her fingers wrapped around the chain. As she lifted it up, the medallion swung round, each rotation catching the sun so that the letters etched into the metal flickered and faded, flickered and faded.

The chain slipped from her fingers without her noticing. Vomit burst up her throat and sprayed from her mouth as she ran from the room, splattering the walls and the lino floor.

Outside, she continued to vomit, her body retching in rhyth-mic spasms, like the death throes of the dog she'd left behind, slowly dying at the feet of its mutilated owner.

# SIXTY-NINE

It was a perfect autumn morning. The grey clouds he'd woken up to had cleared; with the sun came a renewed feeling of optimism as Raj walked up the hill to the top of Greenwich Park. The place was alive with colour. Grass green and lush from recent rain, trees waving in the breeze, showing off their autumn plumes of bronze and red and orange. A final blast before the leaves faded and fell.

He'd arranged to meet Abby in the Pavilion tea house at the top of the park. When he arrived, bang on time, she was already waiting. Sitting outside, cup of tea and a cake on the table in front of her. Of course she was there first. In all the time he'd known her, she'd never shown up late for anything.

'Raj.' She jumped up when she saw him, ran across and embraced him. He hugged her back, holding her a fraction too long. When he let her go, she was still smiling, but he could see the concern in her face too. His fault. Shouldn't have acted so bloody happy to see her. Best not to tell her she was the first person he'd spoken to since Ellen had been in his apartment.

Aidan was gone. Left a message on Raj's answer phone, telling him he'd had enough of being treated like shit. Told Raj not to bother calling back. So he hadn't. Stayed in his apartment instead, drinking beer, avoiding the phone calls from his sister and parents, and generally feeling sorry for himself.

'You look tired,' Abby said.

'Not sleeping so well,' he replied. 'Apart from that, I'm fine. Heard you arrested Collier?'

'That's why you wanted to see me?'

She looked disappointed, although he couldn't work out why. Surely she didn't think... Nah. He dismissed the idea almost as soon as he thought it. They were mates. Nothing more than that. Besides, Abby knew. They'd bumped into each other at a club in New Cross one night. Midway through a long kiss, he'd looked up and seen her across the room, staring at him. He'd been scared at first, but that passed quickly when she raised her glass, gave him a silent toast and winked. They'd never spoken about it since and – thankfully – she'd never told anyone else. His private life was no one's business except his own. He intended to keep it that way.

'Is that a problem?' he asked.

She shook her head, frowning. 'I suppose not. It's just,

sometimes, you and Ellen… Oh forget it. It doesn't matter. Come on. Let's sit down and you can tell me what you want.'

'How sure are you that Collier's your man?' Raj asked.

He sat down, leaned across the table and picked off a chunk of her chocolate cake. She pushed her cup towards him. 'Want to drink my tea as well?'

'Come on, Abs. Don't be like that. Tell me about Collier. And then I'll be on my way again. Promise.'

'Unbelievable,' she muttered. 'Yes, he's been charged. Yes, we think he killed Chloe. And no, we're not looking for any other suspects. Enough for you? Or would you like me to steal files from work and bring those to you the next time? So you can go through them and make sure we're all doing the job we're being paid to do.'

'What about Carl Jenkins?'

'He didn't do it,' Abby said. 'Listen, Raj. We've got enough evidence to prove Collier did it. CPS already has the file and they're going to prosecute. They're pretty confident. Carl Jenkins didn't do it.'

'I'm sorry,' he said. 'I'm not trying to tell you how to do your job. Of course not. And if I'm honest, Abs, I don't think it was Jenkins either. But I keep thinking about how Chloe was killed. It was so brutal. I mean, I can see – sort of – how Collier might have lost it and attacked her in a fit of rage. But to find the wire, to bring it with him to her house with the specific intention of killing her. I can't see it.'

'Maybe you can't,' Abby said. 'But it's what happened.'

'He adored her,' Raj said. 'Would you do that to someone you adored?'

'I'm not a psycho,' Abby said.

'He's admitted everything else, right?' Raj said.

Abby nodded. 'Breaking into her house those different times, yes. Although his motive's not very clear. He's changed his story a few times. First off, he said he did it to protect her. Later, he admitted he was motivated by the desire to get her to notice him.'

'And yet he still claims he didn't kill her,' Raj said.

'Of course that's what he says.' Abby's phone rang. She stood up, walked away from him before answering. The sense of being left out hurt, even though he knew she had no choice.

He watched her as she listened to whoever was calling. Watched her face shift from concentration to shock. The call didn't last long. She hung up and ran back to the table.

'I've got to go,' she said. 'Sorry.'

'What is it?'

She shook her head but he reached out and grabbed her hand. When she looked at him, her face was pale.

'It's Nathan Collier,' she said. 'He's dead.'

# SEVENTY

Ellen stood on the beach, watching a small yellow boat chug its way across the water. A man and woman, both wearing waterproofs, stood on the deck. From the beach, Ellen could make out the sound of their voices but not the words. She wondered, briefly, who they were and where they were going.

Vinny used to speak about getting a boat.

'We live by the river,' he'd say. 'It's crazy not to make the most of that. And the kids would love it.'

At the time, Ellen thought the kids were too young. She worried it would be too dangerous, taking them out onto the swirling, dangerous currents of the Thames. She'd promised Vinny it was something they would do later, when the kids were older. She wished now she'd just said yes and let him do it.

She took out her phone and opened the photo she'd been sent. Stared at herself asleep in the bed, hating herself for not waking. Hating the person who'd done this even more. It was all connected. Chloe, Adam, this photo. Ellen didn't know how or why, but she would find out.

She heard footsteps behind her. Quickly, she dropped the phone into her bag.

A familiar voice. 'They told me you were down here.'

Ger Cox came and stood beside her.

'How are you?'

'I've been better,' Ellen said.

'I need to know what you were doing here,' Ger said.

'He called me.'

'How did he get your number?' Ger asked.

'I came to see him,' Ellen said. 'I was following up Monica's claim that he might have been the person who'd broken into her house.'

'Even though I told you not to spend time on that?'

'I did it in my own time,' Ellen said. 'But I should have told you. Sorry.'

'Sorry's nowhere near good enough,' Ger said.

'There's more,' Ellen said. 'The silver chain by the body. It's not Adam Sharpe's.'

Ger rubbed a hand across her face and sighed. 'Go on.'

She watched Ger watching her. Watched the compassion mixed with frustration in Ger's blue eyes. The frustration she could forgive. The compassion less so.

'It belongs to Jim O'Dwyer,' Ellen said. 'It was his father's. He never takes it off.'

A seagull swooped down to the surface of the water – white against the grey – and rose, moments later, with a fish flapping uselessly in its huge beak. Another bird swooped in, came up empty-beaked and flew away, its angry screeches filling the air. Further out, the little boat continued its journey east. Ellen watched until it was nothing more than a speck on the grey, glassy ocean that stretched from here, across to France and beyond, spreading out across the entire world.

* * *

The murder had happened on Canterbury's patch and the local DCI, William Harvey, made it clear Ellen and Ger were here as observers only. They spent the last hour standing around outside, watching detectives, SOCOs and the local pathologist go about their business.

Everything was spiralling out of control. Ellen was lost, unable to find a way through the mess. Control was everything. Without it, you were at the mercy of circumstance.

She hadn't told Ger about the photo. Wasn't ready to tell anyone about that until she knew what it meant and who had sent it. When she found out, she wanted to deal with it herself. Didn't trust anyone else to handle it the way it should be. By making sure the person who'd invaded her home paid for what they'd done. If that turned out to be Jim O'Dwyer, then God help him. She'd make him sorry he'd ever been born.

Ger had produced a pack of cigarettes, which both women worked their way through while they waited.

'I can't afford to lose anyone else,' Ger said. 'But I don't see how you can stay working on this case.'

Yesterday, she'd really believed the end was in sight. Now, the whole case had blown up in her face. A shit storm with her and Jim at its centre. He was being questioned right now at Lewisham. If he wasn't able to prove he hadn't been here earlier today, the next step would be to transfer him to Canterbury for further questioning. Meanwhile, Ellen was waiting to give a statement.

Ger handed Ellen another cigarette. When both women had lit up again, they talked about Nathan Collier. The call had come in half an hour ago. Collier had used the sheet from his bed to hang himself from the barred window of his cell. He'd tied one end of the sheet to the bars, the other around his neck. Then he'd knelt on the ground and leaned his body away from the window, slowly strangling himself. Another statistic in the growing number of prisoner suicides in the UK.

'Don't you hate it when they do that before the trial?' Ger said. 'Chloe's only chance of justice. Gone. There won't be a trial now. Her poor mother.'

'Must be some consolation to know he won't ever do it to someone else,' Ellen said.

'Suicide's such a cop out,' Ger said. 'Shows what a cowardly creep he was. What's wrong, Ellen? You look shocked. You think I should feel sorry for him?'

'I just think suicide's always sad,' Ellen said. 'No matter what the circumstances. Anyway, Chloe wasn't the only one who deserved a trial. Collier claimed he didn't kill her. Some people might say he deserved the chance to clear his name.'

'You're starting to sound like Roberts,' Ger said. 'Her influence must be rubbing off on you. I thought you were more cynical than that. Collier killed her. We both know that. The trial would have proved it once and for all. Now, Chloe's family will never know for sure. And that pisses me off. It should piss you off too. If it doesn't, I'm surprised.'

The Canterbury DCI came out of the house and started walking towards them. A short, skinny bloke with bandy legs, he walked like he'd just stepped off a horse.

'DCI Cox,' he said. 'A word, if I may?'

Ger threw her cigarette to the ground and winked at Ellen.

'Wish me luck.'

Ellen watched the two DCIs get stuck into the discussion over how the case would be run. In theory, this decision was made higher up the command chain. In practice, if Ger and her Canterbury counterpart could agree first, their recommendations would be taken up by the people who mattered and the case could be conducted in a manner that everyone was happy with.

When Ger had finished talking and started walking back to

her, Ellen could see from Ger's face she wasn't going to get what she wanted.

'Canterbury will take this,' Ger said. 'The murder happened on their turf and, for now, we've got nothing at all linking it with our own investigation.'

'What about Monica?' Ellen asked. 'We should be dragging her in for questioning. She hated her father. She did this, Ger. I can feel it.'

'Your judgement's clouded,' Ger said. 'You're not in any position to tell me what I should be doing right now. Is that clear? As far as this murder is concerned, I don't want you anywhere near it.'

'What about the girlfriend?' Ellen asked. 'Bel.'

'Billy's already onto it,' Ger said.

'Billy?'

'It's his name,' Ger said. 'You got a problem with that?'

She had a problem with all of it. The way Ger had let DCI 'Billy' Harvey take over the investigation without a fight. The way Ellen herself had been sidelined, despite the fact that if it wasn't for her, Adam Telford would still be lying in there without anyone having any idea he was dead.

'I should be part of this,' Ellen said. 'I was the one who found him. I'm the only one who's even met his girlfriend. I can help. It's stupid to put a blanket ban on any input from me.'

And I'm the one who's being stalked by the same person who killed Chloe, she nearly said. Instead, she stopped herself just in time. Ger would use it as another reason why Ellen's judgement was being 'clouded'.

'Give me bloody patience,' Ger said. 'You'll do as I tell you, DI Kelly. You are not part of this investigation because you have a complicated relationship with our chief suspect. Billy knows you've got information he can use. I told him you're ready to make a statement. That you'll tell him everything you know about Adam Telford, his daughter, his girlfriend and Jim O'Dwyer. Is that okay with you?'

'Fine,' Ellen said, knowing she didn't have any choice in the matter.

Ger nodded. 'Good. Let's go.'

* * *

Ellen gave her statement, answered all DCI Harvey's questions and agreed to be available if there was anything else they wanted to know. When she was finished, it was a relief to get into her car and drive away. The journey home was difficult. Traffic was heavy and she was driving with the sun in her eyes. Ahead of her, the city burned bright beneath the setting autumn sun, shimmering and shivering in the hazy light, like a mirage. Unreal, untouchable and utterly beautiful.

# SEVENTY-ONE

It was late by the time Ellen arrived back in London. The guilt gnawed away at her as she parked outside her parents' house. Guilt about her parents, who had looked after her children for the entire day and were too old to be doing that for her. Guilt about her children, who she'd hardly spent any time with so far this weekend. Guilt about the fact she'd arranged for the children to spend another night at her parents' house because she was too scared of what might happen to them if they slept in their own beds.

She climbed out of the car and stretched. Her body ached and her mind was still back at the house in Whitstable. She'd thought of calling into the station on the way back but decided against it. Even if Jim was still in custody, it would be madness to try and speak to him.

She didn't know how she was going to drag up the reserves of energy required for the quality time she'd told herself she needed to spend with her children that evening. She wondered if quality time included pizza and a movie. Decided very quickly it probably did.

Before going inside, she called Abby.

'Monica has an alibi,' Abby said. 'She was with her boyfriend all day. We spoke to him and he confirmed they've been together since last night. Which makes it unlikely she drove out there this morning and killed her father.'

'Unless the boyfriend's lying,' Ellen said.

'Of course,' Abby replied. 'And I'll keep on top of it, Ellen. I promise.'

Ellen had her own keys for her parents' house and she used these now to let herself in. She stood in the hallway for a moment, listening to the sounds of her family inside the house. She could hear her father, in the sitting room, putting on the monster voice she remembered from her own childhood. This was followed soon after by her children's loud squeals. She could see it without having to open the door: her father – arms stretched out, hands curled into claws – chasing the children, cornering them behind the sofa and going in for the Tickle of Death. Pat pretended to be too old for it, but he always joined in eventually.

Further down the hall, the kitchen door was open and she could hear more voices. Her mother and another woman. Ellen assumed the stranger was Marie Molloy, Bridget Flanagan's closest friend and a regular visitor to 10 Fingal Street. Both women spent hours barricaded inside the kitchen, drinking cups of tea and putting the world to rights. As she drew closer, she changed her mind. Marie Molloy came from West Cork and her strong, sing-song accent was as unmistakeable as it was – for Ellen, at least – impenetrable.

The woman in the kitchen, speaking now, had a deeper, richer voice than Marie's and the accent definitely wasn't West Cork. Vaguely, Ellen thought she'd heard the voice somewhere before. She couldn't place it. At first.

When she pushed open the door and walked into the kitchen, the moment of recognition was so sudden and unexpected, she thought at first she might be imagining it.

'Ellen.' Her mother stood up, smiling and oblivious. 'We've been waiting for you. How was your day?'

Unable to answer, Ellen stood in the doorway, staring at the woman. Random images tumbled towards her. Jim slamming his fist into a wall; Chloe's blue, bloated face and her wide-open, empty eyes; Monica smiling at her, dressed in nothing except a small red towel; Jim's chain lying on the floor by Adam Telford's dead body; Monica holding the photo of Vinny in Ellen's sitting room; the confetti of torn petals scattered across a back garden. And the photo on Ellen's phone.

Suddenly, she knew.

Monica was standing up too and saying something. Ellen didn't hear the words, didn't want to. She moved forward, across the kitchen and grabbed Monica Telford by the collar.

'Get out of my house.'

Monica smiled and Ellen's hand curled into a fist that she pushed into Monica's cheek.

'Ellen, stop it!'

Her mother's voice sounded very far away. Ellen couldn't have stopped, even if she'd wanted to.

'Call the police,' Ellen said, rattling off the number for the emergency line.

'Ellen?' Fear in her mother's voice now.

'Now, Mum.'

She repeated the number for her mother and pressed her fist deeper into Monica's face.

'I know everything,' Ellen said. 'You killed Chloe. And you killed your father. I don't know why you did it, but I know it was you. Just like I know you were the person who broke into my house the other night. You think you're so clever. You're not. You're a psychopath. There's a big difference.'

Behind her, she could hear her mother dialling the number, then giving her name and address.

'You're mad,' Monica said, keeping her voice low so only Ellen could hear her. 'Everyone knows it and now you're proving it. I haven't done anything, Ellen. All I've ever done is ask you to help me. It's not my fault you let your own pathetic jealousy get in the way of doing your job.'

She should have felt it then. The fear you were meant to feel when you were in danger. Maybe she would have, if the anger hadn't consumed everything else.

'Five minutes,' her mother said.

She could last five minutes.

'You stay here,' Ellen said to her mother. Then to Monica, 'You. Out front with me.'

Still holding Monica's collar, Ellen dragged her out of the kitchen, along the hall, past the laughter and screams and growls from the sitting room and out into the front garden.

Outside, Monica tried to shake her off but Ellen held on tight.

'This is insane,' Monica said. 'All I did was drop in for a chat. Where's the harm in that? You know, until you found out about Jim, I really thought we were becoming friends. What happened?'

Ellen didn't answer. She scanned the road, willing the response team to be on time. Every detective in CID had a special number they could call if they needed to. Until this week, Ellen had never had to call it before. Now, she'd just called it a second time.

She was still angry, but there was a focus to it now. It wasn't enough that she knew. She needed to prove it. To do that, she needed to show – above all – that this wasn't some crazy obsession of hers based on misplaced jealousy. That's what Monica wanted everyone to think. Ellen could see that. What she couldn't work out – not yet – was why.

She let Monica go, stepped away quickly, unable to bear being close to her.

'Go,' she said.

'Just like that?' Monica asked. Was it Ellen's imagination or did Monica sound disappointed. 'Are you sure you're doing the right thing, Ellen? Just a few moments ago you were accusing me of a double murder and a burglary. I'm confused.'

Ellen heard sirens. Far away but getting closer. She could see how it would play out. Monica protesting her innocence, claiming she'd done nothing wrong. Telling them about her relationship with Jim, Ellen's pathetic jealousy, making it look like Ellen was the one with all the problems.

Monica took a step forward. A memory came to Ellen. That night in her sitting room. Monica's face too close to hers. The smell of her perfume clogging up the air. Ellen resisted the urge to move back, away from her.

'What happened?' Monica asked. 'What did I do to you that was so bad?'

'I told you to go,' Ellen said.

Monica nodded and Ellen thought she'd won. Then Monica smiled.

'Your father told me about his garden,' Monica said. 'Poor man. He seemed so upset. Makes you wonder, doesn't it, what some people are capable of?'

The sirens were louder now, the car screeching around the corner into Fingal Street. The noises mixing with the roaring inside Ellen's head. Monica's face, still smiling, even as Ellen went for her, fist driving forward to smash away every trace of that smug smile.

A hand shot out, stopping her before she could do any damage. A man's voice – her father's – shouting at her, begging her to stop. Her father's hands on her shoulders, dragging her away. Car doors slammed shut, footsteps loud as two uniformed officers came running towards her, batons already out, waiting and ready to stop anything bad happening.

No idea they were already far too late for that.

# SEVENTY-TWO

Monica dried her hair. With the new cut, this took hardly any time at all. When she'd finished, she stood in front of the long mirror, adjusting to the new look. Her long hair was gone, chopped off and thrown onto the open fire, the last traces of it already burned away. She'd dyed the rest of it. Now her crowning glory was short, spiky and very blonde. The colour contrasted with her dark skin, accentuated her cheekbones and the size of her eyes. She looked good. Different, sure, but in a way she thought she'd get used to easily.

She had a TV in her bedroom and this was switched on, volume down low. She didn't need to hear what they were saying on the 24-hour news channel. She already knew. More about the body in the house in Brighton. Police hadn't identified who she was yet. But they would. By the time that happened, Monica needed to be far away.

She'd be gone already if it wasn't for that little diversion earlier. The delay had been worth it. Just to see the look on Kelly's face when Monica mentioned the garden. The fact that Kelly would never be able to prove it made things even better. Monica smiled at her new image in the mirror. Kelly might think she was clever, but she was no match for Monica.

Her suitcase was on the bed, lying open while she packed away the few remaining things she wanted to take with her. She always travelled light and she'd packed quickly. Clothes folded neatly, wash bag and make-up bag both in. And on top of everything, the framed photo of Vincent Kelly. She lifted this out, examining his face, wondering what he'd been like. Good-looking enough, she supposed, in an offbeat, quirky sort of way. Red hair that suited his pale complexion. Strong features and dark eyes that seemed to look right into her.

Her dead husband. Poor Vincent. Killed six months after their wedding. Before they'd ever had a chance to have the children they'd dreamed of having. She'd been pregnant, of course, when the accident happened, but she'd lost the baby as well. Grief ruining everything.

The story felt so real, her eyes blurred as she looked at his photo, picturing herself at his funeral. The poor, pregnant wife. She'd use it to explain why she cut her hair, if anyone ever asked. She would tell them that she'd done it to mark a new beginning.

Putting the past behind her and moving on. Smiling bravely as she said it all, knowing the effect that sort of thing had on the right person.

She closed the suitcase, shutting out the smiling face that was already starting to irritate her. All that bloody self-righteous happiness. People like Ellen Kelly and her husband. Rich, privileged people with happy, loving families – they didn't have a clue. What could someone like Ellen Kelly know about real loss? About how it felt for a little girl to lose her mother the way Monica had? To spend an entire life believing that your mother still loved you, only to find out it was all a lie. For the same mother to laugh in your face and tell you how stupid you were. That *you* were the real reason she'd left. Calling you a horrible, unlovable child who'd made everything impossible.

Her eyes blurred again, more tears. She couldn't stop this time. The terrible injustice would never leave. She knew that. Knew she'd have to – somehow – find a way to live with it. If only it wasn't so difficult.

She walked to the window and looked out, scanning the street. Apart from two drunks weaving their way along the road, it was empty. Lights out in Harry's place, although she suspected he was there. Probably standing at the window looking over at her. Watching. Always bloody watching. After tonight, he'd have to find someone else to watch.

She watched the drunks until they became boring. Then she closed the curtains and picked up the suitcase. It was time to go.

* * *

Ellen sat behind the glass wall, watching Ger fire questions at Jim. He looked exhausted and vulnerable. He didn't look like a killer. Abby sat beside Ger, making notes.

'You say you never met Monica's father,' Ger said. 'Maybe you can explain what this was doing by his dead body?'

Ger opened the file in front of her, took out a plastic envelope with something inside and slid it across the table. His father's silver chain. Jim shook his head.

'I don't understand. I lost it the other day. How did it…?'

Until now, he'd seemed calm, but this time, Ellen could hear the strain in his voice.

'I think you do know,' Ger said. She leaned back in her chair and folded her hands behind her head. 'Come on, Jim. Tell us the truth. You killed Adam Telford. There's no point denying it now. The only thing missing at this point is why you did it. We can speculate, of course. Maybe Monica told you what he did to her. Years of abuse. The story kept you awake at night, you couldn't stand thinking that a man like that had got away with what he'd done. Was that what happened? Or maybe she told you what he was worth, what she was set to inherit when the old man kicked the bucket and you got the bright idea to speed things up a bit? Or was there another reason? Something I don't know about.'

'I didn't kill him,' Jim said. 'I never even met Monica's father. I have no idea where he lived or what their relationship was like.

You're saying he abused her? Well that's news to me. Look, I've already told you. I was working on a job in Bromley yesterday afternoon. Spent the evening with my brother and was home in bed by eleven. This morning I went for a jog first thing – along the river, plenty of people would have seen me. After that, another job in Greenwich. I didn't kill Adam Telford.'

Ellen had stopped breathing, every piece of her focussed on what he said. She thought she knew him. Thought he was telling the truth. Knew he was.

'You said your relationship with Monica Telford ended a year ago,' Ger said.

'That's right.'

'And since then, you've had no contact with her?'

'No. Well, she's tried to see me a few times. Called me and sent texts, but I've not returned any of her calls or replied to her texts. I don't want anything to do with her.'

Ellen started to relax. Ger was going through the motions now. He'd given good explanations of his movements over the last twenty-four hours. They'd find plenty of witnesses to back up what he'd told them. The chain was a worry, but they'd find an explanation for that too.

In the interview room, it looked like Ger was starting to wind things up. She'd put the plastic envelope back into the manila file and was sitting straight in her chair again, like she was ready to finish.

'Just one more question,' she said. 'You told us you'd had no contact with Monica since you broke up.'

'That's right.'

'So can you explain then,' Ger said, 'what you were doing at her house on Tuesday night?'

Ellen hadn't seen it coming. From the look on his face, neither had Jim. She raced through everything that had happened over the last few days. Tuesday. She'd met him the following day. They'd gone for a walk and talked through everything. He'd never mentioned going to see Monica.

# SEVENTY-THREE

Outside, a wind was blowing. Monica tucked her scarf tighter into the top of her jacket. As she did this, a memory came to her. The scent of flowery perfume. Her mother's smell. Sometimes, she imagined the scarf still carried the scent, even though she knew how ridiculous that was. At least she still had the scarf. She'd always loved that scarf.

She walked all the way to New Cross. When she was far enough away from home, she found a minicab office and got a taxi to King's Cross. Inside the station, she looked at the departures board, undecided. Crowds of people milled around her, loud and boisterous as the final hours of their weekend drew closer. She felt separate from it all, isolated somehow, as if there was a protective bubble surrounding her, protecting her but also preventing her from getting too close. She ran through the station names on the departures board, checking the destinations of every train leaving the station in the next hour.

If she left now, it would mean giving up on Jim. Although, if she was being honest with herself, hadn't she already done that? She'd given him so many chances. Every time – every single time – he'd flung it back in her face. It had been that way ever since that bitch Louise came on the scene.

Monica had warned him, again and again, but he'd refused to listen. Insisted the bitch was a dyke and there was nothing going on between them. He was a liar. They were both liars and they deserved what happened. Thinking about it now, her only regret was that she hadn't driven into him that night as well. It would have stopped him breaking her heart all over again.

She remembered coming back from Brighton. Not being able to sleep and going to the park the next morning. Felt like her very heart had been ripped out. Empty and lost, she moved through the park like a ghost.

And then she saw him.

It was warm already. Clear blue sky and a sun that would turn the city into a furnace by the afternoon. A large sycamore tree stood on its own, midway up the hill. As she approached, the air was thick with the citrusy-grassy smell of summer. She breathed it in, thinking of the juice she'd drink when she got to the Pavilion at the top of the park.

He was leaning against the tree, eyes half-closed. Just like the first time she'd seen him, another summer's afternoon, in the Union beer garden. Something woke inside her. To see him here, like this, so soon after what had happened in Brighton. She knew, deep down in her very core, that this was meant to be.

He opened his eyes, almost like he knew she was there. He smiled, and she knew he'd felt it too. When he started walking towards her, it felt as if there was an invisible rope connecting them.

Then, out of nowhere, a child ran past. Brushed against Monica and straight past her, throwing itself at Jim. He grabbed the child, laughing, and swung it high into the air. Another child was there, too. And with the children, a tall, dark, nothing-to-look-at bitch who he took into his arms and kissed as if she meant something. Even though Monica knew that was impossible. He linked arms with the woman and walked right past where Monica was standing. So caught up with what Ellen Kelly was telling him, he never even saw her.

'Are you all right?' A man's voice, too close. Startled, she jumped away from him.

He smiled. 'I'm sorry. It's just, well, you looked a little lost to tell you the truth. It's not very pleasant here at this time of night. I wanted to make sure you were okay.'

He wore a dark suit that looked expensive. He had friendly, hazel eyes and well-looked-after skin. His hair was dark, greying at the temples, but that was okay. Gave him a distinguished air he probably didn't deserve.

When she didn't answer straightaway, he smiled encouragingly, reminding her of a parent trying to get a child to do something it would really rather not have to. One of those, then. The over-protective type that wants nothing better than a woman to save. Well, what the heck, she could do with a bit of saving right now.

She gave him the smile she saved for men like him. Warm but a bit vulnerable, like she wanted to trust him but was scared. Not scared of him, of course, more a general fear of the world itself.

'Thank you,' she said. 'I'm afraid you're right. I was supposed to meet my sister-in-law here but she hasn't showed up and she's not answering her phone. I'm trying to work out what I should do. I only came to London to visit her, you see. I don't know another soul in the city and I've missed my last train home.' She thought of Jim and what she was walking away from and allowed herself a moment's self-pity. Just enough to fill her eyes.

She saw concern in his face. And underlying that, the hint of something else.

'You poor thing,' he said. 'Please, let me buy you a drink. I'm sure between the two of us we can come up with a way to help you. What do you say? I'm Leonard, by the way.'

She shook his outstretched hand, noting the soft skin and the clean, manicured nails. She could do worse, she supposed. She wondered if he was married. Not that it mattered.

'Ellen,' she said. 'Pleased to meet you, Leonard.'

He took her by the elbow, leading her gently, but firmly,

towards the exit.

'This way, Ellen. There's a little bar across the road that stays open late. I'm a bit of a regular. They serve decent food as well if you're hungry?'

And that's how life was, she realised. One day you're one person, the next, you're forced to reinvent yourself. Just because Monica was gone for now, didn't mean she'd be gone forever.

Her suitcase was getting heavy so when Leonard offered to take it, she let him. As she handed it over, she thought of the photo inside. Her ex-husband's face. Ellen Kelly had accused her of breaking into her house. Stupid Kelly. Monica almost felt sorry for her. The detective really had no idea. Monica would never take a risk like that. She was far too clever.

* * *

Ellen bought a pack of cigarettes from the machine in the canteen and took them out front. She planned to smoke her way through the pack until she felt calm enough to drive home. She'd deliberately avoided the car park, where her colleagues gathered to inhale nicotine and catch up on the latest gossip. She had a feeling she would be the main topic of conversation in the smoking area tonight.

At the back end of the weekend, Lewisham station felt like the gathering point for every thug, drunk and petty criminal in South-East London. Outside wasn't much better. Ellen chain-smoked and watched the gangs of drunks marauding the south London streets, squeezing out every final moment of the weekend.

She was trying not to think about Jim. He'd been released – for now – but he remained a suspect. He'd finally admitted being at Monica's house on Tuesday night. Said he'd only gone there to ask Monica to leave Ellen alone. It was obvious Ger didn't believe him. Ellen told herself she didn't care one way or the other.

But there was one certainty and she clung onto this, focussing on it, knowing it was the only way forward. Monica Telford was a killer. Proving that was the only thing that mattered now.

At the bus stop nearby, a group of young people had gathered. They all looked too young to be out at this time of night and certainly too young to be that drunk. The girls were all under-dressed for October. Short skirts revealed skinny white legs that made Ellen cold just looking at them.

One of the girls swung away from the rest of the group, staggered to the kerb and vomited. The sound of puke hitting concrete mingled with the girl's retching and the raucous laughter of her friends, cheering her on. When she finished, the girl straightened up and used the back of her hand to wipe her mouth. Her friends applauded and she gave a wobbly bow before tottering back to join them.

Ellen threw her cigarette to the ground, stubbed it out with the toe of her boot and moved away. The smell of vomit followed her as she made her way around the back of the station to the car park.

They'd been doing just fine, the three of them. It hadn't been easy, but they were coping. And the longer they did it, the longer they got through each day and week without Vinny, the easier it got. Didn't it? The last thing they needed in their lives was anyone else disrupting the delicate balance they'd found for themselves. Ellen, Pat and Eilish. A self-contained unit. The children were her life. She was so lucky to have them. To even begin to want anything else was just plain greedy.

Before she could stop it, a memory she didn't want. A night with Jim. One of their first dates. He'd asked her about Vinny. Not about how he died, but how he'd lived. What had he been like, Jim wanted to know. What was it about him that was so special?

It wasn't something she'd been asked before. While Vinny was alive, no one questioned why they were together. You were a couple and people accepted you as that. Afterwards, all she ever got asked was the stuff she didn't like talking about – how do you cope? How do the kids cope? Does it get any easier? Different questions, each one offering up the same answer: I don't know.

Surprised by the question, Ellen answered without filtering her response the way she normally would. The words tumbled out as she tried to capture the essence of her husband in words. She described how he loved to dance, even though he was the least co-ordinated person she'd ever met. She spoke about his taste in music – a Nick Cave and Johnny Cash obsessive. Dark music for a man full of light. A man who laughed more than anyone else she'd ever met. A man who understood her neurotic need to give her children the security her own early life had lacked.

It was only with Vinny, she explained, that the world made sense. Ever since her sister's death, Ellen had felt disconnected from the world, as if nothing that happened around her could touch her or get through to her. Then Vinny came along and that changed. They married, had the children and, for the first time, her life made sense.

At some point, as she was talking, Ellen started crying. She should have felt embarrassed. Should have apologised and walked away until she could pull herself together. But Jim put his arms around her and held her, telling her it was okay to cry. The way he said it, the way he held her so gently as he whispered to her, Ellen was able to believe him.

She should have known then that Jim O'Dwyer was full of shit.

# SEVENTY-FOUR

Ellen should never have picked up the call. She'd come in early to get some work done before taking Pat and Eilish on the cable cars. Pat was cross because Jim wasn't coming, but Ellen couldn't let herself feel too bad about that. She drew the line at letting a murder suspect anywhere near her children.

Apart from herself, Alastair was the only other person in the office. Alastair was always in the office. Once, Ellen had asked him what he did in his spare time.

'What do you mean?' he'd said.

'When you're not working,' she'd replied. 'What do you like to do?'

He frowned. 'Eat. Sleep. What else is there to do?'

She ended the conversation at that point and didn't raise the topic again.

She went back over every angle of Chloe Dunbar's murder, trying to find a connection to Monica. Two hours later, she still hadn't found anything. Frustrated, she slammed shut her laptop and stood up, ready to leave.

She was about to say goodbye to Alastair when his phone started to ring. She waited. He answered, listened for a moment, then told the caller to hold on.

'DCI Keane,' Alastair said. 'Canterbury. Looking for the boss. Want to take it?'

Ellen took the phone, listened as DCI Billy Keane told her why he was calling.

\* \* \*

'I hate you!'

'Pat, don't be like this,' Ellen begged. 'Please. We'll do the cable cars next weekend. What difference does it make?'

'Because you promised.'

Ellen knelt in front of him. 'Listen to me. Something very important has happened. A woman has been killed and I may know who did it. It's very important I help find that person. It can't wait until tomorrow.'

Pat scowled. 'Bullshit.'

'Pat! Don't you dare speak to me like that.'

He didn't hear her. He'd already turned away and was walking out of the room, slamming the door behind him.

'You can't blame him,' Ellen's mother said. 'It was the same last weekend. Could you not have put it off until tomorrow? That way you could take Pat to the cable cars like you promised and then drop them back here later if you want some time to yourself.'

Ellen sighed. 'It's not about having some time to myself, Mum. I haven't got a choice about this, I'm afraid.'

'Go on then,' her mother said. 'Off you go. We'll be fine. I'll take them back to the park later and then back to mine. Give a ring and let me know what time you'll be back. And you'll stay for tea, all of you?'

Ellen knew better than to say no.

* * *

Ellen drove fast, blue light flashing the whole way to Brighton. Everything she'd suspected about Monica suddenly had substance. Earlier this morning, police in Brighton had identified the body of a woman found murdered in her home. Killed by a series of blows to her head and torso. Post-mortem confirmed the woman had been dead for some time. State pathologist estimated she'd been murdered in the last week of August. Two and a half months ago.

The dead woman was Annie Telford, Monica's mother. Brighton and Hove made the connection with Adam Telford and contacted Canterbury police, who called Lewisham. Ellen was lucky. She'd been in the right place at the right time.

Brighton station was a huge, post-war concrete building in an area of the city that reminded Ellen of Lewisham. Inside the station, she was met at the front desk by a young detective called Victor Rowney.

'Canterbury have tracked down Telford's girlfriend,' he said. 'They're interviewing her at the moment. Annie's landlord has just contacted us. Says he knew her pretty well. I'm on my way to visit him. Thought maybe you'd like to tag along?'

Ellen smiled. 'I'd love to.'

\* \* \*

Carl Jenkins lay on his bed, watching the news. All about a woman's body found in a house in Brighton. Turned out she was the wife of some bloke found murdered in Whitstable the day before. He lifted the remote, pointed it at the TV, about to flick if off when the screen changed. A photo of an attractive, dark-skinned woman with huge eyes and a lots of hair. According to the newsreader, the woman's name was Monica Telford. The police needed to speak to her urgently. At the end of the report, a phone number flashed across the screen.

His phone was on the ground somewhere, beneath the pile of clothes he'd worn last night. When he'd gone out and got so drunk he couldn't even remember coming home. By the time he found the phone, the number on the screen had disappeared. Frustrated, he tried to rewind, but the TV was a basic Freeview box with no rewind function for live TV. He considered dialling

999 – thinking if this wasn't an emergency, what the hell was? – when he remembered something else. The card he'd been given by that Asian bloke who'd kicked the shit out of him.

He ran downstairs into the kitchen. His mother was in there, preparing lunch. She smiled and said something but he ignored her, going to the drawer where he'd put the card, rummaging through it, throwing things out of his way onto the floor, until – finally – there it was.

'Carl?' His mother was shouting at him. She'd had enough. Couldn't say he blamed her, but now wasn't the time to have that conversation. 'What do you think you're doing? Come back here and tidy that mess!'

He wasn't listening. Was already through the kitchen and standing in the small back garden, dialling the number. It rang for a long time and he was getting ready to leave a message when a man answered.

'Hello?'

'Detective Patel? It's Carl Jenkins here. I think I might have something for you. Something important. Are you free to meet?'

Silence. Maybe he'd done the wrong thing. Should have known better than to trust someone who'd broken his nose the last time they'd met.

'Yes, I'm free,' Patel said. 'Just name a time and a place. I'll be there.'

# SEVENTY-FIVE

'Flat belongs to a local bloke called Pete Dahne,' Rowney explained in the car. 'It's one of several properties he owns in and around Brighton.'

'How do we know she was living there?' Ellen asked.

'Clothes in the wardrobe, make-up in the bathroom,' Rowney said. 'There was definitely a woman living there. Two pairs of men's trousers in the wardrobe the only sign there'd ever been a bloke living there. Took us a few days to track him down. Which is why we couldn't ID the victim at first. No one knew who she was.'

'How'd you find him?' Ellen asked.

'He found us,' Rowney said. 'Saw the news, recognised the house and came forward.'

'So where's he been for the last two months?' Ellen asked.

Rowney smiled. Again.

'I thought you might like to ask him that yourself,' he said.

Pete Dahne's house was a large, detached Victorian property on a long, tree-lined road in a pretty part of the city. Dahne himself was a short, skinny man in his sixties with slicked back, dyed black hair and prominent yellow teeth. Introductions out of the way, Dahne led Ellen and Rowney through a big hallway carpeted with a thick, pale pink carpet, into a large sitting room dominated by a grotesque green marble fireplace.

'Take a seat.' Dahne gestured vaguely at some of the over-stuffed armchairs in the room. 'Can I get you both something to drink?'

'No thanks,' Ellen said, sitting down on one of the armchairs.

'Nor me,' Rowney said. 'Good of you to see us on a Sunday, Mr Dahne. We appreciate it.'

Dahne shrugged. 'Just doing my duty. Like I told you earlier, Detective.' He smiled, revealing more crooked, yellow teeth. 'How can I help you?'

Somewhere outside the room, in another part of the house, a young child was crying. A woman's voice, soft and soothing, trying to calm the child.

'My sister,' Dahne said. 'Been living here since her husband buggered off. That's her boy crying. Pete Junior. Poor little fella's teething at the moment. Just two years old and his father fucks off with another woman. Not a word from him since he left.

Too scared to show his face. Knows what I'll do to him when he does. That's not why you're here, though, is it? You want to know about Annie.'

'She was a tenant of yours,' Ellen said. 'Is that right?'

'Not exactly,' Dahne said. 'Well she lived there, yes. But she didn't pay any rent.'

'Why not?'

'I didn't ask for any,' Dahne said. 'I was in love with her, see? Thought I could save her. Stupid. She was beyond saving. Beyond everything.'

Ellen looked at this little man, tears in his eyes as he spoke about Annie. A wave of revulsion made her lightheaded. Another Nathan Collier. Another pathetic man turning some poor woman into a piece of property to be owned and ogled at and Christ only knew what else. Times like this, she pretty much hated all men.

'How did you meet?' she asked.

'A Wetherspoon's pub,' Dahne said. He gave a watery smile. 'Hardly the most romantic of meeting places, is it? Maybe I should have taken it as an omen. At the time, I was so flattered a woman like that could be interested in someone like me.'

'A woman like what, exactly?' Ellen asked.

'Beautiful,' Dahne said. 'She was, I mean even in a shitty pub like that, she was luminous. All dressed up, looking like something from the movies, you know? I saw her the moment I walked in. Course I did. Every man in the place was watching her. She was in her fifties. You'd never think it to look at her.'

'You saw her,' Ellen said. 'Then what?'

'Then nothing,' Dahne replied. 'At first. I'd only gone in for a pint. Don't normally do that, even. But I'd just come from Marley's place. My sister. Things there were tense and it had rubbed off. I needed a pint to calm myself down.

'I'd barely sat down when Annie came over, asked if she could join me. I thought she was taking the piss. I remember looking around, checking to see if anyone was laughing. There wasn't. She sat down, we started talking and that was it. Three drinks later, if she'd asked me to walk to the end of Brighton pier and jump off, I'd have done it. Without even asking why. That's just how it was with me and her.'

'So why put her in a flat?' Victor asked. 'Why not let her move in here with you?'

'She did move in here,' Dahne said. 'At first. But then Marley's husband buggered off and she couldn't cope, so I told her she could come stay here. Annie couldn't stand it. She went sort of mental about it, if I'm honest. The flat at Calvert Lane was meant to be a temporary measure.'

'Not exactly an ideal love nest,' Ellen said. 'But I'm guessing things didn't work out the way you wanted them to?'

'She acted like she hated me,' Dahne said. 'From the moment she moved out, she seemed to blame me. I did my best. I loved her, you see. So even when she was really nasty, I kept going back. It became like an illness. She started seeing other blokes. Taunting me with them. I went over there one afternoon and she had two of them with her. Two young blokes pawing her while she lay on the bed, letting them do whatever they wanted to her. And when I walked in and found her with them, she laughed. Kept laughing when I tried to throw them out and they turned on me. I could hear her, the sound of it breaking my heart while those two bastards laid into me.

'I never went back again. That was four months ago.'

He looked directly at Ellen the whole time he spoke. She felt he was telling the truth but knew that he was possibly just a very good liar. Knew also that Brighton and Hove had already confirmed that Peter Dahne had taken his sister and young nephew to Spain for a two-week holiday during the period Annie Telford was thought to have been killed.

She glanced at Victor, who nodded. They'd got as much as they needed to. At the front door, Ellen thought of something else.

'You said Annie couldn't bear having your sister here. Why was that?'

'It wasn't Marley,' Dahne said. 'It was Kayne, her little boy. He cried a lot, still does as you can hear. Annie couldn't stand it. I found her one afternoon, sitting in the bedroom, with her hands over her ears. When I asked her what was wrong, she got really upset, started crying herself, weeping like a little girl. It's strange, you know, in all the time I knew her, it was the only time I ever saw her cry. What was it about the kid that got to her, do you think?'

A memory came to Ellen. Fragile, half-forgotten. Her baby sister. Crying while Ellen's mother held her, singing softly to her baby, the words lost in the sound of Eilish's wailing. A sound that cut through everything in the small flat they shared, so that no matter where you went, there was no escaping her sister's crying. And then, after Eilish died, the sound of a baby crying would forever be associated with her dead sister.

Back at Brighton station, Ellen called Alastair.

'I need you to do something for me,' she said. 'And I don't want anyone else to know about it. Is that okay?'

After she'd finished, Ellen hung up and went outside. She sat on a wall, lit a cigarette and wondered if anything she'd learned today got her closer to proving that Monica was a killer.

# SEVENTY-SIX

Raj met Carl Jenkins in the Ravensbourne pub across the road from Lewisham Hospital. Jenkins was already there, nursing a pint of lager and looking like shit. He'd lost weight and there was a waxy sheen to his skin that Raj hadn't noticed before. The fact that he had two black eyes and a nose under bandages did nothing to improve his appearance.

'Get you another one of those?' Raj pointed to the half-empty pint.

'Stella,' Jenkins said. 'Cheers.'

Raj returned a few minutes later with two pints. He placed one in front of Jenkins and sat opposite him, waiting.

'On the news earlier,' Carl said. 'The woman on the TV. The daughter of that couple who've been killed. Bloke in Whitstable, his wife in Brighton, you know?'

Raj nodded. He'd been following the story as well. Adam Telford on Saturday. Then his wife's body identified the following day. Killed sometime towards the end of the summer at a flat in Brighton. Police wanting anyone with information on the couple's daughter to come forward.

'What's it got to do with Chloe?' he said.

Carl frowned. 'Dunno. Might be nothing. But it said to call and I couldn't get the number down in time, so I called you instead. Not a problem, is it?'

'Course not,' Raj said. 'But I still don't understand what you want to tell me.'

'It's the woman,' Carl said. 'The daughter. The thing is, I've seen her before. She was a friend of Chloe's.'

Raj nearly dropped his pint.

'Are you sure?'

He'd asked Chloe. Straight out: do you know Monica Telford? When she told him she didn't know Monica, he had no reason to think she was lying.

'Certain,' Carl said. 'She was round at Chloe's when I went to pick her up on Saturday night. I gave her a lift to the station. If fat boy was alive he could have told you about it himself. He met her too. Invited himself along when the girls went out one night, according to Chloe. Stupid idiot had no idea she didn't want him there.'

'Chloe told me she didn't know Monica,' Raj said. 'I asked her.'

'That's because Chloe didn't know,' Carl said. 'She told Chloe her name was something else.'

'What?'

Carl frowned. 'Not sure I can remember. Anna, maybe? No. Anne. That was it. She told Chloe her name was Anne. Why would she do that?'

There was only one reason Raj could think of. Monica lied to Chloe because she didn't want Chloe knowing her real name. And when he tried to think of a reason for that, there was – again – only one answer.

Raj swallowed a mouthful of beer and pulled out his phone.

'Stay here,' he told Carl. 'There's someone I need to call.'

\* \* \*

*The Meat is drilling a hole through my fucking head. I don't even try to stop him. Everything's fucked. I try rolling a spliff. Hands shaking so bad it takes a while. I still have her lighter. The brass Zippo she said belonged to her mother. I flick it open now, light the spliff and draw it in.*

*Three puffs in and I'm not feeling it. Keep sucking on the bastard, knowing it's the only thing that'll keep me from losing it. Standing in the kitchen. Can't remember what I'm doing here.*

*TV on full blast. Newsreader's voice not getting through the Meat's roaring. Her face appears and it's like a punch in the fucking solar plexus. Breath is knocked out of me and I'm on my knees, gasping for air, hand clutching my throat. I'm going to die.*

*Later.*

*On the street screaming her name, banging on the front door.*

*A name in my head. Edges of letters creeping around the music. Emma. No, Emily. It won't come to me.*

*She has a shed in the back garden. Can of petrol there. I cut down the alley at the side of the house, over the gate and into the back garden. Shed's locked but the door's old and I smash through it. Blood on both hands. Fuck it.*

*Grab the petrol and run back out. Into the van.*

*Paradise by the Dashboard Light. Words and voices and music pounding inside my head, drumming against my skull. And mixed up with all of it, the memories. Close my eyes and there she is. Bodies close and tight, just like the song. And when Ellen Foley starts up, it's not her voice I hear.*

*Ellen.*

*My eyes open, the blow kicking in finally, giving me the focus I need. Ellen Kelly. Bitch.*

*There's a rich smell of petrol. I look down, see the can lying on the seat beside me. Smear of a bloody handprint. Hands bleeding. Both of them. Can't remember how that happened.*

*Key in the ignition. I turn it and the engine rocks into life, the Meat gets louder, voice merging with Ellen's, louder and louder, blocking out everything else as the van speeds away.*

# SEVENTY-SEVEN

Bridget was annoyed. Ellen just didn't think sometimes. It was obvious to anyone with half a brain that the children needed to spend time with their mother. Bridget tried her best never to comment on the choices her daughter made. Sometimes that was difficult.

She stood at the sink, watching the children playing outside in the small back garden. Michael was in the sitting room reading the papers and watching Cork play Tipperary in the Munster semis. A recording of a match first played in July. The fact he was watching it now told Bridget as much as she needed to know about the mood he was in. Sulking again over that business with his garden. She thought they'd put that behind them.

She was sorry about the garden, of course she was. Had told

him plenty of times. She knew how upset he was and that hurt her because she loved her husband, even when that was no easy task. But it was only a garden. The longer this dragged out, the harder it was to sustain the sympathy she'd first felt. After everything they'd gone through, to waste all this time feeling sorry about a piece of land, it wasn't right. Everywhere in the world people were dying and suffering. Michael's time would be far better spent worrying about those poor souls.

Outside, Pat shouted something and Eilish started to cry. Bridget braced herself. Sure enough, seconds later the back door flew open and Eilish ran across the kitchen, bawling.

'Pat hit me.' She was weeping loudly, too loud for the tears to be genuine. Bridget grabbed her granddaughter in a hug and looked over her head at Pat. He stood in the doorway scowling, face flushed, ready for a telling-off. She could practically see him getting his story straight, finding a way to show her it was Eilish who'd started it.

She wasn't in the mood for any of that today.

Gently, she unwound herself from Eilish, took the girl's little hand and led her into the sitting room. There were two adults in the house and she didn't see why it had to be down to her to do all the looking after and the refereeing of the endless fighting that seemed to go on between them these days.

'Michael.'

He looked up, face guilty, like she'd caught him doing something he shouldn't.

'Will you watch a film with Eilish? She's tired and I think she needs a bit of time with her grand-daddy.'

Eilish started to protest but Bridget crouched down and whispered in her ear.

'Your granddad is in a bad mood about his garden, Eilish. You know you're the only person in the world who can cheer him up when he's like this, don't you?'

She watched Eilish consider this. Knew she was trying to work out whether the compliment outweighed the injustice of being accused of tiredness when she clearly was not. After a moment, Eilish smiled.

'Can we watch *Frozen*, Granddad? Please? It's my favourite movie ever and you like it too, don't you?'

Bridget backed out of the room before either of them had a chance to change their minds. Closing the door behind her, she allowed herself a small smile. Typical Eilish. Her father's daughter, for sure. Unable to sustain a bad mood for longer than a few minutes. Unlike her brother.

Back in the kitchen, Pat was still standing by the door. Still scowling.

'Oh Pat.'

The scowl wobbled, his chin crumpled and his eyes watered. She crossed the small space and hugged him, whispering soft words, telling him it would be okay, everything was going to be okay.

'I want to go home,' he said, voice muffled in the soft wool of her M&S cardigan.

'Your mum will be back soon,' Bridget said.

She checked the clock on the wall. Five past three. Ellen had promised to be home by three at the latest.

'I'll call her,' she said.

Except when she called Ellen's mobile she got the recorded message, asking her to leave her name and number. She hung up.

'We'll go across,' she said. 'Eilish can stay here with Michael and we'll wait for your mum at your house. How about that?'

He smiled. 'Thanks, Gran.'

She didn't answer, distracted by the smile. His mother's smile. A pity neither of them could find it in them to smile a bit more often. If they could manage that, they might find life a whole lot easier for themselves.

* * *

*Traffic stalls on Kidbrooke Park Road. Wind the window down, take another pull of puff and slam my hand down. At the same moment the blow hits. My head lifts, spins and little red dots skitter-scatter across the front of my eyes.*

*The horn's loud. Keep my hand pressed down until I'm drowning in the noise. Other cars start up and it's like an orchestra, a great big fucking orchestra of rage.*

*Spliff's finished. Flick it out the window and the car in front of me starts moving. Handbrake off and away we go. Slow going, but at least we're moving.*

*A woman standing by a broken-down car. Long dark hair. Heart jumps, stomach does a dance. And then everything settles again. When I look again, she's gone. I think maybe she was never there at all.*

*Ellen Kelly.*

*Petrol sloshing around inside the can. The van sick with the smell of it. Sticks to the inside of my nose and the taste of it coats my mouth and throat.*

*I pat my shirt pocket, check again for the lighter, even though I know it's there. Beside the pack of tobacco and the little hard lump of dope.*

*Traffic speeds up.*

*The electric guitar starts. Keyboard. The beat grows faster. Louder. He comes in slow and low. Then he's speeding up, other voices joining in. And I swear you can feel the heat in the front of the van.*

*I'm shouting the words out now, hot city streets and steaming pavements. Hand beating out the rhythm on the steering wheel.*

*A2 up ahead. Cars flying past. I swing a left, join them. Press my foot down. The van jumps once then lurches forward.*

*Time to burn.*

# SEVENTY-EIGHT

Maybe it was nothing. A coincidence. He heard Ellen's voice, the mantra she'd drummed into him.

No stone unturned. No coincidence too small.

Raj dialled her number. Again. It went to voicemail. Again. He hung up, unsure what to do next. Monica and Chloe. From the news reports, Raj knew Monica's mother was called Annie. The same name, more or less, Monica had called herself with Chloe. Raj worked with an Irish bloke once, Patrick Stewart Maguire. Everyone called him Stewart, even though his warrant card clearly showed his first name was Patrick. When Raj asked about it, Maguire told him he'd been called Stewart for as long as he could remember. He'd been named Patrick, after his father. To avoid the confusion of two Patricks in the same household, he'd always been referred to by his middle name.

Raj wanted to think maybe the explanation was that simple. Even though he knew it wasn't. If she was known as Anne, why tell Ellen and everyone else her name was Monica? More importantly, why did she lie about not knowing Chloe?

He was sitting in his car, parked across the road from The Ravensbourne. Jenkins was still inside the pub, onto his third pint. Raj had left him to it. Come out here, smoked two cigarettes while he called Ellen's voicemail. Then got into the car and realised he didn't know where he was going.

There were too many conflicting ideas knocking around inside his head. He'd lost sight of where this was going. And underlying that uncertainty, a feeling that he was missing something. They all were.

Chloe's stalker wasn't her killer. Nathan Collier. He was in love with Chloe. Obsessively in love. When Chloe started dating Carl, Nathan lost it and killed her. Except he didn't kill her. Monica Telford. She knew Chloe. She lied to Chloe about who she was. She lied to the police about knowing Chloe. Conclusion: she killed Chloe. Why?

Raj punched Abby's number into his phone, hoping he'd get a real person this time, not another recording asking him to leave a message.

\* \* \*

Pat's mood improved in direct proportion to the distance put between himself and his sister. By the time they reached his house on Annandale Road, he was positively ebullient.

They walked slowly, holding hands while he chatted about Minecraft. Bridget didn't understand what it was and didn't care, either. She was perfectly content, strolling along, his hand in hers, listening to his excited chatter.

As they approached the house, it started to rain and they moved faster, hurrying past the white van parked outside, along the driveway to the front door. Under the porch, Bridget looked around for Ellen's car, hoping maybe her daughter had popped home first. But there was no car. Bridget's mood plummeted as she rummaged around in her bag for the key.

By the time she'd found it and got it into the lock, she had already planned the talking-to Ellen was going to get when she finally turned up. The key turned, she pushed the door and they were inside. As she shut the door, she thought she heard a noise from further inside the house. When she listened again, there was nothing.

The hall was darker than usual. She couldn't work out why, at first. Then she realised the kitchen door was closed. Ellen always left it open, enjoying the way the light from the French windows flooded into the hallway, making it appear bigger and brighter.

Pat was already gone, running upstairs into his bedroom. His sanctuary. Recently, she'd noticed he was spending more and more time up there on his own. It wasn't healthy for a child that young to choose solitude over activity and company. Although when she thought about it, Ellen had always been a solitary child, introverted and independent, rarely seeming to need anyone's company. The one exception was Sean, who she always had time for.

Bridget listened to Pat as he moved around in his room above her. The pitter-patter of his footsteps, the click-clatter of plastic falling down as he pulled pieces of Lego from his box and prepared to add bits onto the spaceship he'd spent the last two weeks creating. All this followed by total silence.

She smiled, picturing him crouched down on the bedroom floor, face crunched up in concentration as he put the tiny pieces of plastic together, constructing something magnificent out of random bits of Lego. She would go up to him in a minute, check he was okay and maybe help him a bit. If he let her.

She moved towards the kitchen, thinking she'd make a cup of tea first, steal a moment for herself. Pushing open the kitchen door, the first thing she noticed was the mess. She couldn't understand it at first. Ellen was always so tidy. Even if she'd been in a hurry, she'd never leave the place like this. Drawers pulled open, the contents spilled onto the floor, a chair overturned, lying like a dead person, its four legs sticking up.

Something wasn't right. Bridget stepped back, mind jumping through all the possibilities, reaching the only logical conclusion. A break-in. An image flashed in front of her. Michael's garden, the flowers ripped out at the roots, petals drifting in the breeze like bits of confetti.

Pat.

Upstairs on his own.

She swung around, opened her mouth to call his name. Nothing happened. She couldn't speak. A man stood in front of her. Knife in his hand. Vincent's knife. The man reached out, grabbed her wrist and dragged her until her body was pressed up against his.

A flash of light on steel as he lifted the knife in the air.

Fear like she'd never known before. Legs went but she was still standing, because he was holding her tight as he sent the knife slicing down through the air to kill her.

\* \* \*

Traffic was slow on the way back and by the time she'd reached London's outer suburbs, Ellen was almost an hour late. Her phone had rung several times but each time she'd let it go to voicemail. The caller was Raj and whatever he wanted, it could wait until after she'd picked up her children.

As she approached Greenwich, Ellen called ahead to let her parents know she was nearly there. When her father answered and told her where Pat and her mother were, she decided to detour past her own house first and pick them up.

A white van was parked outside her house, blocking the entrance to her driveway. Irritated, Ellen reversed back and found another space further away.

She'd just locked the car when her phone rang again. Thinking it was Raj again, Ellen answered without checking the caller ID.

'Sorry,' she said. 'I was driving earlier. Couldn't pick up. You okay?'

'Ellen?'

Not Raj. Abby.

'Raj has been trying to call you,' Abby said. 'Monica knew Chloe. Raj thinks she killed Chloe as well.'

Ellen knew that already. What she didn't know was why.

'Raj thinks Monica used Chloe to get at you,' Abby said. 'Because of Jim. She made up the story about having a stalker. When we didn't take her seriously enough, she killed Chloe. She knew if she did that, she'd have our full attention.'

It made a sick sort of sense. Some of the detail was missing, but they could fill that in later. Their priority now was finding Monica.

'Speak to Alastair,' Ellen said. 'Get him to check with all the main train stations, airports and ferry terminals. We've already circulated Monica's picture. Tell them to check all CCTV from the last twenty-four hours. Someone must have seen her. Malcolm's already liaising with other forces. Find out where he's got to.'

When she'd finished with Abby, Ellen dialled Raj's number and put her phone to her ear as she walked the last few metres to her front door. Then she changed her mind and cut the call before he had time to answer. She'd call him later. Right now, all she wanted was to see her family.

# SEVENTY-NINE

The air near her ear whistled as the knife came down. For a split second, she thought he'd cut her ear off. Her free hand shot up. Felt the ear, experienced a moment of sharp relief. He wasn't going to kill her. He was just a kid, disturbed during a burglary.

'It's okay,' she said. 'I won't tell anyone. I promise. Just go and we can forget all about this.'

'Shut up.' He shouted the words and she jerked, stumbled against him. Instinctively, she tried to pull away. Wrong thing to do. The knife came up again. He pressed it against her face, cold steel on her cheek, the sharp tip close to her eye. He was going to cut her eyes out. So she couldn't recognise him if she saw him again.

'No. Please, no.'

Not begging for herself. Too late for that. Begging for the little boy upstairs. A child who'd already lost his father. The man's grip on her wrist tightened, hurting her. Her bones were weak, the doctor had told her that. Not enough calcium. If he didn't let go, the wrist would break. He stank. Sweat and tobacco and something else, a rich, grassy stink that reminded her – oddly – of the city in summertime.

Up close like this, pressed against his damp shirt, she couldn't see his face. The only bits of him she knew were the smell and the heart and the breathing. He could go now and she wouldn't even be able to tell the police what he looked like.

'Where is she?'

'Who?'

He twisted her wrist. The bone cracked and she cried out from the pain of it.

He was screaming at her and she needed him to stop. If Pat heard, he'd come to see what was going on and she couldn't let that happen. She begged him to be quiet, but he wasn't listening. Instead he was dragging her across the hall, towards the downstairs cloakroom.

When she realised what he was going to do, she tried again to fight him off, to stop him. But he was too strong and she couldn't do anything except let him pull her to the cloakroom, let him open the door, take the key before he shoved her inside. She fell to the ground. Pain shot through both knees and up her legs. She scrabbled forward – away from the door, away from that man

– until she realised she was doing the wrong thing.

By the time she'd got up and ran to the door, it was too late. She heard the key turning in the lock and then his footsteps walking away, leaving her locked inside in the dark.

Outside, the footsteps stopped abruptly and she froze, thinking for a second he was going to come back.

'Gran?'

Jesus, no. Dear God, please, no.

'What the…?' The man sounded confused. And angry.

She pictured the knife in his hand. Imagined what he might do with it. The footsteps started again, moving faster now, running up the stairs. She was screaming, begging him not to hurt her grandchild, pleading with him, telling him she'd pay him, give him whatever he wanted.

He was upstairs. Footsteps over her head. Pat screamed, called out for her, his voice cutting through her worse than any knife ever could. Screaming as the footsteps got faster. Both of them running. The man shouting over Pat's voice, roaring at him to shut the fuck up. One more scream from Pat. The thump of something hitting the ground.

And then silence.

* * *

Ellen hadn't expected Pat to come running to her with open arms, but some sort of reaction would have been nice. Instead, it was like they were deliberately ignoring her. Ellen stood in the hall, listening to them moving around in the sitting room. Usually it was her father who played the games. Her mother preferred the more traditional role of mock-authority. Ellen had always secretly suspected her mother would enjoy the games as much as anyone. If she'd only let herself.

'Hello?'

The attack came from behind. Completely off-guard, she fell forward, hands out to protect her face from the parquet flooring. Confused, she thought at first it was Pat. Thought he was playing some soldier game that had got out of hand.

Until a fist came from nowhere, smashed into her lower back, knocking all air from her body. Unable to breathe, she tried to crawl forward, her only thought to get away. Something fell on top of her, a heavy weight. She couldn't move. Another punch to the back then a hand on her hair, head pulled back and slammed forward. An explosion of pain – bright, white, blinding.

Her arms and legs flailed around. Useless. Her fist connected with something. The weight on her body lifted, shifted. She jerked her back up, the person rolled off. The clatter of steel on wood. A knife hit the floor and slid across the hall.

Scrabbling to her hands and knees, Ellen went for the knife, grabbed it at the same time a hand wrapped around her ankle. She swung around, plunged the knife through a pair of dirty denims into the lower part of a leg.

Someone screamed. A man. Not Monica. Ellen tried to strike again, but he was too quick. Kicked her chest and she fell back against the wall. She tried to get up. Still had the knife. Holding it in front of her, slicing the air between them. Trying to stop him getting too close.

White face wet with sweat. She knew the face but couldn't place it. He moved closer, ducking out of the knife's way. She was standing now. Only one thing for it. She dived forward, knife ready, aiming for his heart. Got his shoulder instead. Enough to knock him to the ground.

She threw herself on top of him, fists lashing out, landing punches to his face and solar plexus. She put a hand over his mouth, blocking his mouth and nose so he couldn't breathe. Pressed hard. Beneath her, his body bucked and jerked. Ellen pressed down harder, grinding her palm into his face.

Saliva and snot smeared her hand. She saw panic in his eyes. Good.

'Where are they?' she said.

'Ellen?'

Her mother's voice. Ellen let go. Turned towards the voice. It was all the time he needed. His head jerked up and smashed into her already damaged face. She fell sideways and he kept hitting her. In the stomach, on the arms.

She rolled into a ball, trying to escape the worst of it. The blows kept coming. Something wet ran down her face into her eyes. She wiped it away. Saw blood on her hand. She crawled forward, hands clawing the ground for the knife.

His fists smashed down on her shoulders and across the back

of her head. Bright, white lights – thousands of them – exploded before her eyes.

The lights disappeared, darkness invading every part of her. She tried to fight it, knew she couldn't give in. Pat. He was here in the house. She had to find him. But the pull was too strong. She felt herself slipping, down and away. There was nothing she could do.

# EIGHTY

Raj's phone rang while he was driving. When he pulled over, he saw a missed call from Ellen. Before he could call her back, his phone rang again. Abby this time. He answered the call as he got out of the car and walked towards Ellen's house.

While he listened to Abby – she'd spoken to Ellen, a search was underway for Monica – his phone beeped with a text. Hanging up, his heart soared when he saw who it was from and what it said.

*In Greenwich this afternoon. Any chance you're free? A x*

A white van was parked badly so it blocked Ellen's driveway. Raj stopped beside it. He didn't need to go any further. Ellen was fine. Monica would be found and brought in for questioning. Everything was going to be okay.

He sent a text back, asking where Aidan was, said wherever it was, he'd be there within thirty minutes. Tops. Aidan replied straightaway. Raj read the reply, smiling. He knew the pub. Knew it was less than a ten-minute drive from here. He put his phone away, still smiling as he went back to his car.

* * *

She should have kept quiet. Ellen was winning. She'd heard every bit of the fight, her ear pressed against the door, too scared at first to make a sound in case he hurt Ellen. And then, when she thought it was all over, she thought it would be okay and she called her daughter's name. Big mistake. Now she couldn't hear Ellen at all, just the man, banging around in the kitchen, doing God knows what.

For the last four months, Pat had been asking for a mobile phone. Ellen kept promising him one for his next birthday. Bridget thought Ellen was being too soft. The boy was only eleven. What did he need a phone for? Now she saw how wrong she'd been.

She'd made a lot of mistakes over the years, some she regretted more than others. Right now, there was nothing in the world she regretted more than telling Ellen it was okay not to give in and buy him a phone.

Bridget didn't have one. Told herself she was too old for such nonsense. The real reason she didn't want a phone, though, was the same reason she didn't want Pat to have one. Because she hated the steady, determined way technology was taking over every aspect of her life. If it carried on like this, before you knew it there'd be no room in the world for someone like her. As it was, with things the way they were, she felt her own importance diminishing in the lives of those who mattered most to her.

Her grandchildren were getting older. These days, when they were with her, so much of their play involved gadgets she didn't understand and she lived with an underlying sense of being excluded. Michael told her she was being silly. Said the kids would always need their grandparents, just as Sean and Ellen would always need their parents.

But that was Michael. Always so sure of himself. Never doubting anything. Which was good, of course. Because if it wasn't for that single-minded certainty, they'd never have ended up with Sean and Ellen.

He thought she didn't know. She would never tell him because she knew he wouldn't forgive her for colluding in it. That the only way he'd been able to live with what he'd done was the illusion that he'd done it to protect her. That she was a better person than him because if she knew, she'd surely never have agreed to it.

But she knew. And still she'd let it happen. Most of the time – like her husband, she suspected – Bridget told herself what they'd done was for the best. But sometimes a sense of dread would creep over her, a feeling of unease she couldn't shake off. At those moments, she knew what they'd done was wrong.

She had confessed. Of course she had. Many times. Each time, the priest granted her absolution, forgiving her for that and all other sins. She wasn't sure that was enough. Now, locked in this dark room, she knew. Whatever happened to her this afternoon, it was no more than she deserved.

But not Pat and Ellen.

She prayed, not sure her God was listening, but there was nothing else she could do. She whispered the prayers she'd learned as a child, lips moving over the familiar words, repeating them. *Hail Mary, Our Father, Angel of God my Guardian Dear*. Listen to me Lord, she begged. Save my family. Don't let them suffer for the sins of others. It's not their fault.

The prayers made Bridget feel stronger. She had to believe He was listening. Her faith wouldn't allow for anything else. The punishment was hers and hers alone. By Jesus, though, she wasn't about to let Pat and Ellen suffer as well. She would save them. She didn't know how, but He would show her the way. All she had to do was believe.

\* \* \*

She had lost something important. Not a thing. A person. A child was missing. Pat. She didn't know where he was. She swung around, looking everywhere. She was in the middle of a street, lined either side with identical Victorian terraced houses. Behind one of those doors, someone was hiding her son. She ran to the first house, fists banging on the door, shouting out her son's name. Did the same to all the other houses. No one answered. It was as if all the people in all the houses were stone deaf. Or dead.

She screamed his name, over and over, as she ran down the narrow, empty street. The further she ran, the narrower the street became, until the houses on either side were so close, she could reach out her hands as she ran and touch them.

'Mummy!'

His voice came from further ahead. She peered into the dark gap between the rows of houses, trying to see him. He was down there somewhere. She ran faster. Except it didn't seem to make any difference. No matter how fast she ran, she never moved. And then she fell, face smashing onto the hard concrete. Stunned, she lay where she was, waiting for the first shock of pain to subside.

She woke up.

It was only a dream. Except her face still hurt. She tried to sit up. Couldn't move; hands and legs bound tight behind her back. Her fingers brushed the edge of a wall.

Then she remembered.

She was lying face-down on the kitchen floor. Every time she moved, it felt like she was being stabbed, repeatedly. A broken rib. She'd had one before, remembered the pain. Almost as bad as childbirth.

Her left eye wouldn't open, and the front of her face, across her nose, felt as if someone had smashed it with an iron bar. Grunting, trying to ignore the pain, she managed to manoeuvre her body until she was sitting up. Exhausted from the effort, she lay against the wall, panting.

She could see his feet, moving around the kitchen. He was holding something, shaking it over the floor, sloshing liquid everywhere. Blood blocked her nose and it took a while for the smell to hit her. When it did, the fear was so all-consuming, at first all she could do was concentrate on being able to breathe.

She tried not to make any noise but he must have sensed she was awake because he came over, crouched down beside her, looked at her face and emptied the rest of the petrol on her head and body.

The smell and taste of it was everywhere. Up her nose, down her throat, making her choke and cough and retch, her body slippy-sliding in the oily mess of it. Her eyes burned and she couldn't see properly. Shapes filtered through a grey film. She blinked, but it made no difference.

When he moved, she tensed, thinking he was going to start hurting her again. Instead, he sat down on the ground and slid further back until he reached the island in the centre of the kitchen. Never once taking his eyes from her.

He was breathing heavily, like the effort of pouring all the petrol had exhausted him.

'I'm going to kill you.'

His voice was calm. Surprisingly calm. He didn't look calm. He looked like he was on the edge of something very bad.

\* \* \*

*So fucking tired. Feels like I'm shutting down, all the power inside me being switched off, bit by bit. The music's stopped and everything's gone quiet. I feel distant from it. Like I'm watching it but not part of it. Like I'm having some sort of weird out-of-body experience and the real me is up there somewhere, looking down on this.*

*I try to remember how it got this far. All the anger I was feeling has gone. Like I kicked it out of me when I was doing her over and now there's nothing left. Like it was the anger that was the only part of me still alive and without it, there's nothing.*

*I'm not sure now this is what I want. There's only one thing in the world I want and that's to be with her. But she's gone.*

*'I loved her.'*

*Suddenly I'm talking. Telling this woman about Mon and why she means so much to me. And why I'm so fucking angry that I can't be with her anymore.*

*'She was so scared,' I'm saying. 'She knew you wouldn't stop.'*

*The woman on the ground is frowning, like she doesn't know what I'm talking about. And that does it. I can feel it building up again. The tiredness replaced by an angry energy I need if I'm going to see this through.*

*'You hated her! You fucking bitch. Wouldn't leave her alone. Police harassment. You hear about it all the time. You had it in for her and you were going to make her suffer. She told me what you did. Coming on to her like that, closet fucking dyke. And because she didn't feel the same way, you turned nasty. She was scared of you, do you know that? Every time you showed up, she was in bits afterwards.'*

*And the stupid cunt is trying to tell me I've got it all wrong, but what else is she going to say? I lift up the empty can and wave it at her. Then I tell her what's going to happen next.*

# EIGHTY-ONE

There was a small, rectangle-shaped window over the toilet. Bridget took her shoes off, closed the toilet lid and climbed on top. She wasn't too steady and the effort of getting up here hurt her hip. A deep throbbing in her side that she recognised and knew would get worse until she sat down with her legs propped up on something.

Ellen kept this window locked and Bridget knew there was no key for it. The glass didn't look like it would break easy. She'd kept one of her shoes in her hand. A thick Clark's brogue. The only shoes she ever wore. Using every bit of energy she had, she lifted her arm back and aimed for the glass. The impact, when the shoe connected with the glass, was hard. Waves of pain vibrated through her hand and up her arm. She nearly fell, but managed to steady herself by grabbing hold of the window frame.

The second time, the same thing. A sore arm and the window still intact. Desperate, she looked around for something else. She'd started to smell petrol. At first, she'd thought it was her imagination but the longer she stayed in here, the stronger the smell got, until she knew it was real.

Beside the toilet, a chrome toilet brush sat inside a matching chrome container. Bridget bent down and picked this up. It was heavy, much heavier than her shoe. Awkward to handle, too. Water sloshed out of it, drenching her sleeves, making the lid of the toilet slippy. More water soaked through her tights.

She lifted it and threw it at the window with an almighty roar. The chrome connected with the glass and smashed right through it. The glass shattered, the noise of it mixing with her own voice, still shouting, unable to stop now she'd started. Chunks of glass landed on the floor. She dropped the brush and container, covered her face to protect it.

So much noise she didn't hear the door open. Didn't notice he was there until he grabbed her, pulled her off the seat and dragged her out of the room. Her left foot caught a piece of glass that cut through the soft sole. A trail of blood followed her from the cloakroom, through the hall and into the kitchen where her daughter lay on the ground, face bruised and swollen, with her arms and legs tied behind her.

* * *

'Don't hurt her!'

The way he was holding her mother, manhandling her like she was freight instead of a frail old lady. Ellen thought she knew fear, but this was something new. Her poor mother. The look of terror etched into every line of her dear face. It was unbearable.

Ignoring the pain, Ellen manoeuvred herself into a sitting position. For a moment, the agony blacked out everything else. When she could focus again, she saw he'd pushed her mother onto one of the kitchen chairs and was wrapping the same thick rope around her that he'd used on Ellen.

There was blood on the ground. A trail of red that filtered through the rainbow colours over her eyes. The blood was from her mother's foot. Ellen remembered the sound of glass shattering. She'd thought someone was coming to rescue them. That hope was gone.

Ellen swallowed a few times and licked her lips.

'Please,' she said. 'I understand you're angry with me, but it's nothing to do with my mother. Please, Harry.'

He swung around, angry she knew his name. As soon as he'd started talking about Monica, she'd remembered. The young boyfriend. Deluded fool.

'Where's Pat?' The question was for her mother, but Harry got there first.

'I've already dealt with him.'

A different agony this time. Worse. Ellen shook her head. She wouldn't believe it. Couldn't let herself. Not for a second. Pat.

Her boy. She told herself Harry wasn't capable of something like that, even though she had no idea what he was capable of. She told herself Pat was like her, a survivor. He would find a way to be fine. She would find a way to make him fine.

'If you've hurt that boy,' her mother said, 'I promise I will kill you.'

Harry laughed, but it sounded false to Ellen and she realised how scared he was. That gave her hope.

'Harry,' she said. 'Talk to me. Please?'

Finished with her mother, he turned back to Ellen.

'I'm done talking.'

'If you go through with this,' Ellen said, 'it will be the end of everything for you. Do you think that's what Monica would want?'

It was the wrong thing to say. The moment the words were out she wished she could swallow them back. His face creased into anger, all the softness gone. Cheeks flushed red as he strode over, crouched down in front of her and shoved his face up close to hers.

'Don't you dare, don't you dare pretend to know what she wants. You don't know the first thing about her. If you did, you'd never have hurt her the way you did. You should have left her alone, but you couldn't do that. And because of you, you stupid, interfering bitch, she's gone.'

She thought he was going to hit her again and tensed. It never came. Instead, he stood and moved away. Almost like he couldn't bear to be near her. Monica had certainly done some job on him. Ellen swore that if she got out of here alive, she would find Monica Telford and make her pay for what she'd caused to happen here today.

Harry sat at the table, took a packet of tobacco from his shirt pocket and some cigarette papers. Pulled out three papers and put them together to make a single, longer paper. He sprinkled tobacco into this, then took a small, black, greasy lump of hash from the same pocket.

When he produced the cigarette lighter, Ellen shouted at him not to do it.

'You think I'm going to do it in here?' he asked. 'I'm not stupid.'

He lit the lighter and she had to bite down on her lip to stop herself screaming. The smell of burning hash mixed with the petrol, the air thick with smells that should never be in her house.

Fear, loathing and rage surged inside her.

'Where is she?' Ellen asked.

He'd finished with the joint and put it in his mouth, ready to light. If he lit it in here, if one single bit of burning ash landed on the petrol-drenched ground, it would all be over.

'I don't know.'

'Why not?'

'She doesn't want anyone to know,' he said. 'She's scared, don't you get that? Scared of the pigs, scared of everything. Scared of her old man more than anything else.'

'She killed him,' Ellen said. 'You know that, don't you? She killed him and then she fucked off and left you. If you mean so much to her, Harry, why would she do that? Why wouldn't she take you with her?'

He shook his head. 'She didn't kill him.'

'How can you be so sure?'

'Because she's not like that,' he shouted. 'She's kind and gentle and she'd never do something like that.'

'She did it.'

'Shut up!' He had his hands over his ears, his face scrunched up in agony. As if Ellen's words were physically hurting him. 'She didn't kill anyone! It was me. I killed him, you stupid cow.'

He was lying. She wanted to get him to admit it, but he pushed the chair back and she jerked back, afraid. He stood up, joint hanging out the side of his mouth, lighter still in his hand. He was playing with the lighter. Flicking the lid open and closed. Every now and then, the spark of a flame caused Ellen and her mother to jump.

He walked to the door, turned and looked at Ellen one last time.

'Just remember,' he said. 'This is for her.'

He left the door open and disappeared.

Nothing happened at first. Ellen waited, not daring to breathe.

'Pat,' her mother said. 'He's upstairs, Ellen.'

Ellen pushed herself onto her knees. Every movement was agony but no pain could stop her getting to her son. She shuffled forward. The knife rack was by the sink. Three more big, sharp knives apart from the one Harry had taken.

She didn't know how she'd manage to get them down from the worktop, but she'd find a way. She was nearly there when Harry roared. She thought he'd come back, seen what she was trying to do and turned her head, ready to defend herself.

He wasn't there. Instead, she heard him fall, body crashing to the ground.

And the sudden, shocking whoosh of petrol igniting.

# EIGHTY-TWO

Raj was opening the car door when he heard it. The sound louder on a quiet Sunday afternoon than it would otherwise be. He almost ignored it. Probably would have ignored it another time. It was just today, when so much else had happened, he knew he had to check it out.

The crash of glass breaking. Could be something. Chances were he'd find some local in their back garden breaking up an old piece of furniture, getting it ready for the journey to the dump.

He ran back to Ellen's. If there was no sign of a break-in, he'd do a quick recce of the neighbouring houses and leave it at that. Put his reaction down to an over-active imagination and get back to what was important: an afternoon with Aidan.

The front of her house was fine and he was starting to relax as he made his way around the side. Everything fine here, too. Back across the front and down the other side. A gate at the end led into her back garden. He walked towards that, thinking he'd climb over, take a quick look before heading off.

He hadn't gone far when he felt something crunching under his feet. Chunks of thick glass, the sort you see in front-door panes and on bathroom windows. Looking up, he saw the small window had been broken. Didn't take a genius to work out this had been done from the inside. Not a break-in, then. Someone trying to get out.

Phone in hand, Raj called the station. Told the duty sergeant to get two cars over here right away. While he sorted that, he ran to the front of the house. He'd nearly reached it when the screaming started.

\* \* \*

*Can't control my hand. Get the lighter going, but my fingers won't let it go. It's the boy. Why'd he have to look at me like that? Like I was some sort of monster. Like my old man.*

*I've been trying not to think about it but now it's there, inside my head, and no matter how hard I try, it's like there's nothing else there except the three of us. Me, my old man and the boy with the big, scared eyes.*

*I try to focus the way she told me to. Think of why I'm doing this. But she's not here and it's so difficult – so bloody, fucking difficult*

*— without her. The copper should have kept her mouth shut. Saying those things about Mon, trying to mess with me. I know she's lying, but I can't help thinking about it. There's a riot going on inside my head, building up until I swear it's like it's going to explode. Burst off my neck and blow into a thousand pieces that splatter onto the walls and stairs and floor.*

*I'm spinning around, still holding the lighter, roaring over the noise, trying to block it all out.*

*And then I slip on the petrol. Feet go from under me and I'm falling. The lighter flies out of my hand, and somehow the flame doesn't go out. And as it falls, all the noises in my head start to fade.*

*I roll onto my side, trying to miss it. But it seems to know what I'm doing and follows me. For a single moment, everything stops. Then a guitar starts playing. Chords I know. Someone singing about a heart of gold and lost pride. Dave Grohl. Starts off slow and gentle. A sad song of death and loss. The flame drops down and catches the back of my shirt, wet from the petrol.*

*And suddenly, I'm on fire.*

\* \* \*

Flames lick up the curtains in the sitting room. Thick trails of smoke sneak out under the front door. Inside the house, someone is screaming. A raw, inhuman sound like nothing Raj had ever heard before.

He threw himself at the front door, but it was solid wood. Impossible to break through. Emergency services on their way, but the fire was moving too fast. By the time anyone got here, it would be too late.

He'd seen two wheelie bins at the side of the house. Ran and got the black one. Started dragging it to the front sitting-room window then changed his mind. Pulled it around the back of the house, put it in front of him and ran at the wooden gate, driving the bin right through it.

Around the back. Big French windows. Ellen was inside on her knees. He aimed the bin at the windows, pulled back to give himself enough of a run, and charged. An explosion of glass as the bin connected, smashed through the double-glazing.

Fire moving fast. Air thick with smoke, in his eyes, down his throat, choking him. He grabbed Ellen.

'My mother!' She was screaming, pulling at someone else. An older woman. Raj got the woman first, dragged her outside. Turned around for Ellen. Didn't want to go back in there, but he had no choice. Couldn't see her. Smoke even worse now. The noise of the fire all around him, deafening.

'Ellen!'

He ran deeper into the inferno. Fire blinding him. Coughing, choking, hand over his mouth and nose but unable to block it out. Tripped over something and nearly fell. Ellen. Inches from the flames. He grabbed her ankles and dragged her back.

She was screaming at him, shouting Pat's name, fighting him like she didn't want him to save her. Nearly there. Fire still moving but he was faster. Just. She was heavy, but he was strong.

Her foot lashed out, kicking him in the shin.

'Pat!'

Jesus, no.

'Where?'

'He's upstairs.'

Ellen was still fighting him. He slapped her across the face, stunned her enough to get her outside.

Sirens. Close but not close enough.

Ellen's hands and feet were tied. She was screaming at him and hitting him, saying Pat's name over and over. She couldn't move. He was still holding her. If he let her go, she would fall.

He held her by the shoulders and shook her, hard.

'Ellen!'

She stopped screaming.

'They won't be here in time,' she whispered.

He nodded. 'Stay here.'

Gently, he put her down on the ground beside her mother, turned and ran back inside.

* * *

*Pain like I've never known it. I'm running, desperate to get away from it, but there's nowhere to go. The pain is me. I am the pain. Dave Grohl still singing, loud and angry now, screaming his rage as I'm screaming my pain.*

*Dave asking, did you ever think of me? And it's like he's screaming*

*the words at her. And I'm doing the same. Scream it one final,*
*drawn-out time. And then silence.*

* * *

Smoke disoriented him. Two seconds inside the house and he couldn't find the door. Ellen said Pat was upstairs. He had his sweater off. Tied around his head, trying to save his lungs from the worst of it.

He banged into something. Tried to move sideways, get past it, but it was too big. The island in the centre of Ellen's kitchen. He swung around, searching for the way he'd come in. Nothing. Smoke too black and thick for him to see anything.

Fear and panic consumed him. He couldn't do it. Couldn't save Pat or himself. He was going to die. And if he did, Aidan would never know how he really felt.

That single regret was all he needed. He wrapped the sweater tighter across his nose and mouth, felt his way along the side of the island and shuffled forward, hands out in front of him.

The screaming was worse here. The sound of an animal in agony. Inhuman and unbearable.

Every cell in his body resisted what he was doing. It took every reserve of strength he had to force himself to keep going, deeper into the fire and the smoke and the darkness, getting nearer and nearer to the screaming. The heat was intense, unbearable, boiling his blood, drying all the moisture from his eyes and mouth, burning the back of his throat.

His foot caught on something and he fell. Hit the floor. Tried to get up, but it was no good. He couldn't see or hear or breathe. There was nothing he could do.

# FOUR MONTHS LATER

Monica sat up, panting, snippets of the dream lingering in her head.

Beside her, Leonard muttered in his sleep and rolled onto his back. He threw his arm out so that it lay across her legs: hot, heavy, uncomfortable. She lifted the arm and let it drop by his side.

In sleep, he looked older. Saggy skin around his jaw, which hung open. He was snoring. The sound disgusted her. She thought of Harry, couldn't help comparing Leonard and him. The comparison did Leonard no favours and made her sad. Harry had adored her, would have done anything for her. Did do anything.

She hadn't even spelled it out. He'd just got it. Knew what she wanted and ran with it. Breaking into Kelly's house, stealing the photo of the husband, taking that classic shot of Kelly sprawled in her bed… Monica read in the papers that he'd even admitted killing her old man. Truth be told, she was a bit annoyed at him over that. She'd set it up so carefully, determined Jim would pay for what he'd done to her. It would have worked too, if it wasn't for love-sick Harry. Stupid boy taking the blame for something he didn't do. Anything for love. That's what he'd said, but she hadn't expected him to go that far. The chain fell off Jim's neck the night he called to her house. He'd said some horrible things and she'd lost her temper, threw her wine over him. He'd ripped his top off and managed to break the chain. She'd seen it fall but didn't tell him, knowing it would come in useful some day.

Four deaths. Her mother. The German. Her father. Chloe. Monica rolled her shoulders, flexed the muscles in her upper arms. Such upper body strength. Poor, stupid Chloe. The only one who didn't actually deserve to die. It had worked, though. The moment the poor cow was dead, everyone started taking Monica a bit more seriously.

The chance meeting that morning at the police station was a gift. Monica had read Chloe's story in the newspaper and knew straightaway that was how she'd get to Kelly. What she could never have hoped for was finding Chloe in the reception, waiting to speak to someone too. Monica recognised her immediately. Becoming her friend couldn't have been easier. Chloe was desperate for a female friend and kind, friendly Anne was just perfect.

She'd used the wire on purpose. She'd watched enough crappy police dramas to know that they loved banging on about a killer's MO. Only someone with a total lack of imagination would do it the same way over and over again. Where was the fun in that?

* * *

They'd been in the rental house for a week now. It still didn't feel like home and Ellen suspected it never would. Until last week, they'd been living with Ellen's parents. Her mother had wanted that situation to continue, but Ellen badly needed her own space. This big old house on King William Walk certainly provided that. The rent was exorbitant but, as her mother never tired of telling her, Vinny had left Ellen very comfortably off. And the children seemed happy here, which was all that really mattered. If happy was a word you could use.

The nights were the worst. During the day, he generally seemed okay. To someone who didn't know the boy, there was no obvious sign of recent trauma. The nightmares gave lie to that. He was still sharing Ellen's bed, refusing to sleep on his own. Not that she minded. It was all she could do not to insist that Eilish slept in the bed too, all the better for keeping her safe during the long nights.

Ellen's counsellor, Briony, had recommended someone who specialised in child trauma. On the basis of the sessions they'd had so far, Ellen was cautiously optimistic they would help. Only time would tell, though.

She wasn't sure how she was coping, either. Certainly not as well as her mother, who seemed to be able to carry on as if nothing had ever happened. Time and again, Ellen had tried talking to her about it. Each time, her mother stalled her, refusing to discuss it. 'What's done is done,' was all Ellen ever got from her.

'What's done is done' seemed to be Ger Cox's view of things too. As far as she was concerned, the case was closed. Harry Shields had confessed before he died, neatly solving Adam Telford's murder for Canterbury police. In Brighton, the investigation into Annie Telford's death was ongoing, but Ellen didn't see that being solved any time soon. Single woman, known alcoholic, living alone with no family to care about her, she wouldn't be high up the priority list for a busy force like Brighton.

The day she'd been in Brighton, Ellen had asked Alastair to look up Annie's medical records. Turned out her suspicions were right. Monica wasn't Annie's first child. She'd had another baby before Monica. A little boy who'd died at eighteen months. Sudden Infant Death Syndrome. Ellen hadn't known what to do with the information so she'd kept it to herself. She thought it might go some way to explaining Annie Telford's inability to love any other child, including her own. But maybe she was wrong about that. Plenty of women lost a child and were still able to love. She'd never know the real reason for what Annie did.

As for Chloe Dunbar, Ger had closed off that investigation as well. They had enough evidence against Collier to conclude he was Chloe's killer. In Ger's opinion, the fact that Chloe and

Monica knew each other strengthened the case against Collier. Ger said it explained why Monica had been stalked in the same way. Even went so far as to say Monica had a lucky escape. Ellen knew a closed case reflected well on her boss and it depressed her that Ger seemed to think that was more important than getting to the truth.

Ellen picked up her phone and scrolled through her texts, looking for the one she'd received right before finding Adam Telford's body. She'd tried to trace the number. It was – surprise, surprise – a pay-as-you-go phone. No registered owner.

Ellen didn't need to know the owner of the phone. She knew who'd sent it. Didn't have a single doubt in her mind about that. She also knew, with a certainty that grew each time she looked at the image, that one day Monica Telford would pay for everything she'd done.

\* \* \*

Monica got out of bed, needing to put some distance between them. She went to the wardrobe, opened her bag and pulled out the phone she'd bought a while back. Switching it on, she went and sat by the window.

The apartment was in Cambridge. A new development in a quiet area south of the city. She'd been here four months. It felt like four lifetimes. She'd expected him to be married. He had that look about him. In fact, the stupid sod didn't seem to have anyone in the world. Except for Monica. Or Ellen as she was now. Ellen O'Dwyer. Coming back with him that night had been the easiest thing in the world. Staying was proving to be a little more difficult. But for now, at least, she had little choice.

Outside the street was quiet. She was tempted to pull her clothes on and go out. At this time on a Friday night she'd find a bar open somewhere. And someone to keep her company. Instead, she flicked open the phone and scrolled through to the image gallery. Opened the photo of Kelly lying naked on her bed. Dear Harry, he'd done so well. She did miss the boy.

At the weekend, Leonard had promised to take her to the Norfolk Broads, where he kept a boat. Later in the month, they were planning a trip to his rural retreat in the Yorkshire Dales. A week in the middle of nowhere. She could think of nothing worse.

'Ellen?'

She forced her face into a smile and turned around.

'Hey,' she said. 'It's late. Go back asleep.'

Leonard patted the space beside him in the bed. 'Not without you. Come on, darling. I'm waiting.'

Still smiling, even though it hurt, she walked back and climbed into the bed beside him. When he turned and put his hands on her body, she didn't resist. Leonard was her ticket. A chance to reinvent herself. She'd already decided to ditch him as soon as they got back from Yorkshire. Until then, she would carry on being shy, compliant Ellen. It really was the least she could do.

\* \* \*

Upstairs, Ellen checked Eilish and went into her own room. She put her phone on the table by the bed and lay down beside Pat, too tired to even undress. She tried to relax, tried to breathe with the same easy rhythm of her son's. Tried to empty her mind of everything.

Except each time she felt the first tendrils of sleep wrap delicately around her, a sudden, sharp panic assaulted her. She sat up, hand over her mouth to block the scream. Slowly, the pounding of her heart subsided, her breathing slowed and the world stopped spinning. Pat was still there.

Sweat soaked her body, making her cold now the panic had passed. She pulled up her knees and wrapped her arms around her legs. On the table, the green light was flashing on her phone, telling her she had an unread text message.

The text was from Raj. Just checking in, he said. She smiled and replied, telling him to get back to whatever he was doing with Aidan and leave her in peace. He'd only returned to work two weeks ago following a long recovery from the smoke that had nearly killed him. Saved by a fireman at the last moment.

Pat had been luckier. If you could call it luck. Harry had locked the boy in a wardrobe. Being upstairs, he'd escaped the worst of the fire and smoke. Something to be grateful for, Ellen supposed.

Pat and her mother. Both still here. In the days immediately following the fire, Ellen counted her blessings every single moment and vowed she'd never take anything – or anyone – for granted ever again.

Her bedside table was one of the few pieces of furniture Ellen had been able to salvage from the ruins of her house. She opened the drawer now, ready to put her phone away. A folded piece of white paper caught her eye. She'd almost forgotten. Pulling it out, she switched on the bedside light and unfolded the paper, smoothing it out, amazed it had survived.

*Noreen McGrath, Hope House, Middle Road, Shilbottle, Alnwick, Northumberland, NE66 2TH.*

She knew what she had to do. Knew seeing it now was a sign that she couldn't ignore. It was what she wanted, what she'd always wanted, and there was no reason in the world she could think of to put if off a moment longer.

Underneath Noreen's name was a phone number. Eleven digits separating Ellen from her real mother. It was now or never.

She picked up the phone and dialled the number on the piece of paper. There was a silence, followed by a click as the connection was made. Down the line, the other phone started to ring. Ellen closed her eyes, and waited.

AN IMPRINT OF O'BRIEN